Gwen

'Goldie Goldbloom takes her readers on an exciting journey into the early twentieth century and introduces them to an extraordinary group of artists in London and Paris. Her story is full of surprises, inspired sexual conjectures, moments of pathos and romance, all illuminated by her vivid imagination.'

– *Michael Holroyd, author of* Augustus John: The New Biography

'Erotically and intellectually charged, this is a story of artistic becoming, of life's swirling waters of desire, ambition and the search for aesthetic truth. *Gwen* is a ravishing achievement, a dazzling work of art in its own right.'

– *Dominic Smith, author of* New York Times *bestseller* The Last Painting of Sara de Vos

'This is a masterful book: *Gwen* is brilliant and strange, compassionate and wild. Goldie Goldbloom has done the difficult thing, she has written a book about a very private artist's relationship to her art, her struggles with men and family, her unconventional sexuality and the fusion of these things that Gwen John achieved in her work. This book is startling and beautiful, it is a powerful tribute to a great painter and in the end it brings us back to Gwen John's art, to see it with different eyes.'

– *Audrey Niffenegger, author of* The Time Traveler's Wife

First published 2017 by
FREMANTLE PRESS
25 Quarry Street, Fremantle WA 6160
(PO Box 158, North Fremantle WA 6159)
www.fremantlepress.com.au

Consultant editor Georgia Richter
Cover design Nada Backovic
Cover photograph © Katia Chausheva
Endpapers Archives Musée Rodin

A catalogue record for this book is available from the National Library of Australia

ISBN 9781925164251 (paperback)
ISBN 9781925164282 (ebook)

Fremantle Press is supported by the Western Australian State Government through the Department of Cultural Industries, Tourism and Sport.

Fremantle Press respectfully acknowledges the Whadjuk people of the Noongar nation as the Traditional Owners and Custodians of the land where we work in Walyalup.

A NOVEL

GOLDIE GOLDBLOOM

Goldie Goldbloom grew up in Western Australia. She has received many national and international awards for her fiction and her nonfiction, and is author of *The Paperbark Shoe* and *You Lose These and Other Stories.* One of her stories was selected for inclusion in the *Best Australian Short Stories* of 2015. The National Endowment for the Arts (USA), and the Brown Foundation Fellows Program, Dora Maar House in Ménerbes (France), amongst others, have honoured her with fellowships. She is a professor of creative writing at the University of Chicago and the mother of eight children.

www.goldiegoldbloom.com

This novel was written with the support of
the National Endowment for the Arts,
and the Brown Foundation Fellows Program.

For Shterna, with love

The next tide will erase the way through the mudflats,
and everything will be again equal on all sides;
but the small, far-out island already has its
eyes closed; bewildered, the dike draws a circle

around its inhabitants who were born
into a sleep in which many worlds
are silently confused, for they rarely speak,
and every phrase is like an epitaph

'The Island I', Rilke 1907

A PARTIAL LIST OF THE WOMEN AUGUSTE RODIN SEDUCED:

Camille Claudel, who fell in love with Rodin as a teenager, greeted her models with a cudgel studded with nails, and gave birth to several of his children, so they say, though the children did not live with her and were not acknowledged. She wrote out a contract for Rodin that included the clause, "I will not spend time with other women." He signed, but then crossed out his signature. Or maybe it was she who crossed it out. After sending a bag stuffed with cat shit to a French government minister, she was dragged from her studio and ended up in Montdevergues Asylum for thirty years. Starved to death under the Nazis.

Hilda Flodin, a Finnish sculptor, with a big mouth and big rough hands and a great red bush. She liked to shove Rodin, to push him so he began to fall, and then catch him by the arm and haul him upright again. She got married and moved back to Finland after posing for his lesbian studies. Hit by a bus.

Rose Beuret, de facto wife to "The Sultan of Meudon", crept around their garden, inspecting the hedges to see if there were women hiding in them. Sometimes, there were. Froze to death.

Duchesse Claire Coudert de Choiseul, an American bulimic, became Rodin's city "wife" in 1908, despite her husband writing letters of complaint to both Rose Beuret and Rodin. She bought a gramophone to the Hôtel Biron, and she lay with Rodin under a red eiderdown in the studio, running her fingers through his white hair, listening to Gregorian chants and folk dances from Auvergne. She was as funny and as raunchy as a monkey, and used to tell lurid stories until Rodin burped uncontrollably. Killed herself by drinking a beer stein of lye a year and a half after he died.

Isadora Duncan, the dancer, was called to his studio to model for him, but she smacked his hand when he squeezed her breast. "I'm not a peach in the market," she said. Her neck was broken when one of her long scarves became tangled around the rear axle of a car in which she was riding.

Judith Cladel, his faithful biographer, liked to walk in the garden with him, and feed the ducks small scraps of bread left over from lunch. He, in turn, liked to feel the velvet of her skirt, so that she came to always wear velvet, summer and winter, to please him. This accounted for her faint odour of sweat. Died, in Paris, unmarried, of a broken heart.

Madame Sada Yacco, a Japanese geisha, would not undress but rubbed her silk kimono in circles over his flesh until he cried out. Liver cancer killed her, but she also had cancer of the lips and tongue. In the end she could not drink and her lips were moistened with a cotton ball dipped in milk.

Malvina Hoffman, a sculptor, couldn't stand the way Rodin measured her breasts with an old quill, so she ran off to New York after smashing all the clay models he'd made of her. Died of a heart attack at eighty-one, in her studio, where she lived with a Miss Gullborg Groneng.

Lady Victoria Sackville-West was forced by her husband to burn the nightgown she wore for Rodin. Written on the fabric in Indian ink, the words: *I should like to buy you and have you for keeps. Would you be very expensive?* Died alone with shopping lists pinned to her bosom, in a cottage at Brighton, of dementia.

Hanako, a Japanese dancer, squatted to piss on his floor. Her urine ran between the cracks in the stones, and on warm afternoons, when the sunlight fell directly on the old slabs, it reignited her odour of pineapple and lotus, and he could still smell her, twenty years later. Her real name was Hisa Ohta. Her house was destroyed by an American bomb, in Japan, in 1945.

Rita took dozens of close-up photographs of Rodin naked and then tried to sell them to the newspapers, who refused her offer. She got rich from selling them to all the women in Rodin's life instead. Threw herself into the Seine, but hit a barge.

Anna and Adele Abruzzezi, Italian sisters, one pale and fair, one dark, voyeurs of each other's liaisons with Rodin. They both fell pregnant and gave birth on the same day, in a room and with a midwife Rodin paid for, though it was claimed, afterwards, that they ran away with "Russian lovers".

Corsi, a model with a third nipple. Rodin paid her thirty centimes each time he looked at the nipple on her thigh. Gwen John had one too. Vanished.

Giganty, she of the extraordinary clitoris. Rodin renamed her. Her original name was forgotten. Died in childbirth.

Clara Westhoff, Rilke's wife and a sculptor. Rodin suggested she use kohl on her eyes, but she used a kind of ink that was later linked with her death.

Nuala O'Donel, an artist, grew jealous when she discovered that Gwen John entertained Rodin in her bed and saw him almost every day. She wrote a sad little note, then put her head in the oven and turned on the gas.

Comtesse Anna de Noailles, the poetic daughter of Romanian Prince Gregoire, despite her high birth, demanded that Rodin choke her and slap her face. She looked forward to dying. She was curious about it, so she said. Unsurprisingly, by strangulation.

Marie-Louise Fuller, a dancer, stole an entire box of Gwen John's watercolour paintings, thinking they were Rodin's. Some of them were his, but most of them were Gwen's. It was hard to tell the difference, because they'd been influencing each other for *years*. Fuller died of pneumonia, brought on by the effects of too much damp paper in her bedroom.

Gwendolen Mary John

BOOK ONE: AUGUSTUS

DORELIA IN A BLACK DRESS:

Gwen met Dorothy McNeill accidentally, at a party in 1902. Piccadilly's Café Royal held the celebration of Auguste Rodin's sale of his *Saint John* to the South Kensington Museum. The French Ambassador was there. The entire London art world was there. The *King* was there. Gwen, of course, didn't have an invitation. She was no one. Her brother Augustus, however, was. "Please," she'd begged him. "I want to see the man who is turning art on its ear!" He'd laughed at her, but agreed to sneak her into the Ladies Lounge through the back entrance. Though she was timid by nature, she pretended she was brave and famous and beautiful. She wore her best pink linen dress, the one that was inharmonious with her red hair. She smelled of mothballs and, behind the ears, a bit like lemons and mildew. No one spoke to her. Her skirt was too short, and her gloves far too mangled, and her hair too full of paint speckles for her to be noticed. She dragged a chair into the doorway to the main café, in between the punchbowl and an old man, hoping at least Rodin would come over to watch her drawing the tinkly women who arrived through the front entrance, and who fluttered around the petits fours. *Glacé, salé, sec.* Glazed. Salted. Dry.

For reassurance, she touched the portraits folded into her pocket, one Gwen had made of her mother, and the other, her mother's sketch of her as an eight-year-old child. The two of them sketching each other late one afternoon. Her mother her first art teacher. The forgiving yellow light of autumn, her mother leaning over and gently correcting Gwen's pencilled line, smoothing the lines of concentration on the little face, leaving a pale blue fingerprint on her child's cheek. "You're such a wonderful little artist, Gwennie," she'd said and for some reason, a knot tied itself in Gwen's throat. Gwen hadn't known, then, that it would be the last time she drew her mother. She hadn't known that within weeks, her mother would sicken and become thin and ochred and die. She hadn't known how strange it would be, to regularly find her young mother trapped in the drawing as if she had never died, as if she were still thirty, young, beautiful, smiling, unchanged, still sitting in that spill of autumn sunlight, drawing with Gwen. Or how she too would remain frozen at eight. She hadn't known time could hang, immutable, eternal, in an image. She hadn't known that the knot in her throat would be impossible to untie. She hadn't known either, that when she washed off the smudged blue fingerprint, she was removing the ghost of the last time her mother would ever touch her face.

A small someone wearing a black dress with a white Holland apron rushed into the café and bumped against Gwen, causing her to crush the portraits between her fingers. The girl announced loudly that her name was Dorothy, and said she'd gone to look in the windows of the Museum of Practical Geology after work, seen the world's largest man, almost eighty-seven stone, a gorgon, she said. She'd dodged several dustcarts with their refuse masticators that almost decapitated her, watched the mails being driven out from White Horse Cellar – her favourite thing in the whole wide world was the sound of the post-horn on a foggy evening, which this evening wasn't but it was still a lovely sound, don't you think – she'd admired the horses bedecked with ribbon rosettes and flowers on their bridles, bought a sponge off one of the Hebrew children standing there selling oranges and pencils and brushes to the travellers, had her boots polished *while she was wearing them* by a man in the street, contemplated buying a waterproof cape at Aquascutum but decided it was far too dear for the likes of her, stopped to see the collection of monkeys at the Pantherion, sat for several minutes with the flower-sellers under the statue of Eros in

Piccadilly Circus while wiping the smudges of boot blacking off her stockings with her handkerchief, until the line of Jews and Russians stretching from the Alien Registration Office and the protestors trying to push them into the road had obscured her view of the busy street and she'd finished with her stockings anyway, so she'd wandered through the maze of tiny unnamed arcades and back lanes between Regent Street and Piccadilly Circus and then she'd heard the ruckus. Curious, she'd slipped in through the unlocked back door to the Café Royal, a door that Augustus, as usual, had forgotten to close behind him.

Gwen rolled her eyes. "For goodness sakes," she said, smoothing the crushed portraits over her knee. "Shut up. There's something more important in the world than *you*." She gestured towards the crowd in the next room.

"What's going on?" Dorothy whispered, crouching down next to Gwen. There was torchon lace around the edges of her pinafore. A shop girl in uniform, but a shop girl with money.

"The King is here," said Gwen. She pointed out the big man with his silken top hat tucked under his arm and his drooping moustaches and his belly squeezing out between his buttons, who stood in the centre of the crush. Gwen still hadn't really looked at the girl beside her. She *refused* to look. From the sound of the girl's voice and her incessant chatter, she was probably someone who had climbed out of the dustbins at the Ragged School for Girls in Covent Garden and clawed her way into a secretarial position by sleeping with the manager. Someone well below Gwen. "He came to meet Auguste Rodin."

"Who's that?" Dorothy stood and leaned on Gwen's shoulder to see what she was drawing. Gwen covered the portraits of her mother and her with her hand and tucked them away in her pocket again. She held out her sketchpad instead.

"He's a very famous French sculptor." Gwen's crayonned women were shrill and elongated and ever so slightly absurd.

She turned to brush off this dolt who didn't even recognise

Rodin's name. Glittering black eyes, an extraordinary shade of purple-black, filled with hundreds of shivering candle flames. Skin like an ironed linen tablecloth, richly fragrant: incense, rum, saffron, black cumin, bitter orange, smoked ebony, cedar, cloves, cinnamon, myrrh. Every sound crisp. A fork, falling to the floor, sounding like the bell in church when wine changes into blood. "They're rather dreadful," Gwen muttered, blinking. She felt scorched by the girl's eyes.

"Not at all. They're brilliant. *You're* brilliant," Dorothy said. "You're *absolutely* my heroine! A *lady* artist! What's your name again?"

"Gwendolen Mary John," said Gwen, who hadn't introduced herself, and now had to repeat her name twice because she'd spoken into her hand and Dorothy couldn't understand the mumbled syllables. A *heroine*? It was hard enough being a human being.

"But you're Welsh!" cried the girl, delighted. The shop assistant's smock a costume, a disguise. The prattle, part of her act. "Your accent is quite charming. I don't suppose you ever teach drawing to little sillies like me?"

Dorothy was clearly no little silly. As she asked the question, she lifted an eyebrow and smirked. This was a woman who knew the effect she had on others. Gwen, who had been about to reject the proposal, saw something move in that alluring face and agreed instead, and a handful of florins were poured into her tiny, paint-stained palm, reserving her services for the following Tuesday evening.

"Mister Roodan should come and see what you've been up to," said Dorothy. She was squeezed between the punchbowl and Gwen, her breath all down Gwen's neck, stirring the fine hairs next to her ear, making the gooseflesh rise on her arms.

"*Monsieur Rodin.* I don't think he can see me," said Gwen, shaking her head. She could barely see *him*. "Not back here." She touched the portraits in her pocket and felt emboldened to try to edge her way into the main room.

"You'll get into trouble." Generally, only men were allowed to drink in bars.

"That might be fun," Gwen said. The policy was strictly enforced, but perhaps on this occasion, the rules might turn out to be more flexible?

But within a few minutes, a waiter pushed her chair backwards into the doorway of the Ladies Lounge. "I'm sorry, Miss," he said. "But unless you're wearing a cut-away and trousers … the coppers could be having us up on a charge."

"I told you," said Dorothy, and the girl touched her shoulder.

Ferns ran down the centre of each long table near the bar and the room for the men smelled darkly of the forest, of timber and civet, of leather and bracken and duff. The red velvet chairs were covered in ashen dandruff from the gentlemen's cigars. Great clouds of smoke drifted overhead. Dozens of candles burned in the gilded candelabras, their light bouncing from the mirrored walls to the green marble pillars to the glittering caryatids, all the way up to the golden ceiling.

Two dim gaslights burned behind Gwen in the Ladies Lounge. The chairs provided for the women were unquestioned deal. The room filled with a blur of powdery perfumes, lilac and lavender and lily and rose. The women chattered and ate canapés, jingling their charm bracelets, their backs to the main room. Gwen sniffed, again and again, to see if she could catch a whiff of Dorothy, of the smoked ebony scent of her, the rum.

She sighed. Women could be such a distraction, right when she must not be distracted. She would not allow herself even one more glance at Dorothy. She turned her head to the side. A bearded old man with his top hat clamped between his knees sat forgotten, next to her in the doorway. He had a magnificent white rose in his buttonhole. He looked surprisingly like the King. Gwen, fretting at the impropriety of the arrangement, said, "Sir, wouldn't you be more comfortable with the gentlemen?"

His nose twitched. He leaned further out into the main room and cupped his ear as if to better hear what was being said.

"Sir? This is the *Ladies* Lounge."

"Apparently," said the man, "it's to be the residence of *the Jews* too, whether they be the first Jewish member of the House of Lords and best friend of the King or not."

Baron Rothschild! The newspapers said he was the head of the clique of greedy Anglo-Hebraic financiers who had dragged the British Empire into the disastrous Boer War for their own monetary gains! There were whispers about black magic, spells that had enchanted the monarchy. Behind her, Dorothy gasped and stiffened, then pivoted on her heel and walked away. The Baron's voice didn't change at this affront. It was calm and deep, cultured and infinitely patient as he introduced himself. He didn't have Fagin's accent. His nose wasn't even a tiny bit hooked like Shylock's. Neither was he thin and hunched the way the newspapers depicted him. Instead, he was a well-padded man with excellent posture and the faintest hint of a German accent. But for all that, still a Jew. Gwen had taught Augustus to throw away, unread, letters that arrived for him bearing the name of Jewish correspondents.

Now, her lips clamped around her own name, she inched her hand down the side of her chair and carefully withdrew her skirt from the Jew's vicinity. She felt cold and then very, very hot. She didn't say anything further to the Baron and after another minute had passed, she hitched her chair a few inches in the opposite direction from the traitor.

Just moments before, she had been willing Auguste Rodin to notice her sketching during the party, to address her as a colleague, to show the crowd that a woman, too, could be a great artist. She sighed. She was no longer in the mood to receive Rodin's attention. God forbid he should see her sitting right next to a Jew! Then she was flooded with disgust for herself. Here she was, hoping her position as a woman would be ignored and the great man would give her a chance, all while she ignored the Baron the same way women were usually ignored by men. She spat into her handkerchief. The hypocrisy tasted like frogs.

Rodin was still surrounded by a group of young men, all sculpture students at The Slade, all yelling his name, pushing and shoving. Every so often one of these men would come to get a glass of punch and step on Gwen's foot or drop canapés on her head or spill pickle juice down her neck. She'd called for the manager and the waiter to help her. She'd made angry noises but Baron Rothschild had only turned his head and sniffed. She'd even called out to the pianist who sat bowed over the silent Bechstein waiting for his cue, but with the King and Rodin in the room, all of the staff were busy and the waiters ran past her with trays full of chiming glasses.

"Son of a fiddler's bitch!" Gwen said, after a man stepped squarely on her drawing. All this fuss over the creator of the *Saint Jean Baptiste*. She should never have come. Now that she was here, she couldn't remember what it was about Monsieur Rodin that had compelled her to attend the party. She certainly hated his hideous statue. The bronze looked just like her brother. Legs spread. Beard jutting. A field of crazed energy. Small balls.

She stood up, slid out a hatpin and poked the man who had stepped on her drawing sharply in the back. "You," she said, prodding him again. "Where are your manners?" He didn't turn around and just then, all of the men, more than half of the London art world, raced out onto the street roaring like a single ferocious beast. Even Rothschild stood, released from his exile, and walked through the café and outside. The students unhitched Rodin's gleaming black coupé from the horses and took up the traces themselves. John Singer Sargent swung up to be the coachman. Gwen's brother, Augustus, in front of the others and not bearing any of the weight, had the bit between his teeth and was pawing the ground. At any moment, he'd lift his tail and let fly with a steaming pile of manure. He was the bloody ringleader. Of course.

Gwen and Dorothy walked to the front window and sat back down in the abandoned café. A finger of coffee trickled off a nearby table and tapped against the floor, an impatient sound as if the liquid were waiting for something to change.

Outside, the young men, cheering, waited to pull the coupé down the street. Rodin stood up on the driver's bench, waving to the crowds, kissing his hand in every direction. He had something in his pants the size of a grown squirrel and kept pulling the corners of his frock coat back so that his pleasure was more, not less, visible. Rodin turned and caught Gwen's eye and smiled and her heart leapt. He made a gesture as if he had painted something and nodded his head towards her. He'd noticed her working! Dorothy squealed, "He's looking right at you!" Gwen smiled eagerly and held up her notebook to show that she'd understood his message, but then she caught sight of his abominable squirrel and blushed and looked down. How exposed he was! The display of one's *squirrel* must be a French custom. *She'd* been caught recently rubbing herself intently against a street lamp and almost been arrested for public indecency. Augustus had had to come and convince the bobby to let her go, and then her brother had been unmerciful in his teasing. Everyone expected *him* to exercise his squirrel. If he *didn't* seduce his models, they'd have thought one of the rejected girls had chopped off his manhood. She blamed Queen Victoria, the frigid bitch, who while alive had spread the rumour that a woman who enjoyed a romp in the hay was a whore. Gwen was no whore – she'd had the chance and turned it down – but she was fond of a little pleasure between the sheets, and now, a faint image of Rodin unbuttoning her shirt waist and peeling the sleeves down her arms came to her, unbidden.

"Did your brother leave you money to pay the bill?" called the waiter from behind the counter. Gwen reluctantly turned towards that side of the room. Reflected together with so much gold, she looked as if she were wearing armour. A hero. But a hero has to be brave in some way.

"Why do you only pay attention to me when you want something?" Gwen grumped to the waiter, as she smoothed out her drawing on the counter. The outline of a shoe across the entire sheet. Forgetting that she wasn't holding a pen, she signed her name with the hatpin. Too late, she made a flourish that ripped through the paper and left a long gouge in the marble. She looked at the gouge, licked her finger and rubbed at it. Dorothy offered to pay for the damage and was rebuffed. A white line showed clearly in the deep green stone of the bar.

"Here," said Gwen, handing her drawing to the waiter. "One day that will be worth thousands of pounds, so you'd best hang on to it." In the mirror behind the bar, she saw Dorothy glance at her with respect. It didn't count, looking at the girl in the mirror. It almost wasn't a distraction at all.

One day, Gwen thought, my students will pull *my* carriage down the street, shouting and cheering. One day, I will have glamorous lovers lining up to kiss my hand. One day, I will be brave. And I will take myself to Paris and introduce myself to the man who saw the artist sitting in my dark little corner, drawing. Rodin.

When Gwen was sixteen, Gwen's father hadn't wanted her to go to the city, to The Slade where all the bad girls lurked, puffing on cigarettes and baring their legs, but she had argued and fought and scratched. She wanted the same education in painting technique as Augustus. Though he was younger than her, he'd been sent to school two years earlier. It was Gwen who'd won prizes as a child for her drawings. She'd won a tiny bronze sculpture of a hand that was supposedly by Rodin and she'd sent it to Augustus in London to admire. He gave the ugly prize to a beggar in the street, he wrote back, because it was obviously a fake.

In the same letter, he enclosed a sheaf of his new drawings, which, irritatingly, were miles better than they'd been just six months earlier. She burned the sketches one by one in the kitchen stove, half mad with desire and frustration. She wanted her life to mean something. She didn't want it to be over in a flash, like her mother's. And what would *her* work look like if only she had a good teacher?

Gwen didn't want to sit upstairs with a tin of watercolours and paint sunsets after she'd finished putting the children to bed. She wanted to stride through the academy halls, a modern-day knight, in her brother's high-heeled boots. She wanted to meet Whistler like her brother did, and talk with him as if he were a confidant and a friend. She wanted to learn how to lay oils on a canvas and conjure skin and bones and glittering hair. She wanted to learn to paint eyes, tilted just so, that expressed sadness, or a chin held slightly at an angle, expressing arrogance or temper. She wanted to look on naked bodies and break them into a series of planes like Rodin did on his good days. She wanted brushes that bore the marks of her hands and her teeth, and she wanted the crease on the outside corner of her neck to smell of turpentine. So she locked herself in her room in Tenby and she refused food for fourteen days. On the evening of the fourteenth day, when her father sat outside her door, listening to her weeping from pain and exhaustion, he had broken down and cried through the door, "You may go, you bloody little tyrant! But for God's sake, get up and eat!"

And she had screamed back, "I will be worth it, Father. I will!"

She'd moved to London the very next week. She was seventeen years old, and terrified because her father had told her he wouldn't pay for a thing besides the tuition.

She got down from the train, stepping into mud and gravel and decomposing leaves. Clouds of steam, smelling of wet laundry. People waving. Not to her. She touched her mother's portrait, then picked up her own small box and moved through the stream of people hurrying into the station. They did not seem to see her and she was pushed from one side to the other. Barking her knuckles on a stone wall. Everything rushed and grey and cold. Droplets of moisture furred her eyebrows and trickled down into the sockets of her eyes. She had been to London twice before. There had been tulips then.

She took her time walking to the street where Augustus had his flat. He'd said he would meet her at the station. She hadn't expected him but still it stung. She took a deep drag of the London air. It was cool and thick and full of cinders. It burned her throat going down and her tongue coming back out. It smelled of acorns. "I am going to be an artist," she said to herself. *An artist. An artist.* She thought of the small bronze hand she had won and wished it were in her box and not lost. She wished she were brave and did not tremble quite so much.

She passed a man with a cart selling hot chestnuts. She passed a woman selling Yorkshire puddings filled with gravy. She passed pheasants and geese hanging by their necks from hooks. How would she paint them when she knew more about art? She went along the road and turned right at a sign marked Howland Street. It would be All Hallows' Eve, it would be Guy Fawkes Night, it would be Christmas, it would be Easter. She wouldn't see the ocean for years. It might snow.

Down a little lane she went. To the side there was a courtyard through an arch, and in the middle, an oak tree. A man with a gentle face sat under the tree, reading a book. The masonry looked older than any brickwork she had ever seen, and better laid. She pinned her box to her chest with her elbow and lifted her cold hand and waved to the man. It was an auspicious start. Everything she did in London should be chosen carefully. A sacrifice should have meaning. But the man looked right past her and did not wave back.

She could not put her hands in her pockets because she was carrying her box. Her fingers were blue. Yellow and red and orange leaves fell. Horse chestnut, whitebeam, ash, tree of heaven, Turkey oak, red oak, fig. They carpeted certain parts of the road. Her footfalls were muffled. A leaf stuck to the toe of her boot. A flock of starlings flew out of the whitebeam, each with a bright red berry in its beak.

As soon as she was in her room, she would unpack her paints and warm them between her thighs so the oils didn't congeal. She would set up her easel in the place with the best light and she would clip a fresh sheet of paper to the frame. She would light several candles. She would work all night. Perhaps she would draw the birds with their berries.

When she saw Augustus, she ran to him and hugged him and he rubbed his beard over the top of her head once she had withdrawn the pins from her hat and laid it to one side.

"So, you are really here then?" he asked and she nodded. He had not offered to carry her box up to the rooms.

The fire was already lit though, and her room was warm and there was a small copper kettle singing on one side of the hearth. She found a cup with a blue willow pattern on the table, and a teapot.

"I missed you," Augustus said shyly, coming up behind her and wrapping her in his arms.

"Of course," she said, opening her box. "I missed you too."

The last time she had seen him, he looked exactly the same. But she. She was not the same. He'd seen the prize. And now she would be going to school with him. What did he think of that? He didn't say.

That night and each night afterwards, she lit three candles and put one underneath her easel and one to the side and one on the table where whatever it was that she was sketching lay. She did not go to bed until sleep overcame her. The floorboards were black oak, yellow from smoke and from varnish. The walls were painted puce. The ceiling was made of blackened tin squares. The light reflecting off the walls was green and rippled. If she squinted, it almost seemed as if she was underwater. Outside her window was a huge beech tree. Its leaves had already fallen. It had long sticky buds at the end of each twig. When she was anxious, when she was hot, she put her hands outside the window and wrapped her fingers around the branches of the beech. She never undressed. She never washed. She painted for twenty hours a day or until she fainted. She could not bear to waste time.

"Leave your frock at the door," Gwen said to Dorothy their first day of after-work classes, three days after the party for Rodin. "We shall be studying the human body." Gwen unbuttoned the top of her own itchy woollen bodice and fanned her flushed face with her palette. She had almost translucent skin and the slightest upset turned her face crimson. She wasn't upset now. At least, she didn't think she was, but her nose was a stunning and unaccountable shade of alizarin red.

She halfway hoped Dorothy would do a bunk, run screaming from the terrible lady artist of Howland Street, because even though Gwen needed the money, she also hated giving drawing lessons to incapable, incurious, indifferent little snots, but Dorothy gave her an odd look.

"Hello to you too, Miss John," she said.

Gwen had planned to crunch slices of apple or handfuls of nuts, and force Dorothy to copy the ugliest busts of Roman centurions in the basements of the nearby museum. She'd looked forward to sending the girl with the candles in her eyes back dozens of times until she cried from frustrated pride. Those eyes would be extraordinary, full of tears.

Gwen would laugh Dorothy out of her room. "Call yourself an

artist?" she'd say, crumpling up the girl's sketches and throwing the papers after her. "You haven't even *begun* to see."

Gwen was determined, come what may, to see everything, to see *beyond* everything, to use to the utmost an opportunity she never thought she'd be given. Starving for fourteen days was the least of what she would give up. She'd expect the same dedication from Dorothy. The girl had said Gwen was her heroine. Well, then, she would have to learn that a hero had to be brave in some way. She'd tell her so as soon as she was undressed and exposed, standing cold and barefoot.

Even when she and Augustus were children, still living at home, they had set challenges for each other. Draw love, he'd said to her. Draw hunger. Draw jealousy. Draw lust. Draw sex, she'd said to him and he'd tried and then she'd tried and then their drawings had been discovered by their aunts and the aunts had run away the same day, in horror.

Draw deformity, she'd tell Dorothy.

Sometimes, especially if her students' ribs and waists were distorted from corseting, she had them strip and stand in front of a mirror to sketch the muscles and the bones of their own bodies. She could tell that Dorothy wore her corsets tight, and looked forward to forcing the girl to draw the atrophy of her pectoral muscles, her tiny inverted nipples, her bruised and flaking skin, the compression of her tenth and eleventh ribs. Without regular food, Gwen had shrunk to a size that didn't require corsets. She was glad of her own distortion. Some mornings, she spent a minute or two looking at herself in the lovely old pier mirror, thinking she was *almost,* but not quite, handsome. Other mornings, mornings when her room looked squalid, or when she'd spent the last of her pennies days earlier, or when she had a cold, or when her vision blurred and she felt she might fall over, or when Augustus had teased her about the lamppost incident and offered to take care of her needs himself, she didn't feel quite up to the task. She'd scavenged the mirror from a rubbish tip outside a home in Belgravia, a grave of mirrors, choosing it because the greyish spots and the cloudy haze behind the mercury glass made reflections look as if they floated within someplace far away, someplace not in her real everyday world.

"Are you afraid of me?" Gwen barked at Dorothy when the girl hesitated. "Or a prude? Strip, I said!" It was their first day of classes, a Tuesday evening, and Gwen still had not greeted her student. Dorothy made no move to take off her fancy gown, so Gwen stamped her foot and made as if to run at the girl, to frighten her.

She loved making her students jump. She wasn't quite sure why she enjoyed it, but there was a distinct and particular spike of pleasure each time a quaking girl startled at Gwen's demand to take off *all* of her clothes. Still, Dorothy was no quaking girl. On her lips, the beginning of some unfamiliar expression, surely not a sneer?

Gwen loved to control the things she could control: her cats, her little room, her students, her meals. Her life constantly spiralled into messy disorder. Her mother had died an ugly death when Gwen was a child, a few weeks later her father had abruptly moved the family to a different town, ghastly maiden aunts had taken over the maternal role for six years, her beloved brother Augustus had seduced her at thirteen and then dashed off to art school, only reappearing at irregular intervals to force himself upon her when he felt like it. After Gwen finally escaped Wales for London, Augustus seemed alternately uninterested in her and obsessed, but in no discernable pattern. Even Gwen's favourite tomcat had betrayed her by giving birth to a litter of kittens.

Still, for two years now, since coming to London and fighting with Augustus and finding her own basement room, she'd had peace. She had somehow accumulated a small cadre of lacklustre students who couldn't get a place at The Slade; Whistler had singled her work out for praise; she'd won another major prize for a portrait she'd painted and then it had sold for a good price; she'd made friends who didn't know Augustus or her father or her aunts and who thought her accent charming and her simple homemade clothes winsome and her lack of money merely an artistic affectation.

Now, she refused to be knocked from the sidewalk by crowds. She called out when a lecturer ignored her. She made all her students strip and stand shivering in her cellar, though they were the ones paying her. The pretty ones, she seduced.

But that day in the spring of 1902, when Gwen told Dorothy to strip, the other girl did not do what every other girl before her had done. She didn't quiver or shake or cry out. Instead, she sneered. She didn't startle and this complacency was, in itself, unsettling.

"Make me," Dorothy said.

It was a schoolgirl taunt, but she still didn't open even a single button. Her face had several dimples on each side and she tilted her head and shook out her shiny green-black hair and looked out of one eye more than the other and the corners of her dark red mouth turned up ever so slightly and a tiny wedge of her tongue came out and wet her lips. Gwen's nose shone crimson and sweat gathered beneath her breasts and the hairs on her arms, one by one, stood up.

"I will," said Gwen, her voice flat and inharmonic, then sharp and full of irregular overtones. "I *will* make you." Dorothy was the first woman in two years who had stood up to Gwen, who was more ready, more open to experience than even Gwen herself. She changed everything. *Draw sex.* Well, here she was.

In the strange light that straggled through the filthy windows from the street, Gwen thought Dorothy looked like a serpent, sent to evict her from the tiny Eden she had created for herself in London. The other woman would open her almost black lips and a thin forked tongue would emerge to sample the air and smell what it was, *exactly*, that Gwen most loved. Gwen's sweat redolent with her secrets. What would she lose this time? Did she have anything *left* to lose?

"Strip," gasped Gwen again, all the air gone from her lungs. She was seconds from fainting. She put out her hand and slapped Dorothy's arm, trying to slow her breaths. "Hurry! I don't have all day!" The ocean, the great rollers that rose up from the seabed and moved majestically ahead of the wind until they curled over and crashed onto the pebbled beach. The *crsssh* of the foam on the strand. The hoarse calls of the gulls as they twisted in the wind. The khaki water below the sloping grey shoulders of the cliffs. But the ocean didn't help. On her wall, a drawing from Rodin's party, run through with the hatpin. The tinkly women, those bastions of proper society with their stiff upper lips and iron stays, their willingness to ignore anything that did not conform to their view of the world: *Glacé, salé, sec.* And miraculously, Gwen did not faint and instead, stood glaring at Dorothy.

"I told you to strip, and if you want to be my student," Gwen said, an edge in her voice now that she'd gotten her breath. "You'd better rip off that rubbish right now, or you may as well go along and find yourself a nicey-nice lady painter to teach you."

Dorothy's face broke slowly into a broad smile. "Who says I want a nicey-nice lady painter? Otherwise, why would I have hired *you*?" She peeled off her dress and tossed it onto the floor as if it were worthless and always had been. She unhooked her corset and bent to set it upright on the floor under the easel, and then lifted her arms and pulled off her chemisette. She stood, laughing at Gwen, leaning against a block of wood that until then had looked like an ugly pillar meant to hold up the cellar ceiling, a block left behind when men came to declare the building condemned. She stood there as naturally as if she had sprouted there, as if all the winds in the world would never stir a single hair on her head, as if she were a sprite in her element, and the rejected pink gown was some excuse or a disguise to her essential nature. "Well?" Dorothy said, the girl's eyes locked on Gwen's, a challenge. "Please won't you teach me how to paint, Lady John?" *Please,* sibilant, a long lisped *s*, serpentine.

Sensation receded like water down Gwen's shins until the last gurgle of feeling left her toes. *Glacé, salé, sec.* The edges of the room cackled and swayed. A window opened like a mouth and shut itself again. The walls rumbled. Small silvery fish flickered in her vision and she put out her hand to catch them. The portrait on the wall stretching longer and longer, then rolling up with a snap. The hatpin leaping from the wall, impaling her pillow. Somehow, she found herself next to Dorothy, running her fingers over the girl's powdered shoulders. Dorothy's skin rippling under her touch, as a horse shivers a fly off its hide. "Paint?" Gwen said faintly. "You'll never have a better teacher than me." She looked around and took up a nearby brush, her favourite, softest sable, which she licked and dipped into a smear of Hooker's green on her palette. "Observe my hand," she commanded, and she spiralled the tip of the brush around the girl's breast, binding her round and round with her art, and finally coming to a point. There was very little difference between a hero and a villain, she thought. Which, then, am I?

Gwen's legs were still gone. Her body ended somewhere just below her ribs, in a hot and hazy freshet. Her ears rang. Non-existent things scuttled in the corners of the room, leering at her, dark and treacherous. Dorothy, however, did not seem bound. If anything, she had grown to twice her original size.

Beyond Dorothy's amused black eyes, all Gwen could see was that green snake encircling soft flesh, hissing despite the apple in its mouth. With her last bit of courage, she said, "Dorothy is the wrong name for a girl like you. It's a lie. From now on, you shall be Dorelia."

THE TEAPOT:

Afterwards, people would say that it was Augustus John who had named Dorelia. They would say that the famous young artist had been walking in the street and he had seen a woman pass, wearing a huge black cartwheel of a hat, and that he had gone back and propositioned her, right there, on the high street. They would tell stories about how Dorelia had struggled in his arms and tried to break away but eventually swooned and been borne off to his rooms, to be painted, at the very least. It wasn't an unreasonable guess. Each child Augustus met, he patted on the head in case it was his. The story went that he had a hundred illegitimate children. It was a rumour he'd spread. He imagined himself some kind of ogre Casanova. The truth about the bastards was closer to twenty. Artists and writers and lovers and lost women rumbled up together and dropped their corsets and their stiff cravats and their grip on propriety the moment they laid eyes on him. It was enough to turn milk into cheese, his goings-on. The very trees dropped their drawers when he passed, shedding all sense of decency.

Gussy, Augustus, Gus – her brother – grabbed everything away from Gwen, even this first meeting with Dorelia and the naming of her prize. His gold gypsy earrings shot brilliant lances of light into Gwen's eyes. His gaudy boots sealed her mouth.

Gwen knew that her brother was like Rodin, he trawled for beautiful models and used the women up until there was nothing left but a brittle exoskeleton in the shape of a human. She was not so different herself. And she knew that if Augustus spied

Dorelia, he would demand to have her. And so for several weeks, Gwen kept the news of Dorelia locked in her uncompromising mouth, even after Augustus commented on Gwen's scarcity. "Won't you come and spend some time with your dearlove?" he asked. "You know how much you miss me! You adore me!" And Gwen smiled and nodded but kept her mouth closed over the news of Dorelia. "Are you starving yourself not just of food but of my glorious company too?" She smiled again. "Will you stop smiling, for God's sake! It's not natural on you. You look like a whore with a mouth full of spunk; either swallow or spit it out."

But Gwen did neither and it was only when Augustus grew truly curious and came round to her digs that she had to reveal Dorelia.

At the pounding on her door and roaring of her name, Gwen had turned her nude portrait of Dorelia to the wall and dropped the girl's green cloak over it. "It's my brother. Augustus John. No doubt you saw him at the Rodin party. A painter. Like me. But not as good." Gwen laughed her angriest laugh and turned the key and the door smashed back against the plaster, shoved open by Augustus.

Dorelia looked up at the giant man in yellow boots in the doorway. His huge halo of wild red hair and his flaming beard took up at least half of the space, and the rest was full of his purple velvet suit. "What have we here?" he bellowed. "A coven of jezebels!" He winked at Dorelia and little blue sparks flew in the dank air between them. A match would be all it would take to set the whole shabby room on fire.

"Oh, stop it," said Gwen, flapping at the sparks with her bare hands. She was no stranger to the chemistry between men and women, and both genders were equally delicious to her when it came to loving. *She* fell in love with ideas. *She* fell in love with ambition. She did not fall in love with genitals.

Dorelia, it seemed, was falling in love with genitals. But Gwen was willing to wait to be loved. She was quietly confident that one day, maybe even one day soon, Dorelia would love her too. Augustus had charisma but she had patience.

"This is Dorothy McNeill. My student."

"Dorelia," said Dorelia. She smoothed her hair back behind her ears with the flats of her hands and then extended one paw to be shaken. Augustus ran down the stairs and tumbled from the last step, which was broken. He fell against Dorelia, grabbed the front of her kimono to steady himself, lifted her hand to his lips, flipped it over and sniffed the inside of her wrist. "Mmm," he said, panting. "Quite divine. The goddess of fertility, methinks."

Dorelia waited until he released her wrist and then leaned forward to touch the velvet buttons on his waistcoat. Gwen wasn't quite sure if it was the wide gap between his front teeth that appeared when he smiled, his piercing eyes, or the phenomenal length of his slim fingers that appealed to Dorelia. Despite the clownish entrance.

"I've heard about you," Dorelia said, peering up at him from under the fall of her hair. In all the world, she had the thickest eyelashes of any woman, and she fluttered them at Augustus. They would be challenging to paint correctly. How quickly the little hussy had forgotten Gwen. In that moment, Gwen wanted to stitch Dorelia's eyelids together. With thick black thread and a tapestry needle. Paint *that.*

"I saw the exhibit you and Gwen had at the Carfax Gallery."

"It wasn't really *my* exhibition," put in Gwen reluctantly. She had edged in between Augustus and Dorelia. "It was Augustus' exhibition. I only had two little paintings in it. By *invitation* though."

"Oh, Gwen," said Dorelia, leaning forward. Her kimono gaped open and Gwen pinched the traitorous garment shut. "I thought *you* were the famous one after I saw your paintings. Even though they were so little, such tiny windows, they were so ... serene.

Everyone was talking about you."

"No, no," said Gwen, who did not like to be thought of as serene, who still had visions of threading a curved needle and tying a double knot. "Gussy got all the attention. He's very modern." She glanced at her brother's face, for he had a fearful temper and hated being thought of as the lesser artist, but he was shaking his head.

"Gwen's work is charged with feeling. It's *real* art. Whistler loves her but he thinks I am a whore and I am. My work isn't art. It looks nice over a fireplace, but it's empty of content. It doesn't make you *feel* anything. And that's why the masses love it so. Poor sods."

He exaggerated. He was one of the most popular artists in England that spring. Lords and ladies lined up to have him paint their portraits and he dashed them off, one after the other, sometimes two in a single day. They said he was the most brilliant draughtsman of his generation. They said he earned ten pounds a week and gave it away to his friends. They said he'd paid the entire bill for the Rodin party with the spare change in his pocket. They said he'd received an invitation from the King to paint his mistress in her boudoir.

"But Gwen ... she paints pure feeling." Augustus smiled at Gwen. God! What was it about her damnable brother that the smallest compliment from him made her heart race? Gwen was under no illusions. She took fifty times as long as Augustus to paint a single portrait and though her portraits made people groan aloud with pleasure and something akin to yearning, she was not yet an *artist,* in the way that Augustus and Rodin were artists. And truthfully, the last woman who had been a financially successful painter had been back in the Renaissance. Sofonisba Anguissola.

"What a beauty," Augustus said, transferring his gaze to Dorelia. "I should like to paint you as a Connemara gypsy, with the wind blowing your skirts up and you, exotic, in brilliant red petticoats." Dorelia blushed. "Will you come to my studio?" he asked.

Gwen ground her teeth loud enough for the upstairs neighbour to hear.

Dorelia's eyes flicked towards Gwen. "You're worried about my sister?" Augustus laughed. "Oh, she'll let you come. She *always* gives in to me. And anyway, why just have a pickled fig when you can have a date dripping honey?"

"Gussy!" said Gwen. She was afraid. Her voice was hoarse from terror and something else. "She's *my* student. It's just not done for one artist to steal another artist's model. Just for once, it's not about sex!" *You could paint me instead.* I *used to be your favourite model.* She almost said it aloud. Her heart began to pound. She heard it as a rushing sound in her ears, like water, like the ocean. *Glacé, salé, sec.* What's *really* not done is for a sister to be jealous when her brother loves another woman. Even when that brother has loved her, has *possessed* her, for fourteen years.

Dorelia edged forwards, a moth ready to fling itself on Augustus' brilliant flame. The light from the lantern making deep shadows on her face, her eyes hidden under the fall of her hair. She looked from the sister to the brother. The air smelled of snow, of ice crystals and dust. It was as if their history hung in the air between them. The too-familiar gestures, the possessiveness. Dorelia's eyes moved from left to right, reading everything that had passed between the two. Gwen's face blazed.

"You strip for your brother when you model!" Dorelia whispered, guessing, shivering with horrified delight. Augustus whinnied.

"You could both come to my studio," he said. "We could all strip for each other." He fumbled at his fly buttons and Gwen grabbed his hand to stop him. How he laughed at her stricken face, at the threads of longing and shame that twisted in the muscles of her cheeks. The lump. He had no tactics. What if

Dorelia decided that the incestuous Johns were too much for her, too much for any well-bred Englishwoman? Gwen preferred a steady war of attrition. She would have Dorelia in the end, despite Augustus and his heavy-handed grasping. And she would have *him* too, if she wanted him. Which right now she didn't.

Augustus, oblivious to Gwen's irritation, stood admiring Dorelia with his mouth slightly open. He held Gwen's fist clenched within his, directly over his crotch. She thought he was imagining painting the outline of Dorelia's dark hair, sketching the silk over her full breasts all the way to the hem of the kimono, where one bare foot peeped. The hand with which he trapped Gwen traced, in the tiniest of movements, the figure of the girl like a signum crucis over his groin. Dorelia had a long, slim foot and the tendons stood out over her ankle. She was an ideal model for him, a gypsy queen.

"For God's sake!" said Gwen. "Have you no shame, either of you? You, Augustus, look at her like she's a chop in the butcher's. And you, Dorelia, act like you are a bonbon, crying 'Eat me! Eat me!' What's wrong with you?"

"We share everything, Gwen and I, even our bed," Augustus muttered then. He fumbled for Dorelia's hand with his free fingers but she took a step away from him, from both of them, and then Augustus pulled away from Gwen too. Gwen could not look at Dorelia. "I imagine she wants you but is unwilling to say so. Gwen is a lesbian. Did she not tell you? I'm surprised you couldn't tell. A woman who has sex with other women. Jealous of me. Of us. Spoils to the victor, say I."

He smiled down at his sister and he patted her head. For a moment she felt the soft beard of his fifteen-year-old face against her skin, cold winter air filed her flesh and she smelled bay limes. For a moment, it was night and she was sixteen and a great dark presence descended over her, pressing her down, licking the sweat that had gathered at the base of neck. A finger was pressed against her lips and a practised hand slid inside her nightgown. Her heart fluttered. Her body arced. Her hips rose. She pulled him into her. But just for a moment. To want and not to want. Gwen glanced at Augustus and heard the faintest hiss of the hurdy-gurdy, the dying bray of the dancing bear. Her heart flopped like a mullet on a hook. *Glacé, salé, sec.* She took a breath and then another one. She could not, *must not*, be jealous of Dorelia. She would not lose all that she had gained in this year of freedom.

Augustus snorted. His face came close to hers, so close it was indecent. "I'll have you if I want you," he said. And it was, of course, true.

He struck a match on the sole of his shoe, and put it out with two wet fingers. Then he used the match to draw a quick sketch of Dorelia on the back of Gwen's painting. "And so it goes," he said, applying the last stroke to form Dorelia's décolletage. "I lack Gwen's famous *tone*, but I can dash off brilliant portraits one after the other. I shall draw you wearing the wing of a swan on your head, and the sixty-one-year-old King himself will buy it and keep it in his dressing room where he can look at it as he disrobes and through gazing at your incredible beauty, his facilities will be restored and he will once again stand erect."

"Leave," said Gwen. She struggled to keep on breathing evenly, one in, one out. The air did not seem to be reaching her lungs. "It's inexcusable to draw on my work, Augustus. You might claim my body but you may never claim my work." She pushed him but he didn't move. Mercurial grey spots swam up in front of her, and then fell into a darkly mirrored pool that spread at her feet.

"I will," said Augustus. "In a moment." He took Gwen's face between his hands and pulled her towards him and deep within, something hummed, and her body, for a moment, rose up to greet his. Dorelia gasped. Gwen, startled, pulled back, tore her arm free and slapped Augustus' face. "Don't touch what you don't own," she spat. How could it be that shame and pleasure were so tightly twined together that she regularly mistook one for the other?

"Settle down, little puss," Augustus said, laughing. "I'll come back when your *student* isn't looking."

Gwen wanted something with which to brand him. A poker. An awl. Her hands opened and snapped shut again and again with the wanting of a weapon. Augustus was a lowlife. He would walk out with the woman Gwen desired, and stupidly, she would be jealous, not that *she* didn't get Dorelia, but that her brother could love someone who wasn't her.

Real artists did not lack moral fibre. Real artists aspired to emotional honesty, to freedom, to justice, to humility. Real artists were brave and strode into the unknown without once turning back. Rodin, for example, would never have taken her student, though he would have been the first to admit that Dorelia was beautiful. His daily effort to see the body as a glove for the skeleton had refined him, just as it would refine her. Augustus, when he painted, lied, and so he remained dross.

"Oh don't bother," said Dorelia with a little yawn. "I know this must be how you two argue when you are embarrassed, but it's awfully boring to listen to. I don't care what you do to each other behind closed doors."

Augustus laughed a screaming parrot's laugh. He spilled their darkest secrets and Dorelia yawned. What secrets did *she* have that made the John family's seem so shallow?

Gwen had made a papier-mâché model of her missing trophy and pinned three sketches of children to the wallpaper over her bed. Still laughing, Augustus went to look at the sketches. "Gwen likes children," he said to Dorelia as he lifted his boot and planted it on the model of the trophy. Then he climbed up onto the frowsy sheets to see the children. He tilted a lantern that hung from a nail in the ceiling to cast a better light. "I've tried my best to impregnate my sister but the babe doesn't seem to stick. I'm sure to have better luck with you, darling Hera."

"He's lying." Gwen's eyes flicked again and again towards Dorelia, but Dorelia's eyes were half shut. Her hands stroked the front of her dress, as if she were imagining what it would be like to be pregnant with Augustus' baby. A bitch in heat. It was obvious she was infatuated by the widow with two orphans that lived in Augustus' trousers.

But still Gwen remembered the apple in the snake's mouth, the momentary warmth of the girl's flesh between her lips before she'd been pushed away and the bodice pulled up and the cold goodbye stated. It had not been instantaneous, the rejection. It gave her hope.

Gwen would be a fool to fall in love with a girl who only thought of men. It wasn't an attractive quality at all. And yet she *did* yearn. Was she obsessed with Dorelia only because Augustus wanted the same woman? But she'd wanted Dorelia even before Augustus had seen her. Her mind wasn't clear. She and Augustus were still such babies, fighting over toys, still angry over old hurts.

The previous year, her first in London, when they were both in their early twenties, Gwen and Augustus had tried to share a flat. She had known it was risky. She had known she would wake in the night and he would be there, looming over her, pressing her down, pushing into her the way he had done after their mother died. It had started when they were six and eight, because he was having nightmares. He'd seen the coffin going into the ground, and he'd become afraid of the dark, of the cold, breathing room, of the stillness of the night and the hushed shuffling of creeping things, and he'd come into her room and quietly asked if he might climb into her bed with her, and because she loved her little brother, she had drawn back her blankets and tucked him in and they had whispered to each other all night long. She'd stroked his gleaming curls and held his freezing hands and rubbed them and when she couldn't get them warm, she'd unbuttoned the top of her nightgown and put her brother's hands inside her clothing and trapped them there, under her arms. She kissed his dear little face over and over until he fell asleep. It was her fault, what came afterwards, when they were teenagers, all of it. She'd invited it from the start. Though she knew it wasn't right, the things they did, she wasn't sorry. She wasn't ashamed. What could be more natural than a sister loving a brother?

When she came to London, she had known she shouldn't live in his flat. People would eventually find out or suspect something about them. She wanted to be accepted into the art world as someone who made impeccable paintings of beautiful things, and she was fairly sure that if anything was found out about Augustus and her, it might destroy London's belief in her ability to be this person.

But she was *used* to Augustus, used to the generous splash of his affection, and the first months were so hard, so lonely, that she'd moved in with him despite the risk. She had sewn heavy black curtains for the windows and nailed felt to the door, all the while telling herself it was so that Augustus could sleep better, that the rooms were draughty.

She'd hidden a wooden cooking spoon under her pillow. The landlady had a key. Gwen could say that she had fought back. If someone would be at fault, it would be Augustus, not her. Then she sewed herself a new nightgown that opened with a string at the neck, easier than buttons in the pitch black. The first few times Augustus had come to her bed, he had lain next to her, like an ordinary younger brother, someone who knew what was right and what was sanctioned by church and society, the pure kind of love, and they'd talked about the types of brushes they preferred and where the best canvas could be purchased and for how much, and which students were the finest artists and which the worst, and the virile intelligence of Rodin's new work, and their philosophies of art and what made something beautiful and whether "beautiful" as a word and as a concept was corrupt, and she had nestled into the warm fragrant space under his arm and he had rolled closer to her and by morning, they were both toasty and comfortable and happy. He was like a puppy; delightful, squirmy, fresh. His silken curls her pillow, her breast his.

Each night, they talked and talked until, at some point, about a week after she moved in, the trigger unclear to her, Augustus had taken the cord that tied the nightgown shut between his fingers and he had tugged at it gently until the loops slid through the knot and her heart felt as if it too slid through a knot and came free, and he had slipped his hand inside, no boy now, no cold and shivering orphan, and her body had stilled, the thrill and the pleasure and the shock of this forbidden touch travelling straight to the place at the top of her legs. She'd asked him not to do that anymore, and then he had rolled on top of her and pinned down her hands and said that he knew she *did* want it, and it was true. She did.

Still, she had managed to free one hand and she'd hit him with the wooden cooking spoon and then she'd bitten his cheek, hard, when he wouldn't stop, a man now, heavier, and he had pinned her hands to the mattress with all his weight on his arms, and he had wrenched the cooking spoon from her and thrown it across the room, and then he had forced her, forced her, though she was willing unwilling willing oh god so unwilling her heart yearning and breaking, her body crying out yes no yes no. Even the fighting exciting, every part of her tingling, though she was hurt and her nose was broken and blood ran from Augustus' cheek and great blue and green spoon-shaped welts rose across his head and shoulders.

The next morning, they sat and ate cinnamon toast as if they were an old married couple. She dabbed his cuts and bruises with liniment and he patted her hand absently and said, "Thank you, darling," and she'd washed the dishes in the stone sink and he'd dried them with a towel and stacked them back in the cupboard and all the while, she felt this growing dread that this would be her life, forever owned by her brother, not living the life she had pictured for herself when she moved to London, a life where she was able to accomplish something, a *brave* life where she would be seen not as the sister of Augustus John, but on her own merit, as Gwen John.

She saw that if she stayed, she would forever be that girl lying under Augustus, obscured by him, hidden in his shadow, and so she'd moved out, and Augustus had carried her few things down the stairs, crying.

"Don't go," he said. "I love you." And her heart had almost broken for she loved him too and saw nothing wrong with what they had done, except in the possible outcome if they were discovered, but still her hand slid down the polished walnut railing, sliding and sliding until she stepped out into the sunlight and there were linden blossoms in the trees and tiny white petals on the footpaths and she went to find her own rooms, her own studio, her own little space in the world.

Less than a week later, Augustus punished Gwen by moving in with one of her dearest friends – a girl named Ida – getting *her* pregnant and calling *her* wife.

"I like your brother," said Dorelia, the day when she first met Augustus, as if she had forgotten the tension in the room. As if she did not see Gwen white and quivering, buried under jealousy and desire and shame. Poor Gwen. She was still plotting to get Dorelia into *her* bed.

For Dorelia, the world was always simple and beautiful and safe. Uncomplicated. "Don't fight because of me!" She laughed and opened the kimono a little and a wave of camellia-scented heat rolled up out of the garment. "Birds in their little nests agree, and 'tis a shameful sight, when children of one family fall out, and chide, and fight." It was quite appalling how middle-class and ordinary Dorelia was, quoting hymns at them. "We could have tea, the three of us."

Gwen drew a pin from her own dress, pinched the neckline of the kimono together and stabbed the steel through the silk. She had other uses for that pot of boiling water. "Don't start *liking* him. Gussy is a bastard. And he's *married*." How that had hurt. "He's been rejected from good society for fathering Ida's illegitimate son." It was alright for a man. If anything, it had increased his fame. But what would London have done if *she* had gotten pregnant? Who could they have named as the father? "You wouldn't want that, would you? To be kicked out of good society?"

Augustus, smirking. Watching Gwen. His eyes asking the same question: What would they have done if *she* got pregnant? The air in the room, icy. The floorboards, tilting. His clothes moved a little, shifted slightly to the side, wavered, moved back. Gwen blinked but the clothing still twitched at the corner of her vision. A tiny silvery fish swam across the ceiling.

In the old mirror, Gwen saw Dorelia, not clothed in the kimono, but barefoot and pregnant on a moor, her hair in great snarls over her face, ringed with naked children, wreathed in smoke, stirring the ashes and shivering.

"You'll destroy her," Gwen said. She crouched beside the kettle. Put both hands on the floor in case she fell. She touched the copper handle with one unprotected finger. *Ssssss.* The smell of burning flesh.

"Will you two stop talking about me as if I am not here?" asked Dorelia. She was shorter than Gwen and much shorter than Augustus. She looked at both of them and blinked her almost oriental eyes several times. "It's ever so boring to hear Johns fight. And all that silent yelling in your eyes. Ugh. I like you *both*." Gwen's heart jerked. Other regions of Augustus were affected. "There. That's settled it. Now, can you stop arguing and bring on the tea? Whatever brawls disturb the street, there should be peace at home."

Dorelia would never be an artist if she kept on reciting hymns as if she had been educated inside a Mother Goose book. And she knew nothing about birds in their nests. Crowlings had the habit of throwing the weak ones out, to fall a hundred feet and break their necks. Gwen smiled, picturing Augustus with feathers. She was the oldest in their particular nest. Dorelia, thinking Gwen agreed with her, smiled back.

Augustus picked up two cups from the floor where they lay and looked inside them. "Disgusting. It's a wonder you don't poison yourself, Mary." He pronounced Mary like *marry*. He shook one of the cups and something small fell out and ran towards the wall. He crushed it under his boot. "And no tea again. As usual. You're going to have to run out and buy some," he said to Gwen.

"Oh no! Gussy! How could you? It was alive!" cried Gwen. *She* made soft beds in matchboxes for the cockroaches, and carried them outside before releasing them. *She* tucked the cicadas under handkerchiefs and fed lettuce to the centipedes. Her cat had a pillow filled with hair from the brush, while Gwen slept on her own elbow.

When Augustus was a small boy, he had brought a twin lamb into his room and given it his blanket. He'd found it lost in the market, bleating, likely abandoned by both ewe and shepherd. Its tiny pale pink tongue had stuck out from between its teeth and in order to cry out, it lifted its stomach and heaved its spine and tilted its tiny head back and the sound travelled in waves up its throat until it erupted from its mouth, a shockingly loud and penetrating shriek. Gwen and he had tried to feed it milk and sodden bread. "Poor baby!" he'd said, with tears spilling from his eyes. "You want your mother, don't you?" They'd sat with the tiny thing in their laps all night, deafened by its hideous screams, struggling to keep it covered by the blanket, trying and trying to love it, but it had died anyway. Gwen still tried to protect little beasts, but maybe that's when Augustus began to change, to harden himself towards the death of innocents.

Now, that mad, bad Messiah lifted his foot and hopped in Gwen's direction. He hoisted his foot to show her the crushed remains of the silverfish, dripping from his heel. He stuck his boot almost in her face. She stepped backwards. "What are you afraid of? Me?" He tilted his head and laughed his shrieking laugh.

"How could I be afraid of you?" Gwen said. "You and I share the same sins." It was oddly liberating to talk about it in front of someone else, almost as if their lives were normal lives. But then Dorelia swept in front of her and knelt at Augustus' feet. She was taking out her handkerchief. She was lifting his foot.

"Where are you going, Gwen?" Dorelia asked. She was wiping crushed insect off his boot. His foot rested in her lap. Gwen screwed the key savagely in the lock.

"Getting tea," Gwen said. Her spine ossifying with each word. Her voice sharp and full of splinters. She was two inches taller than a minute ago. Three. "Maybe my upstairs neighbour has some I could borrow? The roaches have carried all mine off, I am afraid. They were last seen heading for Spain, wearing Gussy's nasty boots."

"Could you get me some cheese too? Or some eggs?" Augustus called. Unlike Gwen, he still received an allowance from their father. Also unlike Gwen, he had sold thirty paintings at their most recent exhibition at the New English Art Club and for good money and had the purple corduroy pants and polished mustard boots to prove it. She'd had two paintings in the exhibit, and she'd sold one to her friend and promptly lost the second canvas. As a result, Gwen wore carpet slippers, picked from the same rubbish tip as the mirror and the kimono. It was all well and good being called "a prescient artist" or "a painter of timeless humanity", but accolades didn't pay the bills. Paintings did. And she could not be hurried.

"Maybe some chocolate for the lady?" Augustus didn't seem to notice that there was no heat, no running water, no air and no food whatsoever in the flat. He looked like a flamboyant Jesus but the only person he cared about was himself. He hadn't even glanced at the notice nailed to the outside of the door, stating that the building was condemned.

Gwen flicked one last look at Dorelia's neckline. "Do debase yourself while I am gone," she said. She did not want to be around when Dorelia bent and licked the buttery yellow leather of Augustus' boots. She rubbed her hands together as if she were peeling off filthy gloves and then stalked out the door in search of tea.

"Sweet Aphrodite!" Augustus said, bending low over Dorelia's head. "Divine ardour! You shall jump the broom with me yet." Up close, his eyes were more of a midnight blue.

"Such an Adonis you are. I should like to have *your* cup of tea," whispered Dorelia, lifting her head to look at his face. She was only twenty-one. He seemed infinitely older than her, older and wilder, like a gypsy from the New Forest. He smelled of fallen leaves and moss and the ferns that grow in the darkest places. She took the end of his long hair between her fingers and tickled her own lip with the tiny brush. "What do you think of Gwen's paintings?"

"Ha!" he laughed. "She won't let me see this little sketch she's made of you! But I can do a better painting of you than her, if only you will let me try," he said. He did not want to say that Gwen had won the Melvill Nettleship Prize for Figure Composition the same year he'd won the Slade Prize. Even as he and Gwen painted, out of the corners of their eyes, they each watched the other. He pulled his hair back from between her fingers and she giggled.

"In general then," she said. "What do you think of Gwen's work? It doesn't seem to be like anyone else's."

In answer, Augustus strode across to the painting and turned it around. Against an almost transparent pastel background,

Dorelia had been painted in a corner of the room, her arms crossed over her naked breasts, the fingers of one hand digging into her flesh. Her hair hung down her back and a few strands swept across her face. She did not make eye contact with the painter but instead looked away, seemingly embarrassed by her nakedness, anxious of discovery. In one hand, a crumpled pink ribbon. Her chin appeared to tremble.

"Ah," said Augustus. He took a deep breath. The kettle, on the hotplate, began to whistle. From upstairs, the deep rumble of the treadle sewing machine, *ker-thump, ker-thump*, a heart beating in three, a waltz of construction.

"Well," he said, still staring at the unfinished portrait. "The truth of it is," he cleared his throat and bent closer to see how it was that Gwen had created the illusion of movement, but even after examining it line by line, he was still unsure. "I," he said, and he leaned in again, this time to examine the flatness of the paint on the cheeks, the luminous and sheer layers that gave the impression of a sun rising deep within Dorelia's skin. "I, uh, I convinced Will Rothenstein to include two of her paintings along with mine in the exhibit." He stretched out one finger to test the thickness of the paint, the texture. What was she mixing her colours with? "So she wouldn't starve. The New English Art Club won't work with her after the last time." Who had she learned this technique from? How did she know how to do these things? "She's such an odd duck. Quacking commands at everyone. Complaining about the light." He would have to grill the girl later for the name of Gwen's teacher. Or perhaps she had a notebook somewhere with recipes? "Even if her models are pretty, her paintings of them never are."

For Gwen, standing in the doorway with a saucer of tea-leaves, listening to this blather, the room grew small and dark. Unseen things scuttled inside the walls and chewed the wallpaper. As always, she saw herself moving smoothly backwards, away from whatever small light was cast by the lantern and the greasy shard of window, backwards until she saw Dorelia and Augustus standing together inside a tiny circle, as if at the end of a long tunnel. At any moment she would completely vanish.

This always happened to her in moments of stress. She had the sense that her attachment to the world was tenuous, that at any moment she might no longer exist. It didn't help that she was so small and easily ignored. It didn't help to be bumped into in the street. She felt like a ghost already but she would not allow her own brother to ignore her.

She stamped her foot and called out, "Liar! They begged me to come! " Ever since she came to London she'd carved a sign in illuminated letters into her own flesh: *Artist*. The recognition from Rodin, when he held up his imaginary sketch pad and smiled at her, was what kept her alive and moving forward and facing each day with what she hoped was bravery. I *am* an artist. But now, like a clay man without the name of God on his forehead, she felt herself falling, returning to mud.

"You messed up everything," said Augustus. His very calm was enraging. "You are so antisocial and you work so slowly. You think you send the paintings in but instead they're under your mattress. Then you chastise the senior officials for their carelessness, and then the only portrait that actually made it to the show, you sell to your friend at a tenth of the asking price and the club loses their profit." He turned slowly, looking for a journal where she might have hidden notes about her technique. "I *made* them reinvite you." His voice soft, kind, once again a small boy pleading for her understanding. Apologising.

Gwen exhaled. He was, of course, right. In her hands, the front of the kimono clenched between her fingers. Inside the kimono, plump Dorelia. Gwen could not remember how she had come into the room or what had become of the saucer of tea-leaves.

"Will you draw *me* next Tuesday?" Gwen asked Dorelia, as if Augustus wasn't there. "A nude? Perhaps we could draw each other drawing each other nude?" Dorelia held Gwen's arm, propping her up. Gwen's trembling so violent that they both trembled. "What do you think?" It was a line that had been used on her, by a previous lover, a female artist, most successfully.

"We could *all* draw each other nude," said Augustus.

Dorelia stepped behind a screen in the corner of the room and, underneath the kimono, pulled her dress up over her hips and threaded her arms down the tight sleeves. "Oh no," called Dorelia. "I *couldn't* model nude for a man. But I think it would be terrible fun for you and me to draw each other nude," she said to Gwen. She stooped and picked up the saucer, broken in two halves in the doorway, and swept the spilled leaves into a little pyramid. "No tea for us." She held out the money for her tuition, and Gwen reluctantly took it. The coins were still warm from the beautiful girl's hand. Gwen closed her fingers around the coins and held her fist tucked under her chin until the warmth had faded.

Dorelia stepped closer, fastening the topmost button of her bodice and tying a whitework scarf around her shoulders. "You have paint in your hair," she said, a smile in her voice. She scraped a tiny shard of blue from Gwen's hair and popped it into her mouth. "I am tasting Gwen John," she said. "The famous lady painter of Howland Street."

"Give my love to David, and to Ida," Gwen said. She closed her eyes. Her heart so soft.

"Who is Ida?" asked Dorelia. "Who is David?" Dorelia touched the front of Gwen's dress, startling her. Her eyes flew open. "Gwen? Who is Ida?"

"Ida is Gussy's 'wife'. Ida Nettleship. And David is Gussy's first-born son."

Augustus sat on the step. The new green cape was folded over his arm, hiding the notebook he'd found. Gwen suddenly couldn't bear to look at him anymore. He was everywhere. Looking at her painting, crushing her insects, touching her bedding, moving her paints, claiming her student's clothing, breathing up all of the air in the room, stealing her notebook. He did not have the class of Rodin.

"Please," Gwen said again, but she had no words for what she really wanted to say. Quinacridone red, scarlet lake, dioxazine, manganese blue, cobalt, indigo, burnt sienna, Davy's grey, umber, black. Payne's grey, the colour of rain. She had words for colours, but none for feelings.

"How do you do it, Gwen?" Augustus blurted. "The finish to the paint?" Two years of experiments in that notebook. The thief. She passed a hand in front of her eyes and turned to look out of the smeared window. The glass smudged with fingerprints. Outside, starlings scuffled over a crust of bread on the granite cobbles. He walked out with her notebook, her student and who knew what else.

Gwen went over to erase the charcoal drawing Augustus had made on the back of her portrait, but before she could, she saw that there was some disturbance to her painting, something had been changed. She leaned closer and saw that her brother had pressed his thumb into the wet edge of the paint and left his fingerprint, even here, in her most intimate place, her oils.

Above, the front door slammed. A rainbow of fine threads fell from the ceiling, which was nothing but the bare floorboards of the illegal dressmaker overhead. The bright reds and yellows and greens spun in the dim light, floating down onto Gwen's hair and shoulders, making her cough. When she bent over her fist, the threads fell from her hair and onto the floor.

AUGUSTUS:

My sister was born on the 22nd of June, 1876 in Haverfordwest, in Wales, two years before I was born. Have you ever seen Haverfordwest? There's a castle there. Ruins. And farmers. Lots of farmers with shit on their boots and pipes in their mouths and caps pulled down low so you can't see their eyes. They all speak Welsh. There's a lot of consonants in Welsh. It sounds like they are eating burned porridge and trying to talk at the same time. I got spit all over my face whenever anyone said hello. We moved when I was six.

My sister and I went diving off rocks in 1896. Giltar Point. She was twenty. I was eighteen. There are these cliffs that hang over the ocean outside Tenby, about thirty or forty feet up. I'd been daring Gwen to jump all day and still she swam about, naked, blue and shivering, with a clump of seaweed on her head and draped around her wrist for jewellery. It was only when I stopped daring her that she stood up, climbed the cliff and made a perfect dive straight into the Atlantic, arching out with her feet together and slicing into the water like a blade. Of course, after that, I had to go up and do it myself, but my foot slipped on the ground. It was wet where she had been standing. I didn't leap out far enough and I split my head open on some rocks. I could have died. I think she hauled me in to shore. In the hospital, she wept over me. She demanded that any injury should be hers. She prayed for it. I've never had a single problem from that accident, but Gwen got what she wanted. Now she faints. Her head is strange. It should be me that sees things, but it's her. I have no idea how someone her size could have rescued me.

My sister and I were raised by our aunts, sour old Salvationists who drove us four kids around town in their buggy, ringing their bells, beating on their tambourines, shouting for repentance. In our father's house, at night, they tied our hands together with handkerchiefs so we looked like we were praying. We were forbidden to put our hands under the blankets. At first they put all four of us to sleep in one double bed, the girls at one end and the boys at the other. But later, they wouldn't allow the boys to go near the girls. A lot about Gwen can be explained by those aunts.

My sister would have been the dux of her school in academics if she'd ever gone to school, but our father didn't believe in it for girls. Weaker sex, weaker minds. He ruled the aunts and us children with an iron hand. He believed that girls couldn't learn to read and that an educated woman wanted to be a man and that that was a perversion of God's will. That's why Gwen can't spell. And her grammar is atrocious. She's never even heard of a full stop.

My sister draws inside all the books she owns with purple ink. When we were little, I took many a caning for her doodles when my teachers opened my books and thought, because of the quality of the drawings, that I'd done the defacing. My sister never asked me how this affected me and frankly, I don't know the answer.

My sister went to a lot of different art schools but she never finished at any of them. She got frustrated or broke up with some woman or some man or the school kicked her out or she just stopped going. Even when she was a little girl, she wasted a lot of paper, deciding she hated what she'd just drawn and throwing it into the fire in a fit of rage. She has no idea, none at all, of what she is as an artist. She thinks she still has a lot to learn.

My sister's paintings have been in lots of exhibitions. The New English Art Club and the Salon d'Automne. John Quinn got her into the Armory Show, the International Exhibition of Modern Art, in New York. I would have liked to have been in that one. I could have been if I wanted. I just didn't want to. My sister is the kind of artist who people appreciate slowly. She's not flashy. In fifty years' time, I will be known as the brother of Gwen John. But I've been collecting original Gwen John's since I was ten, so I'll get rich off her.

My sister has squatted in derelict buildings for at least half of her life. Once, she fell through to the floor below. That's where she found her first cat, eating the person who'd fallen through before her. The man had a broken neck. By the time Gwen found him, he was missing all his fingers and toes.

My sister crushes all of her cat's newborn kittens in a paper bag, except for one. Her current cat is the great-great-great-great-great-great-great-great-granddaughter of her first cat, the one that ate human fingers and toes.

My sister works harder than I do but has less to show for it. She paints every day. She experiments with paint and with texture. Her hands are always covered with oil paint and gouache. Her favourite colours are dark green and apricot. Even her best dress is speckled with colour. She wears this disastrous white shirt over her clothes, but it doesn't protect anything. She smells like turpentine and rabbit-skin glue and rotting fruit and gesso. She smells like a sewer on bad days. On good days, she smells like Rembrandt.

My sister reads far more books than I do, and she takes notes, so she can talk about the content later. She talked with Oscar Wilde about his writing, instead of trading jokes or fucking him. Illiterate she isn't.

My sister writes love stories and hides them under her bed. I've caught her writing them and tried to read what she's written but she screams and claws me and bites my hands and shreds the papers. She's very dramatic. And then she faints, so you have to pity her. Sometimes I wonder if it's an act. She says she doesn't believe in love. "It's all a load of codswallop," that's what she says. But there's pages and pages every time I visit.

Our mother died when my sister was eight, after a long

illness. Our mother lay in bed, in the darkness, moaning and moaning and moaning. My sister put cotton wool in our ears so we wouldn't have to hear the moans. She put cotton wool in my ears, and in Winifred's ears, and in Thornton's ears, but there is no blocking out such sounds of agony. When there wasn't enough cotton wool, she made sure we all had while she did without. Even father had cotton wool in his ears. "For God's sake," he yelled at our mother one day, "will you bloody turn them into orphans already!" Even now, you can see the sounds of our mother's moans on Gwen's face. She has never been one to back down from the pain of the world. Her art is better than mine because she paints all the pain she feels, whereas I like to pretend it never happened. For example, I've never talked to Gwen about how our mother's death affected her.

Our father didn't love her. He didn't love any of us. He was a solicitor. It explains a lot. He always did his duty. Sometimes, when we were eight and nine and ten, he did his duty by buying us art paper and crayons and lessons at home. Sometimes he did his duty with his belt. Sometimes, after mother died, he did his duty on Gwen at night, and sometimes he did his duty on me. We never said a word about it to each other, so I haven't got any idea about how that affected her either. And I don't want to talk about how it affected me.

My sister wears a hat that is too large for her small body and tight clothes that are too fancy for her station in life, and rather too much make-up. She gives the wrong impression. Bad men love her.

My sister's waist is exactly seventeen inches around. Uncorsetted. She has almost non-existent breasts. Her nipples are about a thumbnail wide and the exact same colour as the inner corner of her eye. Her hips are so sharp you could use them to cut cheese. *All* of her hair is red. I know because I've been sketching her naked since she was fourteen.

My sister embroiders her stockings with images of open red

slits. They might be mouths. They might not.

My sister doesn't wear undergarments in the summertime. She isn't afraid of small insects crawling across her privates, but she *is* afraid of strong winds and falling down stairs. And she has a morbid fear of circuses for some reason.

My sister doesn't care about things like money and she would starve, except I tell her I have sold a picture of hers and send her a few coins. I have an enormous pile of her paintings and drawings in my studio and I have to hide them when she comes to visit. I told you, I collect Gwen John.

My sister weighs less than a hundred pounds. She has flaming red hair to the middle of her back that she always wears in a bun, with a part straight down the middle, like a little old lady whose head is on fire. She's just a bit over five feet tall. She comes up to my scapula.

My sister loves little children and they are curiously drawn to her. She claims that she doesn't ever want children but she is lying. She puts her nose in the necks of my children and breathes in and sighs. My sister sings quiet little songs to her own unborn babies with her eyes closed. She is my children's favourite aunt. My sister loves things that need her, whether it's small children or mice or little cats or potted ferns. Other than that, though, she has almost no use for anyone or anything else.

My sister won't use certain colours next to each other on the canvas. She lines up her tubes of paint in a particular order and she won't put a tube of burnt sienna next to cadmium for even a second. She washes her hands before she touches the tubes and she washes the tubes too. She scrapes her palette down to the raw wood every single night. She explained her logic to me once, but it was crazy. My sister might be crazy. Actually, I think we both might be.

My sister stole Dorelia away from me, right when we were getting started, back in 1901 or 2. I think she did it to protect Ida, but there was a lot of self-love in there too. My sister really *did* love Ida. She would have crawled through shit for her. My sister was the only one who knew how to calm Ida down. I think Ida idolised Gwen. When she gave birth to David, she only wanted Gwen in the room. After the birth, Gwen had Ida's teeth marks in her hand for weeks. When I was coming home from the pub, it was late at night, I'd been out drinking in honour of the kid, I saw Gwen running down the middle of the street with her arms stretched out wide and her hair down and she was singing at the top of her lungs, "There's a new baby in the world! Wake up! There's a new soul down here!" And I could swear that there were ten inches of navy black sky under her feet.

My sister is in the first photograph we took of our first child. Ida, holding David, on one side, and Gwen, tucked under my other arm.

My sister has the tiniest feet. They are no bigger than my hand. If she *was* flying that night, it would be because her feet, like tiny smelly sparrows, have wings.

My sister and I didn't talk for a lot of years. She didn't like me at all, I think. It was after she broke my nose. She used to beg me. Such a stereotype, the older sibling forcing the younger one. At night, she called out for me until I woke up and came into her room. She needed to be held. She needed to be touched. She was afraid of the dark ever since our mother died. It was as if I had to draw off all of the sad sick energy that she accumulated throughout the day and only then could she go to sleep. She used to kiss me on the lips, over and over, with such intensity. It wasn't my fault. At a certain point, a boy becomes a man and such a thing, every night, it's hard to resist, it's hard to push away when it's offered to you so freely, and she really was beautiful, my sister, in a way that made you think she came from somewhere else, or maybe some*when* else. In the dark, at night, I thought of her as a kind of angel. It was like I was with an angel, not my sister, someone unearthly, someone who wrapped me in soft white wings that smelled of freshly fallen snow, and rocked me through the night. I loved it, I'm not going to deny it. All the boys in school were jealous of me when I told them. My beard came in early because of what we did together. I couldn't stop thinking about her day and night. After a while, I couldn't keep away from her. After a while, we were doing it two and three times a night and we were sneaking away during the day too. You know, I am never going to love someone as much as I love her. She ruined me for every other woman. I wanted to get her pregnant, even when she was fourteen, I wanted to see her stomach swell up with something we made together. I wanted to rest my ear on her belly and hear a heartbeat inside her that was both hers and mine. I wanted her to have a dozen babies with me. I wanted her face to be on every one of those infants. I wanted to suck one breast while the babies sucked the other one. I loved every part of her body from her tiny feet all the way up to her determined little chin. Did you know that she has a red mark underneath her right breast where I bit her? It left a permanent scar. When we paint each other, I always paint that mark under her breast and she always paints the mark she made with her teeth on my hip. That's the truth of this story. I loved her, I loved her, I still love her. And she loved me. It's only wrong when one person doesn't want it but we *both* wanted it. Now I think the whole thing was my fault, probably. I should have been more of a man about telling her to stop. No. It was both of our faults. Things were done that maybe shouldn't have been done. I'm not so sure about that though. It's another one of those things I haven't talked to her about.

My sister loves me, despite not wanting to do it with me anymore. Although that's not true. She wants to. I can see it in her eyes. I love her and she loves me. We don't have to say I love you for it to be true.

I have never seen my sister cry.

My sister doesn't exactly live in this world. It's like she lives in two or three worlds simultaneously. Sometimes she doesn't know which one she is in. Once, when we were swimming off the coast of England, far out in freezing water at dawn, there was a whale that rose up between us and she just swam over to that leviathan and looked into its deep black eye, and it turned to look at her and it rolled over on its side and slapped a flipper down on the surface of the water. It saluted my sister. The entire ocean around it alive, electric, the water felt as if streams of bubbles rose, fast and hard, right through my chest. Afterwards, my sister floated on her back, starring at the pink and blue streamers burning off the morning sky. What are you thinking about, I asked her. I'm thinking about the seam at the edge of the world, she said. Where the day and the night and the world and the sky and yesterday and today and tomorrow are all stitched together.

PAINTING I:

Gwen's new canvas for Dorelia was fine linen, stretched over a wooden strainer and attached with steel tacks, bought from her favourite colourman, Percy Young, not young at all, fifty if he was a day, at his shop on Gower Street near the Tate. The back of the cloth was darker than the front, and stained. She was not sure why, and went to talk about it with Mr Young and after smacking his children and telling them to play outside, he told her that the canvas was sized with hot glue that had saturated the threads. On one edge of the canvas, there was a clean selvage but on the other three sides, the canvas was roughly cut. Gwen used her sewing shears and trimmed the jagged edges, and then brushed a little rabbit glue over the edges so that they didn't fray.

Now, the erased remains of a charcoal drawing are still visible, despite her rubbing, and some of the priming has bled through to the back. Gwen primed this canvas herself, two days before Dorelia came the first time. She used lead white oil paint mixed with kaolin and chalk, and then, with delight and trepidation and with a kind of dull expectation of abandonment, she loosely brushed on a greenish-grey layer that grinned half-heartedly through all the later layers of paint. She had hoped, with the priming, to help the later layers to dry more quickly. She had hoped it would look as if she had painted it all in one fluid rush, rather than painstakingly, slowly, over many nights. She hoped the grey and the faint pink tones would appear clean and fresh and unworked, effortless.

She swipes on thin, dark layers of lead white, bone black and cobalt blue as the mid-tones in Dorelia's flesh and the crumpled dress around her waist. Her paints are thin and fluid, she moves her brush in sturdy swoops, she falls asleep over the painting, standing with her head resting on her arm.

This is how she paints her first portrait of Dorelia, quickly, with her tongue pressed against her front teeth, dizzy, anxious, looking and not looking, wants to touch the real flesh rather than paint it. She paints Dorelia's dimple and twists the point of her brush into the hollow. She paints the mauve shadows beneath Dorelia's breasts. She paints deep violet pleats into the fabric that Dorelia keeps bunched around her hips. Each day, when she rises, she sees that the brilliant hues of the previous day have died overnight, and she layers the painting with varnish, to try to resuscitate the colours. She begins to hate varnish. She hates the yellowish-green haze it creates, the way the varnish darkens the colours without necessarily reviving them. Every time she looks towards the portrait, she finds it hard to breathe. She does not show Dorelia the painting and when it is finished, she stands the canvas against the wall near her bed and sets a candle next to the portrait and she stares at it all night until she finally falls asleep and in the morning she paints over Dorelia with lead white, then turns the portrait around and paints over Augustus' charcoal daubs too.

GIRL WITH A SULKY EXPRESSION:

Gwen was no virgin. She'd fallen in love the year she went away to school, to the Slade, but no one talked about that affair. When her little girlfriend left her, to get married to someone with money and a name, Gwen threatened suicide. She rampaged around the apartment they'd shared. She cried, "But it's *me* you love, not him!" A year later, she had an affair with a man, to test out the possibilities of factory-installed equipment and it was a lovely thing, so she said, though to be honest, she'd already tried it out nightly for years. But a stranger, so she said, was different. And then he too left to get married to another, even as she lived in his apartment, even as she expected to be offered a ring of her own. "Am I always to be the slut, and never the maiden?" she complained to her friend Ursula Tyrwhitt.

"Well, you are, rather," said Ursula, who had no intention of getting married herself. "Whatever happened to that German filly you were seeing?"

"I have mother's ring," Gwen said. "Perhaps I should do the proposing." And at that, Ursula laughed and retrieved her gloves and left, because sometimes Gwen could be such an unholy terror. Sometimes she could be truly frightening. "I would have had you," Ursula called over her shoulder, "had you proposed to me!"

She fell in love so easily, Gwen thought as she walked Dorelia home after a lesson. If only other women fell in love with her too.

"Next Tuesday?" she asked, holding Dorelia's hand for a moment too long, studying the fingers and the curve of the nails, until the small dark woman pulled away and put her hands behind her back. Under a hedge, a song thrush bashed a snail on a pebble, trying to get at the meat. The bird's neat brown body whipped the shell left and right. It paused and spat out a shard of shell, then lifted the snail to beat it again. The thrush's white breast appeared to hover an inch or so in front of the bird itself. Tiny brown arrows flecked the white. Another bird flew down and joined the first.

"But we can't paint next Tuesday!" said Dorelia.

Renaissance painters included thoughts about their subjects' backgrounds, their potential, their sexuality, their scholarship. If Gwen were painting Dorelia, she would include the handkerchief she held crushed between her fingers, with her initial badly embroidered in one corner, the machine-made lace tacked around the edges with extraordinarily long stitches. She would include a book by Henry James. She would paint Dorelia holding an angel with a golden sphere surrounding their heads. She would give her a high forehead, though she didn't have one, and a paler skin than she actually had and a diaphanous gown that would make her appear slim. The fall of light would lie along her body and just touch the ends of her hair. Her lover would be sprawled next to her and her lover would be a small red-headed woman with a narrow chin.

"Your brother has invited me to his party. Shall we walk there together?" The shell split and the song thrush fed the foamy meat to the other bird.

Augustus hadn't invited Gwen. She'd figure something out. She'd find a second-hand dress on Penny Lane or at the St Vincent de Paul's in Queen Square. She'd arrive and then what would Augustus do? The thrushes imitated Gwen's tiny whistling sigh, and then repeated it, once and twice and three times, so that the road seemed full of sighs. The Renaissance-style portrait blinked out. Clouds drifted over the moon and the girls were plunged, briefly, into darkness. The gas lamp's light, at the corner, barely reached more than three feet in any direction.

Perhaps she could ask her upstairs neighbour to make her something very simple, even if it meant she had nothing to eat for a week. But not if it meant something *much* worse. That, she would never do. She had principles. She was not a whore.

The wind carried the smell of fish up from the wharves. The moon slid out from behind its gauze wrappers and its light fell in a slanting sheet on Dorelia's face. In that moment, Gwen stopped loving Dorelia and rather hated her. She was only a clerk's daughter, working as a secretary and living at home, who had actual money for things like clothing and art lessons. Dorelia's head tipped to one side. "What on earth are you thinking?" she said, and her hand slipped inside Gwen's again. From under the hedge, the sound of a snail being rapped against a pebble.

The night of the party, Augustus met the girls at the door of his Fitzroy Street flat. He was wearing an enormous grey Aran jumper and his boots. A parrot perched on his shoulder, nibbling on Augustus' gold earring and shrieking profanities. "Dorelia!" he shouted, ignoring Gwen. "How divine! Arthur, have you met my new model yet? She's going to make me famous! Bring me my sketchblock!"

"You already *are* famous, old boy!" called several men, but they brought him a pad of paper and a charcoal nonetheless.

Outside, Gwen swam through the churning crowd, her hands slicing into shoulders and outstretched arms. Occasionally, she was tossed up and saw Augustus with his fat paws on her model. "Gussy!" she yelled. "You thief! Give her back!"

Dorelia had seen Gwen stroking through the throng and she pulled away from Augustus and reached out her hand to Gwen.

"Gwen?" asked Augustus, looking around. "Gwen is here?" He knew she was, the bastard. "She wasn't invited."

"*I* like Gwen," said Dorelia. "You *must* have invited her! She's your sister!" She kissed Gwen on the cheek and patted her all over as if checking for damage.

"Sometimes she is. And sometimes she's rather more and that's what makes her unbearable," said Augustus, looking away from this display.

"If my canaries die, I'll know your breath is as poisonous as I think it is," Gwen said to Augustus. She could barely breathe herself. She hated crowds. They did funny things to her head. Her heart went flippetty flop. And Augustus was as bad as a crowd. She cracked open a window and waggled the fingers of one hand outside in the cold air.

She pulled free the hand that Dorelia was clutching, rolled up her sleeves, knelt on the boards and hung both arms out of the windows, fishing for a tree to hold on to. Dorelia glared at her – such an odd woman! She waited for a minute with an irritated expression on her face, hoping Gwen wouldn't abandon her amongst all these strangers and then stalked off into the next room, the back of her neck the same slope as a cat when it bends to wash its paw and wipe away ridicule.

"Gwendolen!" called an American who had been after her to do a portrait of his wife. "Miss John!" called Lady Ottoline, who liked her art *and* her body. Gwen brushed past the formidable Virginia Stephen who she thought rather young and rather lovely, past gallery owners and the directors of the New English Art Club and even the art critic Roger Fry. When they called out for her, she pretended she didn't hear them and she ran for the third room, Augustus' studio. She thought that none of those people, really, were interested in her or her paintings. She was not the kind of person who art critics and fancy society wanted to talk with. She was like poor old Baron Rothschild, a social pariah. In the third room, her brother was at the centre of a group of young women, with his arm around Dorelia's waist.

"When *is* Ida going into confinement?" Gwen asked, glaring

at his arm, and she knew, as she said it, that it was a sharp needle in Augustus' side. Poor Ida. If anyone knew what it was like to be run over roughshod by Augustus, it was Gwen. But dear sweet simple Ida always picked herself up and dusted off her apron and smiled again and did her little happy-wife wiggle, whereas Gwen sharpened her swords.

"The little porker is going to pop out some time next month," Augustus said, waving his pipe around. Clouds of smoke and roars of laughter filled all of the rooms. "Ida wants a girl, but I am set on a boy and I shall call him Caspar." He knew Gwen disliked the name Caspar. Or Balthazar. He grinned at her. "Definitely Caspar." He pulled Dorelia closer and kissed her on the side of her cheek and it couldn't have been the first time, because she didn't even blush.

Sometimes, in the right light, the seam across his nose where the doctor repeatedly had to stitch him up after fights with cuckolded husbands could be seen. "You should know better than to come to parties you aren't invited to," he said, seeing the look on her face. It was the right light now.

"Those are the parties I never miss," said Gwen. She stood on her toes as if she might kiss Dorelia too, but then she swerved and instead, bit his ear and he yelped.

"Scorpion," he said.

"Pervert," she said.

"Adopted at birth," he said.

"Product of rape," she said.

They stared at each other, neither one fully enraged. Augustus smiled first. When he smiled, his eyes sparkled and his lips turned up in the most appealing way and his beard seemed to bounce, like a delighted child, in place, all copper coils and gleams of golden light. "You win," he said.

"I wish," she said. "You still have your arm around Dorelia."

It probably hadn't been so very smart of her to rush past Roger Fry in her attempt to retrieve Dorelia. Rodin wouldn't steal another artist's models. But Augustus had no class, so it was all wasted effort. Gwen could see the critic in the next room, whispering to another man, and darting glances in her direction.

"Of course she's mine," roared Augustus. "Every man deserves a beautiful woman."

Gwen put her arm on Dorelia's elbow and tugged, but Dorelia shook her head. The circle of art critics turned to look at them, rings of silence radiating out from this scuffle, touching almost every group in the room.

Gwen snapped her teeth together so suddenly that she bit her tongue.

"What would a party be if there wasn't a little drop of jealousy in all the drinks?" Augustus said. He handed Gwen his glass. On the edge, the prints of his lips. "Happiness to the royal couple," he said, tapping her glass with a new one. "Augustus and Dorelia!"

"Augustus and Dorelia!" roared many in the crowd, raising their glasses and then throwing back their drinks.

"You're a thief," said Gwen to Augustus then. "I have no idea why people ever come to visit you."

"It's the power of my magnificent personality," said Augustus. He'd received one negative review of his most recent exhibition and it turned out to have been written by Gwen. "Dear sweet fat thing," he said to Dorelia, who was chatting with Roger Fry. "Do come away from that nasty man."

"Oh, but I've sold your painting to him," Dorelia said. "The first one you make of me."

Gwen could have wept. Why hadn't Dorelia sold *her* painting to Fry? She couldn't *still* be angry about Gwen cooling her hands outside the windows? Or was it that Gwen hadn't told her that she didn't, actually, have an invitation? Invisible, as always.

"Mister Fry," Gwen said when she had composed herself. "I have a completed painting of Dorelia, should you like to see it."

But the man was walking away with Augustus, Dorelia sandwiched between them. Gwen took one step and stopped.

The painting, anyway, had been painted over. Really, she had nothing at all.

"One of these days," Gwen muttered to her brother's retreating back. "I will stick a knife into your magnificent personality."

Later that evening, when everyone had given up chasing canaries and convened around the fireplace, to smoke and drink port and read from their latest works, Dorelia was invited to perch on Augustus' lap. Arthur Symons blushed as Henry Lamb sat on *his* knee. Tall, slim Henry was impeccably dressed, a purple silk scarf around his neck, an intaglio pin, his long pale hair falling past his shoulders. Gwen, almost hidden, watched as society women pawed her brother's jacket, and as Augustus cuffed men around the ears and kissed them on the lips, merely to make them jump back, confused and laughing. Augustus was far taller than anyone and he spilled out of his chair, his feet cluttering up the centre of the room, his massive head blocking the lights on the mantle.

"Before Goldberg eats all our food or hides it in his pocket, make sure you get yourselves a bite! Don't stint! Aren't we ever so proper?" asked Augustus. "We English. What do we ever talk about but biscuits and horses and ideas?" He brushed back his long hair and raked his fingers under his beard, to fluff it up. "When will we tear down the walls and talk about what is truly important?"

"And what might that be, brother?" asked Gwen. She sat below Dorelia and him on the floor in between two upholstered club chairs. Inside one of them, there was a rustling and a faint squeaking that led her to believe that there was a mouse family nesting in the straw stuffing. "What important subject has caught your attention now?" *Squeak. Rustle rustle squeak squeak.* Perhaps it was only the springs under the combined weight of Henry Lamb and Arthur Symons, but Gwen preferred to think it was a family of little mice.

"Sex!" bellowed Augustus, making everyone jump. "We English are so suppressed! We'll do it, we'll paint it, we'll have a dozen babies, but we won't talk about it in public. What would happen if I came right out and asked you, Gwen, is that *semen* on the front of that hideous grey dress you are wearing?"

The room grew still and hot and within the chair, the squeaks grew louder and louder. Gwen's face turned red and she covered the stain on the front of the second-hand dress with her hand. She was about to say, "No. It's milk. From my cat's saucer," when the room roared to stunned life, everyone shouting at once.

"But that's my point!" yelled Augustus over the others. "We never do speak about such things, and merely saying a word is shocking. There's no hope of smashing bourgeois sentiment, this whole claustrophobic attitude, if we can't even say the words. This, yes," he said, gripping Dorelia around the waist and thrusting into her from below. She squealed and struggled to get off his lap and he grinned and thrust harder. "But the words, no."

The thirty or so people in the room stared at him, waiting for whatever he would say next, and Augustus' eyes glittered in the light from the lanterns and from the candles on the mantle above the fire. Gwen thought of her cat, how her cat would tear apart the chair in search of the mouse family, shred the fabric and paw through the straw until she unearthed the bald, blind, mewling mouse family and tore their heads off.

"Cunt," Augustus said. "Say the words! Penis, prick, testicles, balls. Your turn, Symons."

Symons grinned. "Menstruation!" he said. "Frigging!"

"Fornication!" said Lytton Strachey.

"Coitus!" said Will Yeats.

"Cum!" That was Henry Lamb.

"Getting your greens!" said Dorelia, smiling now.

"Do the mattress jig!" said Walter Sickert.

"Play the bed flute!"_"Quiffing!"_"Poontang!"_"Rutting!"_ "Buggery!" This last from poor old Symons, who never knew where the line was to be drawn. The room lapsed into an excited silence. Buttons were undone, collars loosened. Lytton Strachey would later, playing Augustus, accuse Virginia Stephen of having semen on *her* dress. "I should have been Augustus John," he said about himself. Roger Fry tipped his head back and yodelled. Everyone was ticking with illicit thrill.

"Gwen," said Augustus, "you didn't say anything."

"I don't feel I have to say everything in order to be liberated," she said. A canary swooped down low over her head. "It's not really a matter of saying. It's a matter of doing. And I *have* done." She smiled up at Dorelia and Dorelia looked away, her face turning red.

"But that's where you're wrong," said Augustus. "How can you *do*, if you don't know how to say? For example, I'd very much like to examine this dear girl's fat." He patted Dorelia on her haunch, and she snuggled deeper into his lap, tucking her head under his chin. "If I didn't feel free to tell her about my wishes, in precise language, where would we be?"

"Examine her fat?" spat Gwen. "Her *fat*? That's your precise language?!" She sprang up and went over to pull Dorelia from her brother's grip. "We really must be going." Dorelia hung back but then allowed herself to be lifted to her feet.

"You may not examine my fat," Dorelia said primly to Augustus. "As I have none."

"She's mine," said Gwen. "*My* student. *My* model. *My* friend," she said. *My lover.* One day. "You have treated her abominably tonight. You've practically deflowered her in front of everybody. You've used her to flog your slapped-together *paintings* to people who should know better." In the pool of light around the lantern, Roger Fry uttered a short bark of a laugh and then winked at Gwen. Miniscule particles of dust rose in the air, flashing through the golden rays and then vanishing into the darkness. "I don't know what she will think of our family, or even if she will come back to work with *me*."

"Miss John, if it makes a difference, I wanted to buy your painting first," put in Roger Fry. He *pitied* her. There was nothing worse.

"I'll come –" Dorelia began to say, but Augustus interrupted her.

"Indeed you will!" he said and smacked her hard on the rump again, before pushing her off him. Dorelia staggered and her ankle turned over in her dainty blue leather boot. Gwen held Dorelia tightly by the elbow as if she might blow away, but also as if she were helping the girl, who was limping. She was unsure which of these was the pose she wished to strike, so she aimed for both of them.

"I doubt my sister can give you *that* pleasure. Let me know when you are ready for a *man*, my little gypsy queen." Augustus also stood up, knocking a glass to the floor. He scowled at Roger Fry. The cloying scent of liquorice and fennel filled the room. An oily green liqueur spread across the floorboards.

"Don't forget to send me a message when Ida needs help with the *baby*," said Gwen. This far from the chair, she could no longer hear the mice scurrying and squeaking through the dark interior, but for all that, she knew they were still there, trapped.

The girls walked home in silence, Dorelia rubbing her bottom, taking slow steps. The streets were empty and there was a thick cold fog that cut vision down to a foot at most. It dampened even the sound of their footsteps on the cobbles until it came to seem that they were walking in a pale grey dream. Out of the fog swam a man all dressed in black, with long side curls and a tall black hat, muttering to himself, looking from side to side as if he were searching for something. The girls shrank back against the hedge as he passed.

"It could be Jack the Ripper himself!" whispered Dorelia.

“It’s just one of those Hebrews, the Russian ones. They’re everywhere these days,” said Gwen.

“He looked quite awful.”

“Don’t be scared. They’re harmless.”

“They say, in church, that they are bad. Killers. You know,” said Dorelia. She shivered and pulled her cloak closer around her.

“Hold my hand,” Gwen eventually whispered. “Or you will get lost. You don’t know these streets as well as I do.” It was a silly thing to say. Dorelia had recently moved out of her family home and taken a tiny flat at the end of Augustus’ street, right around the corner from Gwen. Still, as they passed under a gas lamp, Gwen slowed down and held out her hand. Dorelia was more frightened than she cared to admit. Dorelia slipped her hand, gloved in soft velvet, into Gwen’s.

“I was *your* friend first,” she said.

They took a few more steps, Dorelia favouring her bad foot.

“Augustus has no sensitivity,” said Gwen. “Neither of us will be able to paint as we should with him butting in. We should take a trip to Paris. Or to Rome. Just the two of us. It’s the only true way to improve your skills.” Ever since Rodin had seen her, she’d been searching for an opportunity to go to France.

“The Jew didn’t scare me. Not really,” said Dorelia. She took a step and then said, “Did Augustus introduce you to that lovely German in the lederhosen?”

“I hate him,” said Gwen. She stopped walking and turned to face Dorelia. “I hate him so much.” Dorelia could feel Gwen’s hand shaking in hers.

“One can’t reasonably hate one’s relatives, dear,” she said, patting Gwen’s hand, trying to calm her. “And he adores you. Did you not notice?”

Gwen held more tightly to Dorelia’s hand. *More* pity. What was wrong with people tonight? If she was ever to have Dorelia, she’d have her because the girl was madly, passionately, crazily in love with her. Never out of pity. She'd rather die.

"What about Paris?" said Gwen. The wind blew fog in great curls against them, wet and clinging. "This summer, we should take the steamer to France. What do you say?"

Dorelia shook her head. "Mummy and Daddy would never approve."

Dorelia. Rodin. It had become a choice.

"At least let's make a return to some serious painting. Please do *try* to be on time next Tuesday, darling."

Dorelia's mouth fell open. "Did he not tell you?" Gwen squeezed her hand until Dorelia gasped.

"Whatever now?" said Gwen. She clawed at her neck and a wave of such ferocity rolled over her that she panted like a dog that has scented a rabbit. "Let me guess. I suppose he has hired you to be *his* model on Tuesdays. To bash out that dreadful portrait for beastly Mister Fry. There. Am I right?"

They agreed to split Dorelia's modelling time between them, though Gwen wasn't asked if she wanted to give up her model. It was just assumed that *of course* Augustus should have his rights. They agreed that Dorelia was, indeed, an unusually good model, a woman who could almost be cast as anyone, who was patient and serene and divine. Gwen tried not to think what happened when Dorelia was at Augustus' studio and Augustus promised not to think what might be happening when she was at Gwen's studio. Roger Fry bought a sketch from Gwen for five pounds and a painting from Augustus for fifty. Privately, Gwen thought that Augustus had altogether too little intelligence to paint well, and not-so-privately, Augustus spouted that he would cut off the ears of anyone who ever saw Gwen's work next to his and judged him to be the lesser artist. Almost a month to the day after the party, just after Augustus had returned from the Springfire celebrations with his gypsy friends, on the 22nd of March, 1903, Ida John gave birth to her second son, Caspar.

NUN WITH A GROUP OF ORPHANS:

A few months after the birth, when Gwen came to visit Augustus' wife, Ida, there were two lines of nappies hung above the stove and the stinging scent of urine filled the steamy flat. Augustus was not home. After admiring Caspar's toes and grey-blue eyes, Gwen went through to the studio. Light fell from the twelve-foot windows. There were several large canvases, mostly portraits of women, stacked against the wall and one on an easel. That portrait was of the neighbour, an Italian opera singer, Estella Cerutti. There were none of Dorelia. Gwen leaned closer to Estella. Augustus had painted her looking over her shoulder, flirting. Estella's lips pouted. Her hands were held in a pleading gesture. She smoked Turkish cigarettes. She breathed sex. And she lived one floor down.

"Ida?" called Gwen. "Where is Gus painting these days?" She ran her fingernail over the clotted paint on Estella's breasts, nicking off some of the excess. She resisted the impulse to pull out a pencil and add a moustache. One of the canaries Gwen had given Ida to cheer her up flew by, hit the large window, and fell to the sill, stunned. As if the painting had come to life, the singer, downstairs, began to sing her scales. "Do, re, mi, fa, sol, la, si, do!"

"Poor baby!" cried Gwen. She ran and lifted the canary into her hands. There was a tiny crack at the top of its beak and a bead of bright blood. It lay quite still. Its little breast rose and fell, so she closed one hand over the other to keep the bird warm. "Ida!" she called again. *Do, sol, si, re, mi, la, do!* A yellow feather floated to the floor.

In the other room, the baby began to scream. It screamed

and screamed and screamed and Gwen shuddered. "Don't listen to Caspar," she told the bird. "It's not as bad as all that." Downstairs, the opera singer cursed. *Stronzo!*

"It's no use," said Ida, flouncing into the studio, her blouse unbuttoned. "He just goes down to sleep when something always happens! Estella starts her screeching or I lose my grip on the little piglet or Gus demands him for kissing or the canaries make a mess on him. It's impossible! I shan't ever get to sleep again."

"You will," said Gwen. "At least if you are awake you know you aren't dead." When she fainted or got bad headaches, or when her eyes were acting strange, she saw people in strange clothing, women in skirts that were far too short, men without hats, people sitting in the street with their feet in the gutters, huge red banners hanging down from the windows above them. Sometimes she wondered if she had died. Now, she wasn't quite sure the canary's chest was rising. The yellow feather against the black floorboards seemed inspired. Beautiful even. Estella began her scales again.

Ida looked exhausted. Her hair was unbraided and hung in several clumps, her clothing was smeared with jam and fastened with pins, her socks were mismatched and one thin toe poked through a hole in the wool. No wonder Estella had nabbed Augustus. From the other room came the howls of the baby and the deeper cries of his older brother, who had woken up from his afternoon nap too.

Gwen laid the canary on a plate full of ashes, pulled several pins from Ida's blouse and began to refasten the fabric. "Where on earth *is* Gus?" She dragged a cold hand across Ida's forehead and tucked her friend's hair back into her bun.

"I'm awfully afraid," said Ida. "He's off with that Dorelia person again. Why ever did you introduce them?"

Gwen waited for her heart to beat but it didn't. A cold hollow grew in her chest. There's always *someone.* Ida. Estella, Maria,

Susan from the bakeshop. She hadn't minded as much until it was someone *she* wanted. *Dorelia.*

"I'm sure he's just checking in on Whistler," Gwen lied. "I hear the maestro is in a bad way. As are you. Sit down. Rest. I'm going to make you a little pot of soup to build you up. Good heavens. Those boys are quite ridiculous. It sounds like a zoo!" Gwen did not actually know how to make a little pot of soup. Occasionally, she made herself an egg on her gas ring by boiling it for thirty minutes.

She filled a pot with water and dropped in a wilted carrot, a parsnip and a turnip. She looked doubtfully at the dirty pot and then added a potato, before lighting the fire. It was something she could imagine doing for Rodin, in his studio. For Rodin and … she looked around as if Ida could see her thoughts come to life … the babies she would have with Rodin. She took down a willow-pattern plate and set it at the edge of the stove with the canary on it. To warm up. "There you go," she said, smoothing its breast. Then she put her fingers in her ears and waded through the escalating sound towards the boys.

She picked up Caspar, rolled him in his blanket and tucked him in next to the canary. The wet nappies hit Gwen's head and neck as she stood up again. "You can have some soup too." She wiped the tears off his face with the blade of her hand and then wiped her hand on her skirt.

"I'll make you a fortifying cake!" Gwen called to Ida. If only she could remember how a cake was made. No one made statues in honour of mothers and fathers and women who could bake cakes. They only made statues in honour of artists. The nappies slapped her again. "You need a cook!" called Gwen again. "And a nursemaid! I'm going to tell Augustus when I see him."

"I have both," called back Ida. "But I keep on misplacing them." Her voice fading as if she were falling asleep.

Caspar looked up at Gwen and grabbed a strand of fine red hair that had escaped her bun. He pulled her head down towards his and then stuffed his fist in his mouth. She smiled. "Baby," she said. She knew she probably couldn't have babies, not even Rodin's. If she was able to, surely Augustus would have made her pregnant? They hadn't taken precautions. It had been such an odd, hard thing to learn about herself, and the knowledge had left her with a giant yawning emptiness that had only begun to fill when her father had permitted her to come to London, to study art.

Now art had replaced baby-having. Imagine if she lived with Rodin … every day she would be learning more than she had learned in years! An image of him bending over her, his hand on her shoulder. Rodin in her night visions, some unfamiliar French cologne. Maybe a baby on her shoulder, the child of the sculptor? Babies did have rather delectable little faces. She leaned closer to kiss Caspar's nose. Something smelled as if it were burning. It was probably the soup.

"What ever are you doing?" called Ida, awake again, an edge of panic in her voice. "What's that smell?"

Gwen pulled more strands from her bun and shook them in front of the baby's hands and he grabbed at her hair and she laughed when he reeled her in. It was puzzling why the smell of burning was so strong, though the pot was barely steaming.

"It's just food cooking, darling. Settle down. It will be ready soon," called Gwen. Just as she said the word *soon*, a wisp of smoke coiled around her head and an acrid smell filled her nostrils and her ear stung and the baby startled and she realised that her hair was on fire. She reared back into the wet nappies and slapped at her head and a smouldering xylonite comb tumbled from her bun and onto the floor. Gwen stepped on it, just to remove any doubt. The newspapers had been warning about these combs, how dangerous they were, but had she listened? No. Her vanity appalled her. She could have lost all her hair! She might have died and never had Rodin's child!

"How long will the soup be, do you think, dearest?" called Ida.

Gwen swept up the blackened comb and hid it under the vegetable peelings.

"Soon," she said. Her heart fluttered. Such a jolt! She brushed at her scalp and particles of frizzled black hair fell out. *Very* attractive. The soup began to bubble. The baby, in his blanket, sucked at his fist. Estella ran up and down her scales, at ever increasing volume, the bitch. Rain hit the window. It had been falling for weeks. They were saying it was the coldest, wettest June on record. People were escaping their houses on boards pried up from their floors. Tourists were sleeping on billiard tables for lack of rooms. The oldest baby, David, clung to her leg, his saturated nappy at his ankles. Augustus couldn't seem to get his own son's name straight, and called the child Pig Face, and Red Wriggler.

"In Xanadu did Kubla Khan a stately pleasure-dome decree: where Alph, the sacred river, ran through caverns measureless to man down to a sunless sea," quoted Gwen, wiping David's bottom, which was circled with tiny red blisters. He kicked at her and connected with her elbow. "You murderous little fiend," laughed Gwen. He looked so much like Augustus then, the pucker of his full lips, the mysterious slate-blue eyes, that Gwen bent to kiss him. And like his father, the infant reached for the string that held her blouse closed and pulled on it. Gwen almost dropped him.

They had started so young. Maybe Augustus had broken something inside Gwen with all his proddings, the baby-having something that every other woman seemed to have? Maybe it was a punishment from God, although she wasn't quite sure if she believed in a God who was both witness and judge to the smallest, most hidden acts of His children. She laughed at herself for imagining herself giving birth to Rodin's child. Such a dreamer.

Ida noticed Gwen's face. "Perhaps you could help me get the boys dressed? They're holding a Fat Child Competition for all the children born in March, and I do believe Caspar has a chance."

Gwen looked down at the boy in Ida's lap. Caspar's fatless legs stuck out of the charred blanket. His wobbly head dangled at the end of a thin neck and now it bobbled and wobbled and pulled back from Ida's breast. A jet of her milk sprayed out onto the floor and then dwindled, before the baby's head swung back and slammed up against Ida's breast again and he began making greedy gulping noises. David stood at his mother's elbow, thin and dark and ordinary, nothing like his father. He chattered at her. "I want snakes!" he said. Green jelly snakes, a lolly. Twenty snakes for a penny.

In the end, the women carried the two polished and flannelled children between them, each wrapped up against the weather with a piece of an oiled tablecloth they'd cut in half. Down the three flights of stairs, out at the street door and around to the local butcher's, where the competition was taking place.

The butcher stood, handsome and red and curly, in the window of his shop, with a twenty-pound note on his huge brass scale. His bloody apron hung to his ankles. Outside, a crowd of women carrying babies grew large and noisy. "Hurry up and weigh the poor kiddies, will you? It's pouring cats and dogs!"

The rain. At first it had fallen, one and two and five and twenty droplets, tapping on the glass, countable, manageable, but then it had all fused into a single sound, the rough bellow of nature unbound, and it hadn't stopped in days and days. Fast-moving water gushed through the gutters and covered the road in a glassy sheet. Gwen could barely feel her toes, for the cold. "The first baby!" roared the crowd and a juicy-looking specimen was unwrapped and stripped. The butcher pinched the child's flesh and kissed its bald head and then thrust it onto the scale. The crowd roared again. Seventeen pounds!

"Who's next?" called the butcher's son, a miniature carrot-headed version of his father, from the door of the shop. Helling and Sons, so it was painted on the glass. The jolly Butcher

Helling thrust another naked and bawling infant onto the scale. "Eighteen pounds, two ounces!" the crowd screamed and there was a surge of women towards the window, waving babies above their heads.

"Seventeen, six!" bellowed the women. "Seventeen, twelve!" Those babies looked twice the size of Caspar. "Nineteen, one!" The crowd was so large that it spilled off the pavement and into the street, blocking traffic. The omnibus rang its bell. "Hoy!" shouted the driver. "Get up there! You're making the transportation late!" There were no passengers on the top deck due to the rain but from within the carriage came a stream of curses. Another, deeper, bell rang from a second omnibus trapped behind the first one. "Come on, Gwen!" called Ida. "He'll take Caspar next!" Ida stood directly in front of the door to the shop, shielding Caspar's head with the flapping tablecloth.

Behind them, there was a commotion. "Bloomin' hell!" screeched a woman, climbing out of the second omnibus. "Get orf the road, you bunch a witches!" She laid about with her umbrella, thrashing at the stragglers who had stepped into the road. "Get orf it!" Women stepped back onto the pavement to avoid her blows.

"It's us!" cried Ida, but another baby was taken out of the crowd and stripped.

"It *was* us," said Ida to Gwen, bitterly. "We were first. It's not fair."

Caspar cried louder and punched the raindrops with his fists. "Can't we go home, dear?" asked Gwen, plucking at the back of Ida's whitework dress. She shivered.

"Next!" cried the butcher's son, and two mothers standing behind Gwen and Ida pushed forward and one of their babies was chosen instead of Caspar.

"I was next!" said Ida, struggling to turn around and face the woman whose child was being weighed.

"Sixteen pounds, thirteen!"

"Lord fuck a duck!" screamed the woman from the omnibus, thrashing everyone within sight with her umbrella. "It's me own Mister Helling! Me own dear husband!" She fell back into the arms of the crowd but they propped her up and shoved her forward again. The Stepney horror forced her way through the crowd, screaming that Helling was *her* husband, that he lived with her out in her wee home near Shoreditch Road, that he was *hers*.

"Next!" called the butcher's son.

A great line of hansom cabs, the gondolas of London, bobbed in the flooded street in both directions, unable to pass the clot of women, and from between these carriages, came two policemen, twirling their batons and blowing their whistles. The bells of the omnibuses rang and rang. The coachmen yelled to the bobbies from their positions up behind the black-painted cabs. It wouldn't be like this in France. It would be warm and clean and spacious. Rodin would have a quiet studio and the sun would stream in through the windows and he would speak in clever little sentences that would make everything brilliantly clear. He would look into her eyes and really *see* her.

"Mine!" screeched the woman with the umbrella. "The bleeder!" She had made her way almost to the door and now she saw the young red-headed boy in the apron, with his bouncing curls and dewy skin, so like his father. Now she saw the butcher standing in the window, kissing babies, clutching a twenty-pound note and waving it at the assembled women.

"You barstid!" the umbrella woman screamed. "Mister Helling, get yourself out here and answer to your crimes!"

The butcher heard the woman and turned towards her, saw her, flinched. The mothers drove their knees into Gwen's back and pushed past her as if she didn't exist. The crowd drew in their united breath. "Bigamist!" they breathed. "Philanderer!"

"Next?" called the butcher's son uncertainly in his sharp high voice, and Ida chose this moment to push Caspar forward. The baby was swept up and into the shop, though the butcher had disappeared from the window, together with his twenty-pound note. "Dad?" called the boy. "Dad? Whatsa matter?"

Horns blew out in the street, and there came a steady drumming of umbrella handles against the sides of the omnibuses. Wisps of smoke drifted in the air, grey and transparent and shredded. The rain fell through the smoke and the smoke reformed itself after each droplet. It made her sick to look at, the swarming skin of the smoke.

Inside the crowd, Gwen saw one of those black-swathed Jews, a survivor from the Kishinev pogroms, standing perfectly still amidst the swirling, heaving bodies. An enormous silence filled the street. The Jew wore a wide black hat and rain ran over the brim as if it were a waterfall. His hair was arranged in long curls on either side of his narrow, creased face, and it also streamed water, but he did not look bedraggled. There was something in his face that caught and held Gwen's attention. She could not figure out what it was. Slowly, he raised his head and looked in her direction over the top of the crowd, for he was very tall. They stared at one another. He did not smile and neither did she. Without struggling against the pressure of the crowd, his arm began to rise, slicing through the melee, rain sheeting from the corner of his sleeve. He closed his fist and raised his index finger to point at a yellow star sewn to his lapel. The smell of burned hair, strong enough to taste. Gwen had not noticed the star until then. It had some kind of black lettering on it, but because of the rain and the crowd and the tumult, she could not read the words. She did not believe that the Russian Jews had to wear any kind of a sign on their clothing and she was sure she had never seen any of the other Jews wearing it. She put her head to one side and opened her hands in a gesture designed to ask, "What do you want from me?" but the man did not respond. He tapped the star again and lowered his head. The star shimmered for a moment, winked, disappeared and reappeared again, faded, flared up, died completely and vanished. Two police pushed past him and the Jew, too, disappeared from sight. "Come on now, ladies," the police called. "Let us through. How'd you like it if this was your man?" And at that the crowd opened and the coppers fell through, almost to the front. The rain drummed on the canvas roofs of the hansom cabs, the bells on the buses rang. The Jew had been far taller than any of the women, but now Gwen couldn't see him anywhere in the crowd.

"Ida," said Gwen. She was deathly afraid and shivering. "We must leave. Get Caspar!"

"Don't be silly," said Ida. "He's about to be weighed." Sure enough, the emaciated Caspar appeared, naked, in the window, held up by another man, not the butcher.

"Ten pounds, eight!"

The crowd hissed. "Poor love," said the woman behind Gwen. "Shouldn't be out in the rain at that size. What sort of a mother?"

"Ida!" said Gwen. She turned, quickly, to see if she could glimpse the Jew in the crowd and again, could not. "Really!" she said, grabbing Ida's arm and shaking it. "We *must* leave! *Now!*" But Ida would not.

"He married me ten years ago and I've got the brats to prove it." The woman with the umbrella beat on the backs of the women between her and the shop. She beat on Gwen's back and Gwen rounded on her.

"Leave me alone, you beastly woman!" she said. "It's not my fault that your husband found a better wife!"

The woman jammed the spike of the umbrella into the arch of Gwen's foot and Gwen staggered and almost dropped David. "Did something speak?" the other woman screeched and then she pushed roughly past and into the shop. "Mister Helling!" she screamed. "It's the *real* Missus Helling come to pay a visit!"

The crowd roared again. "There he goes! Catch him!" The butcher was seen running further down the street and the crowd raced after him, bowled him over, swallowed him up and bore him back to the constables, bellowing. Ida was, at last, ready to leave and they squeezed past the broad and gloating Mrs Helling into the shop to retrieve Caspar. The butcher's son crouched over the naked baby, crying.

Outside, the police struggled with the burly butcher, and the umbrella woman grabbed at her husband's crotch. "Couldn't keep it in your pants, could ya?" she screeched.

Gwen towed Ida and Caspar through the crowd as best as she could with David in her arms and the crowd shoving in the opposite direction. She looked for, but did not find, the Jew.

"It's perfectly dreadful," said Ida. "What sort of a man does that to his wife? The shame!"

Gwen stopped and stared at Ida. Was she so simple that she didn't see that Augustus was doing it to *her*?

They had arrived at their front door and Ida rummaged through her skirt for her key. "He's a bonny little boy. He *could* have won."

"Ida …" said Gwen. She didn't know what to say. It was all very well having soirées with the literati and rattling off sexual words as if they were gossip; it was fine and dandy to run off to town and to sleep with every model who came through the door, but it was quite another when the result of all this hedonism was women with children and no support, women abandoned without even the most simple of pretext, women dying from backyard operations, children without bread, the loss of homes and jobs and security, the loss of real and stable *family*. "You need a rest," she managed to say. She patted Ida's back. "You need a helper."

"I'd rest better if Augustus was home. I can't help worrying …" She glanced at Gwen. She still hadn't found the key. "That man …" she said. So she *did* understand. "The poor woman. And did you see the look on the little boy's face?"

Gwen had.

"I'll take her away," Gwen said. Her insides hummed with fear and a curious excitement. "I'll take her to Paris." She could paint in the beautiful clean light over there instead of being drowned in London. She could learn from Rodin. "I'll take her away for *a year*. More. Gus will just have to stay home." Even as she said it, Gwen knew that Dorelia was only *one* of Ida's problems.

"Would you? Would you *please*?" asked Ida. "I'll give you money. I'll give you my earrings. I'll give you, I don't know what, but anything, really, if only you'll make her go away." They both knew that nothing would restore Gwen's reputation if she went to France without a chaperone. That her reputation was worth far more than a pair of gold earrings.

Gwen opened her mouth and fished a long black hair out from between her teeth. "You don't need to give me anything," she said, wiping her tongue and then her hand on her shawl. "It would be my pleasure. To help you. To help the whole family." She threw the hair away from her, but it would not be thrown. It clung to her fingers in damp coils. "It will give you and Gus a chance to fall in love all over again." In that moment, she felt almost holy. Almost as if she were once again pure, and her motives were pure.

She rubbed her hand over the letterbox and the hair vanished, and a little image of Dorelia flickered across her mind, Dorelia with her robe down around her waist, a green painted snake on her breast. A tiny shiver settled in her groin, a single throb that completely destroyed her sense of purity.

Ida sighed. "Maybe," she said.

The key was eventually found and the women went upstairs to warm themselves.

Caspar's head lolled back in Ida's arms. He looked drunk. His skin was wrinkled and pink from being saturated in the cold rain. A little of Ida's milk ran out of the corner of his mouth and down under his neck. The women's feet rested on the open door of the stove, their stockings rolled down, their boots stuffed with newspapers and drying on the shelf above. Their mud-spattered petticoats hung over the line with the nappies. Ida wore a house wrap. Gwen still shuddered in her wet dress.

"It's terribly good of you, Gwen," said Ida. "You're such a saint." But Gwen would not hear of her goodness, not with that tickle in her groin and visions of Rodin.

"London is appalling this year," said Gwen bitterly. "Who would *want* to be here if they had a choice? And there's Jews everywhere. All London has become Jewified. France will be warm and Catholic. There will be light to paint by, sunshine, fresh air. It will be lovely. Maybe Dorelia and I will get ourselves a little cat." She hesitated and then said, "I think I'll go even if Dorelia doesn't." But then Ida looked so sad that she said, "I'll convince her parents. Don't worry." There was an irritating sensation in Gwen's mouth, as if the hair was still there. She knew it wasn't, refused to open her mouth again and make an inspection.

"They'll never be at home for you!" said Ida. She peered at Gwen and touched her hand to Gwen's forehead and in this moment, Gwen could no longer bear it, and she put her fingers inside her mouth and withdrew, again, a long strand of black hair.

"Who do we know that has black hair?" she asked.

Ida stared at her. "That bitch," she said, meaning Dorelia, but Dorelia's hair was greeny-black and silken and fine and this was curling and coarse and pubic, though at least a foot long.

"It must have been someone in the crowd," said Gwen, but for the life of her, she could not remember a single woman having black hair. There had been blondes, and brunettes, women with auburn hair and many with grey, and some with red, but in all that crowd, there had only been one person with long black curls. Gwen twined the hair around her finger and then threw it into the fire. Ida looked at Gwen's gesture uncertainly and then got up to get a spoon and a bottle of Mrs Winslow's Soothing Syrup. She tried to get Gwen to take a spoonful of the paregoric, and when she would not, poured herself two spoonfuls and drank them down and licked the spoon clean.

"I wonder if that butcher will have to go to jail?" Ida said, thrusting her breast into Caspar's mouth. "I wonder what will happen to *both* families?" She opened her blouse some more and settled Caspar further into her arms. The fire snapped. The room grew warm. The muscles of her face loosened and soon Ida and the baby were snoring.

Gwen stared at the flames inside the black iron stove, wondering how she could accept praise for taking Dorelia to France, ostensibly to protect Ida, when really, she had an ulterior motive. More than one ulterior motive. When really, she only wanted to become a better artist than her brother. And if, in the process, she was able to ensnare Dorelia, even better. A log in the orange-rimmed fire popped, sounding as if something had exploded, and embers sprayed upwards.

Between her fingers, Gwen twisted a coiled black hair.

PAINTING 2:

Notes for painting the man, the Jew.
Choose a day when you are alone or others will think you are crazy. (*Am* I crazy?)

Method of observation –

1. The strangeness
2. Colour (match the hair)
3. Tones
4. Personal form
5. The star

Method of execution –

1. observation of the 6 points
2. mixing of colours
3. lines in pencil (can you forget his eyes?)
4. background
5. painting of personal forms out of background

Don't think about Dorelia or you will not be able to paint. Think, instead, about Rodin.
You are only free when you have left all.
Leave everybody and let them leave you.
Only then will you be without fear.

STILL LIFE OF BLACK BOX ON TABLE:

Whistler died in July, just after Gwen's twenty-seventh birthday. He'd lived right next to Augustus, and many times, she'd gone in on the way to visit the family, to see if there was anything she could do to help her old teacher. Now, awful Sickert with his fancy pre-primed canvases and his ugly bespoke suits had moved into number eight, like a tailored wool vulture, and started a horrible artists' group in Whistler's former home. And Rodin, of all people, had promised to make a sculpture of Gwen's teacher. And now, instead of raining, London was unbearably humid and sticky and the air was full of fine particles of grit that choked.

The light snagged and couldn't make it to the street. Great drifts of pollen floated in the murky light and gnats swarmed under the streetlights. Baby starlings fell from their nests in record numbers due to weakened bones. Gwen and Augustus both painted Dorelia and both of their paintings were flawed because the sun never came out, though hers was better than his. Augustus painted Dorelia's head slightly larger than life size, her lips pursed, wearing his own black velvet jacket, unbuttoned at the neck. He painted her dimples against the high salmon of her cheeks, what Symons called the "suction of her cheeks". Gwen painted Dorelia half asleep, standing in front of a fire, in a portrait smaller than her hand. A line of brilliant white light ran down the side of Dorelia's face. Before it had even been exhibited, Augustus' portrait was sold for a hundred pounds, and then sold again, to another buyer, for two hundred. Gwen pasted her portrait of Dorelia inside the wooden lid of her paint box and Augustus came to her rooms when she wasn't there and scraped the canvas off the wood and stretched it on a tiny frame and hung it in his studio and critics and collectors all clamoured to buy it, calling it his best work yet and refusing to look at any other portraits, until Gwen found the picture on his wall and flew into a rage and slashed it from the frame with a pallet knife and threw it out of the window. Augustus wasn't sorry to see it go, not at all, and neither was Gwen, once he'd had his hands all over it.

There were Jews, hundreds and thousands of them, everywhere in London that summer, crouching in corners, being run off the sidewalks, overlooked at the markets, miserable and rejected and other. And Augustus was in love with Dorelia and could not leave the girl alone. By August, Dorelia was a fixture at the John's Saturday lunches, Gwen hadn't said anything further about running off to Paris, and Ida was frantic.

Though Dorelia was a talented seamstress, she arrived to lunch in a dress Augustus had given her, a deep red silk with a black embroidered gypsy shawl tied around her tiny waist. It came down low in the front and she had done nothing to cover her bulging flesh. Ida wore a pale blue cotton wrap with wide aqua sleeves. The dress had an aqua sash that she had left untied, and a knitted lace bertha collar. She sometimes wore the same garment to bed. It was very comfortable, she said. Gwen wore the same dress she wore every day, a dark maroon wool that clashed with her red hair. When she'd turned in from the narrow street and gone into the Queen of Hell pub to pick up a pitcher of beer for their lunch, a small child, there on the same errand, had dropped her bottle of grog on Gwen's hem. "I'm sorry, Mum," the child had said, before getting down on her knees to try to blot up the liquid with her handkerchief. But Gwen's hem was rigid with the vinegar she'd been using to sponge off the dress for the past six months and the child had gasped and held her nose and stood up quickly.

"I do think," Ida said to the walls now, "that the boys need some fresh air. Perhaps we might take a cottage in the country for a few weeks. Or by the seaside. We might even go to visit your father in Tenby again. Do you think he might be able to rent a perambulator? One of the lovely big cane ones with the swivel wheel in front and the fringed canopy over the top to protect the babes from the sun? What do you think, Gus?"

"You can go," Augustus said, leaning back from the table and unbuttoning his waistcoat. He took up his concertina and gave it a few trial squeezes before launching into a gypsy tune. "I'm an artist. I don't have to go on family holidays when I'm onto something. It's all coming clear." His eyes rested on the high curved mound of Dorelia's breasts. She scowled back at him. Gwen, sitting next to Dorelia, leaned over and tied a napkin around the girl's neck.

Despite her abundant décolletage, Dorelia would not let Augustus paint her naked. She refused his kisses. And she allowed the napkin to stay tied around her neck, despite how it made her look like a prize-winning pig. All of this gave Gwen hope that perhaps Dorelia, after all, preferred *women*. Like Gwen.

"Where's the pudding, Ida?" said Augustus, as the tune came to an end and he let the concertina fall.

Gwen flounced up and snatched the pudding off the sideboard. "You claim you are a modern man, Gus, but you don't even know how to reach behind you and take up a simple plate of pudding. You need a woman to serve you." She dropped the basin in front of him and it sloshed, a little, onto his lap.

Augustus stroked his finger through the sauce and looked up at Dorelia as he put his finger in his mouth and sucked. "I need a woman," he said. He stuck out his tongue and licked up the sauce from between his fingers. "More than one woman. I've ordered a mighty canvas so that I might paint you spread-eagled. Perhaps in that kimono Gwen gave you. Do you remember that lake in the clay pool, up on Wareham Heath? I'd say the blues are the same."

"Oh! For God's sake!" said Ida and she shoved her chair back from the table. "You're not a husband. You're a billy goat." One of the pins fastening her wrap sprang free and launched itself across the table to land, jibbering, in the pudding. Augustus plucked it out and sucked it clean.

"Wait!" cried Gwen. "Dorelia and I have an announcement to make." She stood up and put her hand on the back of Dorelia's chair.

Ida stilled, her own hand caught in midair. Dorelia turned her head and smiled her dazzling and mysterious smile at Gwen. Augustus looked first at Dorelia, then at Gwen and groaned.

"We," said Gwen, and the *we* thrilled her, a huge electric ripple of excitement and longing running down her legs, "are going to walk to Rome!" *Paris.* Paris. Only ever Paris. Rodin's baby on her shoulder, the art world at her feet.

Ida sat down again and smiled.

"By *we*, I take it you've convinced this dear girl to go with you and be your knavish squire?" said Augustus. "Needed a servant to carry your bits, did you?" His large hands lay coiled in fists on the table in front of him and he frowned at all of the women, busy as flies, they had been, making plans behind his back. He frowned at Ida and then at Gwen, a deeper frown for her.

Gwen smiled. She did not love him anymore, not really. She had found a better man. She refused to model naked for Augustus. She was on her way to becoming more famous than him. She would become one of the avant garde, painting all kinds of new subjects in all kinds of new ways and her brother would be left behind, in horrible, dark, stodgy London, with his squalling brats, copying the styles of painters far greater than he would ever be. She would even have Dorelia. *Her* virgin. Not his.

"Rome!" said Ida. She sloshed a little sherry into a glass and drank it down. Her face bloomed red and tears stood in her eyes. "Oh Gwen! How I wish I were going with you. Remember Paris? Boulevard Raspail? And Rue Froidevaux? And the lovely, lovely walks we took together in the Luxembourg Gardens?"

A few years earlier, after Gwen's first semester in London, Ida and Gwen had spent a summer in Paris, where they'd met Whistler and studied with him. They'd gone, so their friends said, irretrievably to hell. Everyone suspected them of secretly smoking in their flat and of wanting to vote. But then, once she returned to London and rejected Augustus, he made off with *her* friend Ida and installed her as the quasi-married and totally off-limits Mrs John. Gwen didn't like to think about it. Now Ida had two babies who howled non-stop like monkeys and she drank laudanum like lemonade.

"Yes!" said Gwen. She peered hopefully at Ida again, but Ida looked unhappy, perfectly miserable, instead of thrilled. She'd been delighted by the suggestion at the door, the day of the fat baby competition, and later, with their boots off and their feet in the oven. It seemed that no matter what Gwen did for her, Ida couldn't be happy. Friendship was much more complicated than people gave it credit for.

Gwen took Dorelia's soft small hand in hers and held it aloft. "But this time it will just be Dodo and me, walking and singing our way across France until we bump into Italy! I shall paint my way through the summer and by the autumn, we shall both be in the holy city painting frescoes and learning from the grand masters and smoking with the Pope and it will be ever such a marvellous adventure. You can all come to see us once we are settled. You too, Ida. If you feel up for it." Gwen's heart fluttered. She'd have a small stone house with a bright French garden around it, and Dorelia, under an orange tree, smiling up at her, the occasional patter of fruit falling into the long grass. She felt almost certain that she had won. And it hardly mattered about the complicatedness of it all. It *would* be a good thing for Ida. For Augustus. For both of them and for the little boys. Even if Gwen *did* adore Dorelia, even if she *did* want to be Rodin's finest student and lover, what of it? She wasn't just making off with her prize to stick it in Augustus' eye. And it wasn't as if he wouldn't be working and selling his own work back in London.

"Gwen is *very* good," said Dorelia. "To put up with me coming along." She winked at Gwen and for a moment, the floorboards tilted sideways. "To teach me to paint and be an artist. She has already contacted a teacher in Paris. We shall be learning from the very best!"

"We shall become the famous lady painters of Paris and Rome," laughed Gwen, only half joking.

"Who did you write to?" growled Augustus. "Are you abusing my friends again?"

"Rodin," said Gwen. "You told me he said I might model for him."

Augustus frowned. "And what of *my* painting?" he said. "I should also be learning from the very best." His foot drummed on the floorboards, and his knee hit the underside of the table with every beat. The children, in their Sunday clothes, hunched like gargoyles to deflect his rage. The cups rattled in their saucers. "What of my painting of *her*?" He stabbed his finger towards Dorelia. "Her portrait is the greatest thing I have ever done."

Ida slumped further, like a deflated pudding. Above her bed was the portrait Augustus had done of her; the one he'd told *her* was the greatest thing he'd ever done. In it, she wore the same red dress that Dorelia now wore. She stood looking over her shoulder, her hair a dark halo around her head, pregnant, holding her skirts. Even Gwen knew that in *that* portrait the reds were muddier, more brown than crimson, more muted to match Ida's eyes, which were as docile as a cow's. Dorelia looked like a slut in her own portrait, her knees apart, her hands spread, her bodice unlaced. Her eyes as black as a hot seam of coal inside the earth and her dress blood red.

"You have a day or two to finish up," said Gwen, who spent *years* on a single painting. "That should be enough for you." But she had said too much.

"She's mine!" shouted Augustus, leaping from his chair. Both boys slipped from their chairs and hid underneath the table. Gwen froze. Ida, looking down into her lap, moved her hand slowly towards her eyes and scrubbed away the tears. Dorelia laughed.

"I am not yours or anyone's," said Dorelia. "Not yours, Gwen. Not yours, Ida, and certainly not yours, Augustus." She smiled around at them all, a cool unfolding smile that seemed to mesmerise. "I am mine. And I have chosen to see the world a little with Gwen." A dimple appeared in her cheek. She nodded at Gwen, and Gwen opened her hands beneath the table. She would take anything she could get. "The world is not over because we are taking a little walk together. You make it so serious, Gus. I am not *married* to you, you silly boy. I may go if I please. Only Ida may not leave. She made the mistake of matrimony."

"Not *exactly*," muttered Ida, turning her ring around and around on her right hand.

Dorelia leaned across the table and uncurled Augustus' fists and smoothed them out, flat. "It is nothing," Dorelia said and as she said *nothing*, she passed her tiny hands over his large, furry ones, and like a magician, she erased his anger. He deflated, the colour left his face, he relaxed back into his chair. The room became, again, warm and convivial. Gwen breathed. Dorelia still had never seen Gwen's brother in a real temper. Even the babies under the table stilled.

"There," Dorelia said. "Isn't that better? *Much* better?" And she leaned under the table and fished out Caspar, laughing and biting his toes, and the child was rosy and delighted and somehow wearing clean clothing despite there never being any to be had.

"It's hard," said Ida. "I am *trying* to be a modern woman for Gus but sometimes I feel so very …"

"Jealous," said Augustus.

"Tired," said Gwen at the same moment.

"Old-fashioned," said Dorelia.

"Unloved," Ida finished.

"I have boat tickets," Gwen said, after a brief pause. "For the steam packet leaving on Monday night for Bordeaux." She took the tickets from her pocket and spread them on the table.

"Two days!" cried Ida. "How can you give us so little notice? What about your clothes? You'll be horribly unfashionable!"

"I shall wear nothing!" Gwen said and Dorelia whistled.

Augustus got up from the table and put on his jacket. "I'm leaving," he said. "I'm going to the café to meet some friends." He didn't look at the women. Augustus was an unstoppable force of nature, spewing semen down the high street like a broken fire hydrant.

But of course, she wasn't really walking across France with Dorelia to alleviate Ida's pain or to prod Augustus or to save Dorelia from an abysmal mother-and-baby home and the shame of a baby out of wedlock. If it were only those reasons, Gwen would stay at home. It was the other, more difficult to grasp reasons, that were her real impetus for taking the boat to Bordeaux: her own intense wish to be the best artist she could be, her need for light and sunshine and fresh air and the ability to see *everything*, her desire for a teacher who wasn't showing her the same old ways of doing the same old portraits in dark and dreary London, a teacher who saw her and understood. Her fear of the Jew and crowds and horses stamping in the streets and root vegetables that wished to be cooked into soups. Her eagerness to strike out on her own, away from Augustus and away from the strictures of society and away from the London art world that had already condemned her as not-as-good-as-Augustus, or perhaps only not-as-polite. To find a place where she would exist as she, a woman, a person in her own right. The thought that in a different place she could become whoever she wanted to be and escape the history that had brought her to live in the basement of a condemned building. Her hope that never again would she have to walk into one of her lovers, now married, pushing perambulators in the Strand, castrated and namby, and lean under the canopy to admire a child that might have been hers, in another world. And, if she allowed herself to think this one last thought, the vaguest of hopes, the tiniest flutter of desire, that Dorelia might, dressed in simple cotton clothing with her toes sunk into the warm dry soil and her face fanned by breezes from the coast, come to love her, not as a friend but as something more. Because wasn't that what it was all about, really? The terrible urge to be loved, an urge that would sacrifice all in its path?

"Wish us well, brother," said Gwen. She rose and put out her hand, but it was ignored.

"I'll have the pudding when I return, with custard," said Augustus. "You should take a gun, Gwen. Those Frenchmen. Ida, give the girls ten pounds so they don't bloody starve to death."

"For God's sake," said Gwen when the door had closed. "Do stop flagellating yourself, Ida. I think you like making that puddle. *Look at me, the poor long-suffering wife! Pity me, my life!* If you think Augustus is going to give up Dorelia for a heap of shuddering wet fabric on the floor with its dress all unbuttoned and its breasts deflating and leaking all over the woodwork, then you have another think coming. Do you want to be like that ghastly butcher's wife? Get up. Make yourself beautiful again. Put on your stays. Seduce him tonight. Don't let him paint another Dorelia. Lock him in your bedroom. Demand his cock." Dorelia laughed out loud and put out her hand for Ida.

From under her arm, Ida cried louder. "I *am* the butcher's wife," she said. "The ugly one."

"Then get up and find your umbrella and go chase him down and beat him with it, right in the Café Royal, in front of his friends. And don't forget to screech, 'Keep your bloody thing in your pants, Mister John!' Don't forget to grab his balls in front of the whole of High Street. Your picture will be in every paper tomorrow, on the very first page."

Dorelia grabbed one of Ida's arms and Gwen grabbed the other and they hauled her up onto her feet.

"You're such a horror, Gwen," said Ida. "But I do love you."

"And I you," she said. "That is why I am taking Dorelia to France. For *you*," she said. "To stop a husband from betraying his wife is a marvellous thing. I feel like Joan of Arc, saving England, protecting the virtuous! I have always wanted to save someone from harm." And though she knew it was a fabrication, she had almost convinced even herself that she was a saint.

TWO LITTLE GIRLS IN SCHOOL HATS:

The boat left in the evening and by the time it was fully out of the harbour, they could only see the lights of the city as if they were stars, winking out one by one in the fog and the darkness.

People had brought their homes with them: baskets of apples and crates of cabbages, strings of shoes on poles and a metal bucket of used nails, a pile of white linens bundled with string, a rolled-up carpet, a feather mattress, a grandmother on a stretcher. Gwen took out her charcoal and sketched it all in the drenching moonlight, and then she sketched Dorelia leaning against the railing, pointing at something in the distance, nodding off in the deckchair with her hat clamped between her knees. She had begun to really *see* Dorelia; as Gwen sketched, her fingers found, without effort, the unsymmetrical cleft in the other girl's chin, the widely spaced eyes, the upswing of one eyebrow. She felt slightly nauseous from concentrating and from the rocking of the boat and from the petroleum smell that blew back from the stacks and she put away her materials and slipped into the deckchair next to Dorelia and she fell asleep noticing how the silver lines of moonlight rose and fell on the waves, and in the morning, France had already bloomed around them, two low flat ridges of green on either side of the inlet. The ferry blew its horn, and the sound echoed between the cliffs.

The passengers flocked to the starboard bow and pointed. Dorelia smiled. "France," she said. "Home of artists and writers, poets and lovers. Home of *us*. But where has the ocean gone?"

"Bordeaux is not on the coast," said Gwen, and she, too, smiled. "It's on an estuary that becomes the Garonne River, where we shall be walking." She squeezed Dorelia's hand. Within fifteen minutes they would be docking in Bordeaux. The sailors moved quickly across the decks, whistling. "What a good idea this was. Aren't you glad you are not falling into disaster with a married man?" The boat smelled of the soap, of seaweed and salt and a fresh wind and hot tar and canvas and hops. It was loaded with Englishmen and tea and apples and many barrels of beer.

"I love you, Gwen John!" said Dorelia, and Gwen's heart stopped and the boat lurched as it bumped the dock and she stumbled a little. It was pathetic how she wanted to be loved. But then Dorelia added, "For this! For taking me to France!"

The boat nestled against a huge curving dock that looked like a sickle moon. The buildings that crowded the quay were all soft-edged, softly coloured, chalky. There was nothing that glittered or glimmered or shone besides the water itself. The passengers lined up to leave but just as Gwen was about to step on the swaying gangplank, she thought she saw the man she had seen at the fat baby competition, standing off to one side, looking down at the oily green water.

"Sir!" she called, pausing with her hand on the railing. "Monsieur!"

The stranger glanced over at her, jammed his hat on his head and turned away.

"Mister!" Gwen said, and then, in desperation, "Rabbi! Stop!"

"Please, madam, you are blocking the exit." A sailor gave her elbow a push.

Dorelia giggled. "You can't even stop chasing men from the *boat*."

"Oh!" cried Gwen. "Where has he gone?" For the Jew had again melted into the crowd and was no more to be seen. "There was a man," she said to Dorelia. "I think he might be … it's quite ridiculous … I barely believe it myself, but I think he is following me. I saw him a month ago and he tried to show me something, but then we were separated in the crowd. And somehow, I got his hair on me …" It all sounded absurd. Gwen was already on solid land and now that she was, she felt more than a little queasy. Jews made her feel … so odd. So strangely foreign herself. She wished she could take a pallet knife and scrape Jews from the world, like so much poorly placed paint. "Where could he be?" All around them, the sound of cicadas, like hundreds, thousands of clocks ticking too fast, the sound of hours racing past in minutes, deafening.

"Forget him," said Dorelia, taking her by the arm. "We are in *France*! Where's that guidebook of yours?" She began patting Gwen's shawl and her basket and then her bodice and her hips, laughing as she did so.

"Stop," said Gwen, pulling away, blushing and flustered. "I really must find him. He looks terribly worried."

"Alright then," said Dorelia, pouting. At least cicadas had silent wives. "What did he look like?"

Gwen thought for a moment, with her head on the side. "He's tall. His skin and hair and beard and eyes are very dark. He's dressed all in black except for his shirt. He's one of those Jews, the ones from Russia I think. He has a yellow flower or something yellow in his lapel. I noticed it last time too."

Dorelia stared at her. Porters shouted and threw crates and barrels and boxes onto huge wagons. Spars and cleats chimed overhead. Water slopped against the side of their boat with a greedy sucking sound. The cicadas ticked on, louder and louder. One of the barrels of beer escaped its handlers and rolled to the edge of the quay, hesitated there a moment before tipping over the edge with an almighty splash.

"He has those long ringlets beside his face. Do you know what I mean?" Gwen twisted and turned, searching the crowd on the dock for the man. "Look. Like this," she said and she pulled the coiled black hair from her pocket. It was so very *clinging*.

"Let's go," said Dorelia. "There was no one like that on the boat. And you've got nothing to show me." She brushed her hand across Gwen's and the rolled hair sailed out across the river, glittered briefly in the sun, and sank into the deep blue water. Dorelia lifted the easel and slung it across her back. "Feel that air and that sunshine! So lovely on my skin!" Dorelia turned her face up to the sun. "And the colours! Who knew that so many existed in the world! I love France already. Don't you?"

"I didn't see him until the very last moment, and even then, he was on the other side of the boat to us, looking over to the other bank."

"Gwen," said Dorelia. "What colour would you say that building is? Apricot? Peach? And why are the names of colours really the names of fruits? And why *on earth* are the cicadas so loud? And what are we having for breakfast?"

"I think he wanted to tell me something."

"Enough, Gwen. He was just a strange lonely man. You're always seeing something no one else can. Haven't you been reading the papers? His whole family was probably killed over in Russia by the Cossacks. It's more likely that he wants to drop quietly over the railing and drown without a sound in the Garonne than that he has a special message for the haughty and famous Gwen John."

Gwen bent to pick up her basket. She closed her eyes so that she couldn't even try to look for the stranger anymore. It was ridiculous. All Jews looked the same anyway, haunted ghostlings, pale silvered beings on the edge of everything but never really part of anything in the same way she was, but also in a way that was more unacceptable, more deliberate, more devilish. While she would have done almost anything to be loved, she felt certain that the Jews would not. That they held themselves apart *on purpose*. Why? What purpose was there in otherness, in being left out? She had always hated it. The bright day felt, momentarily, cold. It was dreadful to think that she had something in common with the Jews.

She wasn't sure it was the same man as before, and even that first man wasn't important. "I just wanted to entertain you, so I made it up," she said to Dorelia after a moment. She pulled the shawl tighter around her shoulders. "Silly me."

At least the menacing hair had finally disappeared. Her fingers felt every corner of her pocket but it was empty of everything except the portraits of her and her mother. "Such a noise! The cicadas are searching for a female to mate with. Any female," she said. "And they aren't very discreet about it. They're a bit like Augustus!"

"I shall have a baguette, and jam and butter and a freshly squeezed orange for breakfast," said Dorelia. "And a croissant!"

"We don't have enough money for that," said Gwen. She was never sure if she was telling the truth, because the truth and her imagination all got mixed up together. "If you want to eat like a king you shall have to work like a knave." She waved her hand at the easel. "We could either sing or paint, but singing is quicker." She had doubts about her ability to paint on demand, or even make a sketch that resembled the sitter. She thought that if they relied on her talent alone, they might starve.

The two women walked along the crowded quay to where another boat was boarding and they laid down their things and covered them with their cloaks, and then pinched their cheeks and smoothed out the creases in their skirts and the worst of the tangled hair from sitting up in their deckchairs all night.

"Our men folks ain't buying," called a woman who was already on the boat. "Go back to your maison de passé."

Gwen blushed. The woman couldn't possibly mean them. A putain less than five minutes in France. Now she really *did* feel like a Jew. They were always called dreadful names without having done anything. She began to open her mouth to retort, but Dorelia put a hand on her arm and sang out in her strong high voice, "As I walked forth one summer's day, to view the meadows green and gay, a pleasant bower I espied, standing fast by the river side, and in it a maiden I heard cry." It was an old song, one that many knew and loved, and her voice had something in it, a strange sharp yearning that made the people standing nearby turn to listen. Gwen's head snapped around. She watched Dorelia's lips vibrate with the force of the air moving across them. The morning sky, still streaked with pink, was fresh and innocent and clean. The cicadas' song was no longer as loud and now it had faded to be some kind of accompaniment. Gwen, listening, felt a pain in her chest, a hard tight feeling that she could not name. Some men threw centimes at Dorelia's feet. Gwen took a deep breath and joined her for the chorus, "Alas! Alas! There's none ever loved as I!" Gwen looked sideways at Dorelia again, and in that morning sunshine, the girl seemed to glow with such a bright white light that Gwen burned to pull out her crayons and paper. She was afraid to take her hand, afraid even to brush her sleeve against Dorelia's, for fear of diminishing that brilliance, knocking it off as one might knock off the indumentum from a moth's wing or from a rhododendron. The woman who had called out to them came to the railing. "I'm sorry," she said. "I misjudged you from your looks! I can see now that you are ladies." Thank God! Gwen was quietly sure that it was not she who had changed the woman's mind, but Dorelia, bathing in a waterfall of sunshine on that French quay.

Dorelia thought she was coming along to learn how to paint. But why had Gwen brought her along? Gwen could have had Rodin all to herself, but then she could never have returned to England for shame. A young woman travelling on her own was the same as saying a young whore. She could not as easily have made friends with the strangers in the streets, because she, Gwen, was rude and stand-offish and she knew it, whereas Dorelia was simple and generous, a peasant at heart. The trip would be more enjoyable with Dorelia carrying her things, and Ida would feel that Gwen loved and cared about her, and Augustus would be aggravated, but the real reason Gwen had brought along Dorelia was because, without Augustus there, fomenting trouble, Gwen would finally have a real chance at causing Dorelia to love her.

Gwen looked at Dorelia. Her face was in shadow now, under her hat. She looked up expectantly at the deck of the boat. The hair at the base of her neck damp and curling. "Alas! Alas!" sang Dorelia alone. "There's none ever loved as I."

She was not a good person, not really. Certainly not a saint, and definitely not a hero. She did not understand how the greatest passion of her life, art, could so easily be put aside for this other desire. For all Gwen wanted out of her life in that moment was to make that beautiful girl love her.

The woman on the deck of the boat threw down a coin, and both girls swooped. Gwen held up the silver one-franc piece. On one side, a tall barefoot woman walked through a field with the sun behind her. "Breakfast," Gwen said, "and maybe lunch and dinner too." They had no idea how valuable the coin was, but still, they took up their parcels and ran along the broad street, singing, "Farewell to old England the beautiful! Farewell to my old pals as well!"

"We shall get fat!" Gwen interrupted, laughing. She pinched Dorelia's arm and her flesh was soft and warm and sweet smelling. Suddenly, Gwen was very hungry. The feeling of Dorelia's flesh lingered on Gwen's fingers and she popped a finger into her mouth and gnawed on it.

"Then your brother will have more of my fat to inspect," said Dorelia, and instantly, Gwen stopped in the road. Her smile melted into her high collar. She fingered the coin, turning it around and around in her hand. On one side of the coin, were the words *Liberté, Égalité, Fraternité.* Liberty. Equality. *Brotherhood.* Would she never get away from her brother? Perhaps even Rodin would not be strong enough to erase his fingerprints from Gwen.

"Augustus did not come with us," she said. "Don't let's take him with us in our words." The sooner he was banished, the sooner Dorelia might notice *her.*

“Alright,” said Dorelia. “But now, at least, might I see your Baedeker?”

“The guide book?” asked Gwen. “I didn’t bring one.” She had wanted to wander France without a guide, to seem dashing, to make discoveries that hadn’t already been planned out, but now that she was here, standing on the quay, not knowing even which way was south, she felt overwhelmed and unhappy and stupid.

Dorelia looked at Gwen’s face and laughed. “Well then,” she said. “There’s only one thing left to do. I shall copy that woman on the coin.” She bent down, took off her boots and hung them around her neck. Then she grabbed Gwen’s hand and began to skip along the cobbled street again, swinging their arms high. *Too-ra lie ooroo-lai la-ity, too-ra lie ooroo-lai lay!* And Gwen, unsure, allowed herself to be pulled along. Coffee, ripe fruits, baking bread, cardamom, pepper, garlic, olives, rosemary, fish, grease, whale oil, freshly shaven wood, the crisp odour of starched linen as a woman walked past with folded sheets piled high on her head. Vendors called out to them from small carts lined up along the wide boulevard. Gwen and Dorelia skipped from side to side, investigating the handcarts and the barrels piled up along the quay.

They were overtaken by a swarm of men riding bicycles with their bottoms lifted high into the air and their legs pumping furiously and their bells ringing out *tingaling tingaling!* Gwen and Dorelia clutched each other and covered their faces as a huge cloud of dust boiled over them. A moment later they coughed from the odour of sweat. Other men ran alongside the cyclists and motor cars swerved along behind them tooting their horns, with photographers leaning out over the front windows, trying to take pictures. One of the cyclists reached out and held on to an automobile as it passed him and was towed along.

"But what was it?" said Gwen, when the tempest roared around a corner and faded. She wiped the dust from Dorelia's face. "I can hardly see your face."

"That's not such a problem," snorted Dorelia, who did not ever understand the fuss about her beauty.

"It is for me," said Gwen, and Dorelia pulled away.

A man standing nearby said it was something called a Tour de France, a bicycle race around France. This was the first time the race had happened, the man said, but it had caused great excitement in the biking world. Had they seen the man in front, the one with the white coat and the great animal smile? They had. He hadn't seen them and had almost run them down. Gwen had a distinct memory of those brilliant white teeth, those unseeing eyes bearing down on her.

"Will they be coming back?" Gwen asked, but they were told that no, the race only moved forwards and never retreated, in a great clockwise circuit of France.

"I promised myself I'd make friends with freedom and uncertainty," she told the man. "But perhaps not with danger and disruption."

Dorelia laughed. "As if *you* would ever part ways with danger or disruption," she said. "What other girl would take a night packet for France and walk all the way to Rome?" Gwen already regretted *that* lie. "What other girl would live by herself and paint portraits for her entire living and go without stays to the greatest art exhibition ever staged in London? You drink danger instead of tea for breakfast. It just doesn't *look* like danger." She bent and replaced her boots on her feet.

"No," said Gwen soberly. Her chest felt like a balloon expanding. She stood a little straighter to see herself in such a light. "I've never quite thought of myself that way." Maybe the Jew was staring at her because he admired her courage. Could that be it? "I've always been rather in the shadow of my brother."

"It's not hard for a man," said Dorelia. "Bravery is rather

expected of men and there are so many opportunities, but really, they are all such ordinary things. Sail a ship! Whoop-de-doo. Rescue a cat from a burning building. Be honest when you could lie. They barely require effort."

"Was it hard for you to come to France?" Gwen asked Dorelia. She hadn't really thought about how it might feel for Dorelia.

"I know it's rather romantic," said Dorelia. "But I want to fall in love here." She giggled and Gwen looked at her closely, her heart bouncing over cobblestones. "With one of those delicious Gauls."

Gwen snorted. "You don't know the first thing about love. You wouldn't even know how to kiss a girl, much less a man."

"I could never," said Dorelia.

"What?" asked Gwen. "Kiss someone?"

"A *girl*," said Dorelia, licking her lips. "It's disgusting. Abnormal."

Gwen pulled her hand out of Dorelia's. "Do you really think so?" she asked. "Such a bourgeois, you are! I rather like it," she smiled and kissed the air. "Kissing girls. Really? Have you never practised with a friend? Someone with soft lips and a kind heart?"

Still, Dorelia did not seem convinced and so Gwen drew one last card from her sleeve. "My brother is fond of women who enjoy other women. Many men are. I hear Frenchmen in particular." Perhaps Rodin. "I suppose it takes the burden off them, to constantly have to be fertilising things."

Dorelia flared a single nostril. "I don't think it's for me," she said. "If loving women is a requirement for being an artist, I suppose I could *force* myself, but if it's not …"

A mallard hopped down the stone steps from the road to the water. The curled feathers of its tail bounced with each movement of its orange feet. It paused on the bottom step, but then plunged its breast into the water and circled around to face the dock. There must have been little fish, invisible from above, for the duck scooped its bill into the water and then tilted its head back and something could be seen sliding down the inside of its throat. Its head was bright green but around its neck was a coiled black hair, like a necklace, or a garrotte.

"I'm not interested in you that way," said Gwen sharply. "Don't worry."

"You're not?" said Dorelia. She seemed disappointed and relieved at the same time. The duck dipped its head. It took a long time coming back up for air. When it did, it was unable to swallow the little fish caught in its beak for the thread was too tight around its neck.

"No," said Gwen. She glanced at the duck again, not trusting herself to say anything. She could wait. Even the shyest of birds came if the lure was appealing enough. Even Dorelia, she who was disgusted at the thought of kissing Gwen, would one day come begging.

Nearby, a woman was standing at a stall selling seafood. *Clovisses, Portugaises, crevettes, moules, oursins, violettes, pain.*

"Combien coûte votre pain?" Gwen asked. The woman stared down at the bread as if she had never seen it before.

"Let me try," said Dorelia. "Bonjour Madame. Quel est le prix du pain?" she pronounced each word carefully, pointing at the bread. Her accent was better than Gwen's though she knew only schoolgirl French.

"Bonjour," said the woman, shading her eyes against the sun, which was now rising into a bright blue sky. Cicadas chirped, faster and faster as the day heated up, as fast as the ticks of a clock. "Combien voulez-vous payer?"

So it begins, thought Gwen.

Dorelia raised her arms and tidied her hair. She did not seem to be in a hurry to respond to the woman. Her sleeves fell to her elbows and she stretched, as a cat might do, in the sun. The saleswoman was smoking a cigarette, and Dorelia gestured that she would like to take a puff. She took the cigarette from between the woman's fingers and raised it to her lips. She closed her mouth around the paper and inhaled until the tip glowed, and then she blew out the smoke and returned the cigarette. Dorelia wore a faded green scarf around her neck and a straw hat on her greeny-black hair, and her lips, without any paint, were a glittering dark red. Dorelia began to talk with the woman and Gwen, dizzy and lost, watched the girl's lips open and close and her little tongue rise and fall wetly within her mouth. Gwen panted, as if she had run all the way from England. The day was hot. Much too hot. Her own mouth was dry. And still those lips opened and closed and that tongue rose and fell.

Dorelia lifted her hair and flipped it away from her skin. She took off her scarf and wiped first her neck under her hair and then her forehead. She unbuttoned the top button of her blouse. "Aren't you hot?" she asked Gwen, and then seeing that Gwen stood still and pale as if she had sunstroke, as if, at any moment, she would faint, and she said, "But you must have a drink!" She took the baguette and the change from the Frenchwoman, and put her other arm around Gwen's waist.

"You are tired," she said. "And hot! It's much hotter than England here." Together, they made their way to a stone pillar in the centre of the boulevard, where there was a tap and a tin cup chained to the fountain. "I got directions," Dorelia said. "It's as easy as walking beside the Garonne. Though we may wish to cross over to the other side, where there are more towns and the walking is easier." Her arm, around Gwen's waist, burning. Already, Gwen's face had turned an even brighter red and the backs of her hands were burned. Dorelia, of course, was darker than her, like a gypsy.

"I can hold myself up," said Gwen, though nothing could have been further from the truth.

"We can find a place to sit in the shade," said Dorelia. "There's no hurry now that we are here. Didn't the doctor give you medicine for these fainting spells? Give me your basket too."

So first they sat and rested in the shade of a building and

then, when a breeze arose and blew over the river, cooling them off, they began their walk down through the south of France. Dorelia carried the easel and the paints and Gwen's little basket and her own things as well. Gwen kept an eye out for beautiful people to paint. When Dorelia walked ahead of her, she painted, in her mind, a series called *Walking*, all featuring the other girl's swinging hips.

"I know you are looking at me again," said Dorelia, turning around and laughing. "That's what I get for walking with an artist, I suppose. I feel your eyes burning holes in my rear end."

"It's flattering," said Gwen, "that I waste my eyes looking at you." She had lied to Dorelia earlier when she said she was not interested and now she wondered whether the girl believed her or not.

And she told herself, again and again, not to look for the Jew, though every few minutes, she caught herself searching. She did not want Dorelia to think she was crazy.

PAINTING 3:

1. On seeing the subject, note the form, the colour, the tones.
2. Meditation. Decision on the form, the colour etc.
3. The painting (to save time, mix the colours beforehand and lay them on the palette.
4. The Palette:

White from Lefranc is to be placed at the top edge of the centre, in generous quantity. The white of the Jew's eye as he watches.
To the left, yellow ochre, raw sienna, raw umber, cobalt, mineral blue.
To the right, vermillion, Venetian red, Indian red, black for his hair, his coat, his heart.
In the centre, a mass of colour, the fairest of flesh colours, and trailing from it, a long line of black, so that the colour might be spread along it and the shadow be prepared, and the pure tones might be mingled with it as necessary, and so, on the palette, shall appear a tone picture of the Jew.
To the left, a preparation of the colours for the background is to be made in equally careful manner.
Each colour is to receive its own brush.

Wait, like a cat, to take possession of Dorelia.

BUST OF A WOMAN:

In Boisson and Cadillac, Gwen and Dorelia came across sculptures by Rodin, rude things, legs flung wide, so obscene that they both blushed. "What a man," said Gwen. "Such an obsession with *privates*."

"I rather like his work," said Dorelia. "So frank. As if he holds some truth before us and will not allow us to avert our eyes."

That was the moment when Gwen really understood Rodin's sculpture, a moment she would revisit again and again in her mind. The transformation of the invisible to the visible.

In Sainte-Croix-du-Mont, the girls examined their blisters and bathed their feet in the cool and fast running water, before going to explore the local châteaux. Above the front doors of the chateau in Cadillac, two partially draped stone women reclined. Gwen said, "Maybe when we are in Paris, Rodin will sculpt me. Then, perhaps, I will be truly, finally, solid."

"I would rather be painted," said Dorelia. She was half asleep and not paying attention. "Stone women look as if they cannot ever move, but painted women look as if they are simply passing through the frame on their way to somewhere else. I am the moving kind."

"I suppose," said Gwen, "that I am the staying kind."

She found it hard to talk when they were walking, as she was easily tired and grew dizzy on hills, but Dorelia, without saying anything, slowed her steps. Gwen found it hard to talk when they sat and rested too, because she fretted that something she would say might reveal her true feelings, her fantasies, her desire for both Dorelia and Rodin.

"Do you like the staying kind of person?" Gwen asked timidly.

"If it's you, yes," said Dorelia, yawning. "I'm rather fond of Miss Gwendolen John."

"And I am fond of Dorelia McNeill," said Gwen. She examined Dorelia's face for a trace of that earlier disgust but it was not there.

They were directed to a series of caves and Gwen took her sewing thread from the pocket under her skirt and unwound it. "This far," she said to Dorelia, "but no further. I don't want to get lost." They lit a candle and at the scrape of the match, and the whiff of sulphur, a great screaming swirling mass of bats roared around the cave and spilled out of the entrance. Gwen covered Dorelia's head with her arms and whispered in her ear, "They're harmless. If you stand perfectly still, they can see you with their ears, and they won't get tangled in your hair."

Walking along the great river, they barely spoke. Each town appeared around a curve in the distance, like a painting, like something the girls had seen in the National Art Gallery, low to the ground, amidst a haze of green and grey and pink, terracotta roofs and chimney pots floating above the old stone buildings, a single central spire covered in ivy. The river began to smell of fish and decaying plants and now the birds were waders, heron and osprey, that stirred the mud with their feet and speared up kicking frogs in their long beaks. In the shallows, large fish with electric blue fins swallowed smaller transparent fish.

The poorest people lived on the outside bends of the river, where it flooded, in cream stone houses with red shutters, or in houses with green stucco that had mould growing on it, like lingerie lace, as high as the water had grasped. The girls set up the easel on the edge of the river and sketched these old houses. Very often they gave away their sketches and the children ran inside the houses screeching and the elderly parents walked slowly together, holding the drawings with both hands. Once, a woman came out of one of the houses towing two tiny children with terrible scars on their faces. "Can you make them beautiful?" she asked and she held out a cameo carved above a ruby stone.

Gwen sketched the girls with fine skin and rosy lips and lace at their throats. She took out her paints and added the most delicate of colours. She drew the girls side by side, on a swing, their hair streaming behind them, two princesses, an imitation of a painting she had once copied in the National Art Gallery, and the woman hovered, anxious, in the background, terrified that she would never be able to pay for the bestowal of such beauty on her children. But when the woman tried to hand Gwen the cameo, Gwen waved her away and said it had been her pleasure. Dorelia looked at Gwen and said, "That was our dinner," and Gwen said, "We will find something else to eat," and Dorelia looked more fully at Gwen than ever before and saw that she was thin, that she had been giving away more paintings than she sold, and giving what food they had to Dorelia.

In that season, the fields were yellow with barley and wheat stubble, and maroon with grapes, and the pale, dry dirt rose in sheets and snapped in the air each time the wind blew. The girls slept outside, under haystacks, or, if the singing had gone well, in small rooms at the back of public houses, where the horses were kept. They left their shawls behind and they lost their hats and their ribbons and eventually they tied their hair back with string scavenged from the grapevines and they repaired their shoes, first with large leaves and eventually with pieces of wood that they picked up as they walked. One day, both girls looked at their boots, at the wide holes worn through the soles, and they put their fingers through and pretended that their shoes were puppets with noses that grew when they told lies, and Gwen remembered the lie she had told on the first day, about not loving Dorelia, and then they left the shoes lying in the shade of the haystack where they had slept and walked on barefoot.

In Castets-en-Dorthe, Gwen and Dorelia walked past a great

curving allée of plane trees reflected in the river. The leaves on the trees had already begun to turn yellow with the shortening days. It wasn't cold, not yet, but the leaves were a reminder that soon they would need to find someplace warmer to stay through the winter.

The girls no longer needed to tell each other when they were hungry or tired. They knew the tiny motions of each other's bodies so well now that they could tell, from the colour of a cheek or from the movement of an eyebrow if the other needed to relieve herself or if she wanted a drink of water. The silence no longer bothered them. At night, they slept close together under the easel and bundles of leaves, for warmth, and if one needed to rise, the other simply rolled away and rolled back again when her friend returned. Gwen thought that it was not love but it was almost as good as love, this closeness. And she was in no rush. Sometime, sometime soon, the girl would come to her.

It was late September, in the evening. Earlier that week, the locals had begun the grape harvest, the vendange. In the evening, thin lines of fragrant smoke rose straight up from great massed piles of vine and the air smelled of winter and home. In early morning, whole families walked to a single farm, squatted in the rows between the vines with secateurs, and dropped the dark grapes into baskets woven from prunings. The girls hadn't eaten for two days when they tried to join the labour. Their hands were sore and their fingers were thick with sugars. Dorelia, being the less talented painter, had tried to spare Gwen's hands, and Gwen, being shorter, had tried to spare Dorelia's back. The peasants worked quickly, competitively, in a solid line through the vineyards. They chatted with one another, made lewd jokes, called for la hutte, a man with a larger cone-shaped basket on his back into which they emptied their baskets, but nothing slowed down their hands, which flew. By lunchtime, an entire vineyard was harvested and they sat down to eat. Gwen and Dorelia, despite being left behind in their rows, despite men coming back to complete their harvest for them, were invited to join the meal.

The first course was brought out and each of the peasants took out a pocketknife and snapped it open. “Lamproie à la Bordelaise!”

Gwen looked at Dorelia. “Do you have a knife?” she hissed.

“No!” said Dorelia. She picked up the fork and the spoon and began to cut into the food. She picked up a piece of flesh with her fingers and asked what it was.

“Nine-eyed eel, they are saying,” said Gwen. “The name sounds like lampreys? Oh my God!” she said, and pointed. A man held aloft a three-foot eel with its huge bloody mouth open. Thick ropes of slime hung from the eel and wet the earth. The entire mouth was ringed with several rows of teeth. The man made a lewd gesture with his pelvis and mimed the biting of his crotch.

Dorelia pushed her plate away from her.

“They are staring at us!” said Gwen. The ticking of the cicadas seemed to drown out almost every other sound.

“So?” said Dorelia. “We can’t possibly eat the revolting stuff.”

One of the men rose and came across to them. “Would you like my knife?” he asked slowly, as if they were deaf, as if they could not understand things well.

“We are English,” said Gwen. She was terribly hot and sunburned and she had beetles down her dress and briars between her toes. On the plate in front of her lay a greyish pink lump of lamprey. In wine sauce.

The owners of the vineyard were already bringing out other courses, chicken soup with tapioca, a huge roast with vegetables and gravy and potato croquettes and charcuterie and bread and butter and small pots of black olive tapenade and a vat of rabbits cooked in red wine and prunes soaked in

Armagnac. Everything smelled of alcohol and wood smoke.

"Yes," said the man. "But what can you do? It's not your fault where you were born. You are trying to be French now."

"We can paint," said Gwen. "Or I can at least. And she can sing." She gestured towards Dorelia. "The backs of my legs sting from bending so many times."

"I have a tool," said the man as he reached inside his pants. He was already a little drunk and he smirked as he withdrew his hand and opened it to reveal the knife. He was drinking marc, a local vodka and he offered some to them. "What kind of girls are you? To walk across France by yourselves? Barefoot?" He smirked as if he already knew what kind of girls they were.

"I do not need your knife," muttered Dorelia, sawing at the roast with her spoon. It was more food than she had seen in two months. "Or your marc."

The man took Dorelia's face between his hands. "A waste," he said. "If the beautiful face does not match a beautiful behaviour."

Dorelia pulled away but now held the spoon out in front of her, as if it were a weapon. "We are not the kind of girls you think we are."

The man winked at her and licked his lips. "Yes?" he said. "Show me what kind of girls you are."

"Gwen," Dorelia said. "He doesn't understand me. Tell him to go away." She reached for Gwen's hand and Gwen held on tightly.

"It will be alright," Gwen said. "Don't worry. I will take care of you."

"Please," said Gwen. "Leave my friend alone. We must continue walking after lunch."

"But there is another vineyard to do and you have signed on for the full day," said the man and he laughed and pulled Dorelia's head closer to him. Dorelia, who was beautiful despite the sunburn, despite the dust and the dirt and the exhaustion and the lack of soap. "Did you think we were finished with you?"

"Gwen!" cried Dorelia. "Tell him to go away!"

Gwen looked around at the huge meal and the many bottles of wine that had been finished by even the women and children. The sun was three-quarters of the way through the sky.

"We couldn't do another vineyard!" she said, and all of the people sitting nearby laughed and pinched each other and winked.

"Worthless," the man said, letting Dorelia go and snapping his fingers. "We harvest at night and then eat again when we have finished, sometimes at midnight."

"I do not eat meat," said Gwen, and then the men and the women and even the little children laughed at her and said she did not love the cook and they dragged out the cook and the old man in his black checked vest, holding his copper spoon, looked coldly at Gwen's plate and his lips turned down and his hands shook and she was made to apologise to him repeatedly and then an elderly woman dressed all in black leaned forward and cut a small piece of meat off the roast with her own knife and placed it in Gwen's mouth and she was made to chew the dead animal and to swallow and to say that it was delicious.

That night, exhausted, Gwen slid one of the folding knives into her sleeve and told Dorelia to hide under the grapevines when the harvest ended to avoid the increasingly aggressive attempts of the men to touch them, to "help" them, to wind the girls' hair around their calloused fingers, and when the grapes had been dumped into the huge wooden vats and the peasants were again sitting around long tables, eating and drinking and shouting to one another, the girls crept away and slept under the willow trees next to the Garonne. Dorelia whispered that she felt as if Gwen had saved her from something terrible, some unnamed danger. Her face blushed and she appeared to be filled with a great love for Gwen, for the way she had of taking control, of making things alright. She muttered that sometimes she thought that Gwen was unkind, or bossy. But not now. She wished, often, that she did not think many of the things that came into her head. There was something she had said, months ago when they first came to France, that she now regretted and wished she could unsay.

"Gwen," began Dorelia a few days beyond the town of La Réole. Gwen's steps had become smaller and smaller until each step seemed as if her body rocked forward slightly and then rocked back slightly less, like a snail. Hard calluses had formed on her toes and the balls of her feet, but still, the small sharp stones in the road could raise blood blisters. "I am tired. Must we continue past this town? It is larger than the others and it seems to me that the men there will already be drunk. It might be safer to rest here, by the river."

Gwen had begun to think that perhaps it *was* time to rest, time to find a ride to Toulouse and rent a room for the two of them, until it was warm again and the crossing less fraught. She was a little afraid of the Bazadais cattle that were increasingly along the sides of the roads, their large dapple-grey bodies and moody black eyes and terrifying bawls making her heart race. She felt sure that she and Dorelia had reached a point where they would never touch one another intimately and she thought this moment might be when their misunderstandings would erupt. She was already planning their trip back to England.

Though Dorelia's dress was torn and her legs ached and her fingers were stained purple with juice and it had been over a month since she had bathed, she stopped for a moment to thank Gwen for bringing her to France. Her chest swelled. Little tears pricked the corners of her eyes. Gwen almost laughed to see her in such a state.

Both Gwen and Dorelia were afraid of the peasants when they were drunk. They had had several close calls and were not willing to take another chance. Once, when they were exhausted and desperate for shelter, a man, at dusk, had beckoned to them as if he wanted to offer them a room, but then he had turned and walked down an almost dark back alley, twisting and turning, then coming out along the banks of the Garonne and walking along in moonlight for what had felt like hours, followed by a mob of sheep that shuffled silently behind him and nudged the girls in the buttocks when they slowed down. The sheep had odd tawny eyes, slotted and demonic. Every footfall, every echo, had seemed as loud as a cannon to their ears, until the old man suddenly whistled for his dog and an enormous beast with yellow eyes, some kind of domesticated wolf, sprang out of the woods and the sheep parted and the wolf took hold of Gwen's hand in its mouth. Its teeth had rested on her skin, tightly enough to pull her long but not so tightly as to break the skin. Its hot breath had flowed down her wrist.

She had been terrified, though the man seemed old and, between the two girls, they should have been able to fend him off. He shooed his wolf and held out his own hand for Gwen to take, but his hand was missing two fingers and she shrank from it, so it fell to the wolf to lead her after all. And then, when they arrived at his hut, there were two young men there, his sons, both imbeciles, with their straight dark hair falling into their odd eyes and their tongues hanging out. The girls had shrieked and run off into the darkness and neither the young men nor the old had given chase. Even the wolf dog had let them go.

So that night, when Dorelia suggested that they camp outside a village, Gwen agreed. The nights were turning towards winter and the girls shivered as they lay beneath the willows. First the fog walked down the river and began to rise and the thick grey mass of it blanketed the girls and made them damp. Then it began to drizzle. Large droplets came through the branches and fell down the back of the girls' dresses and splashed on their faces and ran into their ears, until at last they were lying in mud. Along the riverbanks, cicadas ticked like clocks that were running down, and the rain fell softly into the water.

"Oh!" said Dorelia, shivering in her ruined dress. "Come here, Gwen, and make me warm." It was not the first time they had embraced but Gwen felt quietly sure that it was the first time Dorelia had *asked* to be embraced and her lips turned up and her mouth widened and she found herself smiling. The tortoise and the hare. Augustus might be the hare but it was the tortoise who won the race.

In the banks of the river, and under the bridges, the house martins and the swallows nestled together for warmth too. The birds murmured and rustled and squeaked. The rain ceased. The river slid by in the moonlight, a silver-black mirror, its sound something like silk or the pleased gurgling of a small child. The stars creaked overhead and from far off, from the village, a man began to sing.

Two or three other voices joined almost immediately and their voices were borne to the girls on the suddenly crisp night air. No instruments played. It was just those extraordinary voices, harmonising, as if *they* were the instruments. The sound echoed between the stone buildings and wound around and around the sky, blue-black with shreds of cloud passing over the moon, purple and a deep midnight green. Gwen crawled closer to Dorelia and put her arm around the shivering girl's waist. The music was a drone, something from some distant past that the English girls had no connection to. It was not a jubilant song, but rather, a reverent one, slow and solemn, a chant Gwen might have expected to hear in one of the twelfth century monasteries they had passed. Dorelia shuddered under her hand. The wind, little tendrils of wood smoke, the fine pale hairs around her forehead, where her flesh had not been burned by the sun.

"It's beautiful," Dorelia said. "But so strange."

The river hushed by. The birds moved in their communal nests. The cicadas ticked slower and slower. The man sang.

Must it be? The other men moaned their harmonies, crisp, painful, sad. Yes, it must! The moon rose above the last clouds and the willows shone brightly in the blue light and still the men sang. The first song finished and they began a round, also without instruments. It could have been a song in Arabic. There were long silences when Gwen thought that they had finished and then the same song would begin again, slower, softer. The voices of the other men now sounded like a single note played on a violin and sustained.

Dorelia moved back into Gwen's arms. "Please, Gwen," she said. She tucked Gwen's hands against her chest. She bent her head and kissed Gwen's wrists. Gwen did not breathe. Her heart rattled wildly in her chest, and in her neck, her veins jumped erratically. The men sang. In the distance came a great roar that drowned out the men's song and up, along the river, came the midnight wave of the Garonne, six feet high, glittering. The boats on the river rose and fell. The birds and the cicadas and even the willows were silent. As the wave receded, the men could again be heard, singing their sad songs in the village.

"I do not understand what they are singing," whispered Gwen. "The words are not French."

Dorelia turned to face Gwen. The moonlight fell through the trees and painted Gwen's face silver. Dorelia lifted her hand. She stroked Gwen's hair. She raked her fingers through the strands and gently unknotted the tangles. She took a handful of hair and ran it across the top of her lip and then she slid the hair across Gwen's lip too. They smiled at each other. The sensation delicious, their senses all sprung alive. The men's song faded. They repeated the same phrase again and again, softer and softer. Then there was a long silence. Gwen found herself holding her breath, waiting for what was next.

Then, in a surge, the entire village joined the chant, and in that moment, Dorelia leaned forward and kissed Gwen. Tears came into Gwen's eyes. The kiss was nothing like she had imagined on the long walk from Bordeaux. "I lied," whispered Dorelia. She touched Gwen's lips with her own and drew away. "I *did* want this," she said. An owl called from nearby and the voices from the village were joined by a woman who sang high above the others, as a bird will soar on thermals tens of thousands of feet above the earth.

Gwen parted her lips to Dorelia's. Then she too pulled back. "I lied too," she said.

Dorelia nodded. "I know," she said. "I have known it all along. Or at least, I *hoped* you did."

Gwen kissed Dorelia's eyelids, and her cheeks and then her forehead and her hands and the soft sweet indentation at the base of her neck. She unbuttoned Dorelia's blouse and peeled it away from her wet skin and then Gwen sucked on the bone that jutted below Dorelia's neck and ran across to her shoulder and Dorelia groaned and she pushed her hips against Gwen and Gwen bit down hard on her shoulder. Now instruments joined the singing from the village, a banjo, or a mandolin, a fiddle and a whistle and a galoubet – faster and louder. Dorelia tasted like the earth, like grapes and branches and soil and sweat. Dorelia's hands moved over Gwen too, touching her everywhere, peeling away the filthy shreds of clothing. The cold was forgotten. The rain was forgotten. A tambourin drum began, and they could hear syncopated claps and the stamping of feet on the earth. Yelps. Cries. The man sang louder and louder and Gwen and Dorelia pressed hard against each other, rubbing, moving body against body. "Why didn't you tell me?" began Gwen but Dorelia put her hand over Gwen's mouth. A woodpecker drilled into the trunk of a tree. Another owl cried. From the village, the music came louder and louder. Dancers came out into the countryside and lay on the ground and began their own explorations of each other's bodies, dark shapes against the dark ground. Birds in their nests, water in the riverbed, owls in the trees, the moon across the dark night sky.

"How could I?" asked Dorelia, after there was a cry from one of the couples. "I was afraid."

"We were both afraid," said Gwen. "Of each other. You are so terrifying, Miss O'Neill. It's a wonder that the dogs don't run away howling."

"Aren't we silly?" murmured Dorelia. "We could have been doing this all along."

Gwen said nothing. She knew it was the waiting that had ignited the other girl. She thought of Augustus, telling her one night back when they still lived in Tenby with their father and the terrible aunts, to draw sex. Now she knew what it would have looked like: willow branches, water, silver moonlight, pebbles in her back and sand in her hair and a rash where something had grated against her hip, a folding easel, autumn leaves, the smell of wood smoke and pond weed and rain. Threads from torn clothing underneath her fingernails, owls.

Another cry came from one of the hidden couples. "Don't worry. They can't see us," she said. "But if you are worried, I will lie on you and hide you with my body."

"Yes," said Dorelia. "Do that. Yes."

DORELIA BY LAMPLIGHT, AT TOULOUSE:

Long rivers of pure light trickled over every surface. Roosters brayed in the barnyards, pigeons cooed, crows cawed, tiny birds within the hedges chimed and tinkled and chaffed. The first farmers walked through their vineyards, fingering the glossy green globes. Night lifted from the bedrock in glazed purple sheets. At seven, the bells of the old Norman church erupted in a raucous cheer for the morning.

The girls awoke, cold and aching from the limestone ledge they had slept on. Now, only the cicadas were not awake in all the wide green world. After the last vibration from the bells faded, there was a waiting silence, as if something might happen at any moment. The stone flags leered. Dorelia leaned over and began to pick pea gravel from Gwen's arm. Gwen brushed twigs from Dorelia's hair. She didn't want to speak. The first ribbons of sunlight draped over their bodies, a cool warmth that crept down their necks. The colour of straw. Gwen was only shivering because she was afraid that Dorelia would deny what had happened between them. But Dorelia smiled at her and tickled Gwen's bottom lip with a fallen leaf and then ducked her head and blushed and smiled again before leaning over and kissing her hotly.

"I'm hungry," said Gwen, though what she *really* wanted was to lie down and pull the leaves over them again. "Let's go into the town and get something to eat." She stood and put out her hand to help Dorelia rise up. They were both naked and now it became apparent that their clothes lay in shreds at their feet.

"Oops," said Gwen. She looked at Dorelia and they both burst out laughing. Despite their laughter, the day was cool and windy and rain threatened.

"Do we have any money?" asked Dorelia, feeling Gwen all over in search of coins, but there was nothing hidden under her ribs, beneath her shoulder blades.

"We're going to have to do something," said Gwen, giggling and squirming. "Um … maybe we can pull together something for me and bury you under leaves and then …"

"And then, what?"

Gwen stood, thinking. Or perhaps she was merely taking the opportunity to look at Dorelia's body in the twinkling French sunlight. Either way, her eyes moved from Dorelia's lips down across her breasts, and then lower, past all her fertile planes, a gorgeous summer's walk.

"I might be forced to borrow something off a washing line," she mumbled. Across the river, men cut the last wheat. Their arms outspread, turning. The long scythes twisted around their bodies and the stalks fell backwards, splayed. "God! How I love France!" she said, and then she snatched the girl around the waist and pulled her down.

"If only you had said something," said Dorelia. "Maybe we wouldn't have had to walk so far."

"I told you I liked women, but you told me it was disgusting. Don't try to pin this all on me." She would have to go back and change every sketch she had ever made of Dorelia

Later that day, much later, they walked into the Musée des Beaux-Arts in Agen wearing the clothing of two peasant women, Gwen in a striped red linen skirt and a pink jacket, Dorelia wearing a checked blue dress and a black jacket. She still had her green scrap of a scarf and she was still carrying the easel and the paints and Gwen's basket, as well as an umbrella they'd found somewhere. And of course, there was more of Rodin's work there. He was everywhere, like Augustus. The thought had come unbidden and Gwen quieted it with a different thought.

But more respectable. More decent. And far, far more talented.

"We smell like fresh air," said Dorelia. She poked Gwen with the umbrella. "Like hay and lavender and rosemary." She sniffed Gwen's hair. "Mmm," she said.

"We smell like sex," said Gwen.

They set up the easel and Gwen began to sketch the marble Vénus du Mas.

"She looks like you," said Dorelia, but Gwen laughed.

"Only the shredded clothing," she said.

"The arms," said Dorelia, jiggling Gwen's elbow. "All over the place. Inescapable."

"Stop," said Gwen. "I can't paint with you distracting me." It was as if she had never been able to see before this moment. Something had changed and she could not name what it was.

She is beautiful
More beautiful than the women of Athens
Most beautiful girls of Sparta
The city without walls
Where girls are like boys
in the mountains
and swim
in the sacred waters of the Alpheus

That was what the man had sung the night before. Gwen had asked at the village, and then asked for a translation into French. She'd had to ask four people before someone agreed to even tell her the words in Langue d'Oc. "It's private," they said. "Sacred. Strangers are not invited. How did you hear it?"

Beside the road, that afternoon, was a tombstone for a tree.

"It was a thousand years old," said Gwen, stopping to look at the mossy stone. "So beloved that it became a family member of every person in the village."

"I will be that loved," said Dorelia.

"You *are* that loved," said Gwen, and for once, she felt that everyone could see her own brilliant fires burning. She felt dizzy with the heat of her passion. The headstone seemed to run with water, so hot she was, so hot she made her own mirages, reflections of the burning sky.

But Dorelia merely looked at her and laughed. "Lust is not the same thing as love," she said.

The red earth lay in crumpled beds. The fields held broken sticks and piles of pruned grapevines. Only stubble remained where once there had been fields swaying with golden wheat. Magpies screamed from between the stones of their nests. The peasants burned the sweet olive wood in their kitchen fires and the air was hazy, narcotic with its smoke. Gwen looked away. "I *do* love you," she said. "I have loved you since the first moment I saw you."

"Such a statement!" said Dorelia. "It's evidence that what you feel is lust. Because loves grows. It doesn't spring on you like a monkey. That's *lust*."

Gwen's chin trembled. In the back of her throat, she could still taste Dorelia's flesh, the sweet fresh juice of her.

Dorelia grabbed Gwen's hand and turned her around and smiled at her. "I *lust* for you, Gwen John," she said.

Gwen smiled a tiny smile. "Oh," she said. "That's good."

Later that afternoon, in between towns, Gwen fell asleep with her sore feet pointing towards a few slight clouds, white streamers in a brilliant blue sky, but she woke up to combed grey clouds, sedately drifting across that vast plain. She had been dreaming of Dorelia, of her body, of the fragrance of her. Waking, her mouth had been full of saliva. She had forgotten her earlier upset over lust versus love. She had forgotten Dorelia's words. She had made herself forget.

Dorelia had not slept. Now, Gwen looked at her through slitted eyelids. She was watching the bees flying in to land on the pebbles that lined the shallows of the river next to a mill. They came to drink, and they clustered thickly on the pebbles, a moving mass of glittering black and yellow bodies, a haze of constant motion, their lacy black wings swivelling in flight. She almost fell asleep again, the humming and the faint scent of honey were so soporific.

"Look!" Dorelia cried, when Gwen moved and stretched, pretending to wake up.

But the moment Dorelia spoke, Gwen's sleepiness shattered and she sat up and hunched over.

"Did you see the bees?" asked Dorelia. Gwen forced herself to look up and to exclaim over their beauty.

She had been resting in the shade cast by the large building and under a fig tree that hung out above the water. On limestone steps that descended to the river, Gwen tore a baguette the miller's wife had given them into crisp and fragrant chunks, which she buttered with the stolen knife. Dorelia added a slab of cheese to each and that was their supper.

"Lust is delicious," said Dorelia.

They smiled at each other then, because despite the lack of love on Dorelia's part, the sex *had* been good. She wished, for one swift moment, that her brother could witness this triumph and then swept her image of him away.

"Are you too tired to walk a little further?" asked Dorelia. In answer Gwen lifted her skirt and fanned her face.

It was cool and pleasant next to the mill. Water fell from the wooden scoops in torrents and a fine spray rose sparkling into the air and the breeze from the river blew the droplets against the girls' hot skin. An ancient jasmine climbed the walls, and its perfume, in the humidity, was dazzling. The scent was strong enough to make them choke.

Gwen reached out over the water and tore two huge black figs from the tree, each as big as her fist. Breaking the stem off hers, she poked a hole into the top and scooped out the flesh with a hooked finger. She licked the juice that ran down her arm. "Dorelia?" she asked, and when the other girl turned towards her, she split the second fig and pressed it to her forehead.

Dorelia lifted her hand, puzzled, to examine what had been done. Gwen took out her sketchbook and quickly drew Dorelia's face, her eyebrows drawn together, the deep purple print of the fig on her flesh.

"Oh!" exclaimed Dorelia. "It's a heart!" She took the pencil from Gwen and drew an arrow through the heart and their initials on each side.

"So, it's love after all?" asked Gwen.

Dorelia shook her head.

Gwen stood up and pulled off her jacket.

"Can you swim?" asked Dorelia. Concern was almost as good as love. "It looks fast. Too deep."

"I grew up next to the ocean," Gwen said. "I would rather be in the ocean than anywhere else. It … engulfs me. It takes me over entirely."

"I don't think I'd like that," said Dorelia. "I like to be me, and not something else."

Gwen stood at the edge of the river, on the old stone steps, in some other woman's petticoat and chemisette, hesitating. She hoped her back, in that late afternoon light, looked like marble, like the Venus in the museum. Something to be stroked and rubbed and smoothed and polished. Then Gwen untied the string and let her stolen petticoat fall. She put one foot into the water. "So good!" she called. It was almost dusk. Her slender calves curved out below the lace on her pantaloons and then swooped in again to her tiny ankles. The flesh tight and shiny and bold. She took two fast steps and then fell headlong into the glittering stream. Dorelia shrieked.

"Oh stop!" said Gwen, surfacing and wiping the water from her face. "It's perfect. At least put your feet in." She rolled onto her back and let the current carry her downstream. Dorelia was a child. She, Gwen, needed someone who could advance her career. Someone who could teach *her*. Rodin. She was almost, but not quite, sick of Dorelia already.

Below her, small shining things flicked in and out of the last rays of light, and there was darker movement, slower, deeper down. Curious, Gwen trod water, trying to touch one of the larger darker shadows with her foot.

"Don't!" called Dorelia again, and Gwen thought how pleasant it would be to find someone who knew she was strong, who knew she was capable. She felt the current slide through the gash in the legs of her drawers, dividing her flesh with a cool silvery touch that excited her. "Whatever it is, it might eat you! It could even be one of those nightmarish lampreys." Dorelia was almost dancing on the bank in her anxiety.

"It's not," said Gwen. She swam closer and splashed Dorelia.

"It's too cold!" cried Dorelia. "Come out! You'll get sick, you silly thing."

With each kick Gwen made, she felt a jolt of electricity run through her body, and so she kicked again and again as the sensation intensified. She opened her mouth and showed her teeth to Dorelia, who moved away from the bank, out of reach of Gwen's splashes. Gwen had a frightening smile. She didn't mind showing that there was something selfish on her face.

"Please!"

With a sigh, Gwen stopped her stroking. Lust might be good enough for Augustus but it would never be enough for her. She dipped her head under one last time and rubbed her fingers through her hair, lifted the heavy strands and squeezed them together, then wrung out the water. She stood up out of the river. The electric sensation drained from her spine and her legs like the water that streamed from her hair. The chemisette stuck to her skin and revealed everything it was designed to hide.

"Can't you at least bring me my skirt?" Gwen stripped off the wet underthings and stood, naked and shivering as Dorelia rushed up with the muddy petticoat and the red linen skirt and the pink jacket.

A door slapped open and before Dorelia could spring away, there appeared in the doorway of the mill the broad old miller's wife in her floor-length white apron and her immaculate white scarf. She, who had formerly been so kind, had been awoken from her evening nap by some kind of erotic rumble, some alien vibration in the air, and good Catholic that she was, she ran at the girls, shouting harsh words, waving a peel, and the girls ran out of the mill yard and into the deep shadows of the road, with Gwen naked and Dorelia occasionally stopping to pick up whichever garment Gwen had dropped in her hurry.

The old woman didn't catch them. They were young and she was old and broad and she'd been napping. She had bread baking in her oven and an apron long enough to trip over. A wagon passed them and then another, going in the opposite direction, but this turned out to be the same wagon, having turned around in the road and come back to help them.

"Good evening, ladies," said the young man who was driving the wagon. Blond hair curled over one amused eye. He took off his hat and smiled at them. "May I be of some assistance?"

Gwen squeaked and jumped behind one of the plane trees that lined the road and Dorelia smiled back at him, all her dimples showing.

"May I help you?" said the man again, his smile even wider. He placed his hat on his lap instead of on his head.

"Yes please," said Dorelia. "I'm very tired of walking. And my friend here is chilled."

"I imagine," said the man and he smiled again and adjusted his hat.

"Oh, *she's* not tired at all," said Dorelia. "She never is. But of course, she doesn't have to carry this dratted easel."

Gwen snorted. "You never *told* me it was too heavy for you, Dodo."

Dorelia frowned. "You should have known. Or *asked*," she said. "Must I always tell you *everything*?"

Gwen stepped from behind the tree. Now the jacket stuck to her damp chest and she had done up the buttons in such a way that there was a triangle of flesh revealed at her stomach. The man looked and Gwen caught him looking. She gave him a stern stare. He laughed. Then he whistled and fanned himself with his hat.

"The things you find on the road these days," he said.

"Yes," said Gwen, ignoring him and talking only to Dorelia. "You have to tell me everything. I want to know *everything* about those I love." She said the last sentence in English, though they'd sworn to speak only French, in order to improve. Dorelia squirmed. It was clear that she was afraid the man spoke English and would understand something about them that Dorelia didn't want him to understand.

"May I offer you *both* a ride?" he asked, still smiling. He never stopped smiling, this driver.

"Yes," said Dorelia, curtseying, just a little.

"No," said Gwen.

The man laughed at Gwen, and then he swung down to help Dorelia into the wagon. He looked at Gwen again, with a question. She wanted to stamp her foot. She wanted to drag Dorelia off the wagon and turn her over her knee and lift her skirts and spank her bare bottom. She thought of that for a moment, her hand moving over Dorelia's bare bottom and running down between her legs and parting the warm flesh there and entering the secret space, as she had done the previous night. She thought of Dorelia's panting, and her gasps and the "Oh, yes! Yes! Gwen, yes!" that Dorelia had cried out at the end.

Gwen shook herself. She wanted, then, to take a giant rubber and erase the man's smile and then, more slowly, his blond curls and his laughing green eyes and his clean white tie and his helpful brown hands and his manly shoulders. When she finished, there would just be smudges of colour left of him, like fingerprints on the back of a finished canvas.

The wagon was already sixty feet down the road. Dorelia twisted around on the bench where she sat, up high, next to the idiot driver.

"She *does* lust for me," Gwen said to the tiny purple bats that were swooping through the darkness as if they could see, scooping up cicadas from their hiding places. "She is just too young to know how to love." She stuck her hands into the folds of the skirt to try and keep warm and felt a coil of something, a small coiled something that could only be a hair, and with a cry, flicked the nasty thing off her fingers and began to walk, hoping to find a haystack or a deserted barn where she could shelter for the night. "*Darling* Gwennie," she said petulantly to herself, over and over.

Beyond the corner, the wagon was pulled to one side under a willow and the man was lighting the lamps.

"Why are you so stubborn?" Dorelia asked Gwen and she put her hands to the sides of Gwen's head and she stroked Gwen's damp hair, raking it back and holding it in a bundle at the nape of her neck. In the lantern light, Gwen's hair gleamed like polished copper. Gwen, surprised, rummaged around inside herself for an answer that felt truthful.

"I want someone to love me best," she said, in a small voice. "Not just lust for me. Lust turns me into a body instead of a person. I suppose…" she hesitated, "I want to be loved as a person rather than as a body." Dorelia had left one of her hands resting on Gwen's cheek. With the other hand, she wound a strand of the hair around her finger and used it to tickle Gwen's ear.

"But I do," Dorelia said. Gwen's lips, from the cold, felt like a deep bruised purple. Dorelia put a warm finger to the centre of her bottom lip and smiled.

"You said *lust*," Gwen whispered. She leaned forward. She was mere inches away.

"No," said Dorelia. "I *love* you. Every part of you." She drew Gwen closer and whispered something in her ear and Gwen flashed a glittering and triumphant look at the man before rushing past him and climbing up into the wagon. She pulled Dorelia up after her.

"I can drive, you know," she said to the man, but she did not touch the reins.

"Such a lovely gentleman!" said Dorelia and she gave her tail a small wiggle, bumping first Gwen and then the driver and then Gwen again.

"If you have worms," said Gwen, "get a tonic at the next pharmacy. But please don't rub them off on the bench. I know it can be itchy, but I am, thankfully, free of them and I would rather not share yours." This was all said in French and when Dorelia asked for a translation and was given it, she fell silent. The driver moved a little further away from both of them.

"Please, Gwen," Dorelia said. "Don't be angry at me."

They drove through the cool night not speaking; the only sounds the slow plodding footfalls of the horse in the dust and the creak of the wagon and the jingle of the harness and the brittle fallen leaves clicking as they were blown tumbling along the road. It was cold enough that even the cicadas had fallen silent. In the light from the lanterns, white powder from the road rose despite the earlier rain, and it swirled and fell and the whitish haunches of the horse rose and fell to, hypnotically, and its tail swished and the edge of the blanket the man had given them to tuck around their legs grew steadily whiter with the dust.

They had just passed one of the open bell towers that was chiming the hour, eleven, when Dorelia asked the man what he did for a living. He said he painted illustrations for advertising.

"What kind?" asked Gwen, curious despite her vow not to say a word to either of them.

"I do paintings of women and children and animals," he said

and Dorelia clapped her hands like a little child. He launched into a description of the masters he had studied, the techniques he used, his preferred materials and techniques, and Gwen fell silent again. He had studied with Rodin!

Reluctantly, she asked him, "What did you learn? What was he like, the maestro?"

The horse raised its tail to one side and let a pile of manure fall without breaking its stride. *Exactly.* Talking about it was not what made an artist a real artist.

He muttered on for a while about energy and life force and animalism, and Gwen turned away, bored. He had not understood anything.

"Gwen?" Dorelia whispered, nudging her in the ribs. "Be nice."

But Gwen's head had fallen on her chest and her hair covered her face like a veil. At every breath, a single hair blew out and then fell back amongst the others.

"It's in the eyes," the man said to Dorelia suddenly in English. "I'd be a fool not to recognise that look. Gender does not matter. The look is the same." Dorelia gripped the slippery leather seat and tried to hold still. Her elbow dug repeatedly into Gwen's ribs but Gwen refused to move. She looked, however, out from under her eyelashes.

"Love," said the driver. "You girls are in love with one another. And more than that. You have acted on that love." He placed his hand over his crotch and raised an eyebrow.

"Let me down," cried Dorelia. "Stop the cart!" But she was wedged between the driver and Gwen. "Gwen!" she said, lifting the other girl's eyelid and poking her eyeball. "Get up! We have to go!"

"Where are we, Dodo?" asked Gwen sleepily. She reached for Dorelia, an entirely inappropriate grab for body parts not touched by friends, and Dorelia opened her mouth to scream in Gwen's face. She lifted her forearms to force Gwen's hands away. They were perched high on a swaying cart. She might have knocked Gwen beneath the wheels. "That's enough!" cried Gwen and Dorelia's hands fell. Her face rearranged itself. Inwardly, Gwen smiled. She had not really been sleeping.

"What is this town?" Gwen asked.

They had entered something rather more than a village and now the cart jolted over cobblestones and the wavering red flames of gas lamps lit the streets. Every hundred feet or so, hazy lemon circles grew larger, shivered and then collapsed in an endless repetition, phantoms of light.

"Toulouse," said the man. "I will bring you to my home, my hotel rather, for I do not own it."

"No," said Gwen, suddenly wide-awake, tired of her game. "My friend and I will get down here. Thank you for the ride."

She put her arm around Dorelia's shoulders and gave her breast a squeeze, but Dorelia twisted away from her and buried her face in the driver's coat. "A male lover is one thing to have said about yourself in the street," she mumbled from between the lapels. "I'm prepared to be called a slut. But not a sapphist. A *homosexual.* That is something else again. People go to jail for less. Poor Oscar Wilde lost everything and still sat mouldering away in the central prison, eating his green carnations and widdling on his velvet smoking jackets."

Gwen did not understand how the feeling between them had fallen away so quickly.

"Take me," Dorelia said to the driver. "To your house. If *she* wants, she can get down here. We are not such good friends that we must always sleep in the same place."

The man looked at their faces as they passed through one of the animated spheres of light. Gwen looked at his. He was sure he was not mistaken, the lout. The smaller, thinner woman, he was thinking, was almost sick with yearning. The rounder, more beautiful one was confused maybe, but she had enjoyed her friend's body, of that he was sure. He was something of an expert in such matters, Gwen guessed. A connoisseur. She saw he wanted to ask if he could paint their stricken faces, but he did not have the skill to paint true emotion and she saw him see, on her face, that she would say no. So they rode along in silence for a while longer.

"Come to my house," he tried after the cart had swayed along for another few minutes. "It's warm, there are beds with sheets, and food and drink. There is a group of wonderful artists there."

Gwen wavered. She was tired. The talk of an artists' salon in a warm room *was* enticing and it had been a very long time since someone took care of her. But then, in the shadowy area just outside a nebula of light, Gwen thought she saw the Jew again. The Semitic head turned as he watched them pass, and when she twisted back in her seat to see him, he raised his hand and waved at her. His mouth opened and he seemed to form her name between his lips.

"Stop!" she commanded the wagon driver. And when he hesitated, she threw herself off the moving wagon, staggered, righted herself and then ran towards the place where the Jew had been standing.

"Gwen!" cried Dorelia, and she tugged the reins above the driver's hands until the horse stopped and then she, too, slid from the wagon.

The driver got down, sighing, and took their packages from the back and laid them on the cobbles. For a moment the poor donkey thought he'd won.

"Goodbye," he said, and he kissed Dorelia in the French fashion as he handed her the easel. Dorelia kissed him back.

"I live in the Rue Dordogne, should you need me. In the house with the large oak in the yard. Bring your little *friend*," he said laughing, before climbing into the wagon and snapping the reins on the horse's broad back. "Au revoir, dear *ladies*!"

"Gone again!" said Gwen, joining Dorelia in the miasma around the gas lamp. "But he left his passport behind. I had it for a moment. I set it down on the wall when the wagon passed, and the wind must have blown it away."

"The Jew from the boat again? Why is he here in Toulouse then?" asked Dorelia. She closed her eyes and passed a hand over her forehead. "Maybe he's a peddler. Do you think he's following us? We *should* have gone with the driver. It's awfully dark here on the street. Did you know that the driver is not French either. He is Belgian. I've never met a Belgian before. From Bruges. It explains his funny accent."

Gwen thought the Jew had not seemed like a peddler. Instead, he looked like a wealthy man who had set aside his clothes for a moment and found them replaced with someone else's garments. He looked confident, determined, sure that everyone would do as he asked.

"It's got to be here," Gwen said.

"He told me his address," Dorelia said.

"You got his address?" said Gwen. She had been bent over, rooting around in a litter of blown papers and dead leaves. "How?" she said. "When?" She took Dorelia's hand between hers and uncoiled the clenched fingers and rewrapped them around her own, chafing the cold little paws. She would paint these lovely hands as soon as they had a room. She stroked Dorelia's face and Dorelia, after glancing around to make sure that no one was there, let her.

"Not your Jew's address," said Dorelia. Her teeth were chattering. "Leonard's address. The *driver's*."

"You asked me something before," said Gwen, pulling away and brushing down the front of her dress. *Leonard.* For God's sake. They hadn't been introduced. How on earth did Dorelia know his name? And now his address as well. "The miller's wife, what she said when she was chasing us?"

Dorelia raised her hand to ward off Gwen's attack but it was too late.

"Perverts, is what she called us. Not just me. Both of us."

THE STUDENT:

After a brief search, Gwen and Dorelia found a deserted spot between a paper manufacturer and a shed that was piled high with rags and they burrowed into them like small animals and tried to fall asleep. Dorelia had insisted that there be no lanterns nearby. But despite the lack of light, just at the chiming of the two o'clock bell the girls were woken by clusters of small brown moths clinging to their faces. When they waved the moths away, the pests came back again, thicker than ever. For an hour or so, they slapped at the little beasts, and then, suddenly, the insects all disappeared and the girls were able to fall asleep again. Around five o'clock, they were woken a second time by a crash and a howl. Lanterns were lit, light spilled out of nearby windows, shutters squalled as they were banged shut in the buildings all around them. A bell rang and then another.

"What is it?" asked Dorelia. "Is it a fire?" For she heard a steady roaring sound.

"The Mistral," said Gwen. Before she was fully awake, the strong northerly gusts blew away her favourite notebook, the one with all of her sketches of Dorelia, and sent it cartwheeling away into the hazy dawn. She'd watched the book go without understanding until it seemed to vault a wall and vanish and then she cried out and ran after it. Larger things flew through the air and disappeared between the buildings. Heavy items, metal and wood and something that said *oof,* crashed into the tin roof. Gwen's hair lashed her face. Dorelia sat up shivering and clawed the rags off herself. The temperature must have dropped thirty degrees. "Gwen!" she cried. "Come back!"

Gwen could not find the notebook. At least she had the original. For now.

"Look!" Gwen said, pointing. In the eerie acid-green light, it seemed as if a black and white dog floated down the street. It did not appear to have feet. For a moment, all sound was sucked from the world. As the dog passed, it turned its head and silently opened its jaws and its teeth were a brilliant, unearthly, glowing blue.

"I want to go to the driver's hotel," said Dorelia, and for once, Gwen agreed, due to the cold, her exhaustion and the terrifying dog's teeth. They ran hand in hand through the early-morning streets, blown along by the rushing wind, pelted by acorns and the prickly seed pods of the plane trees and by leaves and by twigs and by small bones and baby rattles and broken boxes and by scraps of fabrics and aprons torn from washing lines and by apple cores and by a creeping sense that the wind was not just a wind, but a spectral presence.

"It's only wind," shouted Gwen, though it seemed human in its ferocity. Somewhere above them a shutter came loose and banged against the limestone façade in a hysterical frenzy. Not a soul was in the streets. The morning songs of the birds were not sung. The old soldiers with their barrels of water and their long canvas hoses did not come out to wet the streets and neither did the old women with their twig brushes come out to scrub the cobbles. All life had vanished in the face of the Mistral.

"Are you sure it was Rue de la Dordogne?" called Gwen. Their linen dresses were no match for the Mistral. Hundred-foot cedars were bending double.

"Yes!" cried Dorelia. "But wherever *is* that?" For there was no one to ask, no signposts.

By some miracle, they were blown out onto a main road and branching off that road, near the train station, was a little side street with a blue plate on the corner announcing that it was the Rue de la Dordogne. “Here!” cried Gwen and she swung around the corner and was pushed, almost immediately, up against an oak tree in a side yard. They hammered on the front door but no one came, so they went around to the back, where it was more sheltered from the wind, and there, a little old woman dressed all in black unbolted the door.

“You are looking for a hotel?” she asked. She had few teeth and all her esses were hissed. “Leonard? Such a dear man. Yes, yesss. Come in. Let me close the door before the wind closes it on me. Are you hungry? Poor maidens. Let me get you something to eat.”

The girls passed a rolled parchment on the doorpost that had a trident painted on it in black ink. There was something about the old woman, too, that alarmed Gwen. Perhaps it was her bowed legs and her skeletal hands, the way the flesh rose in steep purpled mountains over her veins and fell into dark valleys between. Even the pious black lace on her head and the spun cape over her shoulders felt portentous. Gwen felt some powerful intent radiating from the tiny twisted body, though the woman stood unobtrusively in the corner and spoke very gently.

“She’s a witch,” she whispered to Dorelia when the woman scuttled down into the cellar to get potatoes and two bottles of home-brewed beer.

“Don’t be silly,” said Dorelia in a normal voice. “She’s perfectly ordinary.”

When the woman returned, Gwen tried to figure out what it was that had made her so anxious, and she realised that there was a place on the woman’s chest where the light was distorted. Though the woman wore a black dress, over her heart, the blackness moved and shifted, like a mirage, first grey, then yellow, then black, sometimes taking on a shape like a sun or a star and sometimes appearing as a blur of colour, easy to miss and very temporary, a drift of smoke, a tiny blink of light. This inconsistency, the lack of solidity, is what had alarmed Gwen, for it reminded her also of the Russian Jew, who had a similar mysterious blur over *his* chest. She put her hand in her pocket and rubbed his coiled hair between her fingers. For she had decided it definitely belonged to the Jew.

"An omelette?" asked the woman and the girls sighed and sat down and speared their forks into the eggs. Feeling returned in sharp blue twinges to their hands and their feet and they began to relax. Still, Gwen could not shake the sense that something was deeply wrong.

"She's a wonderful cook," said Dorelia, almost swallowing her fork. "I would like to learn to cook from her. So much better than English mush." The silvery tines came out of her mouth wet with her saliva.

Everything was scrupulously clean and smelled freshly of verbena and lavender. The room had a low ceiling with pots and a lantern hanging from a charred beam. The table ran up against a stone hearth painted with a pinkish ochre that was as wide as the room. Inside the fireplace, bubbling pots swung from iron hooks and in one corner, away from the fire and drawing in the ashes, sat a naked child wearing a black cap, probably a grandchild. The old woman turned a brass handle that projected from the wall and water fell into a huge stone sink under the window.

"Perhaps we could stay here, for just a while. You could paint something for the New English Art Club."

Gwen glared at Dorelia.

She didn't want to exhibit. She wanted to study under Rodin, visit the studios of Picasso and Cézanne and Modigliani, copy the portraits of Velázquez and Ingres at the Louvre. Give birth to the child of a famous artist. Become famous herself. Have her limbs immortalised in marble.

"Do what you want," she said to Dorelia. Gwen put the napkin to her mouth and wept. She could not look at the witch *or* Dorelia.

"Whatever is the matter?" asked Dorelia. "Here we are in this lovely place." She gestured at walls covered with pages from an old calendar, presumably painted by Leonard. Muddy watercolours of French peasants with skulls where their heads should have been. Septembre showing a bawdy clown putting a bony finger to fleshless lips.

Gwen's lungs felt full of sticky smoke. She could hardly breathe. She thought the old witch might be putting a hex on her. Damning her to a life of ordinariness. To *sign painting.* To *calendars.* Listen to the old crone laugh! Why ever had she agreed to come to this place? First she roots Dorelia out of Augustus' nest and then she brings her to another dandy's hive.

Eventually, the old woman turned and saw Gwen's convulsive struggle and she took a towel from above the fire and tucked the warmed fabric around Gwen's shoulders and patted her on the head. It felt like being patted with a bundle of sticks that clicked and knocked and clattered. "It's just the wind," the witch said. She cracked her knuckles and then her neck. "You'll be alright in a while. The Mistral affects everyone in a different way. Murders have been committed under its influence." She smiled. All her teeth were black.

The ancient stone house vibrated in the wind. The walls were close to three feet thick. The beams that held up the ceiling were cedars, two and three feet across. It was hard to imagine the incredible force of the wind, to make such a solid house shake. The old woman had said that the wind was blowing at ninety miles an hour. The bells of the churches had been ringing in the wind until men climbed up and took away the clappers.

The old woman was telling a story about the wind as she climbed the stairs to show them their room. The man next door had walked in on his wife with another man, she said. In a fit of passion, he killed his wife. When the gendarmes came, the entire street claimed that the man had been playing cards in the inn. That it couldn't have been him. That night, the old woman had gone to see the man and said to him, "We know you killed your wife, but we understand. The Mistral was blowing. It makes everyone crazy. You are excused, but you cannot live in this street anymore. We've found a house for you a few streets away."

"Here you go. Number nine," chirped the landlady, more than ever like a crow, her black lips hard and pointed and coming together with a clack. "It's open. Two francs. Payable daily."

In the bed, Gwen's back nested against Dorelia's chest and Dorelia held Gwen close within her arms. It was the first time they had lain in a real bed together. She felt Gwen's sobs in her ribcage, rising up under her chin, though there was no sound. Gwen's head was bowed and almost hidden under the blanket and the bones of her neck rose beneath her skin in a tender arc that Dorelia longed to touch. But she did not try to hush her. "The skulls," muttered Gwen. "Did you not see the skulls on the calendars?"

Dorelia said she had not seen any such thing. Eventually, Gwen's sobs subsided and her breathing deepened. She felt herself sliding from Dorelia's grip and fell, finally, asleep.

Each evening after that, Gwen painted Dorelia in her stolen dress by the light of a small lantern. "You will paint *me* when I am finished," she said to Dorelia, but Dorelia was exhausted after helping the landlady with the cooking and the cleaning. She wanted only to lie in the soft feather bed with Gwen, talking quietly about what she had done that day.

Some mornings, Dorelia went to the market with Leonard in the wagon, and they returned with large sacks of potatoes and onions and shallots and carrots and beets, and once, with several huge boxes of grapes that the entire household mashed with their feet. Leonard, it turned out, was an excellent painter of signs and posters and advertising boards and he was a very good teacher too, with far more patience than Gwen. He'd asked to see Gwen's work but she had declined. She let him wait for her to ask to see his paintings, but she never did.

A month after they arrived in Toulouse, Dorelia received a letter from Augustus. He said he'd told Ida he was *in love* with Dorelia. Poor Ida had to decide what should happen to their family. And Dorelia must, of course, return at once.

"But I couldn't," said Dorelia to Gwen. "He's such a handful of rubies, your brother, but poor Ida ..."

What about Gwen? Didn't she count for anything at all?

"We will be in Paris in the spring," said Gwen sternly. "And you will see the Louvre and we will go to visit Monsieur Rodin and get work from him. We will have an artist's garret and we will paint gorgeous women and we will lie in bed until ten every morning after staying up late." Her eyes darted to the bed when she said *staying up late*. The ferrule on her brush hit the edge of the palette with a repetitive tick, tick, tick as Gwen wiped off excess paint.

Dorelia looked around the crowded room. They were both disastrous housekeepers, but somehow it was worse when there were two people not picking things up, rather than one alone. "Will we share a flat then?" she asked. "In Paris?" Her eyebrows came together and she sucked her lip. "I'm not so sure Mummy expected me to be gone so long ..."

"Don't you *want* to be an artist?" said Gwen.

Gwen spent the day walking around Toulouse, sketching people for three francs a head, or sitting on the hill outside the town, painting the burnt colours of the autumn, colours that made her think of Augustus and his plum-coloured trousers and mustard boots. She missed England, and wrote to her friends from the Slade, that soon she would return. But in the evenings, Dorelia served Gwen whatever she had learned to make that day, quiche and fondue and crêpes and flan, and told her funny stories about the old woman and the stall owners at the market, and showed her the hideous drawings Leonard had taught her to make, anecdotal, melodramatic fluff of the kind Augustus often painted, and afterwards, Gwen washed Dorelia's hair by lamplight, massaging her temples and rubbing the soap into her skin, and then stroking Dorelia's thick black hair dry with the hairbrush, droplets of water falling on the flags like tiny beads of molten gold.

Later, when the household was asleep, Gwen made Dorelia remove her undergarments and change into the pale blue dress she had taken from the washing line near Agen. Then, standing behind Dorelia, she would draw a black ribbon around the girl's waist, slowly, so that the silk hissed over the linen. After she tied the bow, she let her hands rest on Dorelia's waist for a moment. "There," she said each time. "It's perfect." Gwen ran her hands over Dorelia's breasts to smooth the fabric and settle it to her satisfaction. She removed Dorelia's earrings and replaced them with her own. She lifted Dorelia's smoothed black hair and untied the string that held it, the untying itself transfixing, the way the loops slid through the knot and came free.

Dorelia leaned back against Gwen and sighed with pleasure. The tension drained from her shoulders. Gwen's desire for her flowed like a wave through the girl's body, a lamplighter walking through the streets, touching every wick with a flame. Dorelia's fingers shook, her arms, her breasts, her belly, her groin, her spine, the tenderest place on the inside of her thighs. Gwen understood this almost painful sense of waiting and wanting and needing. *Touch me*, that's what Dorelia wanted to say. Her breath came in shallow gasps. Take me to the bed. Force me. *Ravish* me. But instead, Gwen gathered Dorelia's hair together and braided it and pushed in pins to hold it against her head and then went to stand next to her easel. "Now," Gwen said, making herself someone else entirely, someone strange and icy and unreachable. It was if she had stretched a long taut line across Dorelia's body and was waiting to snap it. "Your hand on the chair. Yes. Like that. And lean a little to the left. No, the right, I mean. Push out your hip and bend your head. Exactly."

Once Dorelia was positioned, Gwen began to paint. She took many minutes between each brush stroke. As she finished one painting of Dorelia, she began another, in the same dress, in a similar pose. The smell of turpentine filled the room constantly now, but it was too cold to open the tiny window. The fire grew lower and lower and crumbled into the last embers. The light on the table flickered. Tiny moths danced above the flame. From a nearby room, the sound of bedsprings, soft moans. Gwen looked again at Dorelia. As the moans rose in intensity, she could no longer block out her own rising desire and she let her eyes run over Dorelia's contours, caressing her curves. Her hand hesitated, made a slight stoke on the canvas. Her tongue remembered the sensation of sliding into a deep warm place, of penetration, the wet heat of flesh on her face, the bucking of hips against her cheekbones, the muffled cries of pleasure, the rich fragrance of bread and steak, enticing and delicious, that fell from Dorelia, and she hesitated again, her lips tingling, before allowing her paintbrush to make the tiniest lick on the canvas.

"Every night! For hours!" said Dorelia, tilting her head towards the other room. "Such stamina!" she said, admiring something that to Gwen seemed normal. "You should only paint as long as they go at it in the next room!"

"Don't talk," Gwen commanded Dorelia as she painted. The magic was lost if Dorelia spoke, because Dorelia's working-class accent did not match Gwen's imagining of the mythic Dorelia, did not match her belief about who Dorelia *could* be. It was very frustrating. No matter how hard she tried, she could not connect these two things, the internal sensation of her body and the external image of Dorelia, and as a result, each painting seemed flat and lifeless, lacking in honesty.

"Damn it!" she cried, flinging her brushes across the room and then running to retrieve them before their points were damaged.

"What are you painting?" said Dorelia. "Won't you show me?" She swayed in her pose, hoping for a glimpse of the newest portrait. Four completed canvases were stacked against their bedroom wall. Gwen hated all of them.

"Shut up," said Gwen. "Don't talk." She shook her head to get rid of the real Dorelia's voice and then leaned forward and unbuttoned two of the china buttons between Dorelia's breasts. She licked her brush and smoothed the point and then, touched the brush to the canvas and painted a darker line, a slit. She leaned forward again and slipped her fingers inside the linen bodice. Dorelia looked up and a slow smile spread across her face. Her mouth opened a little.

"No. Look down," said Gwen.

She dabbed her brush against Dorelia's painted face. She waited a long moment, looking at her model, watching for the flicker of animation that had caught her attention. Dorelia looked up again. They gazed at each other and smiled. Gwen still did not move to paint another mark. It was not sex she wanted, exactly. It was something more furtive. Dorelia turned a page of the book she wasn't reading. *Daniel Deronda* by George Eliot. The ferrule hit the side of the palette and the sable scraped across the canvas. A moth blundered into the lantern and the light disappeared with a hiss and then rekindled. The room smelled like powder, like hay that has lain in a field and grown musty. The circle of light grew smaller and guttered again. Gwen's heart beat faster. She began to sweat. The heat. The lack of air. She waited and waited. That look, of anticipation *and* fear, that was the look she wanted to capture. The springs, in the next room, began their rising song. Gwen leaned forward again and slid her fingers inside Dorelia's dress. The linen shushed as it ran across the back of Gwen's hand. Gwen paused. She looked into Dorelia's eyes. She touched the tip of the girl's nipple. Once. Twice. Dorelia panted. Gwen's tongue appeared and she withdrew her hand and licked the tips of her fingers. The candle flickered and the light ran up the wall and back down again. The old house creaked. Gwen slid her hand inside the dress again and Dorelia pushed her breasts forward, holding her breath. Gwen held the girl's gaze. She frowned at her and Dorelia's face crumpled.

"Look down," Gwen commanded.

She pinched Dorelia's flesh and began to roll it one way and then the other. Then she sank her fingernails into the tender skin.

"Oh!" cried Dorelia, and she shrank from Gwen, but at the same time, ground her hips into the rush-bottomed chair. Her face a complicated mixture of emotion.

"Just like that!" said Gwen. "Hold that pose! Exactly like that!"

She thought it might be that the only reason that she ever had sex was to discover what it was to be human and to put it down on a sheet of canvas. It was not a lie then, what her brother had said, that she did not exactly love people. She merely used them. She stabbed the brush at her painting and ruined the tip. She stabbed it again and again, a texture of rage.

THE WIDOW:

One night that November, Gwen woke up with *Daniel Deronda* over her face and her heart pounding from a dream of ghosts and wickedness and thieves and a black dog with five legs that had been chasing her down the street. Outside, the huge clock tower chimed three. Their room, ordinarily stifling, since it was directly above the kitchen fire and shared a chimney with it, was ice-cold and a stream of freezing air swept in from the doorway. The almost-full moon outside the window cast crisp shadows on the Norman furniture. Gwen thought about waking Dorelia, but then changed her mind. Dorelia always rose early to help Leonard with the shopping for the hotel, and the old woman with the cooking. She needed her rest.

Gwen lay and contemplated the ceiling, its crumbling plaster and water stains and the dark carpet of soot above the lamp, and willed her heart to slow down. It had only been a dream. Nothing at all. But despite that, she had the odd feeling of being watched. Every noise was too loud. A cough on the other side of the wall echoed like a shot. The dog barking in the yard seemed like an elephant's trumpet, breaking some important silence. Each scratch from the mice within the walls terrifying. She was afraid even to turn to the side and look around, but reassured herself that no one could be in the room, since she and Dorelia were very careful about locking the door each night. Yet still, there seemed to be stealthy footsteps across the room. A creak from under the window.

Gwen understood at last that she did not truly love Dorelia, that she was fond only of the domesticity, of being able to quietly discuss her day with someone who had heard about the previous day and the one before that. She did not need to be seen. All of their conversations were at night, after the lantern had been blown out. More and more, Gwen felt herself to be unnecessary, unwanted, invisible. It was a miracle that the last portrait had been finished.

Gwen shivered. The cold deepened and solidified. It had a physicality in the room, a malevolent presence. She pulled the quilt higher over her shoulders, and tucked her freezing hands under Dorelia's warm body. She could hear the faint swish of her own blood beating in her ear. She did not want to turn around. She snuggled further under the quilt, hoping that it would deaden the extraordinary heightened sounds. The light in the room changed from pale blue to acid yellow and the shadows leapt up the walls. Ice crystals began to form on the windows, and now, Gwen could see her breath in the frosty air.

Once again, she had the sense that she was being watched. It was unbearable. It might be Leonard. She suspected he might have hidden inside the cupboard near the door but she didn't want to give him the satisfaction of frightening her, so she rolled over quickly and sat up. A terrible sensation of static made all of the hairs on her arms rise and there was, too, a burnt taste in the air, a smell of gunpowder or creosote or tar. Her spine prickled. Instead of being locked, the door stood open, and just within the next room, at the head of the stairs, glaring at her with glittering black eyes, was the old landlady. The odd blur on her chest was now a six-pointed yellow star with the word *Juif* written on it in black ink and this star burned brilliantly, like a lamp, illuminating the outer room. The old woman's face, lit from below, looked like that of a gargoyle, with deep shadows above her eyes and a nose that arched high across her forehead and, as Gwen watched, the woman opened her mouth, and long black hairs unfurled from the sockets where her teeth should have been and detached, with sucking pops, and floated free in the room.

"You are no different than us," she gurgled.

"Dorelia!" cried Gwen, grabbing her arm and shaking her. Outside, the dog barked again and again and an owl hooted and the last cicadas of the year ticked faster and faster and a door within the house slammed. There came the sound of glass shattering. "Dorelia! Please wake up!"

When Dorelia had struggled out of her deep sleep, Gwen pointed at the door but the old woman was no longer there. Still, the door was open and both of them remembered closing it.

"What did you see?" asked Dorelia, who was also shaking from the intense cold that lingered in the room.

"The old woman. I don't know. She had a candle on her dress. No. A star. With the word 'Jew' on it. It was so strange. She meant for me to see her. I am quite sure of it. And her staring! Horrible." Gwen brushed at her arms and found them covered in long black hairs. "I am *nothing* like the Jews!"

"It must have been a dream," Dorelia mumbled. She rolled over and sat up. "Why would you think you are like the Jews?" They'd have to leave for Paris in the morning but Dorelia wouldn't want to go.

"I don't," said Gwen. She sat up and said again. "I'm *nothing* like them." But for just a moment, she understood that she was like the Jews, exactly like them. Only now, fully awake, she couldn't quite remember the connection.

BOOK TWO: AUGUSTE

PAINTING 4:

In 1887, Gustave Sennelier opens his small shop at 3 Quai Voltaire near the École des Beaux-Arts, directly across from the Louvre. It's a crowded little place, two windows and a door under the deep green banner with his name in gold letters, Sennelier. The deepest reaches of the shop, behind the high wooden shelves and the racks, are in permanent darkness. Gustave is a chemist, an inventor, fascinated with pigments, the chemistry of paint. Hue, permanence, chroma, lightfastness, compatibility with other pigments, drying attributes. It's his bread and butter, his quiet obsession. Charcoal, iron oxide, rust. Gypsum, sienna, madder, earth. Paris green and orpiment, poisonous duo. Mercury, arsenic, lead. He grinds each colour on a granite slab, finer and finer, until it is perfect. Pigments from plants, minerals, animal bones. Some of the pigments – carmine, madder, lapis lazuli – can be damaged with improper grinding, so he is gentle, and he twists the glass muller in his old spotted hands slowly, and watches for the moment when the powder is fine but not too fine, not pulverised, not destroyed. With a spatula, he scrapes the pigment into a hill and then presses his thumb into the centre and licks off the pigment. He puts a peck under his nose and sniffs. If it smells right, he strikes a match and lights a candle that stands under a glass beaker full of oil. A chemist. He shaves off flakes of beeswax and melts them in the shimmering liquid, stirring with a wooden spoon, slowly, slowly, there's no rush, there's never a rush, then pours droplets of the linseed oil or safflower oil into the pigment until it is crumbly and dense. He cuts the oil into the pigment with a palette knife. Sometimes he uses hemp oil, or the oil from poppies. Safflower and poppy oil are paler than linseed oil and he mixes these with white pigment, for vibrancy. Jars of honey from the French Alps, powdered egg yolk, gum arabic, they all glitter in the last rays of light, right as the sun sets. He makes just enough, each day, for the few artists who come in and ask for *his* colours, *his* paints, specifically. Van Gogh comes in one day, he's a young man, no one knows who he is, he buys two tubes of paint. He comes back and buys more and brings a friend.

Monsieur Sennelier knifes the stiff paint into fat metal tubes and crimps the ends with carpenter's pliers, twists down the little metal caps to seal out the air, kisses each lid and pastes on his label, each one signed by him, and dated. He has a hundred colours laid out in a fan in the window. No one in Paris has as many as he does. Certainly not the unbearable Charbonnel, with his little tubes of Lefranc paints, hiding in the shadow of the Notre Dame, snagging all the students from the Sorbonne. The thief of his best clients! Monet, Degas, Renoir! The little man, Lautrec! But no one besides Monsieur Sennelier hand-grinds the colours anymore. He takes custom orders for colours that no one else can make. He's in the back of the shop, in the darkest corner, whispering with the artists. He has a notebook full of formulae, a pencil tucked behind his ear. He never smokes because smoking destroys one's sense of smell, and without smell, how would he know if the pigment was just right?

He invents red helios, green cinnabar, Chinese orange, coral pink. He makes a line of watercolours, egg tempera, Indian ink, aquarelles, pastels. Rodin comes back again and again for the grey pastels. Gustave's hands, quick. His eye, always searching. His mind, busy with binder-to-pigment ratios, siccatives, extenders. He buys a grinder with porcelain rollers, so that he can concentrate on his customers, because now he has many. Now, people come from overseas, the horrible English, to buy paint at Magasin Sennelier. Sad little women with holes in their shoes and the blank empty-eyed look of the starving walk across

Paris, from Montmartre and from Montparnasse, in the rain and the snow and they count out francs, one by one from their limp miser's purses, to buy a single tube. And when they do not have enough, they try to bargain with him, offering him buttons, trinkets, a cameo. When he offers to trade a tube for a kiss, they refuse and say that they are not whores. They are artists, they say with a pride that is not indicated in their rags, and he sends them away with a wave of his hand, and off they scurry, like beetles, to buy the cheaper paints of LeFranc.

A CORNER OF THE ARTIST'S ROOM IN PARIS:

Gwen and Dorelia and Leonard arrived in Paris at night, at the Gare Montparnasse, covered in ash and freezing cold, amidst boiling clouds of steam from the engines and flying scraps of paper and the screams of the porters and the shouts of small children who had lost their mothers and a constant rain of pigeon feathers from up near the ceiling, and the travellers fell from the train in exhaustion and stumbled about, looking for their packages and for Leonard, who had momentarily disappeared. It was very early spring and night-time, and their breath floated above them like clouds.

"He's stolen my paintings," fretted Gwen. "My brushes!"

"He's just bringing our things," said Dorelia and so he was.

"There are loads of boarding houses, little pensions all along the roads here," Leonard said when he rejoined them. "Any one of them will take you. I am going to be staying just near here on the Rue d'Odessa, next to the baths. That's where I always stay. I have friends there with whom I share the rent. Do you need me to help you to your lodging?"

Dorelia, of course, wanted help, but Gwen sent Leonard off into the night.

"The first place we find," she said. "I don't care how bad it is." She silently peeled a hard-boiled egg, split it in two and gave one half to Dorelia. "To keep up your strength," she said.

Their bundles seemed too heavy to lift and the cobblestones seemed intentionally malicious, turning their ankles and making them slip. It had just rained and the city smelled of rotting cabbage and urine and mildew. Black mould grew up the stone walls of the buildings and, in the corners, men lounged with their hats over their eyes. In the middle of the street, where there was a wide footpath, a family of gypsies had pitched a tent over a mattress and five of them lay together with their bare feet sticking out from under the canvas, four pairs with the toes up and one set of feet wearing high-heeled shoes many sizes too large.

"Oh, Gwen!" cried Dorelia. "We should have let Leonard help us. I'm so very tired."

"Give me the easel," said Gwen and she pulled it from Dorelia's hands.

They turned into Boulevard Edgar Quinet and there was the first hotel, a narrow four-storey building with a sign out the front that said *Hôtel du Mont Blanc: Vacancies.*

"Here we are," said Gwen. "And think how close it is to the train station! How convenient!"

After paying their three francs, they were sent up to the fourth floor, just under the roof with seven low doors opening off a central corridor. Near the stairs was a single brass tap, with a large galvanised tin standing underneath. Small sticks of firewood were stacked neatly next to the tin. The black painted floorboards bent up at the edges and in the gap between the wall and the boards was collected a moss of fur and dust and grime and litter. There was a steady drip from the skylight. The boards, underneath the leak, were snow white, in a shape like England.

"Which one is ours?" asked Dorelia, but Gwen didn't know, so she knocked at the first door. It was answered by a woman wearing a man's white shirt and black tie, her dark hair cut above her ears. She was smoking a cigarette.

"Yes?" she said. Her voice was husky and deep to match her stocky body, and she wore thick kohl around her eyes.

"Please excuse me for knocking so late," said Gwen in French, but the woman cut her off.

"We all speak English here," she said. "My name is Miss

Hart. Evelyn Hart. And this," she said, gesturing to the room behind her, "is my friend Maggie Goldstein." Maggie wore a low-cut pink negligee and her bottle-blonde hair was spread across the bed. She lifted her hand slightly and waved. Gwen thought, but wasn't sure, that she saw the odd flickering light on Maggie's chest, but she didn't want to stare, as the negligee was transparent, and she didn't want to give the wrong impression.

"I'm Gwendolen John," said Gwen. "And this is Dorothy McNeill. It's a pleasure to meet you. I see you are artists too." Miss Hart's easel stood next to the window. She was painting a nude, apparently of Miss Goldstein, if the thickly daubed yellow paint was anything to go by.

"Isn't *she* a looker?" said Miss Hart, indicating Dorelia. "How'd you get your hands on that?"

"I'm her teacher," said Gwen primly. If she could have shut the door and walked away right then, she would have.

"Uh huh," said Miss Hart. "Of course you are." She was chewing gum. "I'm Miss Goldstein's teacher too. Aren't I, love?"

Miss Goldstein, from the bed, giggled. "She teaches me *all kinds* of things," she said. She had an American accent and enamelled red fingernails.

"Please," said Dorelia. "If you'll just tell us which room is ours?"

Gwen laughed to have washed up on this shore, probably the one place in all of Paris where there was a *congregation* of sapphists. First thing in the morning, Dorelia would be demanding that they move.

"The sixth room is vacant," said Miss Hart, looking Dorelia up and down and whistling. "The girl before you gassed herself, so they've taken out the hot plate. I hope you'll be able to manage."

"Oh," said Gwen. She hesitated. Her heart felt very small. She was afraid of Miss Hart, of her mannishness, and she could feel Dorelia's anxiety raising hot blisters on her arms. Dorelia, no doubt, thought her choice of hotels deliberate. "I don't suppose any other rooms are open?'

"I'm just joking," said Miss Hart and she gave Gwen's shoulder a shove. Ash fell off her cigarette and onto the floorboards and she winked. She took the gum out of her mouth and stuck it to the door jamb. "Nobody has gas piped in. You have to buy the canisters in the market. And if you want to use the toilet, it's down in the yard. Just go on in to number six. We don't bother locking the doors up here. We're all friends."

"What about the keys?" asked Gwen, jangling the set she'd been given.

"All the rooms are the same," said Miss Hart, which wasn't really an answer, and wasn't quite true, either.

Gwen's room had small pink terracotta tiles on the floor, hexagons, and two north-facing windows that looked across many rooftops and towards a cemetery. A large double bed stood at one end of the room and at the opposite end was a narrow stone fireplace. The air was damp and smelled of cigarette smoke. Dead silverfish lay in the corners and the sheets on the bed were rumpled and stained, as if someone had just gotten up. Great flocks of curling wallpaper lifted in the draught from the door and flapped. Hard under the windows, there was a square on the floor covered in multicoloured spots of paint. It was a far cry from their cosy little room in Toulouse, but Gwen loved it immediately.

"It will be alright," she said. "I'll set up the easel right over here."

"No," said Dorelia. "It will never be nice. It's awful."

"Look at the view," said Gwen, and she turned the latch and swung the windows inside the room and they both leaned their elbows on the ledge and looked out. Smoke rose from hundreds of chimneys into the blue-grey sky. A train whistled and clouds of smoke poured out of the open end of the station. Down in the courtyard, a calico cat pounced on a mouse and tore its head off. Invisible pigeons cooed and rustled, and inside the copper gutter scuttled a platoon of rats, their claws scratching music from the metal.

"Paris!" Gwen said. "It's your first time in Paris! Tomorrow we'll get settled and then we'll visit the Louvre and we'll go to see if Rodin is looking for a model and I will buy my very first tube of French paint."

"Suit yourself," said Dorelia and she turned her back on the view and began to pull on her nightgown. "Tomorrow I am going to go find Leonard."

For a week, they both modelled for the women artists on their floor, though Gwen was stiff and irritable and complained that she hadn't come to France to be a lady's model but to be an artist. She avoided the male portraitists one floor down after several had pursued her, demanding kisses, squeezing her breasts to see if she was *developpé*, and worse, much worse, but Dorelia modelled for whoever would pay her. The girls had money now, and they walked across the Seine, past the Notre Dame, and up towards the little fabric shops on the Rue du Sentier. They bought cotton and linen and a packet of needles and two reels of thread. Dorelia was making herself a pink flounced skirt. Gwen, after looking at the watercolours of Cézanne in the Louvre, had muttered, "I prefer my own." But later, she'd admired one of his oil paintings and had sketched a blue dress worn by the sitter, in order to copy the design.

On the way back, the girls somehow got turned around and instead of walking south, walked east and ended up in the Pletzl on the Rue des Juifs. A woman stood to one side calling out "Blumen far Shabbos!" Her black hair was parted neatly in the centre and pulled back smoothly into a bun and it was only when they drew closer that they saw that she was wearing a horsehair wig. She stood next to a green wooden cart with a watering can hanging from the handles. The cart was piled high with flowers arranged on drooping ferns: brilliant red poppies and white marguerites and lilies and bachelor's buttons and cockscomb and love-lies-bleeding. She had two pockets sewn to the front of her skirt and several rows of stitching where the hem had been made shorter so the dress wouldn't trail in the mud. Nearby, her children played at soldiers, three little boys wearing sailor suits and newspaper tricorns on their heads dashing at each other with sticks while a fourth held aloft a French flag.

"I'm an idiot,' said Gwen. "I should have brought my sketchbook."

Behind the woman, a man threw straw onto horse manure and then swept it all into a bucket. Gwen stared at him but he wasn't the Jew she had seen on the boat. They turned the corner and came upon a street simply teeming with Jews, and everywhere were the flashing yellow stars.

"What is that?" asked Gwen, pointing. Many sets of curtains twitched and they were watched from many windows.

"It's just a Jew," said Dorelia. She sniffed. The gutters were overflowing. It smelled of marsh gas and rotten wood and leeches. "I think we should leave, Gwen."

"No, no. I meant those stars that they wear," Gwen said. She would not be drawn away, and even in the crowd, she searched and searched for the man she had seen.

Dorelia looked at her. "What stars?" she said. "You are ever so strange. Listen, I am leaving and you can come with me or not, but I won't stand here on this Jews' Street. Not me. Give me your bundle before it is stolen by these Orientals."

Gwen stared back at her. A bell chimed. The children made another charge. The broom scraped across the cobbles.

"No," she said.

Dorelia turned on her heel but was almost immediately knocked down by a man in a long grey coat riding a bicycle. Her parcels tumbled into the gutter and her knees landed in a pool of horse urine. She sprang up, brushing at her ruined clothing, her face glowing red, furious.

"This is your fault, Gwen John!" she said. "If you wouldn't

always march off like a crazed person without asking for directions, we wouldn't be here! We would be home safe in London instead of walking the back streets of Paris, liable to be..." She didn't say what was liable to happen but the man with the bike dusted off Dorelia's packages and handed them to her, bowing his head and making placatory noises, and then went and bought her a posy of early violets and handed those to her too. "Anshuldikt mir," he said. "Ich hob nisht gevolt ir tzu shodn."

"He's apologising," said Gwen. "He gave you back your fabric. Why are you complaining?" For though she felt uncomfortable around Jews, she was excited about the little neighbourhood and about the possibility of returning to sketch the children and possibly even finding the Jew from the boat. "For goodness sakes, anyone would think you'd been manhandled."

"I *have* been manhandled!" cried Dorelia. "And by a Jew, too! Mummy would die!" She sniffed. "I'm going to leave you, Gwen John. I'm going to leave you here in this street and I'm going to leave you here in France. Just you wait."

"Not such a terrible thing," muttered Gwen. "You might get more of a backbone."

"*I* need a backbone? When you are the one who sits at home, moping about your art, your art, your bloody pathetic little scribbles, and I am the one who has to go out every day to try and earn enough money for food. *I* need a backbone?"

Dorelia's voice hadn't gotten any louder, but it hissed between her teeth and the veins in her neck began to convulse. "You drag me across France with no shoes on, expose me to the roughest elements, claim that you are a high and mighty artist the whole way and never for even a moment think about teaching me a thing about painting and then, when we finally get to Paris, do we see the Louvre? No. Do we go to see Rodin's beautiful sculptures as promised? No. Not us. *Miss* Gwen John hauls us to the Jew Street, to be knocked down by Satanists in grey coats."

"You trumped-up piece of flotsam," said Gwen. She was breathless with anger. "You know how important art is for me. It's my whole life. It's why we came here in the first place. And every day you are grizzling, 'Give me a piece of toast! Why can't we have eggs? It's so cold, dearest Gwenny-poo, mightn't we light the fire? Oh, it's all too hard for poor little me!' Be honest: you regret coming with me and you are resentful that I am a better artist than you and you're ashamed to like a woman the way most people like a man and you've got your hands five fingers deep in good old Leonard's trousers and you are taking it all out on me in all these niggling complaints that make every day so miserable. You're completely unbearable."

The man in the grey coat backed away from them. The woman with the flower cart had rolled it further down the road and sent her children on an errand. Soupy green clouds that had been massed on the horizon suddenly reared up thousands of feet and a cold wind lifted leaves and potato peelings from the gutter and slapped them in the girls' faces. All up and down the street, shutters squeaked closed. Heads turned away. Mothers covered children's ears and eyes.

"I hate you," said Dorelia. No drama. She had *never* loved Gwen. She threw down her package and kicked it into the pool of horse urine.

"I don't hate you," said Gwen, who had thought she loved Dorelia. "I *loathe* you."

Dorelia trembled for a moment and then whirled around and ran back the way they had come.

"Good riddance," called Gwen after the retreating girl, but then she began to cry.

They didn't speak for a week. Their room far too small to hold such silence. The floor full of scissors and rulers and threads and pins and needles that poked their toes and made them bleed. Dorelia went to bed early, long before Gwen had finished painting, and got up before Gwen was awake. She looked more and more beautiful, though she now refused to allow Gwen to touch her at all.

One rainy Saturday when they couldn't bear the tiny room for another moment, they took the tour of the catacombs. At the end of their street, they slipped between granite columns that seemed hardly wide enough for an entrance and climbed down increasingly cold and slippery stone staircases. At the bottom, piles of grey bones were heaped to the ceiling, dead Parisians from earlier generations. The skulls all seemed to be gritting their teeth. Gwen would too, if so many people came to stare at her. She might *bite* them all. Dorelia complained about the smell. "It's just like the caves near the Garonne," said Gwen. "You didn't complain about the smell then."

"That seemed normal," said Dorelia. "This seems ..." But she couldn't say what it seemed like and neither would she stop and look at the tiny roots that had descended from the trees above them on Boulevard Raspail, that had crept down all this way in search of water or nutrients or air.

Candles flickered from notches cut into the stone walls, and as the group turned a corner, Gwen's hand brushed Dorelia's.

"I love you," she whispered. It was too late. She knew it and yet she could not help holding on to the last flag of her previous hope.

Dorelia turned and stared at Gwen, and then very slowly, very deliberately, folded her arms across her waist and tucked her fingers underneath the fabric of her skirt.

"You weren't so fussy in Toulouse," said Gwen. It was cold, very cold, in this underground place and much too dark to see anything. Her fingers and her toes and her lips were completely without feeling.

"It's funny to think of all the dead people piled up here, all the times jumbled together in one place, as if years don't matter at all," Gwen said a little while later. "Can you imagine it? Instead of time being a line, it's just a single dot with everything happening at once, all the births and deaths and marriages, all the people falling in love and falling out of love, all at once and all hidden down here, invisible ..." She couldn't really explain what it was that she meant, and Dorelia stared at her with an odd look and tapped her temple with her forefinger. "Loathing," she whispered and moved even further away.

GIRL PRAYING:

Two months after they had arrived, that Friday, a warm day in May, a letter arrived from Augustus, saying he was coming to get Dorelia in a week.

Why the devil don't I hear from you, you bad fat girl? he wrote. *You sit in the nude for those devilish foreign people, but you do not want to sit for me when I asked you, wicked little bloody harlot that you are. You exhibit your naked fat body for money, not for love. So much for you! How much do you show them for a franc? I am sorry that I never offered you a shilling or two for a look at your body. That was all you were waiting for. The devil knows I might have bought the body and the love together. I am sorry that I was so foolish to love you. Well, if you are not a whore, truly tell me why not.*

It wasn't exactly a confession of love.

Dorelia stormed around the room, railing at Augustus and Gwen for embroiling her in such a drama and complaining that neither John actually knew what it meant to love another human being. The only person Augustus considered was himself. And Gwen! She was an automaton when it came to feelings! Only Leonard was truly human. Only Leonard truly loved her.

Gwen was not delighted that Augustus was on his way. Paris was hers, not for sharing with a brother who did not understand anything about sharing. And the timing was so terrible. Though Gwen wanted Dorelia gone, she didn't want her gone with Augustus.

And too, there was a grain of sadness, for Augustus had not even said a word about coming to see Gwen. She wanted to see him, but she didn't want to have to share Dorelia. No.

That wasn't right. She wanted him to be coming for her, and she wanted to have Dorelia all to herself. But that wasn't quite right either. Did she only want Dorelia because Augustus wanted her too? And was it Paris she wanted all to herself or only Rodin? It was impossible to dig her way to the bottom of everything.

To give herself a little privacy to think, Gwen took Edgar Quinet, her cat, to the Luxembourg Gardens and slept for two nights under a little copse of trees, stripped naked. Even as she went down the stairs with the cat in a basket, Dorelia was shouting at the walls and there was a crash as some object hit the door.

"Somebody's pretty lady is on the rag!" shouted Miss Hart and another object hit the door.

On Sunday morning, when everything was closed and she couldn't even get a cup of tea, Gwen returned to a room full of shredded pink fabric. An open pair of scissors quivered in the wall. Dorelia lay sprawled across the bed, her face raked with claw marks from her own fingernails.

"I'm sorry," said Gwen, laying her hand on Dorelia's ankle. "For everything. My brother really can be too awful." Dorelia kicked at her hand.

"Did you know that bloody Ida is pregnant? Again? How can your brother ask me to be part of such a household? What is that, the sixth child? The seventh? Ida will simply explode one day. Has he never heard of interrupting?"

Gwen began picking up the ruined dress. Edgar Quinet jumped up on the bed and butted Dorelia under the chin.

"He didn't need to with me," muttered Gwen. She hid her face. "Because I can't ever have any children."

"Oh, for God's sake," Dorelia said, and with a sigh, she got up to help Gwen tidy the room.

A day later, on Monday, Gwen came home full of eagerness to share her good news. Though Dorelia and she had both modelled, naked to the waist, for the dreadful Miss Hart and for the equally terrifying Miss Roederstein, they hadn't been able to find someone to model for on a consistent basis, a regular patron. But Gwen had finally finished her new skirt and gone to the Rue de l'Université and asked at the marble depot if Rodin was in need of a regular model. There were other artists' studios there and a woman, Hilda Flodin, had hired her.

Rodin had been visiting Hilda's studio. He wore a white smock and had a large white beard. He had soft eyes. He smelled of pipe smoke and Earl Grey tea and he lisped. He'd talked for a moment with Gwen and touched her hand and asked her to return to model for him as well. In front of this demigod, she felt exactly like a schoolgirl and could not remember simple French words like tomorrow and thank you.

"Come on Wednesday," he'd said. "And we will see how it goes." He'd given Gwen three francs, and said he'd look for her two days later at ten. He had the last two studios at the depot, at the far end, the largest ones, a present from the French government. On the way home, she'd bought a little sausage for Dorelia at the corner charcuterie, and some early strawberries for herself, and a fresh loaf of bread and some butter and a small bottle of wine, and a sardine for the cat. A feast.

She wanted to make up to Dorelia, not as a lover but as a friend, and as she waited for the other girl she made a tiny card, a concertina that opened, window after window, each with a sketch of Dorelia, until the last one, an image no larger than a grain of rice. She washed the sheets and hung them to dry on the roof and she borrowed some lavender water to spray on them when they were already crisp and fragrant. She fluffed up their pillows and laid the card on Dorelia's side.

But Dorelia didn't come home and instead the concierge arrived with a note saying Dorelia would be in much later, that she was "out" with Leonard and that Gwen shouldn't wait up for her, and a telegram from Augustus, saying he'd be arriving on the Monday evening train to Paris, and would she kindly meet him at the Gare Montparnasse?

The floor seemed very slippery to Gwen, as if perhaps starch had been sprayed on it. One wall rose higher and the floor slanted and she felt herself skidding towards the windows. Her heart beat much too fast and she tried to calm herself by picturing the ocean but it had been almost six months since she'd seen the Atlantic. "Oh!" she said, and there must have been some note of panic in her voice, for Miss Hart, from next door, called out, "Is everything alright, Miss John?"

Dorelia would be home any minute. They'd go together to greet Augustus at the station. Gwen brushed her hair and repinned her bun and pinched her cheeks so she would look pretty for the two people she loved best in all the world. She arranged their feast on three plates that had been left behind by the previous occupant, the not-gassed girl. She leaned down and fed her cat – the calico mouse decapitator – the greasy sardine, and then took out her pencil and paper and began to sketch Edgar Quinet eating and later, washing his face and under his tail. The girls had named the little cat in honour of their street. When they'd first arrived, she'd seen him in the courtyard and the next morning, Gwen had lured him in off the roof with a saucer of milk and tamed him with petting and scraps of meat from the butcher.

When it was dark, she lit the lantern and let Edgar Quinet out onto the roof to go and search for mice, and later still, she took off her dress and hung it on a nail and lay down on top of the bed in her petticoat. She dreamed of the walk beside the Garonne and the sunny days and the gentle rocking of the boat and when she awoke, long past midnight, Dorelia had still not come home.

The night breeze smelled strongly of iodoform and pommes frites and something else that Gwen thought might be bodies rotting in the Cimetière du Montparnasse. Cries came from the Asile de Nuit, the dosshouse where women who were unable to pay even the small rent for an attic room lived, hundreds crammed into a tiny space, bitten by fleas and mice and ticks and lice and even by human beings. Gwen's own teeth chomped.

She was glad that she had work modelling and proud that Monsieur Rodin had asked for her. It was, at least, a first step towards her ultimate goal. Of course he had noticed her the moment she came through the gates of the marble depot. He was that kind of man, the noticing kind. Rodin would never look through her as if she didn't exist, the way Augustus did. He would never step on her drawings or bump her off the sidewalk or ignore her in a shop or pass her over for work. No. He had hired her the moment he'd laid eyes on her.

She was glad she could support herself, without help from her father or a brother who loved her in all the wrong ways. She would have worked night and day to avoid going to the Asile de Nuit. Many artists, she knew, worked by candlelight. She'd done some of her own best work, in Toulouse, by candlelight. She'd heard that even the great Rodin, on occasion, relied on a candle with a brass mirror attached to it for his effects. One night soon she would witness Rodin working by candlelight. Many nights. The thought made her smile. On the road to Toulouse, Dorelia and she had passed a cemetery where candles burned on every grave, and each headstone had been carved with an image of the dead. Perhaps, in the light of day, the carvings might not be any good, but at night, lit from underneath, wreathed in smoke, they looked as if the dead had risen and sat surveying the cemetery with calm eyes.

Gwen took out a piece of paper, lit a candle and began to sketch herself in the mirror. She sketched for several hours, deepening the shadows under her eyes, working on the arch of her neck and the slope of her shoulders. At night, her skin was smoother and whiter too. She looked very much alive. She smiled and covered her teeth with her hand. At night, she was beautiful, a siren. She had completely forgotten about Augustus and the train. She had completely forgotten about Dorelia.

On Tuesday morning, Gwen woke up with her head on her desk. There was a pool of congealed candle grease around the candlestick. She sat up with a start. The bed was as smooth as it had been the previous evening. Dorelia still had not returned. Gwen, angry and ashamed, marched next door to bang at Miss Hart's and ask her what she knew. Miss Hart appeared, tousled, in men's pyjama bottoms, a workman's sleeveless undershirt and a pair of carpet slippers.

"Where did she go?" Gwen asked.

"But you knew, all along, that you'd bitten off more than you could chew with that one, right?" said Miss Hart, and truly, Gwen *had* known. Dorelia was not, never had been, in Gwen's league.

Miss Hart told Gwen that Dorelia had been coming home during the day, when they were supposed to be searching for work, with Leonard, and there had been acrobatics on the bed, that's how Miss Hart described it, "acrobatics", as if Dorelia and Leonard were tumblers in a circus, or perhaps trapeze artists, rather than cheaters. She softened when she saw Gwen's stricken face.

"With her, girls are temporary," she said, patting Gwen's shoulder. "Something she'll try before she gets married to someone twenty years older than her, with money in the bank and a nice house. Someone who can give her children." There was tremendous bitterness in the last statement. Gwen thought it might be the reason that Miss Hart had lost girlfriends in the past. "She's not like you and me."

"I'm not like *you*," said Gwen angrily, pulling away. "I *do* like men. Very much, as it happens. I've had lovers."

"Your brother and your father don't count," said Miss Hart, smirking. "We've all had *them*."

Gwen's face turned a dark red and she opened her mouth and shut it again several times. She suddenly remembered that Augustus had arrived at the train station the previous night and that she had forgotten to go and get him. In her gut, a cold hand twisted, and then, just as quickly, a sort of internal blind fell, shutting off this recollection.

She had written words on her the back of her left hand, *I can't, I won't, I'd rather die*, and she stared at these, not understanding how they had gotten there, or to what they referred. She spat on her hand and began to rub at the letters.

"I was almost proposed to," she finally said, in a small voice. She could already hear Miss Hart's voice, sneering "*Almost!*" as she said it. She thought again of Ambrose McEvoy, her beautiful golden boy in his crisp white linens and his straw boater, his smooth muscular stomach and his long adept fingers. She'd thought they would be married, that she'd have his children. She'd been waiting for her own engagement when news came that he'd asked some other woman. The first time she'd been in France, she'd come together with Ambrose and Augustus and Ida. Though, now she thought of it, all her memories of that time were sad ones. Why on earth had she written *I'd rather die*?

"It's something," she blurted. "To *almost* be engaged! And Dorelia loved me. She said so!" Though she wasn't sure if this was true. *I'd rather die*? I'd rather die than *what*? "We were going to go to Rome together. We were going to have a little house in the olive groves. I would paint and she would cook and it would be warm every day."

"Uh huh," said Miss Hart and she pulled Gwen roughly to her and pushed her head down on her shoulder and patted her back. "You bet. It would have been a lovely life."

Gwen jerked her head up. "She's coming back. I'll *make* her come back."

Miss Hart snorted.

"Why don't you get dressed nicely and come out with me and Maggie tonight?" Miss Hart said. "Nothing like drowning your troubles, when troubles come calling."

"Dorelia will be home by then," said Gwen. Her hand hurt,

she had scrubbed it so hard. She had rubbed so hard that small curls of greyish skin had collected on the back of her hand and she had brushed them off. Now she let her head hang over Miss Hart's shoulder.

"*If* she's back by then, you could always stay in," said Miss Hart. The way she said *if* made Gwen think Dorelia had travelled to the Arctic Circle on a sleigh and was never coming back. She tried to swallow. There was something in the back of her throat and she cleared her throat and tried again. It was something cold and wet and full of salt and sadness and no matter how many times she swallowed, it simply would not go down.

Miss Hart raised her arms above her head, linked her hands together and stretched, rather like a cat. Her armpits were full of thick curling hair, like a man's. She was wearing something beneath the undershirt, a twist of cloth, a bandage of some kind that hid and flattened her breasts. Gwen stared, looked away, stared again, tried to swallow, coughed. Miss Hart beat her on the back a few times.

"I'll pick you up at nine then," said Miss Hart. She wasn't a woman for pity. She had far too many hard edges for pity. But there was something in her tone that sounded like she understood what Gwen might be feeling, even if Gwen herself did not know what that was.

At ten that night, Miss Hart and Maggie picked up Gwen from her room. Neither Augustus nor Dorelia had shown up. Gwen's eyelids were red and her face was blotched ash grey but she'd made some effort to appear fresh. She had put on her earrings and she'd brushed her hair and her dress was sponged. She'd taken a carnation off a grave in the cemetery and pinned it to her bodice.

"Hang on a tick," said Maggie and she darted back to Miss Hart's room and emerged carrying a pot of blush and a lipstick.

"Oh! I couldn't paint my face!" said Gwen. She didn't like to stand next to Maggie because of the flickering lemon light on her low-cut bodice. Here in Paris, there were many people with the same odd place on their chests, men, women, especially children. They were everywhere she went. Hundreds of them. The woman at the baths. The man who sold tickets and sweets and toys at the train station. The salesman shucking oysters in the park. Many of the artists who crowded the cafés and the boulevards. A whole line of children going into the local lycée. A little boy sailing a boat on the pond in the Luxembourg Gardens. Gwen had decided not to notice the flickering lights. Or rather, to deliberately ignore their appalling lack of solidity, which might otherwise have made her crazy.

She'd forgotten Maggie and her insistence on painting Gwen's face. The woman's hand was already on Gwen's jawbone, the rouge on her finger in dots like carnelian beads.

"You'll be the belle of the ball," Maggie said, as she daubed Gwen's cheeks and rubbed in the rouge. When she finished, she undid the little black ribbon with the cameo around Gwen's neck and handed it to her, and then unbuttoned her bodice to below the collarbone. Gwen covered her exposed flesh with her hand. Her face reddened even more than the rouge. Maggie took a flower from her own breast and repinned it above Gwen's ear.

"I really don't think I ..." said Gwen, but just as her mouth fell open to pronounce this "I", Maggie ran the tube of lipstick across her lower lip.

"Wait," she said, and then she ran the greasy stick over Gwen's upper lip too and patted the line with a handkerchief.

Miss Hart stood back and whistled. "Just look at you, Miss Fish!" she said. "You'll be hooked in no time."

Miss Hart herself looked very dashing. She wore a tuxedo and a dress shirt with a bow tie. She had a monocle looped into her buttonhole and her hair was slicked back under a glossy top hat. Her Oxford shoes gleamed. For a second, Gwen felt a twinge of attraction and then Miss Hart snapped her braces and guffawed and took both Maggie's and Gwen's elbows and steered them towards the steps. Joan of Arc was burned at the stake for dressing like a man. It was, Gwen thought, dangerous. "Off we go, ladies!" Miss Hart shouted. "Can't keep the gentlemen waiting!"

They crossed the boulevard and there, directly opposite their building, was a nightclub that Gwen had not noticed in the daytime. Now, small lights twinkled around the entrance and couples stood outside, smoking on the curb. Music could be heard, very modern music, tinkling pianos and blaring clarinets, with which Gwen was entirely unfamiliar. The nightclub had a round red door with a grilled peephole in the centre.

"The Monocle!" announced Miss Hart, as they were admitted. The smoky room was full of impeccably dressed men and women who were standing up, drinking, or dancing close together in the middle of the floor. "Home to *so many* of us here in Paris." Gwen followed Miss Hart and Maggie to the back, where they were seated at a table, apparently Miss Hart's regular table, because as soon as they sat down, a waitress appeared at her elbow and put down a gin and tonic. "Anything for the ladies?" she asked, and Miss Hart ordered Maggie a glass of port and Gwen a lemonade.

An elegantly dressed gentleman approached the table. He bowed to Maggie and Gwen and shook Miss Hart's hand. "Would you be so kind as to introduce us?" he asked Miss Hart, nodding towards Gwen. She felt ashamed of her simple old-fashioned dress, and her coiffure, though the gentleman and she both had the same colour hair – a deep and luxurious red that extended even to their eyebrows. All of the women seated around them wore far more elaborate hairdos than Gwen, and far more modern fashions as well. Some women had narrow skirts that ended well above their ankles, something Gwen had never seen. Others were obviously not wearing stays and wore their bodices open far below their collarbones, showing long expanses of curving flesh. She was glad, after all, that Maggie had made up her face, for all the women were heavily painted and looked glamorous in the low light.

Gwen looked down at her hands while Miss Hart introduced the gentleman and then she put out her hand to be shaken but the man bent over her wrist and kissed the air above it. Gwen had completely missed his name. "Will you do me the honour of this dance?" he asked. She could barely hear him over the music and the chatter and the chiming of glasses. This was how Augustus lured Dorelia. All Gwen could supply was kindness, but she didn't understand this *demand* for attention, this refusal to be unseen.

Gwen didn't know how to dance. She'd had the briefest of lessons from Augustus and those were mostly simple country dances, but it seemed the couples on the floor could barely move anyway. They stood swaying against each other, not turning or taking any intricate steps, so she stood up, thinking it was easier to dance than to say no. She'd have to find out the man's name before the end of the round so she could thank him properly. It wasn't like Leonard, it wasn't like that at all to dance with this strange man. It was merely good manners.

She put her hand on the stranger's shoulder and held out the other to be taken, but he pulled her close against him and settled her body between his hips. "That's better," he shouted, placing his hand low on her back, and then sliding it lower still and cinching her even closer. Better for who? "Isn't the music marvellous?" he shouted. He smelled faintly of limes and, oddly, talcum powder. They were the same height, even though Gwen was very short, and together, they were crushed between many taller people, bumped and bullied by elbows and chins and buttocks.

"Good heavens!" cried Gwen. "What a crush!" She couldn't

think of anything else to say to the stranger. She hoped she was dancing well, but suspected that she was merely shuffling her feet to the screaming clarinet. At least she hadn't stepped on the man's toes.

"When did you arrive?" yelled the man. His breath, in her face, smelling of apples and brandy and mint. There were only inches between them. After the cold weeks with Dorelia, it was rather nice to be held, to have a firm grip on her shoulder, but this wasn't cheating. This wasn't acrobatics on the bed. It was a social necessity, a nice moment with a perfect stranger. It was pleasant but it would end and she would go home and Dorelia would be back in the flat and everything would be normal again, and she would be able to show Dorelia that Leonard and Augustus were both unnecessary and that she, Gwen, was all that Dorelia would ever need, and she'd be the perfect perfect perfect friend for her, do everything right and never again say an unkind word or ask her to carry the easel. She smiled and swayed to the music. It would all come right. She wouldn't be left alone.

From many shirt fronts and bodices flashed the familiar yellow blur. She was beginning to think she needed to see an optometrist. Gwen closed her eyes, so as to think, more clearly, about the ways she would make things more perfect for Dorelia. Wood, for starters. They needed more wood for the fireplace. And perhaps more sliced meat. And the occasional bottle of wine, just because. The man pulled Gwen's head closer, to rest on his shoulder, thinking, apparently, due to the closed eyes, that she was enjoying herself and that she felt comfortable with him.

"When did you arrive?" he shouted again. His waistcoat buttons rising up and digging into her as he bellowed.

"A few weeks ago," she shouted back. It was hard to shout with her eyes closed. "Do you mean Paris? Or France? We arrived in France almost a year ago. We walked all the way," she yelled, not entirely truthfully. "You would not believe how beautiful my friend is. Men were chasing her the whole way."

At the man's expression of surprise, she jerked her head upright and took a good look at him. Why had she said such a thing to a stranger? Did she want him to think better of her, for ensnaring a beautiful girl? Did she herself wish to be chased? Was it a warning that she was already taken? Did she, in some way, also want a man? It was very confusing and she found herself blushing as she looked at him.

The man's skin was beautifully smooth and pink and his eyes were blue. The finest trace of kohl lined his eyelashes. He had a great delicacy about his cheekbones and Gwen found herself liking him, thinking him handsome and appealing, though she suspected, because of his feyness, that he might be a homosexual. Not that she had anything against men like that. She rather liked them, if the truth be known. She let her eyes trail along his jawline, admiring his bone structure, and the satiny smoothness of his skin, without even the faintest hint of a beard. Without thinking, she put up her hand and stroked his cheek. Then, with a shock, several things tumbled together in her brain, the height, the voice, the powder, the lack of beard, and she realised that he was not, in fact, a man, but rather, a woman dressed as a man, complete with a lightly pencilled moustache.

"Oh my God!" she said, pushing him away. "What *is* this place?" Now she saw that *all* of the men were women dressed as men, their faces smooth and beardless, their voices high, their hips wide in their altered tuxedo pants. Some of the men even wore skirts instead of trousers with their tuxedo jackets. How she had missed this important observation, she couldn't imagine.

The music stopped to cheers and she struggled through the dispersing crowd to Miss Hart's table.

"Miss Hart!" she cried. "Where have you brought me?" She was furious to be compromised in this way, furious that she should have been brought to such a disgraceful place. Everyone knew that women who dressed like men were doing something illegal and that they could be arrested at any moment. This wasn't anything like the love between Dorelia and her. This was, this truly was, perversion.

And, dear God, if she was arrested, *Augustus* might have to come and bail her out! Who knows what he could reveal to the police about her! About him! How *would* she explain herself? She would never be taken seriously as an artist again if first the business with the inverts was revealed and then, somehow, the incest came out. Rodin would certainly sack her before she even began working for him. None of her friends would ever talk to her again. News would get back to England and there she would be, her bent head covered in a sack, her hands cuffed behind her, a burly policeman on either side of her, etched onto the front page of the Daily News. *Portraitist Gwendolen Mary John arrested for inversion. Captured at notorious nightspot with perverts, consorting with she-hes.* That's what the papers would say. The little paperboys on the street corners would be shouting her name and taking coppers as fast as they could. And that would be the end of everything she had ever tried to do. How easily it could happen.

"It's just the Monocle … I told you earlier today, you silly girl. Our nightclub. A women-only nightclub."

Miss Hart was laughing at her. *She* didn't care that she was sitting in this nest of inverts. No one could help knowing, just by looking, that Miss Hart was an invert. She wasn't hidden at all. But Gwen looked like everyone else on the street. The normal people. For the briefest of moments, she understood Dorelia's horror of being identified as *that* kind of a woman, a lesbian, and divided from those masses who were "normal". She understood Dorelia's wish to avoid being painted with such a damning brush at any cost.

"Take me home," she said. "Please."

"What did you think, little girl?" Miss Hart said. "You rented a room in a building that is filled with people like us. You rented right across from the most infamous women-only nightclub in all of Paris. And you show up with a glamorous, sultry girlfriend in tow. An accident? I don't think so!" Maggie, sitting in Miss Hart's lap, laughed her high, tinkling, fake laugh and upended her glass between her lips.

"But it was an accident!" said Gwen and though tears came out of her eyes, still the silvery, slippery thing in her throat did not dissolve. "I was so tired. It was the first place we saw. We were told any place would do. No one warned me. Oh please, Miss Hart, just take me home!"

But Miss Hart would not leave. She offered Gwen her enormous man's handkerchief and reminded her that their rooms were just across the road.

"Either you are in, and one of us, or you're a weak little sniveller," said Miss Hart. "Ashamed to show what she is to the world."

"I am!" said Gwen. "I am ashamed. Please, just let me go home!"

"I'll tell Miss Markowitz that you thank her for the dance," called Miss Hart. She had danced with a Jew! Almost, she admitted to herself, kissed one! Gwen ran for the door. "Don't say I don't try to make my friends happy!"

"Oh my God!" Gwen wailed as she climbed the stairs to the flat. "I want to go home! I want my *mother*!" And then, remembering that her own mother had died many years earlier and couldn't help her, and that her lover had disappeared with the beastly Leonard and that her awful brother was lurking in wait somewhere in Paris, she began to laugh in hysterical gasps. "Could it get *any* worse?" She tugged at her hair and coughed and ripped at her clothing. "I've turned into a proper infant, crying for my mama." By then, all the u-shaped pins had sprung from her plaits and gone bouncing down the stairs, *ping ping ping*. She sat on the steps and took out a cigarette and lit it and puffed on it angrily. She hoped that Dorelia would come back while she was sitting there, covered in ash, vengeful. *Then* what would be said?

But after a while, she grew cold and her bottom hurt from the hard edge of the step and one of her legs had fallen asleep and so she searched amongst the litter in the corners of the landings for her pins and even bent to pick up the clumps of red hair that she had pulled out of her own head. And twisted around one of her pins she found, again, a long black hair.

Dorelia was lying on the bed when Gwen let herself in. She had one foot crossed over the other and her arms behind her head. The windows were open and the curtains swept into the room and then were sucked out again, to beat in the sky.

"Good heavens," said Dorelia, sitting up. "What on earth happened to you? Has someone attacked you?" she said, noticing Gwen's open neckline, her missing cameo, the startling redness of her cheeks and lips, her handful of red hair.

Gwen fell facedown on the bed. "Leave me alone," she said. All the anger had left her. Instead, she felt as cold and empty as glass. It was almost a disappointment to understand, in the most simplistic way, why she and Dorelia would no longer live together. But still, she did not want to say where she had been, in case Dorelia *wasn't* planning on leaving. She didn't want to frighten her away. "Something … happened," she said, and then thought that perhaps she could even gain Dorelia's sympathy, eke out one more day of company from the girl. "It was a bad man," she said, thinking it wasn't entirely untrue. "I'm alright. Really. Perhaps some tea?"

Nothing was left from the feast of the previous evening. Edgar Quinet had climbed in through the window and eaten it all, so Dorelia heated some water on the little gas ring and poured it into a cup for Gwen to warm her hands.

"I'm terribly sorry, Gwen," she said, when Gwen was settled.

"I know it's a bad time but I have something important to tell you ..."

Gwen thought about her first girlfriend, a tiny, beautiful little girl she had met at the Slade and taken up residence with. She remembered the way the girl had crawled into her bed each night, begging her for kisses, begging for her flesh. The girl had thought that Gwen, older, must be more experienced, though Gwen had never touched another woman. She'd fallen into that love like falling into water, heedless of the cost, desirous only to be immersed, fully, in the experience. When, after several months and much pleading, she had penetrated the girl with her fingers, she had not expected the blood, and had cried, thinking she had torn something or ruined something irreparable. They had consoled one another, the girl telling Gwen that she was an excellent lover, someone that every girl at the school envied her for, and Gwen telling the girl, in mortal fear of losing her love or respect, that she would be fine, that the blood must surely be normal, that it was probably just her period, though the girl had felt a sharp sting, and still felt pain when she moved. Gwen remembered the way they had walked holding hands in the halls of the school, something that was then considered normal between two friends. The school had cracked down on it later when the professors realised that there was something deeper going on between some of the female students, something not so innocent.

She remembered the way she and the other girl used to run their hands over the smooth marble statues, lingering on the impossibly perfect white breasts and looking at each other and laughing; the way they had codewords for things, and when others used these words in normal conversation, how it made them giggle. She remembered the cold stone smell of the halls, like freshly fallen snow at night; the echoes of their footsteps when they stayed behind and walked through the unlit rooms, peering into cases, stroking the curlicues on the gilt frames, trying on the dusty top hats that had been forgotten in the cloakrooms; she remembered the purple velvet coverlet on the girl's bed, stitched with black spiders and red webs, the scent of it something like cinnamon and curry; the smell of the girl's hair, lemons and water from the Avon River, full of decaying leaves; the great peace she had felt in discovering that she could love someone outside of her family.

And then she thought, with horror, of the women across the road, in their decadent nightclub, with all the garish colours slashed across their faces, the lipstick not *quite* on their lips, and her innocent memories of her time at the Slade, and even her memories of Dorelia, turned and curdled and became something she wished she could vomit out.

Dorelia's mouth opened and shut. She talked on and on. Gwen rolled over and sat up. She saw the note about Augustus pinned to the headboard and stood up to reread it. Augustus! Her brother, her lover. Something squiggled inside her, something not entirely pleasant.

Those women across the street were nothing compared to her. For if they were all lined up on a stage and the curtains drawn back and their misdeeds revealed on giant canvases behind each one of them, it was *she* who would look the worst, not them, for all of their man-dressing, women-loving ways. It was she who would have a canvas towering over her, showing Augustus with his pants around his ankles, a leering expression on his face, his huge member in his hand, and her, on her back beneath him, smiling.

On the floor of Gwen's room, between her feet, there was a thin brown and grey snail. It extended its head, just a little, moved its eyes from right to left and then glided forward a fraction, its tail lifted, a small round damp spot appeared on the chalky pink tile, the shell tilted to the left and returned to almost centre, and then the head extended again and the process was repeated. On the floor behind the snail were four increasingly smaller circles where the tile was a tiny bit darker. None of these circles was larger than Gwen's smallest fingernail. The last of these circles on the floor, the smallest, no bigger than a lentil, shrunk, faded, disappeared. No matter how fast the snail moved, there were never more than four circles behind it. Each time, as the snail produced a fifth spot, the last circle behind it faded to nothing.

The next morning, Dorelia and Leonard left for Bruges. Augustus showed up, banging on her door in the middle of the night, drunk and claiming that Gwen had overworked Dorelia, insisting that Dorelia had run away with Leonard merely to get away from Gwen. He demanded a place to stay, despite there only being the one bed, and Miss Hart snorted in the next-door room.

"Go away, Gussy!" Gwen shouted through the door. "I won't have you in my rooms." But the next minute, she opened the door, looked along the corridor and when she saw that no one was watching, let him inside.

Augustus came in and covered her with kisses. "Darling sister!" he cried. "I have missed you unbearably!" He rumbled on about Ida deciding he *must* have Dorelia if he was to be any kind of artist, and about Ida being willing to share him. Gwen pondered this for a moment. Her face was still wet with his kisses. His hands touched parts of her that had not been touched for *months*. Did Augustus want Gwen *and* Dorelia? She looked at his lips and his eyes and his cheeks and it seemed that he was filled with a great passion and her heart leapt and she thought, yes! He *does* want me. But just as she was about to fall into his arms, he began to sing a love song. To Dorelia. The fucking narcissist.

DORELIA:

You go with her to France, both of you wearing white muslin dresses and straw hats with trailing blue ribbons; you think you'll be learning from Rodin, you think you'll be an artist like her, you think every day you'll have free lessons; you think she is incredibly uncoordinated, the number of times you see her trip over her own bootlaces and fall without putting her hands out to protect herself; it irks you that even her subconscious won't allow her to ruin her hands; you think she is conceited when you see the way she stands with her head on the side, one eye closed, examining some pile of stones that was formerly a castle, as if she and she alone knows how to paint it; you think it's unfair when villagers give her the best tomato and the freshest butter and the softest bread after she sketches their heads, because you're an artist too, and how will you learn anything if you are starving; you think some day soon she will stop and show you how to prepare a canvas, how to mix a decent flesh tone; you think maybe if you sleep with her; you think maybe if you tell her you love her.

You think she is boasting when she says she won't sell her paintings until she can sell them for a hundred pounds a piece, and then she sells one for a hundred and fifty; you think you could draw as well as she can if you were given a chance but she never gives you a chance; you think all she has is doggedness, not skill, but there is always some moment when she is painting where she does the unexpected and the image comes to life and the distortion perfectly captures something that was hidden in the sitter and it's all you can do not to weep because how will she ever teach you this slight twist of the hand that even she does not know she is doing?

You think Whistler and Sickert and Fry turn towards her when she enters a room out of politeness but then they push through the crowd to talk with her and don't leave her side all evening; at the Louvre, the archivist comes out from behind his desk and whispers arcane secrets about paint hydration in her ear and the only words you hear are *walnut oil*, and she grips his elbow and smiles and thanks him and it is him who bows to her and she never even has the decency to curtsy; you think Rodin won't notice her mousy figure but he sends for her three times and fucking hires her and you want to kick yourself for not going with her to the Depot because you feel sure that you are the prettier girl and that Rodin would have taken you instead of her and then it would have been you getting the artist's education and not her and you wish she didn't say, when you are fighting, Rodin wanted *me*, as if the great man couldn't have wanted anyone else; and you think she's magicked them all when the women on your floor and the men on the next floor down and Modigliani and Brâncuşi and Roederstein ask for her by name as if she actually was pretty, as if they can't see her receding chin and her watery red hair and her tremendous nose and her sticking out ears and her non-existent tits and her bitter little mouth.

You think she's modest and shy and then you catch her ogling the butcher's balls, and when he notices, she gives him that tiny lift of the eyebrow and a glimpse of her eyes that tips him over the edge; you think she's dour because of the set of her lips but she's always singing these incredibly annoying ditties she claims the sailors in her town taught her and she walks around the cemetery whistling; you think she has no sense of humour until she meets the old cabinetmaker who likes to play with words and they stand in his shop for hours, knee-deep in wood shavings, telling each other strings of puns until she pisses her drawers with laughter; you think she's refined till the day something opens her up and after that you can't get her to stop telling you the crudest jokes and the dirtiest stories; you think she's a victim until you notice that she controls everything, even being a victim; you think she's the lesser artist in her family right up until the day she gets an American patron and her work is collected by the biggest museums in the world and she becomes even more famous than her brother and her best friend is a poet that everyone loves and Rodin makes a fucking statue of her and in the meantime, you have to share her brother with every woman in England. And the women's bloody cats.

You think she is an incredible fake when she begins reading books so she will have something to say to these artists, and you drop her notes into the Seine and are silent while she tears apart your room searching for them, though you want to laugh at all her drama; you think only professors read things like *The Story of a Soul* or *Orthodoxy* and only foolish schoolgirls read things like Rudyard Kipling's *Kim* or Zola's *Vérité;* you think she speaks French like a child and laugh when you hear her say "Please fart again" instead of "Please repeat that" and you think she probably *can't* read all of those books in French, or at least, she doesn't understand what she is reading; you think that in the future, when you see one of her educational books, you will automatically hate it because you heard lines from it at midnight when she woke you up to read a particularly salient passage out loud.

You think she will starve in a garret in Paris but then she writes you a letter from a new address on a nicer street and six months later, from an even nicer address and you find out that Rodin, that fucker, is paying her rent and has given her furniture and beautiful clothing and classes at the best school and meanwhile, you are squatting over a fire on the moors with your unwashed hair falling over your face and two brats squalling in the draughty caravan and you can't help thinking that you chose the wrong sibling; you think she is a whore but it still drives you crazy when she sends you postcards from castles in Brittany, and from hotels in Marseille, and from boats in Dieppe, and from the seaside at Pléneuf, chattering on about how glorious everything is and how marvellous the colours and how brilliant the sun and how warm the sea; and you think it's unfair that no matter what she decides to do, it's always the right thing to have done and you envy her her decisiveness, her single-minded desire to be an artist, because that is how she makes every choice – will this bring her closer to being an artist or not? – because you make choices based on feelings and see where that has gotten you.

You think you won't see her when you move back to Paris with her bloody brother and his screeching mob, but she is everywhere you go: folding a sheet of newsprint into a boat and floating it in the Grand Bassin; seated on a mossy knoll with her legs daintily crossed at her oh-so-slender ankles, eating strawberries in the Clamart woods; in the window of the Bon Marché with a drawer from her bedside table next to her on the floor, a few tubes of paint, an eraser, a folded sheet of paper just barely visible, drawing and redrawing; arm-in-arm with Rodin browsing amongst the antique art dealers on the Rue de Seine on a Sunday morning, Rodin lifting an etching off the wall to examine it, Gwen kneeling to put her hand on the belly of the owner's dog; warming up at the Louvre, sitting on the velvet benches with her knees wide apart, her bare feet on either side of the heating vents; talking animatedly to herself while she sketches some invisible child on a bench in a bright spot of sun in the middle of the Boulevard Edgar Quinet. Hello, my darling darling, she says to you as you pass pushing a perambulator full of noisome bottoms and flailing fists, I do hope you have a *lovely* day, while she is in the middle of having a bloody *lovely* day herself and you have no chance of ever having one ever again. *Fuck you*, you want to say, but you don't, because you still, in the back of your mind, hope she will one day teach you to draw.

You think she's so poor that she'll never eat at the Rotonde, but whenever you go, there she is, her back to the street, her little boots pressed into the yellow sand under the tables, nursing a ten centime cup of ambition for three hours, breaking the ends off the baguettes in the bread basket, every famous artist within a hundred mile radius stopping in to say hello and ask her what she's bloody working on as if it *matters* to them; you drag the babies to the Dôme to get sausages and mashed potatoes one day for lunch and there she is nibbling a piece of mackerel though she claims never to eat anything with eyes, the liar; riding a pony on the carousel in the Luxembourg Gardens, you hear a sound and look across to see her ensconced in the gondola, her feet up, waving to her admirers like Queen Fucking Victoria; on a hot summer day, you stop at the Closerie for a refreshing glass of lemon water and there she is, drawing on a napkin, with the waiter dithering beside her, wiping a wine glass with his floor-length apron for five minutes, unsure whether to kick her out for destruction of property or to frame the bloody thing.

You realise at some point that you were using her to leverage attention from Augustus, that shit, and you also realise that it didn't work, and you know you only went to France with her because you thought you would end up being a better artist than she was, and you also realise that you never really loved her or even liked her, that the only feeling you have for her is a deep-seated wish that she keep her mouth shut and never reveal what has gone on between you because you never want to be known as that lowest of creatures, a bloody lesbian, and you suspect that she will tell her friends and that they will tell their friends and one day it will be all over the papers and you will have to hire someone to scratch her eyes out; you know that she used you too, that she thought paintings of you would bring her fame and so she tried to seduce you and she paid your fare on the boat over from London and she pretended to love you, just so she would see some expression in your eyes, but she wasn't fooling anyone, least of all you, because she's almost like a fucking machine, or a monster, not human at all, in her pursuit of her art; you think that you are by far the more beautiful one, and the better educated one and the smartest, and definitely the better French speaker and that you have the biggest bust and the tiniest waist and that men look at you far more often than they look at her and that you actually read books for pleasure rather than just to impress and that you don't need to take notes and that *still*, she gets all of the attention and that *still*, her brother cares about her opinion more than he cares about your own and even when she is clearly a lunatic, seeing things that can't possibly be there, that have been *proven* not to be there, Augustus is not shy about saying that he thinks her more charming, more deep, more real, more sophisticated, more talented, more lovable, more honest, more believable, more fucking *everything* than you will ever be, and it kills you, it rips the guts right out of you, until you feel like a husk, like someone who used to be someone and is now no one at all.

JEUNE FILLE:

All through that first year she came to Paris in 1904, Gwen searched for the man who had been following her, the Jew. In crowds walking through the littered streets, crushed on the back steps of the omnibus, descending from the train battered by other people's boxes, fighting for the best deals in the handkerchief department of the Bon Marché, she looked for his tallness, his long black curls, his hat made of beaver fur, but she never saw him. He had vanished completely.

She understood vanishing. Living in France felt as if she too had vanished from the world. Now, no one knew her. No one called her name or brought her a flower or sent her a letter. She didn't understand the language and no one repeated their words for her. Men pushed past her to get on the omnibus and squeezed into the last seat seconds before she could. The concierge's husband pretended he couldn't see Gwen and constantly walked into her, steadying himself with brute hands on her bust.

The morning after Dorelia left, Gwen crept downstairs past midday, to get a little fresh air. She had an appointment with Rodin in the afternoon. There were Jews in the street, people who looked similar to the man she knew, but never exactly the same. Paris was *swamped* with Jews. There had been new pogroms throughout Europe. Even the Irish had to flee from Limerick and now survivors flooded the streets as they had done in London, chattering in Russian and Yiddish and German, despite disapproving stares. She peeped at these people from the doorstep. She wasn't hungry. Not even a little. Then she went back upstairs to get her box of paints and her little easel. She returned to the Pletzl and painted the woman with the flower cart and the man with the bicycle and the bundles of wood next to the houses and the little children in their sailor suits and their hats made of newspaper. "I'll paint whatever I *want* to paint," she muttered savagely, over and over, stabbing the brush with each word. "No one can tell me how to be an artist!"

She wasn't exactly sorry that she couldn't find "her" Jew, but still, she wondered what had become of him. She wound the coil of his hair around the handle of her brush and stared down the alleys, always expecting to see him. She wondered, again and again, how to paint the fear she saw in the eyes of the men and the women and the children. She was angry that nothing she had seen in the Louvre had taught her how to paint pain. Nothing had taught her how to fill an eye with fear. And she wondered about that fear. When she looked in the mirror, there was something in her eyes too that looked like fear.

Many of the refugees had the curious flickering star over their hearts. Gwen had gone to the doctor several weeks earlier, hoping he'd say that she had a mild infection, that she needed to apply salt drops to her eyes three times a day, but instead, he'd looked at her oddly and recommended a psychiatrist. Gwen had been insulted. She wasn't making it up! She wasn't *so* crazy in the head. It was the *doctor* who needed to see a psychiatrist and she told him so, although in her uncertain French, it came out all wrong and the man had reddened and called for the concierge and had her ejected from the building. Gwen had hit the concierge with her umbrella and *tried* to explain, but she was no match for the old Frenchwoman's strength. Later, she'd screwed up her eyes and looked into her little mirror, wondering if she would see the star over her own breast.

"Why are you so obsessed with the Jews?" Monsieur Rilke, Rodin's poetic new secretary, asked her as they stood outside the gate to the studio that afternoon. He'd come out to meet her, apologising for his Master's absence and offering her a slip of paper with a pass to return to the studio. Rodin had cancelled their meeting; he was busy meeting collectors and gallery representatives and wealthy patrons.

Rilke had noticed the way her eyes followed the Jewish peddlers, lugging sails and planks and baskets of bricks and kegs of apples down to the nearby river. Gwen was glad to meet the great man's secretary. She liked Rilke. He didn't talk about the things other people talked about. And there had been, somehow, some form of recognition between them and both had stayed to talk.

"No reason," she said. "Except that they are so strange. So picturesque."

"Why don't you draw them?" he said. "You sketched a horse, a nun and a child while you were waiting. But even though there are Jews back and forth all day in front of the gate, and you turn your head and watch them, no drawings. You would think, since they interest you, you might at least make a sketch."

"No," she said. "I am not *that* interested." It wasn't *adults* that interested her.

On the way home from the Pletzl that same day, Gwen had seen a line of children waiting outside the nearby school. She thought they might have been there before, maybe for weeks, but she wasn't sure. No one waved to these children, or called to them. They did not speak to each other, or throw things, or push on each other's satchels. They stood quietly, even sadly, waiting. They wore shoes that were the wrong sizes and cardigans that were missing buttons and scarves that belonged to older people. The little boys wore men's caps and the little girls wore women's coats. The children formed an island of silence and she put down her easel and leaned on it, staring at them. She hadn't needed to tramp across Paris on a day when she had an important appointment. She had Jews right here, right outside her doorstep.

All of these children had the odd yellow flickering over their hearts. From what Gwen could tell, most of the people with the heart lights were sad, or afraid, or terribly lonely, much like herself. Perhaps all Parisians were morose. She felt quietly certain she too had the star, though she could not see it in her mirror.

"Do you see anything on my dress?" she had asked Rodin's secretary later the same afternoon. The Master had received a commission, said Rilke, to create a bust of Whistler and he was searching for a model. He was my teacher, said Gwen. I loved him. I'll tell Rodin, said Rilke. He'll want to know. But was she hungry? Would she like a piece of cheese and a Reine des Reinettes apple? They sat in the last spot of sunlight in the mossy central courtyard of the Dépôt des Marbres and ate the simple foods and she showed him some pages in her sketchbook and brushed the marble dust off the knees of his trousers and Rilke read her "Mécontent de tous … meprise" from Baudelaire's *Poèmes en Prose.*

She wrote his words into her notebook, thinking to reread them later, in bed, as the only prayer that she then felt capable of saying. *Dissatisfied with everyone and dissatisfied with myself, I should like to find redemption, I should like to take some pride in myself … souls of those I have loved, fortify me, grant me the grace to produce something that will prove to me that I am not the least of people, that I am not inferior to those I despise.*

But after she'd written down the words, they seemed to her weighty and profound and she could not simply close the covers over such thoughts, so she tore the page out of the book and folded it in quarters and slipped it into her pocket with her other treasures.

Rilke was murmuring about a little cottage he'd originally been given in the Master's garden, on the hill descending from the Villa des Brilliants in Meudon. He received two hundred francs a month for letter writing, and free food and a bedroom, a study and a dressing room. The first night he'd slept in the cottage, though he couldn't find the door because there wasn't one. The building lay open to the wind. And a massive dog had climbed into the bed with him and drizzled silvery saliva tracks on his chest until morning. When the poet rose in the pale light of dawn, he'd trodden in several piles of swan shit. Despite the fascinating Khmer Buddha and the equally fascinating Rodin, Rilke said he'd been forced to move to the Rue Toullier, wedged in between the Asile de Nuit and the Maison d'Accouchement. With women, she said in response, it was always either babies or madness.

"I don't suppose you have any stewed apples?" asked Rilke, who loved them.

"Can you see anything here?" Gwen asked, pointing to her chest. She had no interest in his personal affairs. And since she couldn't have babies, the only option open to her was madness. "A star?"

The thin elegant man blushed to be directed to her breast. A homosexual then. He plucked a mushroom from among the mosses and turned it upside down. "You see, in a single night, all these gills are formed. That's good work. Rodin taught me that."

He was writing a book about Rodin, so he said. Sometimes he was too friendly and sometimes entirely distant and he barely held her fingertips between his fingers when he shook her hand though he stared for many minutes at the lace on the edge of her sleeve. He didn't sniff her perfume and he didn't smile and he didn't do any of the things she expected men to do when they had a picnic with a woman. He showed her a photograph of a clock he had placed above his desk, shield-shaped and solemn. He was, she thought, most definitely one of those men who preferred the company of other men.

"You didn't even look at my bodice!" Gwen accused several minutes later. She tapped him playfully on the arm.

Rilke turned his head partially in her direction and glanced over her shoulder at an enormous marble eagle that lay with its beak pointing at the clouds, abandoned in the grass. The sun was setting. “There’s nothing there,” he said, but still offered her his handkerchief so that she could scrub at her breast, at the invisible star.

“Perhaps,” he said, “you might try reading the thirtieth chapter of Job before you go to sleep. I find every word of it true and most helpful when I am confounded by this city.”

Weeks had passed since then. She still hadn’t met with Rodin. Gwen put her hand in her pocket and folded the single coin left there between the portraits and the pass to Rodin’s studio. She felt weak, barely able to walk, so she sat for a while on a bench in the middle of the Boulevard Edgar Quinet, under the plane trees. It was not a hot day. Sparrows hopped along the edge of the cobbles, picking seeds out from between the cracks. She felt burdened, her arms as full of turgid blood as sides of beef. It should have been good to be out in a shaft of sunlight with her hair brushed and a straw hat pinned to her head, but instead, even the light lay on her shoulders like a yoke. A group of six nuns passed by, singing some kind of dirge. Her own cat came out of the courtyard and rubbed against her ankles and she bent down and stroked its fur. In her pocket, the original pass in Rilke’s handwriting, asking her to return to Rodin’s studio. Written weeks ago, essentially worthless. And a portrait of her as a young girl, thin and pale, a few weeks before the death of her mother, before she knew that terrible things happened in the world. A bundle of radishes on a passing cart the reddest thing she had ever seen, and the most round.

Spring was almost over. The street seemed empty. The line of children standing next to the road, waiting. The tulips gone. Just yellowing leaves and headless stalks. And the daffodils. If she didn’t find work with Rodin, she might starve. He’d noticed her before. He’d cared. But now she’d been forgotten again.

She might not be able to stay in the little room. She’d never learn to paint. Soon, without food, she’d lose her last chance to stand at the feet of real greatness and discover what went into being an artist. Nobody wanted to paint a skeleton. Certainly not Rodin who was known for his love of plump haunches. And Gwen could hardly walk for hunger.

Across the street, those terrible children. Motionless. The breeze didn't even lift the hair from their foreheads. They were thin but they must have had sources for food, cheaper than the little restaurants and markets that lined the streets.

She stood to ask the oldest girl, a ragged but defiant person of about fifteen or sixteen, where she found food in Paris. The girl startled. She looked behind her. She looked to the side and then to the other side. There was something about her that Gwen couldn't quite put her finger on.

"Are you talking to me?" the girl asked, though she continued to look from side to side, to see if anyone noticed them talking. She tapped a fingernail against one of her front teeth. She was dark haired, and up close, perhaps only twelve. She wore a mauve jacket over a purple skirt, and a yellow leather belt tied the jacket to the skirt. Bound around her neck, an indigo scarf. She spoke carefully and she had an accent, perhaps German, which made her French sound odd, even to Gwen, who was not perfect in her pronunciation either. The girl's eyes turned downwards at the corners, and this made her appear even sadder than the other children.

"Yes. I'm talking to *you*," said Gwen. She waved at the line. "Why are you all just standing here?" The simple motion of waving had almost knocked her off her feet. She held on to the base of gas lamp. She put her other hand in her pocket and touched the pass. Why was *she* talking to these strangers? These *Jewish* strangers?

"We're waiting," said the girl after a moment. She darted glances at Gwen and spoke at an angle, her feet pointing towards the cemetery rather than towards the street, as if she were speaking to someone else. She looked like a younger version of

Dorelia. The sun painted her hair green and blue and black. "For our parents." Eight buttons down the front of her jacket, buttons covered in the same darker purple fabric as the skirt. Perhaps dioxazine purple mixed with mineral violet.

"But where are you going?" asked Gwen.

The girl stared at her. "Away," she said faintly. The shifting light over the girl's heart solidified. It was clearly a yellow star, the same yellow star that had been on the witch's chest on that terrifying night, the same yellow star as the man with the side curls. Gwen stared at it, at the frayed edges, the large stitches in grey thread holding it to the girl's coat, at the inked word – *Juif* – and she lifted her hand to touch her own breast. Her fingers tingled.

The girl moved from foot to foot, uncomfortable. She lifted her satchel to cover her own star. Several more sparrows landed on the nearby road and joined the little flock that was already there. A horse pulling a wagon with exceptionally thick wheels clattered by and all the birds flew up to the rooftops.

"My name is Gwendolen John," said Gwen, putting out her hand to be shaken. The note and the single coin left behind in her pocket. "What's yours?" She half expected the girl to say *Dorelia.*

In a place where people turn away from one another, a single word of kindness can sound like a shot. Heads turned all along the row. A green omnibus passed the line and rang its bell and the children jumped. Gwen saw herself reflected in the windows. She didn't remember looking quite like this reflection. The thin hair. The loose blue dress. The shaking face. The tall girl patted the shoulder of the boy who stood next to her. "It's alright, Naftali," she said. "That one's not for us."

Gwen's hand still hung in the air between them and all of the children stared at it until Gwen retrieved her property and hid it behind her back.

"My name is Renée," the girl whispered then. She cleared her throat and said it again, much stronger. *Renée.* She looked quickly at Gwen. Right at her. As if she was as solid as bronze. The resemblance to Dorelia, then, was uncanny. A much smaller girl who had been standing behind Renée peeked out at Gwen. She grinned. It was shocking to see one of these sombre children smile.

"Hello, Vin Lin Zhon!" she said. "My name is Giselle." She was young enough to have a lisp, and was very obviously Renée's sister. She stuck out her hand. Her wrist, pitifully thin. Like Gwen's own. They did not have some secret source of food. She and the children were all alike then, in their poverty.

Gwen bent down to take the small girl's hand.

"Hello, Giselle. It's very nice to meet you," she said. "Perhaps you should call me Mademoiselle Marie instead? It might be easier. My middle name is Mary." They couldn't be waiting to go into a school. Their ages were too different. And it was already the afternoon. The story about waiting for parents some falsehood invented for safety. Instead, they must all be waiting for an omnibus or one of the yellow electric trams than rumbled through the neighbourhood.

"I'm going to model for a sculptor some day soon," she told the children. "And then I will have food."

They stared at her.

"You're not very pretty," said one of the boys.

"You don't look quite well," said a girl.

Renée pursed her lips and closed one eye. "You might be able to," she said. "If you perked up a bit. Pinch your cheeks. You look haggard."

Gwen frowned.

"That won't do," she said. "He won't hire me if I look bad."

"Then eat," said the girl with an anger Gwen couldn't understand. "Go home and make yourself a meal. It's not like anyone is stopping you."

Some of the children turned away from Gwen. Many of the girls had coarse black hair, curling down their backs. Gwen waved but only Giselle lifted her hand to wave back. "Goodbye then," called Gwen. "I'll see you tomorrow!" She knew that simply speaking to the Jews had changed her.

LA PETITE MODÈLE:

Of course, she didn't make a meal. She had no money. She lay upstairs for several days, not eating, not painting, staring at the ceiling. Dorelia was gone. Augustus was gone. Her chance with Rodin was gone. Gwen found she could not pick up her paintbrush or even her sketchbook ever since her vision of herself on the stage with the giant canvas looming over her. The image of herself at Augustus' knees. The only thing she had been able to paint were the Jews in the Pletzl, but now, every time she touched a brush or opened a tube or stood a canvas on her easel, she felt nauseous. She chewed the salted plums and crackers and thin slices of orange that Miss Hart slid under her door, suspecting, from the sounds of retching she heard every morning, that Augustus had gotten Gwen pregnant.

One afternoon, lying on her bed, sketching her empty room, she discovered that she was not drawing the room at all. Instead, she had drawn the painting from her vision. In horror, she tore the page from the block and crushed it between her hands and threw it under the bed. Later the same day, she knelt beside her bed and fished out the crumpled paper and lit a match and held the flame to the paper until thin lines of black smoke coiled around her hand and the flame caught and the paper flared and twisted and crumbled to ash.

During this period, Augustus came many times to her flat in search of news of Dorelia, but she no longer let him in. "Attagirl!" cried Miss Hart. "No one has to fuck their brother!"

Six-year-old Augustus in a long white nightgown haunted her dreams, begging to come into her bed. He was twelve and he dove, again and again into the ocean and emerged, shaking the water from his hair in an Elizabethan ruff of droplets and she dove in after him and they were both naked as seals. He was eighteen and his shadow ran up the plastered wall and he held out his hand and stamped his foot and tried to teach her how to do the danse apache, the tough dance between a pimp and his whore that he'd learned in the dance halls of Paris. Then he was twenty-two and they lay in bed together, in his flat, and she hit him with a wooden spoon. But she was almost twenty-eight now, and he was twenty-five. He was a father, a man with a wife and a home and a mistress, and she was not his lover. He wanted her help. Not her. How could she open her door to that?

Once, when he was knocking, shouting at her through the door, words rose into her mouth, but they did not spill out. The cat jumped down into the room with the tail of a mouse protruding between its teeth. A cold Atlantic wave rose over her head, a white nightgown swung past her, a wooden spoon. She looked at the calendar and was surprised to see that it was almost summer. A chunk of plaster as big as a canvas fell from the ceiling and landed on her one night. She hurled the pieces out onto the roof and watched them melt in the rain.

Augustus still lurked outside her door waiting for her to come out. Every day, he slid a few coins under the door, a handful of crackers, a slice of cheese. She hadn't eaten in a week. Since burning the sketch, she hadn't drawn a thing. She sat on her bed all day and moved her feet, hoping to see the little snail she had once seen. Miss Hart climbed across the roof tiles and smuggled in a canteen of sweet milky tea. Her head was light. Her heart beat fast. She fainted. Got up. Fainted again. Rilke climbed the creaking stairs to deliver a note with a new appointment to meet Rodin. She thought it was a dream, fainted, got up, saw that the letter had not vanished, that it was real. The cat was so hungry it bit her fingers and drew blood. Protein. One day Miss Hart told her that she could come out. Augustus had gone to Belgium. The next day was her new appointment with Rodin.

Miss Hart looked her over after helping her dress and then took out a few coins for a cab ride. "You'll never make it if you walk," she said. She offered a lipstick. She offered an apple and Gwen hid it in her pocket for Rilke.

In the cab, Gwen planned what she would make for dinner with the money she would earn when Rodin gave her regular work. An omelette. Toast. Butter. She waved to the man unloading the dripping rib cages of cows from his wagon and she waved to the woman who was twisting hempen rope between two hooks. She smiled at the postman wobbling through the streets on his yellow bicycle and she made the cab driver stop so she could pick a red poppy from between the cracks in the street, to tuck into her hat band. She pinched her cheeks, not once but many times. Near the Quai d'Orsay, while they were waiting for a string of trolley cars to pass, she saw another line of solemn children with yellow stars waiting for something and she called out hello to them. "Call me Mademoiselle Marie!" she said. "You will be seeing me every morning! I am getting work with an artist!" One girl, about twelve, laughed out loud. "Mademoiselle Marie," she said, "artists do not have money." Her older brother put his hand over the girl's mouth and told her to hush.

By the time the cab came to the end of the long Rue de l'Université, Gwen's cheeks were rosy from the fresh air and her eyes were shining and her hair had been burnished by the wind from the river and tendrils hung around her face. Light poured between the clouds and splashed the buildings, the trees, the river, everything. She felt ecstatic and full of energy. She felt as if she had swallowed the spring.

"I am here!" she cried, ringing the bell. "Today is the day that I will model for Rodin!"

Only after Monsieur Rilke unlocked the gate to the Dépôt des Marbres did Gwen begin to feel trepidation. She remembered the huge chunks of marble and cranes to lift them from her earlier visit. The piles of marble dust, drifting. Everything was covered in this fine white dust. There were twelve large studios arranged along a grassy pathway and within these studios men and women cut and chipped and drilled and shaved. Giant callipers stood between small plaster and clay models and the much larger marble sculptures. Half finished, these sculptures were armless or lacked eyes, or their skin was rough or they had great chisel marks down their raw chests. Gwen walked past them and her earlier mood of joy and delight drained from her.

What had she been thinking? Rodin was famous. His statues stood in the squares and in the galleries and museums across France. Even if he gave her regular work, what could he possibly see in *her*? He was a symbol of the entire art world, and she was damaged merchandise. She turned around to leave but Rilke stood in her way, his arms crossed.

"I brought you an apple," she said, holding it out to him. He smiled as if he understood her real reason for turning. "Go on," he said. "Remember you heard it from me ... you are perfect for this job."

At the steps of Rodin's studios, she hesitated and then sat down on the listing stone doorstep. Between the pocked marble, tufts of cold moss. Floating, just above the field of green, tiny flowers. A scent of rot. Her heart beat very rapidly. The blood sloshing from chamber to chamber. She thought again about not going in, of returning to her little room and only modelling for the familiar women on the fourth floor. She wouldn't exactly starve. But perhaps she wouldn't exactly live either.

It turned out that she had arrived much too early. Despite having asked for Gwen at ten, Rodin never came in to the studio before two. His home was in Meudon and he worked there in the mornings, before taking the train or the ferry, the Hirondelle, in to the city, where he worked until dark.

At first, Gwen hoped Rilke would come out and talk with her as he had done the previous times. Then she peeked into all of the other studios. A tall Scandinavian woman was friendly and looked her up and down with frank interest, but others ignored her, or worse, asked her to leave. She only had a small piece of baguette left and she had spent most of her money on the cab ride. She was hungry, but worried that if she left to get something to eat, exactly then would be when Rodin would arrive. The marble smelled liked the catacombs, of bones and smoke from beeswax candles. Tired, hungry, anxious, Gwen leaned back against the floor to ceiling glass wall at the front of Rodin's studio and fell asleep in a spot of sunshine.

"Come along now." It was Rodin in his long white smock. When he spoke, his beard wagged but his lips weren't visible. "Let me help you up," he said, offering his hand. His touch felt as light as paper, and his flesh was cool and dry. "My little English model," he said, smiling. "I am glad you have arrived safely. You and I have a lot of work to do."

His voice was deeper than she remembered from the first times she'd heard him, and he spoke slowly in French. He took out a pipe and knocked it on one of the huge pieces of stone that lined the studio. His hands were coarse, lined and scarred. "Come over here," he said, and he stood her beneath the tall windows overlooking the river and swung one open to the breeze and the light and the smells. He held her jaw and turned her face this way and that. "Yes," he said. "Very good. Now take off your clothing."

Gwen glanced around the studio. Such a large space. What she could accomplish if she had such a light-filled room! Drawers and drawers filled with plaster hands and feet and fingers and toes and ankles and arms. *Mes abattis*, Rodin called them when he noticed her staring. My giblets. Many men and women chipping at stone, perched on ladders, or moulding plaster at nearby tables. Some of these people looked in her direction. A few smiled and did not turn back to their work, but instead stood with their hands on their hips, watching to see what would happen.

"Here?" she said. The windows, at least, did not face the street. "You must be joking."

"Monsieur Rodin?" A secretary, not Rilke, stood at Rodin's elbow. "May I read you this letter?"

"One moment," he said to the secretary, holding up a finger. "No," he said to Gwen. "I'm not joking. I never joke. Where else would you pose? There are screens." The screens he pointed to were few and low and sheer. Several of the nearby men snickered.

Gwen put her hand to her throat and began to thread the first button of her blouse through its hole. She was kind to her models, set them in screened spaces with a warm fire burning nearby, and as a result, they all looked bovine.

"Faster, my dear," said Rodin, and then he began to talk with his secretary, his beard rising and falling, the white hairs in his ears bristling, something about a foundry stealing his mould and casting illegal reproductions of one of his sculptures. The secretary, a middle-aged man, good-looking, tall and serious, a Monsieur Gillet, read aloud from a series of papers. Rodin, his head tilted to one side, tugged at his eyebrows and listened.

Gwen's carefully pressed clothing fell in a pile at her feet. She bent to pick up each item, to fold it and lay it aside. She had never posed naked for a man before, and certainly not in front of a man close to her own age, like Monsieur Gillet. She took off her bloomers last of all, with her back to Rodin, drawing the cloth down over her hips, lifting one foot and pulling out first that leg and then the other. She folded the pantaloons in half and then in half again. She held them against her stomach.

"It will not do!" Rodin barked suddenly. Gwen, startled, dropped the pantaloons. The entire workshop fell silent. "I will not allow them to steal from me as if I am an imbecile! Tell him that I will be taking him to court unless he comes and explains himself to me, like a man!" Rodin chomped on his unlit pipe, drew heavily, took it out of his mouth, looked at it with great disappointment and then lay it down on a table.

It was cold in the studio and Gwen was freezing. Her feet, on the stone floor, burned. She hugged herself with her arms and danced from one foot to the other. She would have to rethink her methods of painting, that much was already clear. Demanding that they strip was not enough. Strip in front of others. Strip in the freezing cold. Some of the students, on their ladders, laughed at her again. Laugh at her models. Scream at them. All for the look in their eyes. The pantaloons were splayed on the floor, gaping. With her foot, she pushed their legs together. She coughed.

"Oh yes," said Rodin and he turned his great shaggy head towards her. "Que c'est beau! Pardon me, my dear, I had forgotten you. Turn around, please. Not the whole way. Ah!" he gasped and began to mutter to himself. "... like sun breaking through clouds. And those slim legs, those clever little feet. With feet such as those you could have climbed and lived in trees. Bend over. Are you a dancer? No? An artist. Oh, you like to draw, you say. An amateur with a paint box? Very well, then." He had still not asked her to stand back up, and so she stood with her head down and her rump facing the great man for many minutes. Between her knees, she saw that he was studying her closely. Monsieur Gillet returned but this time, Rodin waved him off. Someone began playing the Steinway grand piano she had seen on the way in. More minutes passed and still Rodin stared at her bottom. *Orpheus, Alceste, Iphigenia.* Gwen did not like to think of all of the men on ladders who could possibly *also* be staring at her in this ridiculous position. She could not imagine the strange Jew requesting such a thing, even though he did seem to want *something* from her. But she would do the same to her own models. She would paint them filled with shame.

Now Rodin took a sketchpad and began to draw her bent over. The pianist switched to Haydn. Rodin asked Gwen to spread her feet. He made one rapid drawing, tore off the sheet and threw it on the floor and began another. A slender woman ran in and picked up each sheet of paper before Rodin could step on it.

"Lie down," he said. Gwen eased herself facedown onto the ground. She was very stiff and the stone was intensely cold.

"No," he said. He indicated a wooden bench covered with a rug behind her. The top was higher than Gwen's waist. She looked at it.

"The stairs," he said. He reached for his pipe, looked into the end again, shook his head and put it down. Gwen did not see any stairs and she didn't quite know how to ask where they were. After a minute, Rodin looked up at her and saw her still standing in the same position.

"The stairs!" he said again, but louder this time, and the pianist stopped abruptly. The men on the ladders burst out laughing. Rodin looked up and shook his fist at them. "Back to work, you layabouts!" he shouted. The same slender woman ran in carrying a set of wooden steps, which she placed near the bench.

"Thank you, my dear," said Rodin. He touched her hand as she went out and closed his fingers around her hand, holding her there for a moment. She smiled. "It was my pleasure, my Master," she said. A little shiver ran over Gwen and something moved in her stomach. She frowned at the woman.

"Such a back, don't you think?" he asked, pointing towards Gwen. "Her spine!'

"It's very beautiful, my Master," said the woman, and then she slipped from his grasp and left the room, but not before cutting her eyes at Gwen. So, he painted rage, jealousy, desire. He painted what she *wanted* to paint.

Now Gwen climbed onto the bench and lay down, curled up her side. She faced the wall, showing Rodin her back. The woman's face hung before her eyes, and Rodin's hand holding the woman's rose up, the vision enlarged, grew damp and swollen and hot, and then resettled. Gwen was still very cold and began to tremble uncontrollably.

"Not like that," said Rodin. "Lie down as if you *desire* something. Open yourself for what is ready, waiting for you." He opened his arms and splayed his legs, then pulled his hands quickly against his chest. "Grasp it!" he commanded.

Gwen rolled onto her back and opened her legs a few inches. She held her arms above her until she could hold them there no longer and then she dropped them. The rug was terribly itchy and she tried not to wriggle around or to scratch. Her teeth chattered, but she burned with an intense excitement. Here, finally, was a teacher who could guide her to be the artist she wanted to be, who could answer the questions that plagued her.

"No, no, no!" he shouted. "Here, between my hands, is life!" He held his hands a few inches apart in front of his face. "Roiling, slippery, beating life! Can you feel it?"

Gwen nodded but she had no idea what he was talking about.

"Now eat it!" he said, and thrust his fingers into his mouth, licked them and swallowed.

Gwen blinked and tears came into her eyes. She put her hands up to her mouth, and timidly put one finger inside. She looked up at Rodin, expecting to see that she had already failed him, and was surprised to see him soften.

"Poor little English model," said Rodin, coming to her side. "You do not know what I mean, do you?" He pushed her legs together and held them closed with his big hand. Gwen dashed at her tears. She was humiliated and oddly thrilled to see that this too, he painted.

"Sit up," Rodin said. He wrapped her in a blanket. "You are shy, it seems. And I have been a terrible host," he said. "Perhaps you would prefer to model for me somewhere more private?" He glanced up at the young men on their ladders and they slunk down the rungs and disappeared from sight.

He took her by the hand and led her through the main studio to a secluded area in the second studio, with a large Norman wardrobe at one end and warm thick carpets underfoot. It was heated by a small stove that stood in the centre of the space. The chimney ran up through the roof. A fire burned inside the stove and on the top, a kettle bubbled. On a table stood a mechanical device, a record player, and piled next to it were a stack of recordings.

"Better?" Rodin asked, dusting a wicker chair for her to sit in and bending to look into her eyes. He stroked her head and then patted it, as if she were a puppy.

"Yes," she whispered, wondering at his method, curious to see what would happen next. First the dark emotions, then the light? In her excitement, she forgot about being hungry and weak and cold.

"Tell me something about yourself," he said. "Why did you come to Paris? Who recommended you to me?"

She reminded him that they had met briefly as he exited Hilda Flodin's studio. She had not wanted to mention that it was Augustus who had made the initial recommendation, but his great grey eyes widened and he became very excited. "You are the sister of the great Augustus John, not so?" Rodin was a friend of Augustus, and now he remembered that Gwen had studied under Whistler at the Slade and that he had asked to see her so that they might discuss Whistler's techniques, his penchant for tone. "He wouldn't have wanted a statue of himself," Gwen said when Rodin mentioned his recent commission. "With a tap in his tummy."

Rodin seemed to be very impressed by painters and writers and artists of all types and he encouraged her to keep on talking, to tell him about all of Augustus' painterly friends, even though she blushed and stuttered and forgot every shred of French grammar she had ever known.

"But how perfect!" he said. "I have been commissioned to make a sculpture in honour of Whistler and here I have his own little student in front of me. You will do very nicely indeed. What is your name again?"

But he, like Giselle in the morning, could not pronounce Gwen's name, and so she became Marie to him too.

"A hot cup of coffee for Marie!" he shouted. "With milk and sugar!"

A different woman appeared with a press that she filled from the kettle and within a few minutes, Rodin handed a cup to Gwen with a smile. "Soon all will be right with the world," he said. He took a small flask from the pocket of his smock, unscrewed the cap and splashed something brown into Gwen's cup. "One must take care of one's models," he said, before sitting beside her and asking her about her family, and about Wales, where she had grown up, and inquiring after her little cat, Edgar Quinet. It was more conversation than Gwen had had in several weeks.

"He's ever such a clever cat, sir," said Gwen. "Whenever I sing him 'Ben Bolt', he frowns at me." She imitated the cat's purring and his frown and Rodin laughed. She wished that she could talk about art with the same ease with which she talked about cats. She wished she felt free to discuss the way he had bossed her around at first, humiliated her, and only then been kind, painting all of it, every emotion that crossed her face, the way she held joy and rage and fear and delight in her spine and her neck and her cheeks.

"I will call you Marie, but you must call me Maître," said Rodin. "Everybody calls me that. Even my wife." Rodin, like Augustus, had not exactly *married* his wife.

"Yes, my Master," said Gwen. It was an odd name for a person who was discussing cats, but then, she had not his greatness.

"Now," said Rodin, "I see that you are feeling more in your body. Come, let us see if you can model properly for me."

It was the first time anyone had noticed that Gwen was not fully present in her body and requested her return to the world. A great tremor went through her, of shock and of pleasure. She wanted to model well for Rodin, who had taken the trouble to see her as she really was. Now, when he asked her to lay on her back and spread her legs, she did so with great energy, spreading them as wide as she could and holding them there with strength. She thrust her arms into the air and snapped them back against her body. She tensed the muscles in her calves and raised her legs. She crouched on one foot and held the other high above her. She bent backwards like a bow and thrust her pelvis forward as he asked.

"Yes!' cried Rodin. "You have it!" He threw paper after paper onto the floor but no one came to carry them away. "Again!" he cried. "Kneel!" he commanded. "Turn your head! Excellent! More! That's right! Perfect!" He did not seem old to Gwen. He seemed like a young man, vigorous and sizzling.

When she was finally in a position that satisfied Rodin, with one foot high on a block of wood, and he had sketched her several dozen times that way, he went away, asking her not to move, and came back carrying a small damp sack of clay. Pinching off pieces of the worked clay, he layered them onto a base he had created of solid clay. Every so often, he walked over to Gwen, and corrected her shoulder, or her jaw, or her thigh with his muddy hands, moving her slightly to the left or to the right. He measured her with the great brass callipers standing next to the wall and carried the measurement back to his sculpture. Every ten minutes or so, he swung open the door to the stove and threw in a few more sticks of firewood. As the clay on his maquette dried, he took a swig of water and spat it at the statue. Droplets fell on the hot stove and sizzled and steam rose in the air, clouds of pale blue steam that twirled around above their heads and eventually were lost amongst the dark rafters. The clay model began to look more and more like Gwen. Every pore of Gwen's body felt open and juicy. A feeling rose in her chest, an ignition, to see herself portrayed in three dimensions, unlike in a mirror or in a painting. She felt as if some internal part of her had been ferreted out and replaced with something more basic, more crude and vital and alive. Her face glowed with sweat, the inside of her thighs ran with moisture, and now the room felt hot, very hot.

At one point, the concierge came in and said it was time to close, but Rodin asked for the key. "Leave us alone," he said. "I will close up."

When everyone had left the studio, Rodin covered the clay maquette with canvas. He dipped his hands into a basin of water and rubbed them briskly together, then dried them on a linen towel. He picked up his pipe and put it down again. He brushed the front of his smock and shook it out and removed it, hanging it on a peg. He leaned down and put another few sticks of firewood into the stove. Then he dipped the linen towel into the bowl of water and twisted it between his hands until many drops ran from it. He twisted it again. His hands were wet. His skin shone in the candlelight. He brought the damp towel over to Gwen. She was still leaning back on one hand, her back arched, her legs spread. He touched the cool towel to her forehead and then to her cheeks. "You are so hot," he said gently. "Your flesh is burning." He ran the towel along the inside curve of her back and Gwen almost fell from the shock of the touch.

"This is beautiful," he said. He rubbed the towel along her back again. "This arch. The strongest thing in nature." Behind the towel, every fine hair on Gwen's back rose up. Rodin bent and blew a stream of his breath across where he had just run the towel. Gwen cried out from the pleasure of it, the silvery aching coolness on her inflamed skin and even then, even in that moment, the thought, *I will run a cold towel over my models' hot bodies too.*

"And this," he said, running the wet towel along the crest of her hip. "I am in love with bones." He paused to blow on her hip. "*And* with women," he said as she shuddered. "Women are so very remarkable. Extraordinary, their bodies. I hope you know," he said, "that your body is a construction beyond imagining."

"My Master," said Gwen. "May I stop holding the pose? May I sit?" Her arm was trembling. Her whole body was trembling.

He ran the towel under her breasts and blew a stream of cool air across her chest that raised her nipples.

"You are a very good model," he said. "You can hold a pose much longer than most. But yes. Of course. Come sit here next to me."

He patted the bench very close to his side. Gwen sat towards one end, at the far end of the bench, her legs shaking and her heart in disarray, and he turned to look at her. "Are you afraid of me, my little Marie? I am just an old man. Sixty-three years on this earth," he said. "And very harmless." His voice was soft. His brilliant eyes sparkled with laughter, though the corners of his mouth, beneath its whiskers, turned down. He was much older than Gwen had thought, his long hair white, fine lines around his eyes. More than thirty-six years her senior, six years older than Gwen's father, and yet he seemed as if he had just been drawn from the kiln. His breath smelled of bread, like something rich and fragrant and hot.

"Yes, sir. I *am* afraid," said Gwen, though it wasn't quite the truth. She shook not from fear but from desire. She burned to run home and take out her own stick of charcoal and to make demands of her own models. But it was not something a woman should show, that intense ambition, it was not feminine, it was not proper, so she looked down at Rodin's hand on the bench. There was still a little clay at the base of one cracked fingernail. His fingers so strong that veins snaked across their surface as if they were really biceps. "My Master," she corrected herself.

"Have I done something to make you afraid?" he asked. The sun went behind some clouds and the studio became momentarily darker. The clay lay in the small cove at the edge of Rodin's thumbnail. Gwen shook her head. She would like to take his hand in hers and remove that small piece of clay with her mouth. She would like to *absorb* him.

"Come," he said, and he patted the bench beside him again.

Gwen slid a few inches towards him. His hand, now, was close enough for her to touch, to take up if she wished.

"Are you hungry?" he asked. "You are very thin. I have something here somewhere. Some cheese and bread. We could eat together if you wish."

Still Gwen could not speak. It was not only food she had lacked for so many weeks.

"Look at me," he said. Her head was bent. She lifted her eyes. He was looking at her with eyes that glittered darkly between eyelashes that seemed sentient. It seemed he was saying something to her without speaking. She looked down and then looked up again, to see what it was in his eyes. His eyelids heavy over the grey irises, and full of creases. His pupils enormous. In the centre of each eye, a reflection of Gwen's face.

"My little model Marie," Rodin said. "We will learn so much together, you and I. We will find out how to take something cold and make it burn." He smiled. Gwen looked down and smiled to herself. Yes! Yes, she would make it happen. "So shy!"

"My Master," she said. "Please. Don't play with me this way." She wanted, more than anything, to learn how to see the hidden world all around her. But her education was not, she thought, what Rodin had in mind.

"Do you not want to be touched?" he said, and without waiting for her answer, he moved away. "Oh no!" she said, leaning towards him, and then he reached around her naked waist and slid her closer on the bench. Underneath her thighs, she was slick with sweat. Now, she could feel the heat of him through his clothing. She felt, between them, a kind of electricity pass. "Are you a virgin?" he asked. Her fingers tingled. She looked up and saw a bullseye mirror reflecting the two of them sitting so close together, hand in hand, and she thought of van Eyck's *Arnolfini Portrait*. The marriage.

They worked that night until close to midnight. Rodin placed a candle in a wine bottle at her feet and one at his elbow to draw by. Everyone had left the studio, and even the concierge had given up and retired to her little room at the side of the gate. When they finished, Gwen felt that she should always remain naked, that it was the most natural way to be, and she delayed getting re-dressed. It felt almost as if she could *see* with her skin, as if everything that happened in the air was communicated to her clearly, in images, through her flesh.

She went over and looked at his sketches. Their simplicity. Their energy. The movement shown with one or two lines. The obvious knowledge of muscles and sinews and tendons and bones, and she told herself she would go to the market and buy an anatomy book. But she also saw that he had communicated her yearning, her wish for something she did not have, and she studied his drawings without finding out how it was done.

She spoke with Rodin about when she should return and about what poses she could practise, to strengthen herself for him. She hoped, when she returned, that they would talk about drawing, about how to capture hidden motivation in a gesture. Truthfully, she could not remember what had become of her clothes and was sure Rodin would remind her. But eventually, she had to ask him and he scratched his head and smiled. "I do not know," he said. "They must be here somewhere." They searched the studio by candlelight, the eerie shadows from the marble statues rising high on the walls and looming overhead like dark wings. Barges passed, whistling, on the Seine. "I have surely missed the last train home," fretted Rodin. He seemed, then, like a small boy. "I will have to take a carriage and Madame Beuret will be very angry with me." Madame Beuret was his wife, Gwen gathered. "Perhaps you can borrow one of our costumes?" He led her to a Norman wardrobe, almost as wide as the entire room. In the centre of the blackened door was a deep oval containing an image of Joan of Arc with her cropped hair, holding a spear in one hand and two lilies in the other, all in carved relief. Around her head were star-shaped ventilation holes. On one side, just above the iron strapping of the hinge, an incised *J*.

"She is my hero," said Gwen softly, her fingers on the girl's throat, on the unopenable buckles. "I want, more than anything, to be as brave as she was."

Rodin turned the great key. "But she was a virgin, my dear, and had taken a vow of chastity." Gwen did not remove her hand from the saint. She traced the unmoving hair, ridged like a frozen field, March, maybe April, still very cold outside, pale lemon spears rising up blindly through the dirt, not knowing what lay ahead. One end of the wooden hair cut bluntly across, truncated. Perhaps broken and then sanded smooth again. How did she go from being a frightened girl to being immortalised in wood and stone and clay? A wingless creature rising, always rising. Her face so cold and smooth and certain.

Rodin smiled. His neck was bent. He was much too close. "Come inside. I cannot see in the dark. Could you look?" He took Gwen's hand and helped her up into the wardrobe and then climbed in behind her, blocking her exit. He put his hand on her naked shoulder. "Marie," he said. She turned. He stooped and in the darkness, felt for her face. She stepped backwards, away from his hand and into hanging fabrics, soft and dusty. Perhaps Joan was not brave at all. Perhaps she simply did not know when to retreat. Rodin closed the door to the wardrobe, the key grated in the works and now the darkness was only pierced by tiny star-shaped beams of light. By this light, she could just make out his body, his great leonine head, the short, thick arms and the broad chest. Slowly falling particles of dust. "Marie," he said again, his voice curiously muffled by the fabrics.

Gwen's heart pounded and she felt she could not breathe. No stone soldier, she. Under her bare feet soft quilts and pillows, perfumed velvets and silks. Dorelia, for a moment, standing close to her, the warmth of her body and the delicate scent of her flesh. Dorelia as a young girl in a purple dress standing in a Paris street, waiting for something. She had let Dorelia down but Dorelia had *abandoned* her. Dorelia was somewhere else with someone else. She meant nothing anymore and Gwen heard again the turning of a key, the scraping of iron as it raised tumblers, the soft click as the bolt shot home.

Rodin stepped closer and his hand searched for her body. He was breathing fast. Hangers scraped on the rail over her head and she was brushed by something studded with fur. The bright star-shaped streams of light made it hard for her to see in the darkness. They seemed to move, to circle and then, one by one, they disappeared. She was no longer sure which way was up. The darkness *was* velvet and fur. It was silk. She stepped forward and stumbled against Rodin.

He braced her, and she felt the strength of his arm, the sinew and bone that supported her. She was surprised at this hardness, and at his lack of breasts, his sheer size, the warmth of his body, his smell. Rodin kissed the top of her head, then took her face between his hands. "Open your mouth," he whispered. He waited patiently for her to comply. Her blood, pounding so hard, made her arms twitch. One of his knees made a creak as he bent lower. His heart was audible, like a horse, in the far distance, cantering over turf. It beat steadily, reassuringly in the dark. He, at least, was calm. For a brief moment, she saw Dorelia's face bathed in blue moonlight, and then Rodin's incredibly soft and mobile lips touched hers. Until that moment, she had thought she knew all there was to know about kissing and being kissed.

The skin of his hand, chapped and roughened from the clay, felt exquisite as it moved across her body in the pitch-blackness. "My Marie," he said softly, cupping her cheek in his warm and callused palm. "My little model. How small you are compared with me. And how perfect nevertheless." He touched her everywhere, slowly examining each part of her, as a blind man might, perhaps not intending her arousal, perhaps merely learning her by touch. Perhaps this was the way of a sculptor, to learn with the hands before the eyes.

And then, before she was ready, Rodin pulled away and unlocked the door and stepped outside. She stumbled out after him, blinded by mere candlelight, forgetting she was still naked. Her whole body chiming from his touch, loud with sensation. Every part of her ringing and ringing. "Sir?" she said, putting her finger in her ear. She couldn't quite hear. "Master?" Had she done something wrong?

"I must get a carriage," Rodin said. "I can't be late." It turned out he knew where her clothes were after all, and he handed them to her in silence and watched her tie the tapes and fasten the buttons.

"I will write you a note," Gwen said. She was still unsure of what had happened, if he was pleased with her or not. The sudden departure.

"No need. I will see you tomorrow," he said. "At two." Then he kissed her quickly on both cheeks, handed her five francs and sent her out into the night.

PAINTING 5:

She takes out her charcoal and her paints the minute she gets home and begins to sketch him from memory. She no longer sees the looming canvas, she no longer sees Augustus. She paints until she hears the birds in the trees and light falls in a soft wave into the room and the cat drops through the window and weaves between her feet. Already, the way she paints a line has changed. Already, she is trying to capture energy rather than image.

face. chin. top cushion. under cushion. cheeks. honey pot. lower cheek. jam pot. lower cheek. jaw triangle.
measurements. jaw limit to muscle line. muscle line to square of chin. square of chin. square of chin to muscle line. muscle line to jaw limit. jaw limit. jaw limit to upper cheek. upper cheek to slope. slope to eyebrow. eyebrow to hair.
placing of mouth. measurement from end of muscle line.
face. eyebrows to eyes. *tranches de potiron* [slices of pumpkin].
life to mouth. calm. firm. silent.

elderberry fish flying

leave those

CAT CLEANING ITSELF (EDGAR QUINET):

Gwen sent letters begging Dorelia to come back to Augustus, even though earlier, she had convinced Dorelia to come to France by telling her how ignoble it was to flirt with a married man, to lure him away from his wife. Now she lay awake at night making excuses as to why a man *must* have two wives. Perhaps the first wife was never really a wife to begin with? Perhaps there was never any intention of staying with the first if a second should come along that was better in every way. The French had different attitudes towards love outside of marriage than did the English. It was an honoured institution.

Gwen might have been called a hussy in England but in France, mistresses were given their own homes, an education; even the Prime Minister was not ashamed to let it be known that he had a lover in a flat in St Germain. And though she loved Ida and understood the situation would half kill her, Gwen rationalised the return of Dorelia to Augustus. Knowing, as she did it, that she was also arguing for her own future position in Rodin's household.

19 Boulevard Edgar Quinet
Paris, France
May 1904

Dorelia, something has happened which takes my breath away, so beautiful it is.

Ida *wants you to go to Gussy – not only wants but desires it passionately. She has written to him and to me. She says, 'She is ours and she knows it. By God, I will haunt her until she comes back.'*

She said also to Gussy, 'I have discovered I love you and what you want I want passionately. She (Dorelia) shall have pleasure with you, eh?' She said more but you know what I mean.

Gus loves you in a much more noble way than you may think – he will not ask now because he says perhaps you are happy with your artist and because of your worldly welfare – but he only says that last because he knows you – we know you too and we do ask.

You are necessary for his development and for Ida's, and he is necessary for yours – I have known that a long time – but I did not know how much. Dorelia, you know I love you, you do not know how much – I should think it the greatest crime to take with intention anyone's happiness away even for a little time – it is to me the only thing that would matter.

I point out your happiness and the highest happiness – I know of course from one point of view you will have to be brave and unselfish – but I have faith in you. Ida's example makes me feel that some day I shall be unselfish too.

I would not write this if I knew you had no affection for Gussy, but you are his, aren't you?

She told Dorelia that she should come on the first train back to Paris. She told her that she would meet her at the Gare du Nord and introduce her to Rodin and give her money to go to London, to Augustus. But when Gwen convinced Rodin to go with her to meet the train, Dorelia had not arrived. Rodin left early, nervous not to be seen in public with his model. Gwen stood on the platform, waiting until the final person got off and the engineer climbed down from the engine and all of the boxes had been claimed and the last of the steam had risen to the top of the glass roof and twirled around the vent and been sucked outside into the night, and then she turned and went back to her empty flat.

A letter was waiting for her at home. Dorelia had written back from Bruges, where she was living with Leonard, suggesting that Gwen was in an ecstasy, from opium use or some other stimulant. *What on earth has happened to you, Gwendolen John?* she wrote. *Have you gone crazy in the few months since I have been gone? What is this talk about making off with the heart of the greatest artist in Europe? Do you truly think he will stay with you for longer than a week? You do know, I hope, that your sensual charms are quite lacking.*

And do you honestly think that now I am with Leonard, I want to hear your brother's proclamations of love?

Gwen only read half of this letter before she took all her paintings and sketches of Dorelia to the shipping agent, and had him crate them up, to be sent to England. She would be glad when they were sold, glad when she no longer had to look at Dorelia's secret love face, the face she made for Gwen only.

Returning, she sat at her little table under her window, with Edgar Quinet brushing against her legs, understanding cat that he was. The second half of Dorelia's letter was just as bad as the first. *I am tired of being weak,* Dorelia wrote. *Of depending on people, of being dragged this way and that by my feelings, of listening to everybody but myself. I must be free – I will be.* What was this spell the Johns had on her, she asked. All of them? She must be rid of it.

Gwen had been working on a portrait of herself next to Rodin, in the style of Van Eyck. She stood up and looked at the canvas. It suddenly seemed absurd to her, unoriginal and melodramatic and clichéd. She'd be better off painting Edgar Quinet, the cat. Rodin had *laughed* when she told him about her little *chat*. He would not laugh if she showed him *The Rodin Wedding*.

She rummaged in her box of paints, took out a tube of china white, squeezed a large amount onto her palette and began, methodically, to paint out everything she had done. When she finished, she put away her materials, opened the window to air out the room and sat down to read the rest of Dorelia's letter.

Dorelia had shown Leonard Gwen's letter despite her warning not to, so there was a letter from Leonard too, angry and hurt. Gwen had written that there was "no greater crime than trying to ruin someone else's happiness", and yet here she was, doing exactly that! And he, Leonard, did not agree with Gwen on the point that this was the greatest crime either. He believed there was one greater crime: to do things that are against the rule of nature. He said her letter was deceitful. Gwen hadn't written on Augustus' behalf. Really, her letter was filled with the love of one woman for another. It reeked of unnatural passion.

A great coldness, as of a bucket of water, dashed over Gwen's head and ran down her neck, pooling in her stomach. The icy sensation seared, burned, then melted, sending painful waves of embarrassment throughout her body. All that time in Toulouse, he had been *judging* them, judging *Gwen*, specifically. He had not lured Dorelia away. He thought he had *rescued* her.

Gwen's shame was rapidly replaced with anger. She stamped her foot and crushed Leonard's letter in her fist. How could loving someone be a crime? If so, then every man was a criminal and every woman deserved to be in jail. What did Rodin think of such things? She wanted to know, but suspected that he would be generous, curious, erring on the side of sensory pleasure rather than religious dogma. She sat down to write again to Dorelia, and she added a page of rebuke for Leonard at the end.

The laws of nature are infinite, she wrote to him. *You do God and nature an injustice to limit them.*

In the end, under a barrage of letters and poems and entreaties from Gwen and Augustus and Ida, Dorelia was lured to Ghent, to meet Augustus. And Augustus was, as always, irresistible to her. A mountain couldn't have withstood the onslaught. He was like the Mistral, maddening. A week later, on August 1st, 1904,

Dorelia returned to England, to live in "wonderful concubinage" she said, with Ida and Augustus and the howling babies.

Dear Mrs Harem, Ida had written to Dorelia. *I heard from Gwen. Gwen says you "have given in". Were you then holding out against Gus, you little bitch? You are a mystery, but you are ours. I don't know if I love you for your own sake or for his.*

His, wrote back Gwen, when she heard.

How delightful to have a drawing given you by Rodin – does he give all his models drawings? Augustus wrote to Gwen.

I have given my teacher a painting of Edgar Quinet, she wrote back. *My cat. Rodin is teaching me to see the body as I never have before.*

Dorelia, standing on the platform of Bruges station as she departed for England, had written to Gwen on a postcard.

When Gwen turned it over, all it said was, *How* is *the cat?*

Rilke, writing for Rodin, sent Gwen notes almost every day. *Will M. John please come to the studio at 2 PM tomorrow?* and she wrote back, *It will be my pleasure*. She wrote Rodin other notes too, notes that she read to him when they were inside the wardrobe, from memory, and which he stole from her mouth, interrupting her with his kisses. Now, when Gwen arrived at the studio, she had to pass a group of young women who waited outside the door, waiting to see Rodin. "But where has he been?" one asked. "He has completely vanished," said another. A fire leapt in Gwen's chest. *She* was seeing Rodin for ten and twelve hours a day.

And she waited for the day she would receive a different letter, telling her that Rodin would be coming in early from Meudon, to visit her in her flat. This she planned to burn in the fireplace.

THE NOVICE:

Gwen now posed in the morning for Hilda Flodin and then walked across to Rodin's studio at two and posed for him, although he was often called away or travelling.

"Quite the little lovebird, you are," said Hilda to Gwen one day as she posed, naked to the waist, under the studio window. Hilda was Finnish and had a heavy accent. She was in her mid-thirties, tall and muscular, with very fair hair, what was described as Rodin's "type". She was an excellent sculptor and was working on a sculpture of Gwen for the next salon.

"I don't know what you mean," Gwen said. Gwen was not Rodin's "type". She was short and very thin with small breasts that she pinched at night, to make sure they didn't shrink.

"Every woman in Paris has fallen in love with Rodin," said Flodin. She drove the chisel deeply into the marble with one stroke of her hammer. "But none of them know details about him like you do." She tapped the chisel again, and a small chunk of marble fell onto the ground.

Gwen blushed as red as a peony. "You know details about him too," she murmured. She couldn't move as she was posing, but she wanted to turn around and hide her face.

"I am his assistant," said Hilda. "And I have been his lover too." She smiled, thinking of some memory. She spread her legs, steadying herself for the next stroke. "He still comes when I command." She snapped her fingers and laughed.

Gwen was silent. This was not something she wanted to hear about Rodin. She remembered instead, a story he had told her of being invited to Hilda's studio and arriving just in time to see Hilda on her knees, scrubbing the floor, with her skirts tucked up around her waist. He'd laughed and laughed, but now Gwen frowned.

Gwen felt as if Rodin's every casual touch lit her on fire and she craved his company so much that she had begun writing him daily letters, asking to see him more often, begging him to come to her room, proclaiming her great love for her Master. Their relationship still had not been consummated and she ached for him to pierce her body, to fully own her. Twice more, they had stayed late and climbed into the Norman wardrobe with its tinkling bar of old bottles. And many times besides that, he had kissed her openly as he sculpted, reckless of the many young men on ladders who were easily able to see what they were doing. Sometimes his kisses were tender and gentle, but many times, when he was inflamed by his work and from concentrating on her body for such long periods, he would yank her head back by the hair and kiss her roughly, driving his tongue repeatedly into her mouth. It wasn't very English. None of her other lovers had ever done such a thing. It was almost a sign that he wished to penetrate her in other ways. This, too, she came to beg for.

"Surely you cannot command the Master?" said Gwen now, still frozen in her position. Hilda hit the chisel again, but this time, she missed and hit her finger.

"Women have ways," said Hilda, putting her thumb in her mouth to soothe it. "I am surprised you do not know. From what I heard, you had a woman living with you when you first arrived. A vixen." She slitted her eyes and smirked at Gwen.

"Who told you that?" said Gwen. The conversation had run away, out of control. "Oh!" she said, rubbing her elbows. "I am aching all over from standing in this position so long. Please let me finish early today."

"There's nothing wrong with loving women. Don't be ashamed," said Hilda. "I like women myself." She reached out and touched Gwen's bright red hair. "So soft. They smell so good. Malleable. There are things women do to each other that a man would never think of doing." She flexed her hands and then gave Gwen's hair a gentle tug.

"I am going to take a walk. My apologies. I need a little fresh air," said Gwen, brushing her hair back and winding it into a bun. She hurriedly pulled up her bodice and fastened the buttons. On the days she modelled, she left her stays at home.

She thought she might walk to the bridge and watch the boats pass underneath, a scene very similar to the Asian prints Rodin had in his studio, but then, in turning, she noticed that Hilda had a new screen next to her fireplace that pictured exactly that, a bridge, a river, a boat passing underneath. It was a Japanese screen, very delicate in colour and form.

"How beautiful!" exclaimed Gwen. "It's new! Wherever did you find it?"

"It was given to me by Rodin," said Hilda. She stroked the head of her sculpture. "It's the most beautiful of its kind I've ever seen. Has Rodin given you presents too, little lovebird?" Her hand slid over the head again and again. Gwen could not take her eyes off Hilda's muscular hand, as it flowed over the head and then tightened around the neck.

"He gave me a drawing," she said, her face closing. "And the wicker chair I sat on when I first came to his studio, as I didn't have anything to sit on in my room."

Hilda smiled at Gwen with her head on one side. "Is that all?" she said. "Just that dusty old thing? It's a wonder you haven't already broken through it."

"I have only just met the Master," said Gwen stiffly.

"The marks on your neck say otherwise," said Hilda.

"My Master is very generous with *everyone*," said Gwen. "At the end of the night, his pockets are always empty and Monsieur Gillet screams at him for losing all of his cash. Just yesterday, I saw him give ten francs to a clochard in the street outside the studio." Gwen did not accept money from even Augustus anymore, though Augustus continued to send baskets of food and packages of warm fabric. But Rodin was different. The beautiful fire screen rankled. "He pays my rent," she added softly.

Now it was Hilda's turn to be jealous. "Your rent?" she spat. "Are you his whore then? His cinque-à-sept?" She slapped the sculpture.

"His five-to-seven?" repeated Gwen. She was not familiar with the expression.

"The woman that a man visits from five to seven, after work but before he returns home to his wife."

Gwen shook all over. She had just received a note from Monsieur Gillet in Rodin's name, that he would be visiting her at her room next Friday evening, at five. She had been excited and had begun to clean her room, in anticipation, though she could not imagine Rodin in her tiny, dark room. Edgar Quinet left mouse bones on the bedspread; there were dead termites in the corners. Her sheets had not been washed in months because they still smelled of Dorelia.

"No," she said, shaking her head and blushing. "I am not that type of woman. A cinque-à-sept. No man may treat me that way!"

"Ha!" said Hilda. "We are *all* like that, us women! How else should we make our way in the world? We must take what we can get from those who have it."

"I am a painter," said Gwen softly. "I paint portraits. I support myself."

"Paintings won't support a baby! How will you look walking around Paris, modelling nude in men's studios, with Rodin's brat sucking on your tit? How many Mary Magdalenes can you pose for?" Hilda had a way of striding about the studio, flashing her unshaven legs, smacking objects with the flat of her hand as she passed them. Her voice was loud and her accent stronger than ever, full of tees and spit.

"I can't conceive," growled Gwen. She wouldn't have minded getting pregnant by Rodin. Feeling something that came from him swell inside her, fill her entirely. It wasn't possible but he didn't know that.

"Look at you! You're practically panting, just thinking about having his child!"

Everything she saw now, even terrible things, turned her mind to her Master. She painted Rodin beside her on her walk to his studio, imagining the warmth of his hand within hers. She imagined him lying down with her at night, his body curved around hers and she positioned slippers she'd bought for him next to her bed, just so. The advertisements plastered on the sides of buildings made her want to run out and buy patent medicines for him, Le Chat soap, sugared almonds, Boston garters, absinthe, cocaine tooth drops, the Vital Power Massager that promised to make him a manly man even after hours of activity had depleted him, shoes with lifts for the arches, Suchard chocolate, tickets to the wild animal shows that passed through, butter from Normandy, a bottle of Schneider beer, a badger brush for his beard, a moustache trainer, an electric belt and suspender, a jar of tapeworms, a bag of Climax Plug, a felt toothbrush, Mariani wine, an X-ray, a clock, a camera, a coat. The children she saw each day, lined up waiting for whatever it was they waited for, became her and Rodin's children, and she imagined herself tidying them up to see their father. "You must brush your hair and your teeth," she told the tallest girl, the one called Renée. "And put a ribbon in your hair. A purple one." Renée made a face, but the next day, Gwen brought her a purple ribbon.

The school year would start soon, but the children just grew more and more untidy. Gwen couldn't understand it. Some mornings, as she passed, she saw that Renée was holding a young baby, a newborn. Gwen imagined it was her own child. She imagined Rodin fathering the child and herself pushing this object formed from their passion out of her body, into the arms of the local midwife. She felt within her the hollow space from which it had emerged. She pictured bundling the child up and handing it to Renée and asking her to watch it while Rodin sculpted the new mother's torso. First rubbing her body with fragrant oil and then massaging her thighs. Only then would Rodin lower his head to her full breast and suckle, drinking the milk that leaked from her, milk that was rightfully his. Only then would he smooth the rumpled skin of her belly and kiss it. "The home of my children," he would say, kissing her hip and touching himself.

She lived in a world where only Rodin and she existed for many months, where either she was modelling for him or locked in the cupboard with him or getting ready to see him or writing letters to him or waiting outside the gate to catch a glimpse of him. She dreamed of the giant callipers he used to measure from the crown of her head to the point of her chin, the poppets Rodin began with, a phallic clump that formed the shoulders balancing a ball of packed clay that gradually transformed into a head. She imagined he might one day make a sculpture of the two of them kissing. She'd seen other sculptures of couples kissing that she suspected were his previous lovers. She woke thinking of the way he scooped out the arches of the eyes with a quick reaming movement of his thumb and she felt his thumb reaching within her.

And then, one day in early January, 1905, just as she came out of her flat, singing a nursery rhyme in French, Augustus was coming up the stairs. He'd run off from Dorelia and Ida and returned to Paris. He grabbed her by the arm and dragged her back inside her room.

"So, you give it to him but you won't give it to your own brother?" he said.

"I am not seeing anyone," she protested, the room roaring, the windows flashing past her, faster and faster.

"You're a liar," he said. He fell on her as if she were a piece of furniture.

That afternoon, she had brought Rodin a scarf she had knitted for him, in soft red wool and garter stitch, but he hadn't opened the package. She'd been shaking and hadn't wanted to undress for him, and they'd walked around each other for almost an hour, like cats, neither able to please the other, and then Rilke had run in, crying that a crazy person had attacked *Le Penseur*, climbing the iron railings outside the Panthéon, and chopping up the plaster cast of *The Thinker* with a hatchet. Le Rodinophobe had been captured, but the statue was destroyed. Rodin had clapped his hands to his head and shrieked and pinched Gwen's arm and crushed Rilke's balls for delivering such bad news.

Gwen was cold and bruised and she had wanted to wash herself, but there hadn't been enough time after Augustus left if she was to make it to Rodin at the appointed hour. Then Rodin had claimed, after sniffing her décolletage, that she smelled strange and of course she hadn't been able to say anything about her brother, and then he'd asked about the marks on her arm and her neck jealously, as if she might be seeing someone else, and in the end, he had refused to even go near the wardrobe, just when she most needed to be held. And before she could wash at his little copper sink, Rodin had demanded that everyone leave and he'd locked the door himself, screaming that no one wanted him to succeed and they were all murderers.

Then, just as Gwen left the Dépôt des Marbres, she saw the tall Jew walking away from her, strolling towards the Seine. "Stop!" she called. She dropped her umbrella and ran after him. He was very far away, and perhaps she had been mistaken in his identity, but it seemed to Gwen that he heard her call and he hurried along, much faster than before, almost running. He rushed ahead of her, always on roads following the course of the Seine, and she came after him, as best as she could.

"Please stop!" she cried again, but the Jew turned onto another street, and kept up his fast pace. They came close to the hideous almost-new Eiffel Tower and Gwen wondered if perhaps he was working there, painting the beastly iron struts, but the Jew continued past. Though she'd been running for what felt like ages, she had not gotten any nearer to him, and then, suddenly, she *was* closer. The man turned away from the river and headed back into the maze of streets that led to Montparnasse. He stopped outside a large building, a velodrome being built for the sport of bicycle racing.

Panting, she caught up to him. "Why are you following me?" she gasped. She leaned against a wall, and coughed. Red spots swam before her eyes. Time seemed to pass. The light slipped, every edge had a hard white outer line, there were streaks of black dust across the buildings, moving and shifting. Only now did she realise that she was in a lonely part of the city with a man who may not have had the best of intentions towards her.

The Jew stared and stared at her, his face almost skeletal, his eyes huge and dark and moist, as if at any moment he might begin to cry. "Tell me!" she said. "For ages, wherever I go, there you are. Your hair! Your passport! That crazy yellow star! You have frightened me!" Inside her chest, she felt a sharp stab of something, a momentary flash of awareness or of some other almost ungraspable thing.

But when the Jew continued to stare at her, now with tears rolling down his face and catching in his long beard, Gwen suspected that perhaps he did not understand French, and that whatever she had felt was entirely inappropriate to the moment, and she put it away from her. Remembering that she had seen him first in England, she made her little speech in English, but he still didn't respond to her.

"England?" she said. "France? Poland? Germany? Russia? Deutschland?"

When she said Deutschland, he nodded his head. Now he looked away from her and fingered the lapel of his jacket. The wool had tiny shreds of thread jutting from the fabric where something had been picked off. There was a pale yellow haze over the whole area. Up close, it seemed as if he had spilled paint on his dark clothing and then carefully rubbed it off. She liked the effect, and thought about trying it in her own work. Would she scumble the paint with a piece of cheesecloth? Would she stab at it with a dry paintbrush or ponce with wadded paper?

But "Munich?" she said, still trying to connect with the Jew, though he seemed lost in his own world. "Cologne? Berlin?"

The man looked straight at her then. He didn't nod his head, but once he'd captured her attention, he pointed at the building she was leaning on, the ugly concrete bicycle stadium with its blank face and rounded walls. Then, without any warning, he turned and ran through one of the entranceways.

Gwen was winded. She couldn't chase him, but on the other hand, he couldn't come out without her seeing him. And what was to be gained from staying there anyway? He couldn't speak English or French and she couldn't speak German. Was he spying on her because he needed something from her? Did he plan on stealing her paintings? Taking something more personal from her? The air, that day, was very still and cold. The light was quick. A last cicada, secreted somewhere warm, ticked. Several cabs went by with their tops up, the cabbies wearing scarves and coats and gloves. It was winter again. Almost an entire year had passed since Gwen came to Paris.

Gwen waited, but she was chilled through. She didn't have a coat or a scarf or gloves yet. Rodin had said that he would give her some money to dress herself warmly and stylishly, and her friend, Ursula, in England, had sent her several pounds for her birthday. She leaned against the cold, stuccoed wall, thinking of which colour gloves she would purchase at the Bon Marché, and wondering which colour Rodin would most appreciate.

The Jew, however, did not emerge. There were workmen in the building – she could hear their hammers – she would go inside and see if she could find out anything further.

He was seated inside on one of the bleachers that lined the

frame of an oval track, awkwardly angled as if he held a child in his arms. He sat, looking blindly towards the middle of the stadium. His shoulders curved around his chest. One of his hands made a repetitive stroking motion. His back heaved. He looked quite mad.

Gwen stood below him, on the wooden track. She rubbed her hands on the cloth of her dress and felt the faint grasp of the fabric on her skin, a sense, through her fingers, of the red plaid weave. "Rabbi," she called up to him. The ceiling was very high above them, and made of blue glass and everything was bathed in an eerie undersea light. Her voice echoed throughout the empty stadium. "Rabbi, please! I don't know why you are upset. Did I scare you?" For this was the only thing that Gwen could think might have happened. If he were the victim of one of the Russian pogroms, or some other tragedy, perhaps having a tiny woman chase him through the streets, shouting, was terrifying.

The Jew struggled to stand up on the concrete step. He looked as if he were remembering, his face blue, waxing and waning with every memory. As he straightened, he groaned and arced his back, and then repositioned his arm to protect the invisible thing cradled inside the curve of his elbow. He shouted something. He looked down at her, and seeing no response, he gestured at the thing in his arms and then shouted again. Still, she didn't understand him, and now he became quite frantic, shouting louder and louder, over and over, a stream of words that she couldn't understand, this verbal torrent striking her frankly in the chest, *pushing* her, so that his terror became her terror too. She wasn't even sure he was speaking a language. The sounds he was making became a blur, a wordless scream that filled the stadium with echoes. A sound that filled her like water, as if the air of the stadium, liquefied, blue, boiling with horror, poured down her throat and began to drown her. Though she tried, she was unable to close her mouth and her lips stretched, wider and wider, until they began to tear at the corners.

The workers stopped their hammering and stood with their heads cocked, not staring at the man but staring at her, at Gwen. "It's not me," she shouted to them. Her words came out garbled, full of hot liquid. "It's him." She pointed above her to the Jew. Now, sometimes, she thought she could almost understand what he was saying. "Hilft unz", could that be "Help us"? Why should she? She was no friend of the Hebrew race. And just as she thought this, the Jew changed languages, or at least, she thought he changed languages, because she could no longer understand any part of what he was saying. Now, he also lost interest in what he was saying and long gaps stretched between his phrases, but at last, the workmen had laid down their tools and were coming around the track. Surely they would help her with the Jew. It seemed obvious that the man needed to be locked up. He needed a doctor, a sanatorium, an asylum.

He was screaming "Aiuto!" which might have been Italian, though what it meant, Gwen wasn't sure, and then, again, the man's language dissolved and became a series of wordless cries.

But then he began to scream in English and in French and now Gwen knew what it was that he was saying. "Help us!" cried the Jew. "Help us! Don't deny that you see us, like all those others! Please, for God's sake, there are women here, children, grandparents! Have mercy!"

As he screamed his eyes rolled back in his head. He fell forward and his face hit the railing and he tore at his hair. Tiny yellow flames sprang up in every corner of the liquid stadium and spun, whirling like leaves, higher and higher, and as they passed through the blue light, they became a brilliant acid green and then Prussian blue and then, in the shadows, yellow again, twining thicker and thicker until they became a great tornado of fire, a massive rope of fire twisting up towards the roof, and now children's voices, their cries and their shouts, could be heard, and a massive roar arose, as if a crowd watched a race and cheered wordlessly, mindlessly, for the winner. The Jew, above her, wailed and his head flopped and hit the railing and the railing sang a searing metallic song and blood sprayed from the Jew's face and his hands, flying out and spattering Gwen and the glossy new wooden track.

"Stop!" Gwen cried, ripping at her clothing where the blood had landed. "Such filthy behaviour!" She tore off her sleeve and threw it down. "I will *never* help you! I hate you! I hate all of you! We have *nothing* in common!"

The roaring grew louder and louder and now Gwen covered her ears with her hands. In front of her, illuminated for the briefest of moments, a spider on a thin line of silk. The track buckled under her feet, rose up like yellow teeth, shattered, and she fell.

PAINTING 6:

Do not let the world overcome you.

(dangers)
being *amoureuse*. my painting. unkindness of people. impoliteness of people. *les partirs, les retours*. fatigue.

~~*la stupidité du monde. manque de temps dans mes affaires.* my own mistakes and weaknesses. want of money. ill health. my sins. fear of the world. pleasures of the world. kindness of the world. success in my painting.~~

smoky corn and wild rose

faded roses (3 reds)
nuts and nettles

cyclamen and straw and earth (large slabs)
faded primroses and dandelions
(on straw and earth.) on nasturtiums.
milky bluets [cornflowers]
grey and yellow plaid

THE CONVALESCENT:

When Gwen awoke, she lay on her side in a pale room with high ceilings. Sunlight fell onto a limestone floor between two shutters that had been propped open to let in a little light and air. She was resting in a snowy bed, far softer and more comfortable than her own. In front of her, there was a small, very fine dresser and standing on it, in front of a huge old mirror, were two Grecian sculptures of young women. A faint scent of beeswax and lemon. A bright fire on the hearth, snapping, golden embers rising up the chimney. A warm eiderdown. A nightgown that was not her own.

She fingered the sheets. A kind of heavy linen, embroidered with red initials. R.B. She knew no person with the initials R.B. It was very puzzling. She rolled onto her back but her head hurt in that position, and she put up her hand to find a bandage on her forehead over a large swelling, and then, rolling onto her other side, there sat Rodin, dozing in a wicker chair that matched the one he had given her, one leg crossed over the other, his unlit pipe lying in his open hand.

"My Master!" she said in surprise.

"You haven't been eating," he growled without opening his eyes. "What do you think happens to little models who do not take care of themselves and eat proper meals? They faint in bicycle stadiums, that's what."

Gwen sat up quickly, but her head whirled and she had to lie down again.

"Oh, my Master," she said, remembering. "Something terrible happened! There was a Jew in the velodrome. He went mad, right in front of me. It was awful. Did they take him away?"

Rodin patted her hand. "Nothing but the dreams of anorexia," he said. "The fearful intoxication of wasting muscles."

"No, sir! Master!" Gwen said. "It was not a dream! See, I still have his blood on my hands." She pulled her hand from Rodin's and held it out for inspection.

"You fell, my little Marie, ma petit soeur. You hit your head. Of course there is blood on your hand."

"But the Jew," she said, tearing at the sheets, swinging out her legs to stand. "Someone should shut him in the madhouse. Such a barbarian!"

"You are lucky that you were carrying a letter addressed to me. The workmen carried you to the studio, where the concierge recognised you." Rodin gently put out a hand and pushed her back toward the bed. He pulled the sheet over her and tucked in the blanket. The slippers he wore made of carpet, the pattern a blur of pinks and greens and reds.

"But could that man find me here?" Gwen felt a rising panic. She tried to rise and Rodin tucked the blanket tighter.

"You are safe," he said calmly. "We were told that you were crying out and that you fell and hit your head. If you would like, though," he said, "I could inquire."

He did not believe her. That was obvious. She wanted to cry. When she closed her eyes, she still saw the twisting column of yellow flames rising into the blue dome, and she still heard the terrified screams of the Jew. A dream? No dream she had ever had was as vivid, as nauseatingly real.

"You must eat," Rodin said. "This has happened before. You models are all alike. You starve yourselves. And unfortunately, you can only stay here one day. Though Madam Beuret is away, visiting her family, she will return tomorrow in the afternoon. She would not be pleased to find one of my models in her bed."

"Where is this place?" asked Gwen and Rodin smiled.

"My home," he said. "In Meudon."

Gwen had been very curious about Rodin's home, the Villa

des Brilliants, just outside the city overlooking the Seine, but she had not yet visited his house. She had not felt welcomed or invited.

"Is this your bed?" she asked shyly. A clock over the fireplace whirred, getting ready to strike the hour. "You sat up in the chair? I am so sorry. And you have the grippe as well."

"I did not say I did not sleep in my bed," he said and his face wrinkled in a boyish grin. "I did not think you would mind." He sat down on the edge of the bed, and the springs squealed and he lifted first one foot and then the other and took off his slippers. "Madam Beuret made these for me, twenty, thirty years ago. She is a good woman," he said, as he examined them. He held the slippers out for Gwen to look at too, and then he bent and pushed them under the bed.

Gwen blushed all over. The room swam, for a minute, and she put out her hand to steady herself, and Rodin moved a few inches until his right hand touched the edge of the smallest finger on her left hand. His hand was large and solid and rough, a workman's hand, covered in cuts and scars, the skin deeply pitted, each pore visible. Only now did she notice that the pillow next to hers bore the impression of a head.

"But who took off my clothes?" she whispered. "And dressed me in this nightgown?" A plain white nightgown for a woman even smaller than she, a nightgown that pulled tightly across the chest. "Surely not you, my Master?"

Rodin smiled. "Would you *like* it to have been me, ma chère Marie?"

Gwen, ashamed, hesitated and then nodded. On the other pillow was a long, curling black hair. Gwen took it and wound it around her finger. Not Rodin's. His hair was white. Not hers. She had red. And not Madam Beuret's. Her hair was grey.

"I have never done this," Rodin said, looking out across his garden. "Bring a model home and put her into my bed. No model has ever come through the door of my home before now.

It might be a mistake, a terrible mistake." He turned to look at Gwen, and in the beautiful, clean light, a halo formed around his head, and all his white hair glowed red. Gwen gasped.

"You look like a saint," she whispered. Within her, something came loose and rose, floating, spiralling, circling higher and higher. The ring of black hair around her finger unwound and fell free.

"You look like a *wife*," Rodin said, his voice low, and her heart beat very fast and tremulous, and she opened her mouth a little, to breathe. "Will you be my little wife tonight?"

"But I couldn't," Gwen said, her words shaky. Each heartbeat choked her, strangled her voice. "Your wife. She will come back. She will know. It's not right." An image of Dorelia sitting in Augustus' dining room in London, and then, Ida's face, her haunted, jealous face, ragged with pain. "I can't."

Rodin rubbed his eyes and ran his hands over his head. "She is not *really* my wife," he said. "We have never married, you see. And she took the servant with her. No one need know what happens here."

"*I* will know," said Gwen.

"Yes," said Rodin. "We will both know. And so too will Madam Beuret, eventually. There is no keeping anything from her. She is aware of what I do in my Bluebeard's bedroom."

She hoped he meant the Norman cupboard and not this room. "Have you told her," asked Gwen, and she filled with a cold that seemed like it would never go away. "About us?" She pulled up the eiderdown and covered her arms.

"Marie," said Rodin, and he pulled at the sheet and the eiderdown, pulled them down to her chest and then to her hips and then drew them slowly past her feet, taking his time with the revelation. "She knows everything and she allows everything. You do not have to worry." He lifted the edge of the nightgown and rubbed slow circles on the bridge of her foot with one fingertip. "Is it warm enough in here for you, to do without the eiderdown?"

At his touch, Gwen shook.

"You are cold," he said. "Do not tell me that you do not desire me. I know it's not true. You have written me as much in your letters, though you do not tell me to my face."

He lifted the nightgown higher, and ran his hand up her calf. He tickled the inside of her leg with the ends of his beard.

"See. You are always so worried but I *do* read your letters," he said. He waved his hand as if to fan the pesky sheets of paper away and then he leaned toward her. His great grey eyes looked into hers. "And I *do* love you," he said as his face grew closer and closer to hers. "Do you love me too?"

Rodin's hands were in her hair, his lips so close to hers that she could feel, brushing her skin, his breaths, the warmth of them. She hesitated. "More than you can imagine."

He unbuttoned his trousers and let them fall. His grey socks were tied at the knees with red ribbons and the ribbons were too tight. They had left deep red lines in his flesh. A yellow toenail had carved its way through the end of one sock. She missed the salt-grass marshes, the cliffs, the cold, cold sea. Despite herself, she missed the familiar darkness of her brother's room, its smell of kerosene and sweat. She missed the familiarity of Dorelia and Augustus, the ease of bodies she knew by heart.

Leaves and small twigs hit the window and pattered against the side of the building, one and two and ten and twelve. The wind got louder again. She had turned and now she opened her eyes and she saw, reflected in the mirror, Rodin's thighs and the coarse curling grey hair at the base of his belly and her own strange face. How odd she appeared. How different from the last time she'd looked at herself.

Rodin sat, again, on the bed, and his weight tilted her towards him and in one practised movement, he turned and lifted her into his lap, pressed her close against his chest and covered her eyes. Beneath her ear, his heart ticked fast, as fast as hers.

"Say it," he said, his lips in her hair. "Tell me that you love me."

Her whole body flushed red. She couldn't see anything and yet, she felt so very observed.

"Sir, there are so many other people here with us." Augustus. Dorelia. Ambrose. Her little girlfriend from the Slade. All standing around the bed, waiting for the inevitable comparisons.

Rodin sighed. "Yes," he said. "There always are. Begone, you Bogeys!" he shouted, and he flapped his hands and she laughed.

She pulled his head down and whispered in his ear, "You are very lovable."

He kissed her eyebrow. "You will have to do better than that to get what you want," he said. He kissed her earlobe and the back of her neck where the short reddish curls clung damply to her skin and then he undid the buttons of the nightgown, one by one, his kisses following his hand lower and lower, until she felt him rising beneath her and she shifted her weight in his lap, and then he whispered, "Look at me and say it." She had done almost the same with Dorelia. And Augustus.

Rodin turned her body so that she straddled him and then tilted her chin up with his hands so that she gazed into his eyes, blushing, suffused with heat. Now, he rocked her in his lap, his great hands on her hips, pinning her to him, and there was no moving away. He pressed up and against her, hard and urgent. "Oh my God!" she gasped. This was not the unwanted attack of Augustus or the blushing passivity of Dorelia. She tried to lift herself off Rodin but he pushed her hips down again, ground her into him. He reached under her nightgown and parted her knickers. His hand on her.

"Tell me!" he commanded.

"I would do anything for you," she said, with her face pressed against his chest.

She felt as if her heart or her lungs or some other vital organ was lodged in her throat, perhaps all of them at once. Her legs ached from being stretched apart in such an awkward position.

And yet, and yet. It was nothing, *nothing*, like what she had experienced before. "Please, my Lord, please, I beg of you, do not make me wait for you this time."

Later, they lay in the damp, tangled sheets, naked and panting. She had pretended to come, but he had known that she lied to him, and so he had tried, several different ways, to please her. "Show me how you do it," he finally asked, and then he watched her touch herself, watched her body arc up from the bed and shake, and then he had held her and kissed her and done the same thing to her himself, again and again, first with his hands and then with his mouth, and it was better, far better, than anything she had ever experienced on her own.

"There is still a whole night ahead of us, my little wife," Rodin said. "The sun has barely gone down. But perhaps you are hungry."

She laughed and agreed that she was hungry, so very greedy that she could eat *anything*, but he, not understanding, began to stand up.

"Wait," Gwen said, pulling him back and laying her head on the soft bed of his body. His hair full of white marble dust, all his creases too. The trails of her sweat visible on his flesh. "Just now you called me your little wife, but earlier you called me your little *sister*. Why would you call me that, your sister?"

Something passed over Rodin's face and his lips closed. He sat on the edge of the bed and gazed out of the window, at the royal blue sky and the silver stars that were beginning to appear there. "My sister's name was also Marie," he said. "Like yours. But she died. I worshipped her. I still do, though it's been more than forty years. You look similar to her, your legs, your chin, even your eyes. I saw it on the first day, when you passed me going into Flodin's studio. Seeing you, it was almost as if my Marie lived in a different time, just as she was when I lost her."

"How odd," Gwen said. "That you have the name of my

brother and I have the name of your sister. How incestuous we are." A cold sliver of moonlight came between the curtains and passed between the two of them and Gwen reached out to take it in her hand and there, instead, between her fingers, was the black hair.

"Do you love him?" asked Rodin, his hand tracing circles on her thigh. "Your brother?"

Now it was Gwen's turn to look away. The answer was yes, but it was so complicated. "He did things ..." she began and then stopped. "*We* did things ..." Outside, an owl hooted, terrifying the mice that ran between the garden rows. She wound the coarse hair, again, around her finger. "Awful things." She glanced sideways at Rodin. He did not seem to be passing judgment. He nodded his head.

"And sometimes," she continued. "Not such awful things."

She could not bring herself to say anything further.

"Ah," he said. "I still think of my sister, nearly every day. Perhaps my love for her is the reason I have never married."

Gwen began to cry silently. She sat up and turned her back on Rodin and wrapped her arms around herself. Her face, in the mirror, completely unfamiliar. "I don't want you, if when you are with me, you are thinking of your sister." Though she could not promise him the same thing. She wound and unwound the long black hair, pulled it so tightly that it cut off circulation and her finger swelled and turned a blackish red.

"Come back," Rodin said. "Please don't go away." He waited for her to turn back to him but she did not. "I don't think of my sister when I am with you, little one," Rodin said, very gently. He was so close behind her that his breath stirred the hair on her neck. "I think of *you*. Do you think of your brother when you are with me?" The face, in the mirror, opened its mouth and showed its teeth. A shadow movement, a barely visible shiver in the glass.

"Oh no!" cried Gwen, and she turned and buried that face in

Rodin's chest so he should not see her expression.

"Then it is not what you think. You are not my sister and I am not your brother. We are not doing something wrong, something immoral. You can let go of your sadness from the past, and I, too, can think now of a happier Marie, a new Marie, an angel returned from heaven to bring me great joy. A Marie who shares my passion for art, for drawing. A real artist of the body." Gwen lifted her face and smiled at him. "And of pleasure," he added, grabbing her arms and pinning her down. "After I finish the little statue of you and it is shown in the Paris Salon, you and I will go to see the Pope in Rome," he said. "And he will give us his blessing on our marriage." Gwen's heart leapt. To be Rodin's wife! For all the world to see that he loved her.

"I will be the best wife ever," she said. She squirmed under his hands, arching her body up to rub against his. "You will sculpt and I will paint in Italy and it will always be warm. But if we have to travel elsewhere, I will not allow you to catch cold. I will keep you warm by pasting myself on you. I will cling to you wherever you go, a Marie coat."

Rodin laughed again. "But how will you do that if you can't even get out of my bed?" She wrestled mightily against his grip, twisting and turning, biting his fingers, kneeing him, throwing first one leg and then the other over his body, and still, despite his age, he held her down easily, laughing. Augustus had done the same thing to her, and it was ... she didn't want to think about him. Better even to think of Dorelia. *Begone, you Bogeys*, she said silently, and she beat her hands in the air.

"Such a little hellcat!" Rodin said, thinking she was fighting him off. And then he frowned. "But what is this?" he asked, pulling the black hair from her finger. "You wear a ring? Are you someone else's woman?"

"I found it ..." she began to say and then laughed. "So absurd. Throw it away! It's rubbish."

Rodin dropped the hair on the floor and wiped his hands on

his shining thighs, and began to tickle her. She was gasping for breath, giggling and struggling at the same time. "Your pleasure will be greater when you are full of air. Keep laughing!" he said. Pinning her hands to the bed above her with one of his, he tickled her until the tears ran from her eyes, and she was rosy with sweat and oxygen, and then he spread her knees with his. "Just like a fire burns hotter with every blow of the bellows."

SELF-PORTRAIT, NAKED, SITTING ON A BED:

From then on, all that winter and into the spring of 1905, Rodin came to Gwen's room almost every morning. He no longer worked at home in Meudon. He was restless. He could not stop himself but neither could Gwen. Instead of painting, she modelled for him in the afternoons at his studio, and afterwards, they lay in the wardrobe for hours, making love, talking, fantasising about their joint futures. Her memories of him from that time were of his deep warm voice in the cedar-spiced darkness, so utterly unlike Dorelia's high voice that she was never confused. If Rodin was called away on business and missed their afternoon appointment, Gwen waited for him in the garden of the studio, and walked him to the train in the evening. They sat in the twilight, and she showed him her drawings and he pointed out places where her line had faltered, or where she had not quite captured an angle, and she felt at last that she *was* an artist, a scientist of tone and planes and light. She hid the long black hair within her clothing, twisted into a ring for a giant, and only took it out when she was alone. She avoided looking in mirrors, and took her own narrow spear of glass outside and left it in the corridor.

Rodin told her she must keep herself and her room clean for him, and she began to go the baths on Rue d'Odessa every couple of days, waiting until the railway workers had left. She came to love the building instead of fearing it, because it meant that Rodin would be pleased with her. The pale blue-green tiles that looked like dripping water running down the face of the Bains made her skip. The echoing grotto with its ferns and pillars and classical busts and the feel of the water closing over her head reminded her, somehow, of Tenby, of good days when she was small and going to the beach, days before her mother died, days before things became complicated with Augustus. Days when she was only a little girl with pleasure on her mind.

She puts perfume under her skirt. She picks up the bones that Edgar Quinet leaves all around the room and she scrubs her pale pink tiles until they shine. "Such a respected visitor," says the concierge knowingly. "What do you two do up there all the time?" Gwen tells the old busybody that Rodin is teaching her to draw, and it is true. Very often, they stand at opposite ends of the room, both naked, and each sketches the other. She draws his eyes. Their heavy lids, the pale eyelashes, the eyebrows like wings. She draws his head. The halo of his hair. She traces his outline with her eyes, lingering, sketching the muscles of his neck and shoulders, his upper arms, his chest. The chalk in her hand, the quick strokes, the blunting of his angles with her thumb, his hips, his long, lean thighs and his calves, a slash of red where the ribbons cut into his flesh, his old feet and then back up to the place where his legs come together. She sets aside the chalk and takes up her charcoal, the hardness pleasing between her fingers, watching him watching her, she draws and then has to erase what she has drawn because it's all changed, and he watches her hand circle and circle over the page, the long stiff charcoal wedged between her flesh, the repetitive motion, he watches her erase some part of himself, swallow it up, and he makes a sound that is not exactly a sound and then his own hand moves, and now she must erase his arm, his hand, and she laughs and protests and he exaggerates his movements, makes it harder for her. She comes and winds the black hair around the base of his flesh and she sketches as fast as she can. Out of the corner of her eye, she sees something, she doesn't see something, it's happening all the time now. She hears a meow, a shadow passes over her work, and it's only Edgar Quinet. The cat jumps into the room and springs onto her bed, staring.

"Angel's feet," Rodin says, not looking at her drawing. "Such toes as would have grasped the primordial branches."

"But what do you think?" she asks him.

"Here," he says. "And here and here. This feels alive to me. The light and muscles and feeling all in motion. But here …"

And she? She spreads her legs and touches herself and he draws picture after picture. She has no shame. She would do anything for him. He tells her to dry her fingers on his drawings, and then he folds the papers and pushes them inside his waistband. After he leaves, she pulls the curtains closed over windows that reflect the entire interior of the room, the scattered sheets of paper on the floor, the wadded sheets, the easel with its splayed legs, her.

One day, though he was in his mid-sixties, Rodin carried a heavy box up the five flights of stairs and put it on her floor. "What is it?" Gwen asked, as he began unpacking several pieces of machinery. "Is it a present for me?" She was thinking of the Japanese screen.

"Lie down," he told her, and he cranked the handle on the machine. It made a loud noise and Edgar Quinet hissed and ran for the window. "You will like this, I promise," he said. She had liked surprising Dorelia with twists on their lovemaking too. In some ways, pleasuring could be more delightful for the one who delivered the pleasure. "It's a new invention. I bought one of the first ones, thinking you, my voracious little wife, would enjoy what it does." He laid the head of the machine between Gwen's legs. As the noise rose, she began to move her hips and writhe on the bed. "What is it?" she cried. Her thoughts of Dorelia, of their evenings in Toulouse, fled. "What is it? Oh my God, my Master, what are you doing to me?" She tried to close her legs but he would not let her. "Shit!" she cried, a word she had never said.

"Fuck!" An animal growl came from deep within her throat.

Miss Hart, next door, banged on the wall between them. "Whatever that is, I want some too!" she shouted, and then Rodin and Gwen giggled and tried to be more discreet. "I shall gag you," said Rodin, and he took off one of his long grey socks and ran it between her teeth, and knotted it behind her head and she thought, for a passing moment, that perhaps she was some kind of experiment for Rodin. There was something familiar in the way he tried something and then tried it slightly differently and then changed it again, always looking for a particular effect, always keeping notes, which reminded her of the hours in the studio.

And she wondered, too, if perhaps this was what he was teaching her. To be methodical. To experiment. To test her materials. To keep on trying. She began to make copies of her drawings and to colour each one slightly differently, looking for the subtle differences in form and tone that were induced by miniscule changes. She kept notes. She made recipes for particular shades and recorded them in her notebook. She showed Rodin what she was doing and he nodded his head. "Yes," he said. She did not need to hear any further praise.

He was not much for criticising. He didn't say to think of the Old Masters or say anything like they said in the schools. But in a moment, he could make her see how good or how bad her work was ... if she wanted to do an arm, he told her to make a complete portrait of the arm. Not think of theories or maxims. Simply, to observe the grace of life. Make it without timidity. Not to be preoccupied by details but not to leave gaps.

Though the machine consistently pleased Gwen, often many times in a row, she asked after a few weeks for it to be taken away. "I prefer your hands and your lips and your beautiful thing," she said to him. "Even if I don't always come, it's still *you* that is touching me, and there's something in that." Miss Hart, calling from the other room, volunteered to take the machine away for them, as Rodin might slip, she said. They left the machine outside for her, at the head of the stairs, and the next evening, Gwen heard it start up in Miss Hart's room. Maggie had, by that time, gone back to New York, and Miss Hart, it seemed, missed her.

The next morning, Gwen and Rodin were noisier than ever, wrestling, tickling, laughing, shouting, crying out. The double bed Rodin had bought and had installed for Gwen creaked and shook and hit the wall, plaster fell, and one day, the bed itself broke with an almighty crash. They continued though half of the mattress was on the floor. "For God's sake!" called Miss Hart, banging on the dividing wall. "You torturers! At least share a little!"

Rodin had given Gwen a romance novel, *Pamela*. Instead of reading it after he left, she read a few pages out loud to him, just as she and Dorelia had liked to read aloud to each other after they had made love. Though she opened her windows and held a glass to the wall and tried to listen, Miss Hart could only catch every second or third word, and in her frustration, one day she threw the vibrating machine out of the window and down into the courtyard. "What happened?" she yelled. "Damn it! Don't leave me hanging! Bloody artists!"

The concierge wanted to know what on earth the contraption was and when she found out, she had a repairman come and fix it and she took it into her own room, though she still fined Miss Hart five francs for damage to the houseplants and Edgar Quinet refused to go into the courtyard for weeks.

Lying in her bed, Gwen told Rodin about the children she had made friends with, both the family who waited near her room, and also the much longer line of children near the Quai d'Orsay. Each day they looked thinner and thinner, she said, as if they were not eating. The baby that Renée carried never seemed to grow at all. It could not even hold up its head. He had never noticed them, Rodin said. She must draw those extraordinary families for him. But Gwen never had time to draw the Jewish children. She was, those days, fully occupied with Rodin. On a rainy day, she stood outside without an umbrella for half an hour looking into the window of a jewellery shop where engagement rings were displayed, choosing the one that would look best on her finger. She was no longer sure if it was summer or winter, if it had rained or was sunny, because she was so few times outdoors. She mistakenly ordered a new heavyweight dress in pale green patterned wool, for winter, when it was late February and the temperature was rising.

She showed Rodin the new dress and he put his hands around her tiny waist. "Give me your fingers," he said and he lifted them to his nose and then to his mouth. "You have been touching yourself again!" he said. He took hold of the top of the new green dress and he jerked hard, downwards. The dress ripped open and Gwen fell towards him. The silver buttons Gwen had chosen so carefully tinkled under the bed. "Oh!" Gwen cried. She put her hand up near the neck of her chemisette, but Rodin took hold of that and tore it open too. He pulled the garments down her arms and twisted them behind her, so that her hands were caught behind her back.

"I will give you many dresses," Rodin said. "But you cannot have this one. You have soiled it, ruined it by your behaviour, you bad child. You will get nothing from me today."

"Please, my Master!" begged Gwen. "I tried not to. But it was so hard! I fell asleep thinking of you and when I woke up, I was already in the middle. I couldn't stop."

He towed her to the bed and slipped the twisted dress and chemisette over the mahogany bedpost, so that Gwen was tied there, unable to move.

Rodin often punished her when she touched herself at night. He made her lie on her hands, and sometimes, if he visited her at night, he tied her hands to the headboard and left her there until he came again in the morning. Sometimes she cried a little, but usually she told herself that she deserved such treatment.

Then, when Rodin returned, he would take her forcefully, against the wall, or facedown on the tiled floor, without waiting for her readiness, and afterwards, she would feel the shape of him within her for days as she walked through the streets and sat for other artists. He demanded this of her, this fear.

Sometimes, when she confessed that thoughts of him had filled her head and she had been unable to resist satisfying herself, Rodin teased her, bringing her right to the edge and then backing off, repeatedly, torturing her with waves of agony and desire. “Beg me,” he would tell her then. “Get on your hands and knees and beg me!” And she would kneel at his feet, naked and weeping. “Please my Master! *Oh, mon tendre amant!* Please allow me to come! I can’t bear waiting for one more minute!” Looking down at her kneeling, Rodin would smile and unbutton his trousers. “Perhaps you can earn yourself a little pleasure,” he’d say.

“Don’t do it, Gwen!” Miss Hart would bang on the wall. “Don’t lower yourself to *that*!” Gwen, on her knees, would shake her head gently, very gently. “This?” said Rodin, pulling her head tightly against him until she gagged. “How can there be an end to love like this?” It was love then, and not lust that he felt.

But still she did not tell him that she loved him.

THE ARTIST IN HER ROOM:

It seemed to Gwen that her brother had been right, back in London, that the entire world was full of sex, for now, wherever she went, she saw men and women in the process of luring one another to bed, and every object had potential, a carrot at the epicerie, the stone pestle at the pharmacist's, the leg of a chair, the rumbling of the omnibus and the rocking of the tram. Dogs and cats and pigeons and mice and even butterflies and cicadas and gnats, they were all doing it, blatantly, publicly, right in the street beneath the eyes of strangers. Now, Augustus' party and all their frank talk seemed like a dismal shadow in the face of actual sex, actual love.

"It's so beautiful," she exclaimed, one evening after Rodin had bought her some pink paper flowers from a little shop near the train, and they were sitting on a bench, watching clouds of moths fly up into the air and copulate. "How free they all are to express their love! Why must *we* be so careful that no stranger's eyes fall upon us?" On warm nights, she walked to the Luxembourg Gardens and stripped beneath the bushes, and then lay down, imagining Rodin penetrating her, their love as natural as that of the feral cats that screamed and fought beneath the shrubbery. She rubbed soil into her skin, pressing it against her breasts, thinking it a proxy, since man was made of mud, and Rodin's hands were often full of clay.

Even Edgar Quinet came home one night and made a strange and terrible noise and then gave birth to three little kittens, evidence of sexual exploits and a gender Gwen had been unaware of. Ida gave birth to another boy and then Dorelia wrote her a letter with news that *she* was making a *petit,* and seemingly within a month, she had given birth to the child, Pyramus, alone, in a gypsy caravan up on the edge of Dartmoor. Gwen knew why she and Rodin did not have a child but still hoped that somehow, it would happen. "Don't worry," Rodin had told her their first time. "I'll make sure you don't get pregnant." Though he hadn't used a barrier of any kind and definitely didn't interrupt anything.

"I don't want children," Gwen told Rodin the morning after she got the notice about Dorelia's baby. She erased the memory of Caspar tugging her hair, the good clean smell of him under her chin. She tried to erase her memories of the Jewish children and their hair ribbons but she could not erase Renée.

Gwen had lain awake all night wondering if somehow, Dorelia's baby would have her red hair or her small turned-up nose. It seemed right that *something* Gwenlike should have been transferred to Dorelia's baby. She felt very odd, shy and sad that morning, and within her belly, there was a strange empty sensation. She kept Rodin waiting at her door while she washed the last traces of tears from her face. She did not want to pose for him. "I don't want babies even from you, my Master," she lied. "Do you want children from me?" Cicadas could lay as many as two hundred eggs at a time. She'd read that somewhere. Some species could lay eggs nearly continuously.

When Rodin shook his head, horrified, Gwen felt something slide from her, like Rodin's semen, but much colder. She felt very old and tired. "The drawings I pose for shall be our babies," she declared. "Immortal and beautiful and wise." There were whispers that Rodin had two children with Camille Claudel, an earlier lover who had gone insane. She of the kissing sculptures. That Claudel had had to have abortion after abortion. Her children were being raised in a convent. Rodin refused to see them.

"Marie," said Rodin. He pulled at his eyebrows. "I will be going away again soon. To London. Or perhaps Spain. I am not sure. I am becoming busier than ever. The world never stops bothering me."

"When will we be travelling?" said Gwen, delighted, clapping her hands. "I must have new dresses made. It makes a difference where we will be going. I know you prefer me in red, you bad man. But perhaps I should wear a more modest pink? I have never been to Spain but I hear that it is very hot."

"My dear," said Rodin, and he did not need to say anything more. He travelled often, but never with her. "I will miss you terribly, of course."

"When?" asked Gwen again, but this time, she did not really wish to hear the answer. He did not want anyone to know about their love, except perhaps Rilke. Dear Rilke, who smilingly brought her the most ribald of letters and carried hers back to Rodin. Gwen understood about Rodin's wife. Of course, *she* should not know *everything*. But Rodin hid Gwen even from his friends, as if he were ashamed of her, as if she could not compete with their wit and their brilliance and their wealth. As if she were a common whore.

"Soon," said Rodin vaguely. "I will let you know." The day Dorelia had left for Bruges, she too had said, "I will let you know."

"But what will I tell my ladies?" asked Gwen, meaning the five women she posed for when Rodin did not need her: Miss Hart, Miss Roederstein with her pocket watch and trousers, Germanic Miss Gerhardie with her love for burlesque, the celibate Miss Bowser, and Hilda Flodin, who just the day before had given Gwen a cigarette and then lit it from her own. "Do you know what that means?" Hilda had asked, blowing the smoke out of the window and then inhaling deeply again. "It means I am going to kiss your favourite lover."

"Don't be ridiculous," Gwen had said. "Rodin would never kiss *you*."

Hilda was the closest thing Gwen had to a friend in Paris, and they often talked about Rodin now, racy talk that aroused them both. Gwen had shared these discussions with Rodin, and also her feeling that Hilda was attracted to her. What she hadn't shared was her own disloyal attraction to Hilda, though it was obvious to Rodin.

"Wouldn't he?" Hilda had asked. "Kiss me?" She had smiled. "We'll see," she'd said.

Now Gwen said, "*Oh mon Maître*! You are the whole world to me! Promise me that you won't kiss anyone else on your trip, or if you do, that I will never know about it!"

Rodin looked at Gwen thoughtfully. "Who have you been talking to, my dear?" he asked.

Gwen did not want to say.

"Let me guess," he said, pushing her onto the bed and pinning her body under his. He pressed himself against her, but she lay still and did not rise under him sinuously, like a seal, as she usually did. Gwen did not struggle or attempt to wrestle him off. She did not smile. For the first time, she thought of Augustus here, in her room. Is this all men wanted from her? Did no one value her as an artist, not even Rodin?

"How many guesses do I have before I owe you a penance?" he asked. Augustus. Auguste. So easily confused.

"Just one, my Lord," she whispered, and he sat up again and patted her on the head.

"Hilda, of course," he said then. "But you do not understand what she and I have been talking about, little one. Just wait and you will see. It is not what you think."

"Please, my Lord," Gwen said. "*Please* only love me. Am I not enough for you?" She was not so stupid as to put that crowd of beautiful women waiting next to the studio out of her mind. And many times, when she was trying to explain something to Rodin about her painting, she lacked the words in French and ended up saying something like *I paint to make it pretty on the legs the light with muscles jumping* and his face screwed up in an effort not to laugh at her. If only she was more fluent in French. If only she progressed as quickly as he wished her to. If only she knew the language that other artists used with one another, instead of her own invented words for the things she discovered.

"You are more than enough," Rodin said. He leaned forward and kissed her. "You are very much." He was already putting his overcoat back on and taking up his umbrella. "Sometimes even too much."

"My Lord," she cried as he went down the stairs. "I will send you letters! Leave me your address when you go! You will not forget me because I will travel with you the whole way there, in my words."

He stopped and looked up at her. "I have had special boxes made," he said. He loved her! How could he not? She was sincere, devoted, earnest to a fault. "For your letters. I have ordered my secretaries to lay your letters flat in the boxes so they are not ruined. Your words are very precious to me."

"I will write you more! I will write you hundreds of letters! Thousands! But must you go now?" she said and she put out her hand. Edgar Quinet wove between Rodin's feet and ran down the steps to the street, but Rodin returned to Gwen's room.

A RAG DOLL:

That afternoon, when Gwen, still aching pleasurably, went to Rodin's studio, the concierge gave her a note that said Rodin would not be in and that she should go to Hilda Flodin's studio instead. The curtains were drawn across the tall glass windows in the front of Hilda's studio and it looked as if no one was there. Gwen tapped timidly on the door. "Hilda?" she called. "Are you in?" There was no sound of hammering from inside, but she thought she heard someone breathing just on the other side of the glass, so she pushed the door open and went in.

Inside, the studio was dark and draped with red paisley shawls. Tiny candles stood in tea saucers on every surface, and lit the studio with a mysterious shifting light. Rodin stepped from behind one of the shawls with a sheet wrapped around his waist. He looked like a Roman senator, serious, proud, degenerate. "We'll have more privacy here than in my studio," he said. Gwen laughed. "Mon Maître!" she said. "What will we be doing together that needs such privacy?" Gwen ran towards him, peeling off her skirt and bodice and letting them fall. "Wait, little model," said Rodin, when she pulled at his drapery. Hilda stepped from between the shawls. She was also coiled in a sheet, and she smiled at Gwen's surprise. "It is my wish that Hilda should see our lovemaking," Rodin said, when Gwen crouched, hiding herself.

"No! Please!" she said.

"Don't you want to please me?"

Gwen did, truly. She stood and pressed herself against Rodin, but Rodin pulled her arms away from her sides and turned her body towards Hilda. "My Lord," Gwen said, squirming, twisting in his fists, trying to hide again. "I would do *anything* for you but this."

Hilda came then, and kissed her cheek. "Please, Gwen," she said. "I have been wanting this so badly. Each time you sit for me, all I can think of is our Master deep within you. My best work has been made, dreaming of that image."

"No!" Gwen pulled out of Rodin's grip and buried her face in Rodin's shoulder, but he held her away from himself and shook his head. "For me then," he said, and she slumped against him. Would one woman ever be enough for him? What if they were caught? It wouldn't be Rodin who lost everything.

The crank of the gramophone. The eerie scratch of the needle, the loss of colour in the room. Gwen turned to see two Hildas, one facing her, one not. The Hilda facing her opened her mouth and licked her lips. She drew a hand holding a powder puff slowly across her neck and then down her throat. The crumbling white cross bright on her lunar skin. She lowered her sheet to the ground and stepped out of it and the other Hilda did the same. A mirror. Between the racks of hanging pastel vestments and silver embroideries and shawls there was a huge rococo mirror. The room so claustrophobic, strings of tiny mirrors spinning in the heated air, flashing candlelight, the scratching needle of the gramophone, tentacled spider ferns reaching out from the corners, faintly chiming bells, the melting wax, the smoke. Hilda's damp hair coiled in hooks around her face. Her breasts bound now with a sheer veil, unwinding with each step. Gwen couldn't help herself, she looked, wanting to see the pale nipples revealed, *waiting* for the silk to fall. "Gwen," said Hilda, her voice smoky and stoppered, all sound absorbed by the soft draperies. The veil seemed to fall in single images, below the breast, below the rib, below the hip, below the knee. "Don't turn away from me." Each spinning mirror reflecting a tiny section of body for a moment, a finger, an earlobe, a toe.

Hilda touched Gwen's shoulder and ran her hand down to the

root of her spine. She touched Gwen, again and again, a sculptor luxuriating in a gorgeous physiology, swimming through the arc of the sacrum, the valley that falls between the bones of the iliac spine. Then she moved her hand lower. "You have us all buzzing around you like bees, little lovebird," she said, and with each circling motion of her hand, she shoved Gwen rhythmically against Rodin's body. Rodin's chuckle coming as if from the ceiling and the floor simultaneously, as if from some place far away in dark and distant space. Without warning, Hilda slapped Gwen and she stumbled forward. "You bad girl," Hilda said. "You wanted my Master all to yourself." Rodin and Hilda laughed, and then Rodin nodded his head and Hilda knelt behind Gwen and licked the insides of her thighs, higher and higher, her tongue as rough and barbed as a cat's. Gwen could barely stand. Her legs shook. She closed her eyes for a moment and when she opened them, the flames had created black shadows on Rodin's face, his eyes were huge and black, his mouth a giant black slash. The embroidered shawls tangled themselves together, undulating. The faded eighteenth century priestly vestments ballooned out and sank to their knees. In the corners, Hilda's statues stared from empty eye sockets that looked like hundreds of profaned mouths.

Rodin pushed Gwen down onto a pile of pillows and carpets. "How are you doing, little bird?" he asked. "You were so worried this morning. Do you know now, that I love you?" Gwen looked from him to Hilda. Why did Hilda have to be there? Gwen had tried so hard to be enough for Rodin! Now he knelt over her hips. He slapped her thigh with his cock.

She was so dizzy. They must surely open a window soon. The snakelike shawls alive and jeering, the candles skewing sideways, the light in Flodin's cave demonic. Pale heads floated above the chasubles and thin white hands plucked at the fraying embroidery. Warm brandy dripped on her lips. The edges of the room grew soft and blurred, rose and sea-green and mauve and apricot. Rodin's hand slid between her legs, the sweet slick sound of herself, Hilda's laugh. "A peach," she whispered in Gwen's ears. "A ripe peach that we *both* shall eat. Kneel, Gwen. Rest on your elbows," she said. But Gwen couldn't move. The lights spiralled around her head. She closed her eyes but the room rocked faster and faster. The costumes hung over her, leering, their dark velvet bodies and lace wings leaking perfume, their hangers squeaking faintly. When she opened her eyes again, she had somehow been turned and now kneeled with her rump in the air, leaning on her elbows. Her right hand rested on a nail. The point cut into her. She tried to move her hand but her limb was numb and unwilling.

Hilda lay beneath her, drinking something, making unfamiliar sounds, a muffled sort of crackle. The sound of flesh being licked. "Oh!" cried Gwen, lowering her hips. "Yes!" She only wanted Rodin, she had promised herself she would only respond to him, but her body betrayed her. Each time a shiver ran through her, she drove her hand against the nail, to remind herself that it was not Hilda she wanted. To remind herself that she was not the kind of woman who would sleep with two people at once. She cried out as the nail drove further into the meat of her hand, and Rodin, misunderstanding, stepped behind her. A cry of pleasure so similar to one of pain. The heat from his body scalding her thighs. His hands gripped her hips as she bucked against Hilda's mouth. "My turn," he said, and Hilda rose. He pulled Gwen sharply back against him and plunged deeply inside. Bright lights exploded in her head. A huge wave ran up her back and down her legs. "Oh my God!" she cried out. She fell forward onto her face and Rodin fell forward with her, covering her slight body with his great weight, shuddering and cursing.

Augustus, no little child but himself a great and hairy man, running his hands over her, panting, begging, rolling her over and ripping off her nightgown, taking her from behind, crushing her against the pillows in his London flat, whispering, "I know you like this, you little slut." And she did. Oh, how she did! A new series of tremors, even stronger than the first, passed through her, and now, ashamed, she screamed out, "No! No! Stop! Please!" As Rodin thrust into her, even as she cried and struggled, she could not stop imagining that somehow the man raking her shoulders, biting her neck, twisting her breast in his paw was her brother.

"You have never been done this way, have you?" whispered Hilda. "You are still a little girl. Half a virgin."

This was the painting Gwen would paint now, if her flaws were displayed on a stage on a giant canvas behind her. She outlined it on the pillow with her unhurt hand. Rodin kneeling in front of her, his club-like prick in his hand and her, sprawled on the floor, her legs flung apart, a sound like the ocean rising from within her. His head pressed against her cave, as if he were drinking from a great mottled shell. It would not be Rodin she painted between her legs, though. It would be Augustus. The only difference between the two paintings the colour of the man's hair. Rodin's hair white. Augustus' hair red. Even their names the same. How had she not seen it before? And with that, she crushed her hand against the nail and bore down on the tiny metal spire until it entered her flesh, tearing through the delicate muscles she had worked so hard to build.

She must have tightened, for Rodin gasped and then pulled back and rammed into her so hard that she thought she might split in two, so hard that she felt something within her shatter, and then he let his full weight fall on her and his legs jerked and his breath came out in a violent gust smelling of garlic and fried smelts. "This little bitch is almost perfect," Rodin crowed to Hilda. "She could do it for money!"

Gwen's whole body throbbed. Every part of her felt as if it had been burnt by a brilliant fire, a fire that had torn off her skin and left her bare. "Don't get up," Hilda said. "I have food." Rodin began to snore lightly on Gwen's shoulder. She tried to slide out from under him, but her hand was still pierced by the nail.

Hilda brought out oysters and pineapple and fenugreek leaves. "Come on," she said, and she woke up Rodin. "There's still pleasure to be had." She fed dates mixed in milk and cinnamon to Gwen. She poured some liquid into a glass and drank from it and then passed it to Gwen and then to Rodin. Schubert's "Ave Maria". That was what had been playing. Gwen's head swam. Her chest burned from the alcohol, and she cradled her hand in her lap. It hardly bled. On her palm, a single bright red spot.

Hilda lit a cigarette and sucked on it, then handed it to Gwen. "What is this?" asked Gwen, for it did not smell like tobacco, but sweet, in the way that a decaying corpse is sweet. She took the cigarette between her lips and drew in the smoke. The odour made her feel even dizzier, cloudier, the world roiling and faint, but it also made her hand less painful, so that now the piercing did not remind her of Augustus. When she looked at Rodin she saw only Rodin, only an old man that she loved without an afterimage of her brother. She no longer noticed Hilda sitting next to her, or the heavy antique clothing murmuring or the dark mouths gaping in the corners.

Rodin lay next to her, awake, fondling himself and she reached out to assist, but Rodin pushed her hands away. "Put out that drug," he said to Hilda. He rose and from behind the shawls, he took a sketchbook and his charcoals. "I'm too old to continue. Now I want to watch you," he said to Gwen. "And Hilda. I want to draw you making love."

Gwen looked at Hilda and a sharp lance of pain ran from her hand to her elbow. Weren't they finished with her? Would she not be allowed to get up and get dressed and go home and tend to her wounds? It was all she wanted. But Hilda opened her mouth and showed teeth the colour of cooking oil. "Oh, Gwen," she said, the teeth coming together and the tongue rising and falling and the lips flapping. "We are here merely to do our Master's bidding. Will you not have me when our Master wants to see our lovemaking so much? You liked me well enough before."

Gwen shook her head. She squeezed her palm and the drop of blood in the centre swelled and then rolled, very slowly, to the edge of her distal palmar crease, the place where her heart line ended.

"If you really loved him," said Hilda. "You would do it."

"I want one," said Gwen then. "I want one of his drawings." She sat up and looked around for a piece of cloth with which to wipe her wound.

"Give your little bitch what she wants and I'll get started," said Hilda, gesturing towards the sketchblock but Rodin frowned and shook his head.

On the floor next to Gwen's legs lay Rodin's gold pocket watch, opened and forgotten. The minute hand jerked forward. No ticking was audible. After a moment, the slender hand twitched again. Did the golden case also jerk a little, did it shudder as the minute hand moved forward? Or was she mistaken, had the hand moved backwards? Two golden orbs, linked in the centre, dark to light, burnt umber and ultramarine, phthalo blue and permanent rose as it warmed up and breathed its first breaths. *Was* it breathing? Something whirred, the watch emitted a shrill cry. A foetus of a watch. Its long gold chain snaked across the floor and ended between Gwen's thighs. She drew the cord towards her and wiped her blood on the heavy interlinked circles.

"I want one," said Gwen again, her voice softer, her tone quieter, though what she meant to do was not diminished. "To remind myself of today. Of everything." She pulled the chain towards her, and lay the watch on her stomach. The gold was warm. Its ticking could be felt through her body. She squeezed her torn palm and let droplets fall onto the engraved case. I wish to turn your sketch of me into a painting, she said or didn't say to Rodin. A giant man rutting between her legs, a man with two heads, one white, one red, a single spine and no eyes at all.

Rodin looked down at her. He hummed a few bars of "Ave

Maria". Give me my watch he said and when she drew it to her breast and clamped its golden mouth to her nipple, he bent and yanked it out of her hand, the chain sliding through her fingers, link by link, until it was all gone, until she could no longer hear the ticking. No, she said, no, I don't like you, no I don't want to do this, no no no, this is all wrong, this is not what I wanted. My lover wants everything from me but wants to give nothing of himself? Not even one of his paper children? Had this always been true? Gwen struggled to her feet though the room held her down and breathed on her and demanded that she remain.

One, Rodin blurted then. Just one. He does not want his lover to have even *one* portrait for herself? Then she is merely an experiment. Any woman could have taken her place. Any body parts. Hilda's busts with their gaping mouths and their hollow eyes, succubi perfectly poised, clay bodies built at the perfect height for him to rape.

Gwen felt intensely cold. Even her shins, which never, in her whole life had felt cold, were chilled.

"May I have a blanket?" she asked, folding herself onto the floor again. She shivered and shivered and her teeth chattered. Rodin sketched her shivering, he sketched her cold flesh, the raised bumps on her nipples. Though a woollen cape hung from the rack next to him, he made no move to pass it to her.

"Our Master does not like drapery on his women." Hilda knelt between Gwen's legs and ran a piece of peeled ginger between her folds. She could smell but not feel the stinging root. Rodin smiled at Gwen. She looked away. Augustus' face hid within Rodin's whiskers. She had wanted to stay standing, if only her shaking legs could have supported her. She had wanted to run. Instead, she covered her eyes with one arm.

"Please, my little model, won't you do this for me?" It was the voice Rodin had once used to seduce her in his room, soft and tender, so similar to Augustus' voice as he broke down her resistance, as he claimed her body as his territory.

The sober women walking through the streets, their baskets in their hands, their crisp white collars and cuffs starched and ironed fresh every day, they were not like her. *They* didn't walk through the streets holding the pounding shape of their lovers within them. *They* didn't walk home carrying their upright baguettes imagining they transported their lover's member, salivating at the thought of that springy dough in their mouths; *they* didn't walk the streets leaking cum. *They* didn't have bite marks on their breasts, shredded dresses in their wardrobes. They walked alone with their own thoughts, their own wishes and desires.

"Put your arm down," Rodin ordered. His anger, too, just like her brother's.

Gwen lowered her elbow and glared at her Master. She slowly lifted her hand, palm outward, so that he could see the mark of her violation. I don't want this, leave me alone, it's too much, she said or didn't say, but Rodin flapped his sketchbook at the two women and said, hurry up now, don't make me wait, and Hilda bent and began to hum, her mouth against Gwen and the room moved and Gwen no longer lay on the floor, the real Gwen that is; instead of lying on the floor she was rocking near the ceiling, as if she were in an invisible boat or a cradle, watching the Gwen who lay below. Neither the Gwen above nor the Gwen below spoke so that anyone could hear. Rodin drew rapidly, changing paper each time Hilda changed position. The room was so hot and airless. He looked up at the ceiling and she thought perhaps he saw her there, but no, he looked right through her, absently stroking himself. Even at rest, he was not a small man. Now, she saw the Gwen that covered her head with her arms was pleasing him. At least one of them was pleased. Hilda bent lower over Gwen, her head moving quickly. The Gwen on the floor struggled not to groan, not to arch her back. She had wanted to be the best model for Rodin. She had wanted to be *perfect* for him. Now, the Gwen who watched didn't care.

She wasn't thinking about the women in the street anymore. Instead, Augustus filled her. For all that he had harmed her, at least he was honest in his lechery. At least, when he said he loved her, he meant it. The Gwen below shouted out loud, and pressed her fingers into herself, making tiny animal noises. "Oh, Augustus!" that woman cried, and in her thrashing, she felt the edge of some fabric and pulled it and covered herself with her skirt.

Hilda rose from between Gwen's legs and wiped her face on Gwen's thigh with two quick motions, right and left, as she might clean a palette knife on a rag. Then she jerked Gwen's skirt away and tossed it in a corner. "No coverings," she said. "You'll ruin it. Why do you think we are doing this? It's not for *your* pleasure, despite your moaning and carrying on. This is for Art."

Rodin clucked his tongue and continued to sketch.

"Keep going," he said. "Switch. You do her."

If my mother could see me now, how would she draw me?

Throughout everything, Gwen had always thought that her mother would still draw her as she had, back then, when she'd been little, an innocent child with dimples and a head of shining curls, chewing on the end of a blue pencil. Even when her original drawing had become crushed and stained and feathered and worn, Gwen felt that her mother was following her, smiling on her efforts. But now, the Gwen who bobbed at the ceiling saw a pale blue sketch of herself climb out of the other Gwen's body, as if a slim blue skeleton were emerging from her chest, one bone at a time. The blue child peeled itself away from the Gwen that lay on the floor, tearing itself free little by little. The drawing shook itself off. It frowned at that other Gwen and then lay back down over her as if she could protect the woman underneath, and they became, together, a double image, the mature Gwen and her six-year-old self fitted together, arm to arm, leg to leg. But then the child disappeared under Rodin.

"No!" cried the watching Gwen, reaching out for the little girl. Only a small part of the child could be seen, an arm, a few curls of hair, a toe. She was trapped under the great man, being entered by him at the same time as he entered the older Gwen. And with each of Rodin's thrusts, as if he were a giant caoutchouc, his body first smudged the child's blue lines, then erased them. Stop, cried the only Gwen capable of speech, the watching Gwen, but all that was heard in the room were the old man's grunts. Please stop. I'm begging you to stop. Now, the child lacked fingers, and her head, which appeared every so often from beneath Rodin, had no mouth, no nose, no ear. Her hair was missing on one side. Now each time the old man plunged into her, whole limbs disappeared, and the watching Gwen screamed. When there was nothing left of the small blue child, as if she were suddenly boneless, every part of Gwen's body collapsed in on itself and she fell down from the ceiling and into that other hollow version of herself on the floor.

Gwen looked up at Rodin and bared her teeth. "Get off me, you bastard," she hissed, and he patted her on the head. "Little hellcat," he said. "You know you love this." Then she kneed him hard and beat at him with her forearms and Hilda pulled the Master away and they both stood at a distance, panting and laughing.

"Your turn Hilda," he said, pushing her forward. "She'll do you now."

Gwen, reluctant until then, sprang up and dragged Hilda down, kneed the other woman's legs apart and speared her with three fingers. "More?" Gwen said, and before Hilda answered, she jammed in another finger.

"More," groaned Hilda, spreading her legs wider. She was not wet. She was acting. Gwen looked up at Rodin again. His hand raced across his paper. His mouth hung open. Hilda was tall and muscular, her torso as ridged as a man's. She twisted from side to side, screwing her body down onto Gwen's fist. "Your thumb,"

Hilda gasped. "This is why we are here. Don't disappoint him."

"For you, *Master*," Gwen spat, then forced her knuckles deeper. With a hoarse shout, Hilda swallowed Gwen's entire hand. Her eyes glazed over and she rocked herself from side to side on Gwen's fist.

Rodin, watching from the corner, rubbed himself against the edge of the table, mewling like a cat. In the candlelight, his hair shone with a ruddy tone. Image after image fell from his sketchblock. *Mine*, thought Gwen. I have earned them. She reached out to claim a page and saw that it was only a sketch of her legs. She took another paper and another and began to cry. They were all of disembodied legs and pubic arches. None of them contained a face. Her body, her eyes, her mind, had all been completely erased with the child's.

STREET AT NIGHT:

Now, every day when Gwen had to return to the studio to model for the Whistler monument, she begged Rodin to make arms for the sculpture. Now, when she saw Rodin's assistants taking a leg, a foot, a hand, a thumb from the drawers, she wanted to run at them and smash the shapes, grind them under her heel until they returned to dust. "Why do you have so many?" she asked Rodin. In answer, he asked her to pose with her legs spread and one heel under her buttocks and he sculpted her legs with her sex bulging forward and he cut off the rest of her body and then he displayed this horror in a gallery and let it be whispered that it was her body, *her* sex. Strange men bent and touched her bronze cunt and laughed.

"Please," she begged him. "Just make the arms." If she could have found other work without starving, she would have.

There was always some reason that Rodin couldn't create the arms. Not right then. Perhaps never. Didn't she think she looked better that way? She didn't. She couldn't. Didn't he understand how demeaning it was to be simply a body? Didn't *she* understand how there was nothing *but* body? Augustus at least drew her face. *He* had listened when she had spoken about the children. But Rodin refused to talk about them at all.

On her way home from Flodin's room, leaking, sore, sad, she'd seen her line of children and ran to them only to see that more than half had vanished. "No!" she'd screamed. "No!" The remaining children had stared at her, their little mouths open. The wind had blown. Birds skidded sideways off the roofs, and fluttered in disarray before clawing their way back onto the tiles. In a distant street, something metallic fell on the cobbles.

She'd dropped her own key onto the cobbles and knelt to find it. Her back bowed, her hair fell loose over her face, the stone was cold under her palms. Rodin would not help her save these children. He couldn't see them, the way he couldn't see her.

Now, when she thought of Rodin, he reminded her of the worst of Augustus, but unlike Augustus, he didn't acknowledge her talent, her artistry, her humanity. She stopped blocking her memories of children and began to block her memories of Rodin. Not a great man at all. No. She had travelled so far to get away from Augustus, and yet Rodin was only an older French version of the same man, cruder and crueller.

Then, in the late mail, Gwen got a letter from London. Augustus, Dorelia, Ida and the five children had all decided to move to Paris, and would be arriving in a few weeks, in the bitter summer of 1905, and did she have any suggestions about where they should stay? She took out her scissors and cut the letter into tiny pieces and threw it out onto the roof tiles. She would have liked to shred herself.

Rodin, misunderstanding Gwen's upset about the arrival of Augustus, suggested that she move to a new unfurnished room, bigger, with more light, a little closer to his studio and further away from where Augustus would no doubt rent. He offered to buy her new furniture, a shelf, a bed with a mattress as soft as the one he slept on in Meudon, sheer voile sheets, or silk ones, a desk to work on, paintings for her walls. *Whatever you give me it will not be enough to pay for what is gone.* In the end, she asked for a room with high windows on a nicer street, a fine etching from two hundred years earlier, the little sculpture he had named *Joan of Arc* in her honour and Rodin's favourite cane-bottomed chair. She bought herself three small ferns for her window ledge and a tiny brass watering can and she tried not to look when she passed the street where the whores plied their trade. I am not, she told herself. I am not I am not I am not.

"Why are you panicking? Your brother can't harm you now," Rodin told her one afternoon as they lay in the new feather bed he had purchased for her. He pulled her head onto his chest and she shuddered at the rubbery texture of his skin. "I will protect you." What had become of her desire to be an artist? What had become of the Gwen who had moved to Paris to build her own skeleton of ambition? Was she, after all, only Rodin's whore?

Gwen turned and hid her angry face on his shoulder.

"Thank you, my Master," she whispered in his ear. "But, I am thinking of something else, right now."

He begged her to tell him what it was, so there should be no secrets between them, and she snorted for all that would remain unsaid, and then suggested that perhaps Dorelia would be willing to replace her, to make the third in the type of threesome that he had so enjoyed with Hilda.

"I know her," she said, and then blushed for the implication.

"She is pretty, you say?" he asked. "And young?"

But then Gwen changed the conversation, for it was clear that Rodin did not care who he slept with if he would take even a woman he had never met, as long as she was pretty. Gwen's own selection by him had nothing to do with her ability to paint or to sculpt. This was not what had drawn him to her. It was simply because she was pretty in a certain way, and young. He was only infatuated with the *shell* of her, the husk that held the real and unknowable Gwen.

After Rodin left, Gwen opened the windows to release his scent and she tidied her tubes of paint and she lifted the cloth off her canvas and she began to paint the two-headed man, but her heart wasn't in it. The portrait was not in her style. The harsh colours, the whiff of freak show was all Augustus. He'd eaten his parrot, she heard, before sailing for France. Just paint your emotions, said Rodin. After a few minutes, she put down her brush and picked up her palette knife and she ran it through the canvas, just below the twin heads.

Now, in the evenings, Gwen stayed up late, reading books she had borrowed from Rilke and writing letters to Rodin, describing what she had learned.

"I want to be clever," she explained to Rodin when he complained about the flood of letters, sometimes two or three a day. "I want you to be proud of my work." Rodin had two types of women, she had noticed. The *pretty* type and the smart type. The pretty type of women revolved into and out of his life. The smart type stayed as regular fixtures. She was determined to be seen as the smart type.

"I *am* proud of you, little sister," said Rodin. "Most especially when you are *painting*. I would prefer that you spent your time painting rather than scribbling your missives to me, no matter how delightful they may be. It has been an age since you showed me something new. What are you working on these days?" He put his hand on the cloth cover to her easel as if he would lift it and Gwen sprang at him.

"No!" she said. "You can't look." Her palette knife still dangled from his throat.

Gwen told him then that most mornings she lay in bed, dreaming. She told him she wanted to paint something that was truly her own work, in her own style, and she believed it would arise out of the intensity of her feelings for him, quite naturally. He knew she'd sketched him but he didn't know she hadn't painted anything besides the gargoyle in close to a year. She told Rodin that between their afternoons and modelling and writing him letters, she did not have the time for a major work. She was as busy as any wife, she said. The *real* truth was something she did not say, not even to herself: she did not have the heart to begin a new painting. Now, for her, Art was covered in dirty fingerprints and dried body fluids and it reeked.

"But then, what's this?" asked Rodin, pointing to the covered canvas.

"I have begun a self-portrait," she said, making it up in her head as she spoke. "Something similar to what that man, Picasso, might do, a simple interior in very pale tones, like a Japanese print, with a woman, me, sitting next to the window, sewing." All the body parts included. And the face.

"When will you show it to me?" he asked. His hand still lay on the cloth, his blunt fingers pleating its surface.

Gwen shook her head. She took her earring out of her lobe and reinserted it. She did not like to think of Rodin's rejection of her art. Her palette knife, a blade of deep crimson steel, didn't really run through his throat. It ran through her heart. She would never be able to show him her serious work. Perhaps it was true what they said, that nothing grew in the shade of a large tree.

She had thought that she had made a wise decision to work for Rodin, a decision that would be conducive to her growth as an artist. While it was true that she had learned how to *create* pain and joy and desire and fear in a model, she had not yet learned how to paint it. She had learned how to draw quickly, she could capture expression and gesture and energy, but she was not a practising artist. She was some man's toy, instead.

"It's not ready yet. I will show you soon."

That afternoon, Gwen lifted the cloth herself. She looked at the ruined canvas. In the end, she had hacked at the gargoyle's neck with the palette knife until she had almost decapitated him. She took the painting off the easel and slid it under her bed. Then she took out a new canvas, one much smaller than she was used to, and put it on the easel. She felt as if, by stabbing the painting, something had been released in her. She opened her window and the curtains began to blow in with the gentle breeze. The time rang three. From down the street, she heard little children's voices. The school had let out for the afternoon. She thought about Renée and she thought about Ida's children, and about Dorelia's little baby, who she had never seen. She thought about Rodin's golden watch. She thought about the thin blue-boned drawing of herself as a young girl. She thought about the odd empty part inside of her that was not a woman, nor yet a man, the neutered place that could, despite everything that had happened to her, still paint something beautiful.

She angled her wardrobe door so that she could see herself in it, sitting next to the window. She laid out a sewing hoop and a needle. Working in china white, she made some basic outlines, planning the final shape of her portrait. She tilted the door a little more so that she could see, behind her on the wall, Rodin's portrait, the first she had ever made of him. It was perfect, even though she had learned new techniques and greater skill from Rodin over the previous months. Yes, he was brilliant, but she too had talent. She smiled to herself. Rodin would see that she would be a perfect partner for him, someone intelligent who shared his understanding of the world, his beliefs about art and beauty and love. Who was even sympathetic towards his unusual passions. Not merely a toy. One day, one day soon, he would look up and discover that his little model was also a great artist.

Later, when that portrait was finished, she began another one, this time painting herself reading the book *Critique of Pure Reason* that Rilke had loaned her. She made herself diligent, collected, capable, calm. She put everything Rodin had taught her about drawing into this second portrait, and then she glazed it with everything she had learned about passion and pain and disquiet and loss. A year might have passed while she waited for an opportune moment to show Rodin her painting, looking forward to hearing his compliments. Though she did not like to paint and still struggled with hands and motion of any kind, she knew that her composition was good and the concept would please Rodin. In the corner of her room, she found a snail shell, and she stooped and picked it up. The animal had fled and the shell was empty, a coiling maze within. She held it to her ear, but it appeared the ocean, too, had vanished. She thought, when Rodin saw her painting, he would be impressed.

When drawing, I must not only have a knowledge of the human form, but also a deep feeling for every aspect of it. I must incorporate the lines of the human body, and they must become permeated with the secrets of all of its contours, all the masses that it presents to the eye. I must be able to feel each plane at the end of my fingers. All this must flow naturally from eye to hand. Only then can I understand. What is drawing? Never once in describing the shape of the mass may I shift my eyes from the model. Why? To be sure that nothing evades my grasp. No thoughts about the technical problems of representing a body on paper can be allowed to arrest the flow of my feelings about the flesh, always from eye to hand. The moment I drop my eyes, that flow stops. I must try to see the figure as a mass, a volume. The object, always, is to test to what extent my hands already feel what my eyes see.

But a few days after Gwen moved into her new room on Rue Saint-Placide, on the day when she had planned to show Rodin this portrait, an American woman visited Rodin's studio and kept him so late that he missed his appointment with Gwen. Claire, the Duchesse of Choiseul. She had huge buttocks, a tiny waist like a hornet, a mound of teased red hair, and grog berries bloomed on her nose. Everyone except for Rodin knew she couldn't possibly be a duchess but she ran on and on about all of the important people she knew, and all of the artists who had painted her portrait. "You will sculpt me too, won't you, Monsieur Rodin?" she said, pushing up her weighty breasts with her hands, purring. She did not wait to be invited, but draped her arm around his shoulders. A body. Not a brain. "Oh, my dear! We are going to be such great friends!"

After she ate anything, even a grape, she ran to the toilet to vomit, and blamed it on her caesarean. She wore hats with feathers so large they were at risk of flying away. She painted her lips. She painted her eyes. She painted her nails. She painted the truth. She danced the bourrée, a high-kicking folk dance from Auvergne that somehow seemed like a cancan when she lifted her feet and waggled her rear. She talked and talked and talked and could not be stopped. She was closer to a music hall girl than a duchess.

Gwen hadn't even fully unpacked in her new rooms and the door wasn't locked when Augustus showed up, banging on the door and demanding to be let in. "I'm *home*!" he shouted. "C'est moi! Votre cher petit mari!" Edgar Quinet's tail fuzzed up. Gwen's tail, if she'd had one, would have fuzzed up too. She sat very still in her cane-bottomed chair by the window, slowing her breathing, thinking only of the children in the street, Renée in particular. The girl still reminded her of Dorelia, a younger Dorelia, with cropped black hair and a dimple and slanting oriental eyes, but without the prickly bits. Though the physical similarity wasn't the whole story. She couldn't quite put her finger on where the resemblance truly lay.

She had begun spending time each day, reading with the Jewish girl, discussing ideas. Gwen was teaching Renée to draw, just as she had taught Dorelia, though the Jewess was afraid to touch the tubes of paint and disliked the smell of turpentine. Gwen's mother had taught Gwen to paint in a room full of light under the gables of their old house. She'd laid out the colours and squeezed a little of each, in sequence, on a board, and allowed Gwen to try out whichever she liked. *Patient.* That was the word for the way her mother had been. She'd quietly sung "Ben Bolt" and "To the Great Ships Down" and "Fair Olaf" as Gwen made her first painted lines on paper. Gwen's own dedication to the Jewish child wasn't altruistic in the way her mother had been towards her. If Augustus or Rodin *did* show up, Renée would be there. A hedge.

"Gwen!" shouted Augustus again. "I know you're in there! I can *smell* you! I can hear les soupirs d'une femme se caressant." He rattled the handle and the unlocked door sprang open and Augustus strode in.

Gwen closed her eyes and pretended to be sleeping in her chair. On the back of her eyelid, images of their last meeting: a hand on her arm, a shoulder, a corner of a bearded face, a bottle of wine, blood on an edge of a sheet. She couldn't move. Was it a possum or a bear that played dead?

Augustus lifted her eyelid between his thick fingertips and peered into her eye from an inch away. "You're faking," he said. "You were always horrible at it. Come on, don't you want to come and see Ida all bloated with a new little beast? We'll get some sausage on the way, some beer and some bread. You can climb all over Dorelia, if that's what will tickle your fancy. I'll share. Give us a cuddle, then."

He put his arms out, expecting her to step into them. "Be careful!" said Gwen. But he pulled her up to standing without even a glance at Renée, and he pawed Gwen's bodice and pressed himself against her. "The child!" said Gwen again, pointing. "It's not fitting …" She turned her back on Augustus and opened the window and leaned out to breathe something that wasn't haunted by his stench. She could not, could *not*, feel anything for him without betraying Rodin. She could not feel anything for him without betraying herself.

"You won't fob me off," said Augustus. "There could be an elephant in the room and I'd still have you."

"I have a beautiful view," Gwen said. She was ashamed that Renée saw her like this. "In the courtyard. See that little boy?

He's the concierge's child. He tortures my cat, Edgar Quinet, and the concierge does nothing to stop it. Such a cruel little brat." Augustus hugged her fiercely from behind, hauling at her skirt, devouring her neck. "I'd like you to meet my friend, Augustus, if you'd leave off for a moment."

"I've found a studio," he said, gripping her jaw in an effort to turn her face towards his. "Less than five blocks from here. We shall be neighbours again, you and I!" When he saw he could not move her, he smacked her on the rear and she fell forward, hitting her forehead on the window frame.

"*Will* you listen?" She whipped around and kicked out at him, hard, striking him in a place that brought tears to his eyes too. "Get your hands off me. I am not your *property*." But where was Renée? The door of the wardrobe was slightly ajar. It was better for her to hide from Augustus. He was dangerous. And Renée looked so much like Dorelia.

"You're the only one in the whole world who knows how to handle me!" he laughed, but he stepped away from her with his hands in the air. Gwen pushed the door to the wardrobe shut but it immediately reopened. "Ida and the kidlets are going to stay by themselves on the Rue Dareau. I just signed on rooms for Dodo and her two bubs, behind the cemetery, near your first flat. She must have gotten confused and thought you were still living there." Gwen tried to close the door again, but there was strong resistance from Renée. "Has she not had a letter from you, explaining that you have moved?"

Did Dorelia try to rent a room near Gwen on purpose? And why wasn't she living with Ida? From Ida, she'd gotten the impression that Ida and Dorelia had been *very* intimate. It would be too complicated if Dorelia should suddenly show up and expect to be readmitted to Gwen's bedroom, as if nothing had happened. Such an incestuous family. Why *had* the Johns come to Paris? In the crack between the door and the frame of the wardrobe, Gwen could see Renée's ivory face:

stark, brittle, furious.

Augustus prowled around her room, picking up objects and laying them back down again. He swooped past the easel once, twice. He was obviously intrigued by its little cloth cover. He stopped at her desk and picked up the second page of a letter she was in the middle of writing to Rodin and read it out loud.

I had the intention of going to Rue de l'Université without being called since I have waited for you for so long. Now it's a quarter past one. I still have the thought that you might come before work until it reaches a quarter past one. But how can I go to Rue de l'Université without an invitation? I would be like a scared puppy.

Augustus snorted. "God! How women write to their employers! I should be ashamed to be so abject," he said.

He replaced the letter and flicked through a book that Rodin had marked for Gwen and all the bookmarks fell fluttering to the floor. Edgar Quinet darted out from under the bed and pounced on them. Augustus gave the cat a kick with his boot. "Scat!!" he said. The good little cat clawed his trousers, raking his leg through the cloth. From within the wardrobe, a growl.

"What? Is your damnable cat just like you, Gwen?" Augustus roared. He knelt on the floor, fishing under the bed for the cat. "Where's your broom? I'll give the beast what for!" But Quinet was too fast for him and ran behind Augustus and out of the open window and down across the slates, just before his hand touched the gargoyle canvas that Gwen had forgotten under the bed. "Blast!" said Augustus and then he threw himself into the wicker chair.

The door to the wardrobe creaked and swung slowly open. Augustus swivelled to look at it.

"So," he said, completely ignoring Renée, who stood perfectly framed within the open door. "You have a double bed now and there are dents on both pillows … who's been visiting you?"

"Renée," said Gwen. "But she doesn't sleep over. The cat

sleeps on my other pillow." She stood directly in front of a sketch she had made of Rodin, naked, standing with his feet splayed, and she worked at the pins that held it to the wall. It was for this reason that she had not tried to stop Augustus when he reached beneath her bed. "And I am getting old and need more space to stretch out." She was thirty.

It would be terrible if ever her brother suspected her of anything with Rodin. It would terrible if he recognised the dreadful bronze legs. Her earlier calm began to slide from her. There would be no end to the gossip, with Augustus gleefully spreading most of it himself. And Rodin would be furious at her lack of discretion.

"You and the women. So now it's Renée," said Augustus. "I have no idea why you don't adore the males of the species, like every other woman. *Won't* you give your old brother a kiss? We could get inside your wardrobe and close the door and no one would see."

"No!" cried Gwen. Renée stepped out of the wardrobe and walked towards Augustus. "Go back!" Gwen cried again. Her whole body convulsed. She put up her hands to cover her eyes.

"You were never so fussy in the past," he said. Renée went straight to the chair where Augustus was sitting. Then she sat down in the chair, directly on his lap and sank right through him.

"We are too old for that now," Gwen said quietly. "And you have two wives and hundreds of children." Augustus and Renée turned to look at her at exactly the same moment. She saw Augustus with one eye, and Renée with the other. She tilted her head to the left. Augustus came into focus. When she tilted her head to the right, Augustus vanished, and she could only see Renée. Behind Renée, through the window, Gwen saw a long red banner unfurl with a broken black cross on it. When she moved her head back to the left, the scene through the window was the same, but there was no red banner. She moved her head, back and forth, both fascinated and horrified. She was, most definitely, crazy. In the end, she moved so that she could see Renée and not Augustus, Renée and the long red banner.

Something in her odd twitching reached Augustus. He tilted his head backwards in the chair and closed his eyes. He sighed. She was not sure, but there was the tiniest glint of something underneath his eyelid, trapped underneath his eyelashes, something shiny. He sat up and wrapped his arms around himself. "I'm cold," he said. "Why is your room always so bloody cold?"

She could simultaneously smell *his* rank odour, something like a feral animal, a fox, or a wolf, and *Renée's* own odd scent. In a single chair, both Augustus and Renée. A split through the fabric of the world. She felt her eyes being lifted up, to look out beyond the window, beyond the strange twinning. She could hear the tramping of many feet, boots, a military step. She struggled to remember what they had been talking about and thought it would always be correct to talk about his narcissism. "Ugh. Even when we aren't talking about you, it's still all about you."

"Well then," said Augustus, rising, pale streamers of some translucent matter sheeting off his body. "Won't you at least come with me and say hello to Ida and the babes?" Renée remained seated in the chair, her chin in her hand, an odd look on her face, as if she had been stung on the lip by one of the tiny bees that made their home under the eaves.

Gwen was convinced that she should go to visit a doctor. She wished she were well and ordinary; how she longed, in that moment, for a quiet home with a husband and children and washing on the line, and a tea kettle singing on the hob. Renée lifted her head and smiled at Gwen. Outside, a loudspeaker played a military march, but when Gwen looked at Augustus, the music stopped instantly. It was not good to be different. It was not pleasant at all. There was something wrong with her. She had a tumour. Brain damage. A psychiatric illness. She had been deceiving herself. She nodded to Augustus and moved as though through dense underbrush to get her umbrella, and quick as a wink, Augustus engulfed her in a second hug that almost strangled her. “Can’t fob me off!” he said, laughing and mussing her hair, pressing his lips to hers. “Best brother ever!”

“Get off me,” she whispered. Her hand had clenched automatically when Augustus touched her and now the drawing of Rodin she gotten off the wall was crushed. In the tussle, she passed the paper to Renée. “I’m glad the whole family is together again here, but please,” she said, “I’m not used to company anymore. I’m not used to *you*.” Again the long stare between them. She straightened her back. “I need space. Time.”

“When will you show me what you are painting?” he asked.

She did not want to show him how her work had advanced, but Renée pulled off the cloth and Augustus turned back to look at the small canvas.

“Oh my God,” he said.

He didn’t say anything else for perhaps ten minutes. He pulled the chair over to the easel and sat down in front of it and leaned forward to within a few inches, examining her brushwork, the tiny bubbles in the surface that seemed to trap and diffuse light, the muted colours. Renée stood at his shoulder, but faced Gwen and smiled at her and tapped her forehead and made the universal sign for craziness.

“It’s good,” Augustus said. “It’s … well … you know yourself how good it is, Gwen. But why is it just a room? Even if you can’t afford an model, at least you could paint yourself in the room.”

“But I am,” she said. “You just can’t see me.”

He stared at the painting, leaned closer. “I suppose, yes, that’s true. Some sense of yourself at any rate. It’s as if the room is waiting for something. Or perhaps someone.”

She nodded. “I really wish I’d been able to –”

“Just be happy with it,” he said. “I know you aren’t ever happy with your work, but this might be the best thing you’ve ever done." Renée nodded, but then stuck out her tongue at Augustus. "It's not finished."

Augustus turned to look at Gwen. Her hand was over her mouth, smothering a giggle. She felt rosy and happy and knew her eyes were sparkling and she also knew he knew, right at that moment, that something had changed for her.

"What's going on?" he asked. He was no worse than Rodin and possibly better.

"Do you think that there could ever be people," she paused and corrected herself. "*Children.* Children who are somehow in two places at once?"

"Yes," said Augustus immediately. His own devilish crew were notorious for being in two places at the same time, but he couldn't have known what she'd meant. Still, Gwen smiled at him with a blistering smile. She wasn't crazy. It was all possible.

"Do you know something?" she asked him. "I love you so much sometimes."

He looked at her again. She knew her face was clear and her clothing was of good quality and of recent manufacture. A man's silk umbrella leaned against the wardrobe. Gwen's room was very large, larger than Augustus', and it was furnished with simple but well-made furniture. On the wall over the fire was an etching by Albrecht Dürer; she'd say it was a very fine copy. Augustus walked over to take a closer look, puzzled. Her etching did not look like a copy because it wasn't.

"Where did you get this?" he asked, touching the paper. Renée shrugged and Gwen put her finger to her lips.

"One of my painter ladies," Gwen whispered, all the mirth drained from her voice. The temperature had changed in a split second. Tiny silver frostblossoms began to form on the windows. She could not meet Augustus' eye. "The lady couldn't pay me, so she gave me her etching." Despite the rime on the glass, Gwen was sweating. Augustus' face folded like a ruler and he squinted at the etching.

"*He* must have owed you a fortune," he said flatly. The pronoun hung in the room. Renée clapped her hands and danced a tiny jig, and Gwen pressed down on the girl's shoulder, to quell her delight.

"I don't remember," said Gwen. "It's pretty, isn't it?" She spoke as if she had no clue of the etching's value or provenance. She ignored his suggestion that a man had given her the etching. Renée shook her off. Pimples rose all over Gwen's tongue as it flapped inside her mouth.

Augustus turned from the etching and looked slowly around the room again. He stared at Gwen and frowned. "You're seeing someone," he said. She was surprised to see a flush rise up his neck. Jealousy? "Someone *rich*. There's someone been coming here. I just know it. Is it the beast on Rue de l'Université? Not Rodin? I'll be keeping my eye on you, sister. If you won't tell me who it is, I will find out for myself."

Augustus liked my painting, Gwen wrote to Rodin that evening. *I had planned to show it to you but now I must finish it quickly as he claims to have a buyer for it already. Why didn't you come today? Why do you hurt me so? You are like a little child that loves to torture small innocent animals.*

Neither before or now or later are solid, she wrote in her diary. *Time is a human invention, as ephemeral as light.*

Gwen was still posing for the Whistler monument, and now Rodin was also making a new bust of her. As she stood, with her knee raised awkwardly above her head, the Duchesse of Choiseul looked over the pile of recordings and the old-fashioned gramophone. "How the great man owns such rubbish is beyond me," she said. The next day, she came in with a new machine and new recordings, replacing Rodin's classical music with her own tawdry cakewalks and sultry singers. She had boxes of wine and champagne carried in and the empties piled up inside the Norman wardrobe and rutted in the corners, multiplying faster than rabbits. Kneeling down so that Rodin had a superb view of her mountainous cleavage, she cranked the gramophone handle and then draped herself in a shawl and danced for him. As she danced, she removed gloves the colour of new butter and dropped them in his lap, and then she removed a handkerchief from between her breasts and dropped that in his lap too. Gwen waited for her to drunkenly unclip her fake red hair and deposit *that* in Rodin's lap. Rodin had a horror of the unreal. Had he noticed the ghastly fake bun or been aware that the Duchesse had already gone grey and that her red hair, unlike Gwen's, came out of a bottle, it would all have been over in a moment.

Gwen, naked, cold and in the Whistler pose, fumed. The Whistler monument still lacked arms. Rodin was besotted with the awful bitch and had no time for such niceties. *The Influenza.* That's what all the staff called Choiseul. In her letters, which Gwen now wrote twice a day, she complained about the Duchesse and about Augustus' suspicions about Rodin, but her complaints went unheard. She wrote to him about the children and asked him if he believed in ghosts but he ignored that letter too. It was as if Rodin no longer cared what Gwen said, whether she wrote that she loved him or was angry with him, whether her brother lay with her each night, or told the newspapers about their affair. It all seemed the same. It was enough to make Gwen spit. People whispered that the Duchesse had drugged Rodin.

Rodin, abashed, dabbed at his statue of Gwen, looked at the Duchesse as she swirled between him and Gwen. He smiled weakly, added a piece of clay and then removed it, sat down again. The music was deafening. "Perhaps you could lower the volume?" he asked, but the Duchesse twirled on, as if she had not heard, obscuring Gwen with her outstretched shawl.

"Come, come," she said to Rodin, heaving her chest as if she had actually *done* something fatiguing. Rodin couldn't take his eyes off her cleavage. Gwen coughed. He glanced at his skinny little model and then back at the shuddering mountains. "Too much work makes for a very dull Jack. Surely that's enough for today?" She offered to take Rodin out to dinner, to introduce him to her important friends, and Rodin, like a chastised child, took off his smock and washed his hands.

"My Master," called Gwen, still naked, draped with the heavy entanglement of the linen sheet. It had been only weeks since Gwen and Hilda and Rodin had lain together in the same sheet in Hilda's studio, next door. It still *smelled* of them, for God's sake. Rodin came back to her.

"Yes, my little Marie, my little sister?" He smiled at her, a real smile without a trace of worry, and she frowned back.

"Monsieur Rodin! We must hurry!" called the Duchesse.

"When will you come to visit me?" Gwen asked quickly, in a whisper. There were still things to learn about drawing. "At home? My little affair misses you." She glanced downwards, to let him know what she meant. Rodin slipped his hand beneath the drapery and squeezed her little affair absently, as if it were a rubber ball. Or the teething ring of a baby.

"Monsieur Rodin! I must insist!" screeched the Duchesse. "My car is already here!"

"I cannot … just yet," Rodin said to Gwen. He sniffed his hand.

"Dorelia …" began Gwen.

The Duchesse stood in the doorway, beckoning impatiently with her perfumed, velvet glove. Her diamonds blinked with malice. "Write to me, dear Marie … I …" But he did not finish that thought, before the Duchesse had her claws in him and was dragging him away. "Ha ha! Hahaha!" she laughed. "Why *ever* do you talk with those skinny young things? Nothing between the ears but sawdust! Just pay her and let's be on our way. Important people are waiting for you."

Rodin put his hand in his pocket and pulled away to return to Gwen. She felt her last shred of self-respect slip from her shoulders, slide all the way down her body, tumble onto the floor and shatter. Not in front of this woman! But indeed, Rodin took out several coins and laid them in Gwen's palm. She let them fall through her fingers, clattering and chiming, rolling under the wardrobe. Rodin's face crumpled.

"Marie ..." he said. "I must ..."

"I could perhaps share you with Flodin," said Gwen quickly. "But not with *that*." She inclined her head towards the Duchesse and then, once again, the Duchesse stood between them, bulging her evil breasts, pushing Rodin away with the sheer force of her corsetry.

Gwen mixed the ink with a spoonful of water and stirred it with the butt end of her pen. She changed the nib and dipped the new one into the ink and pressed the point into the paper. The light burned low. Gwen's pen scratched and scratched. Her stomach growled. Edgar Quinet, curled around the candlestick, tried to catch the nib.

My Lord,

I felt despair in the street when I left like that without even having been kissed. I thought about killing myself or rather, I desired that someone would kill me. I have not had this thought for a long time, or a despair like this. It seems that all the courage and patience that I've struggled to cultivate has left me. I thought that you would at least try to make me happy; my little letters should have shown you a bit how desperately I need your affection. But today you did not even kiss me. You paid me in front of her, as if I am a harlot to you. An employee.

And you forgot, again, to ask me about my painting. I am not only your model ...

When she finished the letter, she folded it in half and then, holding her pen in her left hand, she carefully wrote Rodin's name and a fake address for herself on one side. She put the letter in her pocket and then she opened the windows and leaned out on the window ledge.

"Come, Quinet," she said, patting the parapet. Her cat jumped up but did not go out onto the slates. "Look how beautiful all of this is. I should be the happiest artist in the world." She sighed.

Fireflies rose above the crumbling roof tiles, tiny pinpoints of light against the navy sky and the pale smoke rising from thousands of chimneys.

"Maybe happiness is only for a moment," she said. "And isn't something that lasts. Maybe, if we knew in the moment that we are happy, that this is it, that things will keep on moving and changing, that at no other time will we ever again get to experience this joy, then even right at that moment, we could not be happy." She put her hand in the cat's fur. Far down below, the concierge and her husband murmured as they lay in bed. An occasional word in the husband's deeper voice rose clearly. Strawberries. Cotton. Fourteen. Beer. But their voices got quieter and quieter and then fell silent. The whole city, all of Paris, a ghostly blue ruin.

Within days of the shame of the coins, the Duchesse had sent away Rodin's faithful assistants, Maillol and Despiau, and when he asked where they had gone, she said that they had run off with some of his bronzes and that for the life of her, she *would* make his studio more efficient. Now, when Gwen arrived for work, she had to hand a slip of paper to the concierge, signed by Rodin, saying that he required her that day. The work on the monument fell further and further behind, to the point where Rodin sent the terrible armless plaster maquette to the Paris Salon, instead of the full-scale marble statue he had intended.

Each time Gwen disrobed to pose, the Duchesse came and sat in the wicker chair and cranked the handle of the dreaded gramophone. Sometimes she invited her society friends to come and sit with her and watch Rodin as he attempted to sculpt Gwen's body. "One knows how these little sluts are. So grasping. And Monsieur Rodin is such an innocent. She could steal everything from him in a moment!" The women all laughed in their high fake voices and waved their long coloured nails in the air like scimitars. "My dears," whispered the Duchesse, "have you seen how Monsieur Rodin modelled the whore's legs?"

No longer could Rodin stay late at night with Gwen, working by candlelight. It wasn't very long before he abandoned work on the monument, since his work had always been connected with passion, and without access to Gwen, he was unable to access the passion that drove his best work, and Gwen too, exhausted, angry, jealous, could not paint.

Rose Beuret appeared for the first time in the studio, shuffling in wearing a pair of old carpet boots that had no heels, and a dress from the middle of the previous century, and she hissed at Gwen. "I know all about you," she said. "And you, I don't mind. But *that* witch!" She spat towards the Duchesse. "She, I wouldn't use to sour the cream." The Duchesse, for her part, asked Rose to polish her shoes for the following morning and offered her a few centimes, as if she were a servant, and the faithful old woman sat on the floor after they left, in the midst of all of the dust and crumbs of clay, and wept.

Gwen's heart flinched. She pitied Rodin's first mistress and also respected her, for her ability to allow Rodin his freedom. In many ways, she was similar to Ida. Gwen pulled Rose up from the litter and brushed down her dress. The old woman's hair fell over her face. Gwen slid a pin from her own chignon. She held it out in front of her for a moment. It was a humble U shape made of cheap metal. Nothing special. The old woman, too, stared at the pin, and then Gwen took a handful of the grey hair and smoothed it back into the bun and twisted the pin to secure it. Nothing was said either before or after.

But in Gwen's heart, an unbearable weight lingered. For if Rose was Rodin's Ida, then she, Gwen, was his Dorelia. In order for Gwen to have the happiness she imagined with Rodin, this patient old woman would have to die.

Rose patted her hair and then turned and walked towards the tables where the maquettes were kept. Each day, she faithfully wetted the pieces of clay, and re-covered them with canvas, making sure they would be ready for Rodin when he returned. Rodin had once told Gwen that Rose had been an artist too, when she was younger, but she had given it up to support him and now all she had left was this, the quiet rounds in the deserted studio.

Gwen watched her. It was almost unbearable. The slow and painful drag of the canvas across the clay, the clink of the brass bell inside the pail as it refilled with liquid, the religious anointing of the earthen heads with sprays of water, the old woman's sighs and the *shuff shuff* of her slippers.

There was something mesmerising about the whole process, but something eerily familiar too. It was only later, as she ground her ink and lit the candle and bent to write yet another letter to Rodin, it was only then, when she heard the scratch of the pen across the paper with a sound that was so reminiscent of the shuff of the slippers, that Gwen laid down her head and let her own tears flow.

PAINTING 7:

Some things I have found out but it is satisfactory to have them confirmed and to be able to express them well. For instance, were I to say "A Cat or a man, it's the same thing", you might look surprised. I understand that it is only an affair of volumes. The physical object is of no importance.

We are the same. Rose. Me.

But I will be God's little artist: a seer of strange beauties, a teller of harmonies. A diligent worker.

I will not give up.

SELF-PORTRAIT WITH LETTER:

Sunday

My heart is hurt by disappointment. You know that without you, I cannot exist. This week, it was difficult for me to work. I was very tired from all of the noise from the women. Do you know that I earned forty francs, but I have not been paid yet, so I am very hungry and you know how that affects me!

Last Thursday night, I dreamt that you were with me, pleasuring me as you do, and I came, but only in the dream. I did not wake up. How I wish that you were with me, to make me come but when I am awake this time, so I can feel you all through my body.

I am suffering and I am going to start to die if you do not come quickly to my room.

Your Marie who waits for you.

Monday

Miss Hart told me that she would be terrified if I go out tomorrow. Because of the strike, I am going to stay at my place and give my room an extra cleaning.

I'm not going to put this small body which belongs to you in danger and oh! I love my life! Too much maybe, but it's your fault because it's you who made me know pleasure and happiness.

I dreamed again last night of you, that I went into your workshop and you took my hand and the little tremor of pleasure when I touched your hand woke me up. I wish I had not woken up so soon! But also last night, my brother came to visit. He managed to get a spare key from the concierge and when he opened my door, it woke me up. You, better than anyone, know how this upsets me. I do not wish to be desired by him. I am no longer sure who I wish to be desired by, except by you.

Oh my dear Master, still I thank you for letting me write to you, morning and night. Oh my lover, my Lord, I wait for you to enter me again – my body trembles from pleasure – my body which is linked forever to yours now and to no one else. Please protect me and preserve me as you promised.

From your Marie.

Tuesday.

My dear Lord,

I hope you have a good fire this evening. I lit mine a while ago but I'm still cold. I will be happy when tomorrow evening comes. It's hard for me to write in French, but oh, it's natural for me to want to be with you, and to write to you, because you are the man I love. I have begun a new painting of my room, and I am sad that you are not in it. I have put your wicker chair in my painting, and I am sitting there, waiting patiently for you to come and take me, the way that you do, the way that I like.

It's good and charming and satisfying to be in your workshop, even when you are far from me and I am far from you there. If you become cold towards me, though, my heart will break. I don't know why this thought came to me, because I have so much happiness these days, and I am full of joy right now, writing to you. Perhaps it's only because I am so happy with you, that I fear the loss of my happiness.

There are weaknesses in me that you have graciously pardoned in the past, my Lord, and as time goes by, more of these are revealed. I like it better that you know them than not.

When we love, we want to seem as we are, not more or less. There is great pleasure in knowing that you know me well, despite everything that has happened to me.

I'm going to read a bit from the books you gave me now and pretend that you are here listening.

I hope, my Lord, that you have the indulgence to read all the

things a heart full of kindness and inspired by your love could write in these outpourings. I would not be this happy if you did not read my letters.
Your Marie.

Wednesday
I received your card this evening, my Lord, when I came back from my session. It gave me great joy to think that you had taken the time to dictate the letter to your secretary. I was so glad that you had written to me, that I made a drawing of myself, holding your note, so you should see how pleased I was to receive it.

At first I thought I saw your writing on the envelope but now I see it was not that, but only a note from Monsieur Rilke, letting me know that I will be in receipt of some wood for my fire. I am most grateful, my Lord, for anything.

I do not wish to complain at all, my Master, but between us there is a great love, and it is hard to bear that I see you so little now. Please do not leave your little Marie alone, at the mercy of any person! I have been doing as you said, bending, going to take the baths, cleaning my room, and I tell myself that this would all make you happy with me, but in my heart I know it's not enough. If only you were here to see it all with your own eyes. If only I could hear it from your lips. My little affair is not yet tired! Come soon to tire it out, my Master!

My dear Lord, come to kiss and take me! I know that you read my little letters in different states of mind – with impatience or with kindness – but please please, never forget your little model. You are the beauty and the pleasure of my life. I always have a pain at the bottom of my heart when you leave me for too long, My Lord – I am sorry to say – I feel a bit famished and abandoned.

Good night
from,
Marie

Thursday

My beloved Master,

Yesterday that woman looked at me with such menace while opening the door for the first room at your studio, my Lord. I fear that she may be reading my letters.

I am going to Luxembourg Gardens. Thinking about this woman puts me in a fever. In the gardens, I still think of you calmly, my Lord, and my pestering thoughts are at a distance when I am there.

Think of me when you are in bed. I kiss your portrait before I turn out my lamp. Do not go to bed too late, my Master, or you will be too sleepy to think of me.

From,

Marie

Friday

The only thought that prevents me from being completely ill is that you will come, now that I ask you, the first day you return from Belgium with that woman. You do not want to make me die, do you, my Lord? I was so disappointed when you did not come today, that I ran to your workshop. I am weak like a shadow after waiting for you all week. It was then that Monsieur Rilke told me you and she had gone to Belgium.

Oh my dear Lord, let me have confidence that you will come to me the first day that you return.

I'm going for a walk tomorrow in order to be pretty for you Monday or Tuesday or whatever day you return. And if you don't come soon, I'll know I'm not wanted in life,

Marie

Saturday

Did you know that I have been banned from your workshop? I am not just one of those models who you may ban whenever you wish. I am an artist, just like you. There is a note at the concierge's, in that woman's handwriting, that I may no longer enter. So perhaps you did not know of this. I am sure you couldn't have.

Please do not forget your little model (and so much more!), Marie

Tuesday

I was angry this afternoon, that I could not see you. Me, who belongs to you! You see everyone else, but not me! You see that woman constantly!

I was seen in your garden today.

I didn't see you. I arrived late in the day because I was lost first in the Clamart woods. I thought I would somehow remember the way from the previous time, but of course, I was not awake then, and today I had to run out quickly from my room, without getting proper directions. Afterwards, I got lost in the country at Meudon and somewhere else. I believed I would arrive very quickly if I took the train to Clamart – only now do I know the road. If I had remembered the road then, I would have found your pavilion very quickly, but I did a large loop instead.

I think you were at dinner when I was looking in your garden. I climbed from the bottom of the cliff to the top. People could not see me like that. I stayed hidden until it got a bit dark and then I dared to cross the little path, hoping you could see me in the darkness. It wasn't completely dark and I saw a part of your garden that you did not show me the last time I was at your house.

I was astonished. Truly, it was very beautiful when it appeared in my sight all of a sudden, at sundown. It was the copse of trees and the statue.

When I was looking at that, all happy, I heard voices coming from your museum or close nearby. I tried to distinguish your voice from the others. But all of a sudden, I was scared because I heard steps coming out of your museum and heading in my direction. I was afraid and fled.

Your, Marie

Thursday

Today I saw you in your garden at Meudon!

I wasn't close to you. I was in the bush to your left when you look out at your garden, next to the door. You know the laurel bush that descends and separates the wild land from the other garden?

I trembled so much when I saw you that I could no longer stay standing and for a moment I desired that you would see me and the moment after, I was afraid that you would be angry – it's like that all the time with us! Sometimes I took steps towards you, but then I hid myself afterwards. Oh! I was happy and afraid at the same time. Oh my Lord, your dog came to call you to the table, I think, and you spoke to it and then you left.

When I did not see you anymore, I became distressed – I came closer – I wanted you to see me.

I went up until I stood at the gate into your garden.

When the sun went down, I became brazen and I even crept up and looked through the little holes in your door, and I saw you seated at the table – it was indiscreet, I know, but the daylight had already ended.

I left when all the lights went out in the house.

Oh! I was so alone, my Lord! I did not like to think of you lying in our bed with someone else in your arms.

My Lord, let me write to you always! Don't become bored of my letters. I think that if I was not allowed to write to you, my Master, I would die. But I don't want to write them if they annoy you. That would make me ashamed.

Marie

THE PILGRIM:

Gwen felt by art alone she could alleviate some of her pain. Painting, though hard for her, took her outside of herself and allowed her to see the world as others might see it. Instead of seeing one world, the hard one she inhabited, she was able to see it multiplied, as if in many mirrors, each world different than this one, each part of something infinite and ungraspable.

When she felt most sad, most alone, she opened her window and sat opposite her little table and her wicker chair and drew the empty room. Many mornings, waiting for Rodin, she was sad, for he didn't always come. Many mornings, she sketched her room with a golden sheet of light falling through the window, slantwise across her table. Sometimes, she set her red teapot on the cloth. Sometimes, she added the book she had been reading. Once, Rodin left his furled black umbrella, and the next morning, she included that in her drawing. Once it was her summer parasol and many times, her blue cloak lay draped across the chair. Her pencil did not move quickly. Her hand did not skate across the page. First the window with its gauzy curtains, then the eaves, the wallpaper, the mouldings, then the table, the chair, the floor. Always the same image. Only when she had sketched the entire room and Rodin was not sitting in the chair, one foot crossed over his knee, an unlit pipe in his hand, only when the room had been proven, by her drawing, to truly be empty, could she allow herself to cry.

On evenings when she thought she might see Rodin, she walked to the Rue de l'Université, cleanly dressed, and stood in an alcove opposite the Dépôt des Marbres, waiting. If Rodin walked out unaccompanied, she came to him and they walked together to the train under the deepening night sky. "What did you draw today?" he asked her every time. "I am still drawing my room," she said and he sighed. "You should go outside. You should draw the children in the street. The doves. The cats in the alleys. The women with their brooms. The old soldiers. There is nothing living in your room."

It was not exactly what he had meant to say, and yet it was true, too.

And one night, several months after Rodin had begun to walk out with the Duchesse, he caught hold of Gwen's hand and said, very seriously, "I will not look at another drawing of your room. The next time you come to me, show me something lively."

For many days after that, Gwen roamed the street, looking for people or animals to draw. She could not get back into her former habit of sitting for the lady artists in the morning. She did not want to stay in her room knowing Rodin wouldn't come. And the fresh air was good for her. She brought home some spring peas and a few new potatoes and boiled them on her gas ring and ate them with butter and licked her fingers afterwards. She had been hungry and she had surprised herself with that knowledge.

She did not initially think of drawing the children though she still spoke to them each morning. They looked unbelievably wretched. They were not fit subjects to bring to Rodin in their mismatched shoes and their collapsing socks. But one morning, near the Quai d'Orsay, she noticed that the line had grown *much* shorter. "Where are Gerard and Michel?" she asked the oldest child, Francine, a girl of about seventeen.

"They left on the train."

"But who will watch the little ones?" Gwen asked. Her brushes jutted from the pocket she had pinned to her skirt and the children nudged one another and pointed when they thought she wasn't looking. "Why don't your parents come to help them?" Never once had she seen these children with a mother or a father. Now that she thought of it, she realised that there were fewer and fewer people with the flickering lights left in Paris. It had been a long time since she saw *any* adults with the glowing stars, and even amongst the children, only the youngest ones were left. Francine was an exception.

"Where did *everyone* go?" Gwen asked. She pulled a brush from her pocket and two other brushes fell out into the street. She stooped and picked them up and wiped them carefully on her skirt, before replacing them. The children's legs were almost *transparent*. The brushes a ruse to take a closer look. There had to be somewhere to file a complaint about the appalling neglect.

"On the trains," said Francine again.

"But then they would still be *here*," said Gwen, pointing at the ground with the brush. "And they are not. Which trains do you mean?"

"The ones that go away and don't come back," the young woman said, and Gwen stared at her. She seemed to be telling the truth. As Gwen watched, Francine put down her bundle and opened it and took out a hard piece of baguette, which she broke into three shards and shared with her siblings.

"Are you hungry?" asked Gwen softly. She had fresh figs in her own little bundle.

"No," said Francine. "We have enough." She was proud. But they *were* starving. It was clear to Gwen now that something dreadful was going on, some appalling crime was being committed against these children. Francine's wrists stuck out of the ends of her cotton blouse and her bones stretched the skin taut across them and now that Gwen was noticing, she couldn't *stop* noticing. Francine's face was blue and her eyelids were the colour of crushed mulberries. Her belly stood out. Gwen saw the cruelty of hunger, that the children all appeared to be fat when, in fact, their legs were so thin that under their loose skin, she could see the momentary ruddy blush each time their hearts beat, and the grey flush of pallor half a second later.

"I can't carry this anymore," said Gwen, laying down the figs in their red checked cloth. "It's much too complicated when I am painting. I don't have enough hands. Would one of you carry it for me?" She could deliberately forget the bundle and they would eat the fruit so it did not rot. It was not much. It was not enough. But she could come the next day. She would come with the police.

The children looked at each other. "No," Francine said. "We can't leave here until the train comes. We are waiting, you see."

"But what are you waiting for?" asked Gwen. She nudged the bundle towards the children with the toe of her boot.

"Our parents," said Francine. "When the train comes, it will take us to our parents." What sort of parents left their children alone in the city? Were these parents working in the countryside each day and then returning at night? She thought of all the times she had accompanied Rodin to the train station in the evening. Had she seen any of the children then? No. It couldn't be allowed, this outrageous abandonment of children. En masse!

Many times, Gwen had sat on a wall looking over into the Seine and people had gathered about her, saying, "Poor girl! All alone on the streets of Paris." But she was an artist and thirty years old and had regular work. She had food and a room all to herself. She *wanted* to be alone in the streets of Paris. Or, at least, she didn't mind so long as Rodin came *sometimes* to her rooms. And truthfully, she was never *really* alone anywhere. She had a family. She had Miss Hart and Miss Roederstein and Monsieur Rilke and even Augustus would never let her starve. But these children?

"How long have you been waiting?" she asked Francine.

"A long time," Francine guessed. "Years?"

Gwen had already been in Paris for more than two years. The first day she had arrived, these same children had been standing at their corner. It had been early spring then and now it was almost winter. Then, she had passed the children without noticing them, but slowly, over the years, she had come to see them as the most important part of her daily landscape. It was them and them alone that called out to her every morning. "Hello, Madame Marie!"_"How beautiful you look today!"_"Are you going to your artist?" Where once she had been afraid of their Jewishness, now she thought it might be the very thing that bound her to them, for she was just as invisible as they were. And there was something about the way they stood all alone in the street that reminded her of her own isolation.

"You've been waiting here for *years*? I am going to inform the authorities!" Gwen said, and at that, Francine laughed a hard sardonic laugh that did not match her age, and all the children snickered into their hands and bounced on their toes and bumped into each other, as if she had said something funny rather than threatening.

"It is the authorities that sent our parents away in the first place. This is not news," Francine said. She spoke slowly and very clearly, as if Gwen were hard of hearing or exceptionally stupid. "Soon they will send us away too." Why were they all so apathetic? Why did they all stand there like wraiths, uncaring, unconcerned, more interested in a small twist of paper blowing along the street than in normal childish things? How could they be so immune to this absurd situation?

"Even if the *authorities* don't care about the welfare of little children, I *do*," she said. "And I will ask Rodin to help you," said Gwen. Each time she looked at the children, she felt a strange sensation in her lower abdomen, a cramping similar to that which she got once a month, a dragging and pulling. "He knows everyone. He must know someone who can find your parents." She thought it might be what some women felt in the days before they gave birth. She had heard about it from Ida, before David was born. Contractions.

"*Auguste* Rodin?" sneered Francine.

Gwen couldn't see the children's faces, for they turned away from her now and pinched one another. Smothered laughter. Whispers.

"Yes," said Gwen. Francine seemed wary of her. She also turned away and told her younger siblings to look at the boats passing by in the Seine. "Look!" she said, pulling them over to the parapet. "Tugboats!"

"*Auguste* Rodin is dead," she said over her shoulder.

"No!" cried Gwen. A small skiff passed under the bridge, not a tugboat. For a moment, fear had shot through her, but the news of Rodin's death would have been everywhere. There would have been black flags hanging from half of the windows in Paris. Gwen looked across the Seine. No black banners. But for a moment, three long red banners with broken black crosses at the ends. She blinked. "He's not dead. You are mistaken. I saw him a few days ago." More laughter from the children. They thought she was one of those women who wandered the streets, shouting at strangers and insisting that there were elephants in the dirigibles of Santos-Dumont that were going to be placed on the spire of the Eiffel Tower.

"Perhaps," Gwen said, trying hard to sound ordinary, trying to sound like someone's genteel mother, "you mean a different Auguste Rodin?" Tomorrow. She would bring help.

"Per-haps," said the girl, but she did not turn around. A long barge slid by with kegs stacked on its deck. The children waved but the bargeman did not sound his horn. He was looking straight up to where they were all standing. Gwen waved her hand and the bargeman pulled a cord and the foghorn bellowed. "I meant Rodin the artist. The sculptor. Who did you mean?"

Cicadas ticked down next to Seine and a pleasure boat with a high mast and a flapping canvas sail stalled and blew its whistle. Shopkeepers cranked open their awnings after the weekend. Gwen felt the earth shudder beneath her as the bridge lifted. She put her hand into her pocket and took out her sketchbook and she flicked through the pages until she found a drawing of Rodin.

"The artist," she said. "This man." She held out her sketch. "The man who made *The Poet*, maybe you know it as *The Thinker*? In front of the Panthéon? The famous Rodin."

"He died," said Francine, tapping the sketch with her finger. "A long time ago. More than twenty years ago. He gave his house to be a museum. It's right next to the Invalides."

"No," said Gwen. "He is not dead. And he does not live next to the Invalides. You are talking about a different man."

The girl snorted. "He didn't live in that house. That was his workshop. He lived in Meudon. Everyone knows that. Even Jacques knows that!" Her little brother nodded his head in agreement.

The earth shuddered again as the bridge swung down. After a pause, the cicadas resumed their ticking. Boats kept on sailing back and forth as if everything were ordinary.

Gwen looked at the little girl. She looked closely at her clothes and at the clothes of the other children in the line. The newsboy on the corner blared news of a new war. *Les operations militaires. Les forces allies approchent des faubourgs de Rostov. La guerre aero-navale à l'ouest. Une declaration de Gandhi. Un premier train de prisonniers liberes arrivera prochainement.* There was a story about a monster, a doctor who had killed many people and stolen their suitcases, and then tried to burn them in the oven of his house.

A tickling shivering thing ran up Gwen's arms and down inside her clothing. She scratched at herself. The ticking of the cicadas rose to a crescendo and then came to a stop. Another boat whistled. The river slid slowly vertical. Her body canted to the left. Everything in front of her was blurry and only from the edge of her eye could she see. She tried to take a step and fell to one knee. Over everything lay a blurry orange haze flecked with black. All she wanted, she suddenly realised, was Augustus.

There had never been a newspaper stand on the corner.

"Don't play with me!" shouted Gwen and the smaller children crouched and covered their heads. She looked at them, at their pale pathetic faces turned up in fright, and then she backed away and ran through the streets to the children near her own home, children who would not deceive her. "Renée!" she said, angrily, catching the oldest girl's arm. "What year is it?"

"I don't know anymore," said Renée. Gwen snorted and stamped her feet.

"I am *not* mad!" she said. The terrible sounds from the Asile de Nuit assailed her. "What magic is this?"

"Perhaps you are senile and you have forgotten everything?" said Renée. "That happened to my grandfather. He couldn't remember which year it was. Or even the day. He used to put on my grandmother's dresses but the buttons wouldn't fasten and then he would walk out on the streets like that and we would have to go and get him. Sometimes the gendarmes brought him home. He had purple eyes, circles around his eyes I mean. You are lucky not to be Jewish, because they put old people in the back of a truck that has gas in it and then you are dead. Don't get in the back of the trucks, that's what they say. Trains are safer." She looked at Gwen's horrified face and blinked. "But you don't look old enough to be senile. My grandfather was fifty when they shut him up in the truck and you look like you are only twenty."

What imaginary world did these children think they lived in, where an old man could be gassed? "I'm thirty," Gwen said. "And I'm not senile."

Renée nodded her head. She patted Gwen's arm. "You'll be alright," she said. "Maybe you need a cup of tea?" She fished around in her pocket and brought out a heel of bread. "You haven't been eating."

"What day was your mother taken away?"

"It was a few weeks ago, in the morning," said Renée. "The first night after the full moon. In July."

Gwen passed her hand over her eyes. What day had it been when she was at the Velodrome? Surely not mid-July? The face of the Jew at the Velodrome, his mouth open and his eyes rolled back, swam in front of her. Why was she remembering him now? *She* wasn't the crazy one.

Gwen jammed her hand into her pocket, searching for the portraits of her mother and her but when she pulled out her hand, she found a circle of black hair tangled around the papers. With a cry, she threw the packet away from her, into the road, but when she opened her hand, the hair was still there. Now a crowd had gathered around them and some women began to talk of calling the police.

"Call them!" cried Gwen, rounding on the women. "Let them come and find out the whole dreadful story! These children have been abandoned with no food! They've been here for years!"

"Tut," said one of the women. She was short and round and had a clean white apron tied around her middle. "These girls get strange when they lose a baby." She drew closer. "Did you lose your own baby?" she asked.

"What?" said Gwen. A baby? Why did the whole world want to talk about babies when she could never have one? "I'm not talking about myself."

The woman attempted a smile but in the middle, her lips collapsed like a soufflé and her expression became rather more sad. "I had a miss myself," she said. She put out her hand, palm up, as if to calm a flighty horse.

From a distance, the roar of a police motorbike. Gwen covered her ears and turned around in a circle. The crowd muttered. The Jewish children stared at her with huge eyes. A word floated in the air. *Salpêtrière.* A burly man pushed his way to the front and crossed his arms over his chest. Another word. *Hysteria.* And another. *Lunatique.* The blowing of a horn, *pee-PAA, pee-PAA.* "Shhh," Gwen said, putting her finger to her lips. "Shhh. You'll scare them."

"Come on, dearie," said the woman. "You'll be alright. Let me just take your hand. What's wrong, now, won't you tell us?"

Gwen pushed the woman away and grabbed Renée's arm. "Do I seem strangely unfashionable to you?" she whispered. "Because *you* seem strangely dressed to me. Your skirt is too short, and your shoes are all wrong. Even your haircut."

"Well," said the little round woman. She had fallen onto her bottom. "Excuse me! I was just trying to help!" Several people helped her up. A police officer swerved across the street on a black motorbike with a sidecar. The sidecar shaped like a coffin. Painted just behind the window, a red cross. A minute later, four officers came barrelling around the corner pushing a cart with two large back wheels and a single, smaller swivelling wheel at the front.

"Don't worry, now." One policeman unlocked the handcuffs that hung from the wagon. Another opened a hood and tightened the bolts. "We'll get her off the street. Make way for the professionals." Two of the police officers came towards Gwen. They carried small cudgels. "Don't get too close. She might bite."

Sleeping in Renée's little brother's arms, a baby. It had not aged a day. Gwen pushed aside its nightgown, and there, attached to its belly, was the dark umbilical stump, two years after she first saw Renée in the line.

Gwen put her finger to her eye. "I see," she said. "I see how it is now." She laughed and the crowd drew back. Renée looked at Gwen sadly. She had pushed her siblings behind her and now stood with her arms outstretched.

"It is *both* years," Gwen whispered. "At the same time."

It was fortunate that Monsieur Rilke was on his way to bring her a last note from Rodin before the poet left for Germany again. He saw Gwen being strapped onto the cart and claimed her. The police argued with him. A danger to the community, they said. Hysterical, they said. Hungry, Rilke said. English, he said. Rodin's model, he whispered.

They took her down off the cart and apologised to her, though she was still wild-eyed. She crouched down and grubbed amongst the papers in the gutter, retrieved a small bundle and lodged it in her pocket. Money was exchanged and warnings issued.

"I won't tell our Master," Rilke said to Gwen as he helped her up the stairs to her room.

"Did you see the children?" Gwen asked.

In answer, he offered her a piece of cheese.

Augustus was called and he trundled up the stairs and leaned over her bed and stared into her eyes. "Children from the future?" he said. "Why not? My poor dear girl, if anyone could see them, it'd be you." She sighed and rolled over and curled around his great forearm.

"Gussy," she said. "We are just the same, you and I. Thank you for believing me. It gets so tiring trying to convince people."

"What is it like then, the future?" he asked. "What are people wearing?"

She told him stories about the children for hours and he sat in the wicker chair, quietly smoking until she was drowsy. As he walked out the door, Rilke turned to him and with a quizzical look, tapped his temple. Augustus shook his head. "No," he whispered. "She definitely sees them."

GIRL WITH A BLUE SCARF:

A few mornings later:

"I don't think I should talk to you," Renée says. The baby, on her shoulder, cries thinly, and flails an arm. She tucks it neatly inside the nightgown again and traps the limb next to her body.

"Please let me at least give you some milk," says Gwen. "For the baby."

The following Sunday:

Apples and socks.

They don't talk. Renée takes the apples and leaves the socks. But when Gwen returns a few hours later, the children are all wearing the new socks.

Thursday:

"There is ink on your fingers."

"I write a lot of letters. At least three every day."

She offers Renée a bucket of hot soup and four spoons.

"You are a horrible cook. Haven't you ever heard of using salt?"

But the bucket is empty when she returns.

Friday:

The soup has salt.

The children sit on the ground playing with the top Gwen gives them. They seem, somehow, more solid. She can no longer see the privet through their chests.

A full week goes by:

"Who are you writing all those letters to?"

"Monsieur Rodin." She misses Rilke, who was sympathetic. The replacement secretary puts on gloves to take her letters from between her fingers and won't let her talk with the Master.

"You write him more than one letter a day? When you work for him and see him anyway? Don't you run out of things to say?" The girl is humouring her. Gwen knows she doesn't believe Rodin is a real person, alive.

Don't upset the lunatic.

In the first week of February:

"I am making soup instead of art. I hope you are appreciative."

"You could draw me."

It has never occurred to her. Gwen runs to get her charcoal and her paper. A tempest roars through her head all the time now. A vital scouring wind that erases everything she knows about the world, or everything she thinks she does.

As she runs, the long shadows of the great plane trees that shade the centre of the boulevard flash purple over her face, and then she is blinded by brilliant sunlight and then purple shadow passes over her again, each flash leaving an afterimage inside her eyes, to be replaced by the next. The scent of fresh linen and lavender water and steam. The evening is changing into the clothes held out for it by the trees.

Monsieur Rilke returns from Italy or Germany or wherever he has been. In 1906, in March, his father dies and he stays again in Paris, though he has a five-year-old daughter in Germany. And then the child is six and seven. Her name is Ruth. Even the homosexual has his own child. Rilke once said that about dusk, that the evening is changing into clothes held out for it by the trees. He brings Gwen notes from Rodin again, but she knows Rodin is not in France. Who, then, is writing these notes?

Everything is changing. The sky, the earth, the trees, the world. And her. *She* is changing.

She draws the children every day now. She cannot stop.

Sitting in a window seat of the department store near her room, where she can see if Rodin or Rilke or Augustus are coming, she folds a sheet of the company's stationery in half and then in half again. She turns the paper ninety degrees and folds it two more times. Opened, the page is divided into sixteen squares. She fills each square with the faces of the waiting children.

Her mother's portrait is ruined. So is hers. The papers were wet when she fished them from the gutter, the colours have run together, the fibres mildewed. She fills the empty space in her chest by writing four letters a day to Rodin. Then five. She uses pencils and ink and paper and brushes she pilfers from his studio. Rodin never visits. Rilke never climbs her steps, puffing, with a note in his hand. He is spending half a year in Italy and half a year in France. She can't tell if she does not hear from Rodin because no other secretary besides Rilke is willing to talk with her or because Rodin no longer loves her as he once did. To find out, she haunts Rodin's home, his garden, his train station, his studios, his doctor, his dentist. She befriends his Spanish hairdresser so that she can make a pillow from the hairs he draws from the brush after the great man leaves. Rodin walks past Gwen with his white hair in fresh and jaunty curls without saying a word, as if she is, once again, invisible.

"You have bored him to death," says Renée, and abruptly, Gwen stops writing letters, and begins, again, painting.

Rodin returns to her room.

"Show me what you are working on," he says, and Gwen could almost weep in gratitude.

"Compose yourself," says Renée from near the window where she stands, watching. "No one likes a crier."

PAINTING 8:

Rule 1: The drawing is the complementary of the atmosphere.
Rule 2: The atmosphere is the motif and its world seen at a distance.
Rule 3: The blackness is the drawing or the turning of the leaf of the drawing.
Rule 4: The drawing is the discord.
Rule 5: The world cannot be contained.

There cannot be rules.

RODIN:

Good morning, young man. How delightful to meet you. Just sit yourself down there and I'll be happy to answer your questions.

Gwendolen Mary John? Never heard of her. A student of Whistler? The sister of Augustus John? I'm not sure that I remember … almost a child, you say? My secretary will know. You should ask him. A simple little girl, one of my models, well, I have fifty or sixty of those, it's no wonder I can't quite recollect.

Not much to look at? Quiet? Working as a model so she wouldn't starve? Well, what could I say to that? Of course I would have taken her on. I'm humane. I don't even like to cut my beard.

I have an entire book of the models I hire and look, you can see, she is not in there. The Whistler monument? That was some other girl, some English woman I hired at the last minute. The statue looks like Marie? I don't know why I called the model Marie just now. I don't know any Maries. Are you suggesting that I know a specific girl named Marie?

Look, I'm a man in the public eye, and there are women, lots of women, who will say that I touched them, I slept with them, I kissed them, all that kind of thing, but at the end of the day, I go home to Madame Beuret. Too much sex wastes the powers of a man. I'd be a fool to indulge. I haven't done anything wrong. I'm an innocent man.

But alright, I'll humour you. Let's just say that there was this girl, this Marie, and let's just say I had an affair with her for a few weeks or so. Well, she'd have to have been something special. I wouldn't waste my time with someone ordinary. I'm a famous man. I could have anybody I wanted just by snapping my fingers. People, I am sure, talked about the Duchess. Any lover I had wouldn't need to be a sculptor or an artist or even a good model. No. The thing I find most attractive in a woman is her willingness to submit to me. You can feel that the first time you meet, in the way a woman takes your hand. I'm not saying I ever had an affair and I have no idea why you keep on pushing this Marie person, but I will say this: if anyone ever deserved a mistress, it was me.

Now, if I had a mistress, I'd choose one with blue eyes and long legs and a kind heart. I'd set her up in a nice little flat near my studio and I'd pop in to wind down after work and I'd let her bathe my feet in a bowl of ice-water with slices of cucumber floating in it and I'd brush her hair by the window and weave violets into her curls. I'd send her interesting books, make sure she had plenty of wood and encourage her to sprinkle her thighs with attar of roses. On her birthday, I'd buy her a nice etching. And a bottle of perfume. I'd bring her bones for her cat. And a wind-up mouse. I'd try not to let it mean anything, the sex, I'd try to think of it as having one's teeth cleaned at the dentist, a service provided by a professional. I would try not to fall in love with her and I'd make sure she didn't fall in love with me. Love is too complicated to confine to an hour after work.

And if one day she asked me if I believed in parallel times, well, I'd listen to her, and technically, I'd agree. *Technically*. I'd make sure she understood that. Because of course there's no such thing, really. I'd only say it to humour her, as an exercise of the imagination. So that then, if one day she pointed to the corner of her room and claimed to see some child that wasn't there, some child from the future or the past or whatever she dreamt up, I could laugh and walk away and call the police on her, get her carted off, because I only agreed with the idea of two times coexisting *technically*. Only the insane have visions of things that don't exist. Not the sane. Which is why, if such a thing had happened, I wouldn't have seen anyone standing there. No child with a blue scarf around her neck, no mulberry coloured dress, no hair cut short with a knife, smiling carefully at me, not expecting to be seen. No. I wouldn't have seen a thing. The craziness was all hers.

Who could continue seeing such a person? It would be absurd. And possibly dangerous. No matter how much one had liked them previously. There's talk about insanity being spread through the air by invisible microbes. That's what they say. That one breathes in and the particle enters the brain and multiplies there, like a peasant, and soon enough, there is lunacy.

That's what happens when women fall in love with me. They go insane. I have no idea why, but this is all conjecture since there never was any model called Marie. But if there had been, I'd probably have ended up making hundreds of sculptures of her hands and of her feet and of her thighs. I'd probably need to draw her in every possible position and I'd be likely to carry some of those drawings around with me, to remind myself of all that I loved. I would treat her like the daughter I've never had. Like my own sister. Send her to the best school. Buy her a beautiful doll with dozens of dresses. Smuggle little tins of caviar into her room and eat it out of her cunt. A man can't do that with his wife. Frenchmen! Such grand passions we have! But of course, I have never done such a thing and there is no Marie and there never was.

THE FRIENDS:

By the late winter of 1907, Gwen no longer begged Rilke to let her in to see Rodin. He'd denied her in the newspapers. He'd rejected her Jewish children. She read the words she'd copied down that spring day in 1904, over and over: *Grant me the grace to produce something that will prove that I am not the least of men, that I am not inferior to those I despise.* Still, she'd moved, with Rodin's assistance, to an even larger room in the Hôtel de Montmorency-Bours on Rue du Cherche-Midi, this one with a vestibule and a tree in the courtyard and a double helix of marble stairs that spiralled up the centre of the building. After looking over several of her drawings of Edgar Quinet, Rodin had suggested she attend the Colarossi art school near the Sorbonne and when she protested that she couldn't afford to, had paid for a year of tuition in cash. She began to paint two new pictures based on earlier sketches, both titled *A Corner of the Artist's Room in Paris.* She knew they were good work, but he did not want to look at them. All he wanted from her was sex. She was, to him, merely a pair of legs joined at the top with a convenient pocket for his spunk.

Gwen's paintings sold now and for good money. In London, people had come to an exhibit at a new gallery that included her work and they spoke of her as an artist to watch. She had become the hero of her own story, though she had never felt less heroic. Rodin, when he argued with her about paying for the art school, called her his *belle artiste.* He sculpted a bust of her that was shown in the Paris Salon and made a small copy of it for her birthday. She placed it on a plinth above her shelf of books, all of which had been given to her by Rodin. It didn't even have shoulders.

Gwen avoided his Saturday salons, when Rodin chatted with impeccably dressed and highly educated women. She had tried hiding in the back of one of these salons, waiting for all the garrulous and grasping women to leave, in the hope Rodin would turn back and give her a kiss, or at least, squeeze her hand. But instead, he had simply turned the key in the door as he passed through, and, shamefaced, she'd had to pound for the concierge to come and let her out.

She still waited outside Rodin's studio, hoping to escort him to the station, but many days now, he passed her by without waving to her, and once, when she had run at him and tried to give him a letter, he had turned away, and said, "I can't. I can't. The Duchesse ..."

Gwen glared at him with eyes that could have conjured a guillotine glittering between them, then turned on her heel and walked away laughing her thin high laugh. "You will come to miss me," she called back to him.

She no longer lived only for the times when Rodin came to her door and knocked and spent an hour or two with her. She liked his company, she supposed she even liked *him.* But she was busy with the children.

"Try to balance everything," Rodin said. And she tried. *C'est a se les prendre et a se les mordre.*

After a year of no visits, it seemed the old sculptor forgave her for her momentary lapse of sanity, and now he sometimes came twice a week, sometimes, twice a month. Once, Rodin came when she was with Renée and didn't want company. Slow footsteps. Stumbling on the stairs. The creak of his lungs. The hoarse coughing. The pause outside her door. The timid tap. Her own restricted breathing. The thump of her heart. The unexpected leap of satisfaction when the familiar feet descended the stairs and climbed into the motor car and the engine wheezed to life and he was driven away.

Rodin could never stay fully away from her. She was confused by this and continued to write to him, telling him about her day and her great tangled love for him, pleading for his company. "My dear Master" ... "My beloved Master" ... "Lord of my heart" ... "Honoured and cherished friend".

"Enough," said Renée, who now came up to her rooms and sat in Gwen's cane-bottomed chair, posing for a painting. "You are not chasing *after* him. You are chasing him *away*."

They had agreed not to discuss whether Rodin was dead. The entire situation with dual times existing at once had caused her, repeatedly, to be sent to the asylum. Now she didn't often discuss it. It was too confusing even to think about, so she simply put it away, like one might put a difficult or painful book back on a shelf. And in painting together with Renée, she was able to achieve a semblance of peace because there is no time in a portrait.

Every week, Rilke climbed the stairs to her room and knocked on her door. Both Augustus and Rodin told her that *they* would turn her into an artist, but Rilke had recently asked her what she thought. "I will turn *myself* into an artist," she said. "My paintings hold *my* memories of people, not theirs."

"True," he said. "But you will have to extricate yourself from under both of their thumbs in order to trust yourself enough to believe in Gwendolen Mary John."

How he knew about her brother, she could not understand. She had never discussed Augustus with Rilke.

"Show me your pantry," Rilke said at the end of each visit. "What did you have for breakfast? Dried apples are good for the heart. Have you been taking the iron tablets?" He hooked a bone out from under her bed with the handle of his umbrella. "Tell me you didn't feed the cat that soup bone I gave you?"

In Rilke, Gwen had found a true friend, someone who, like her, sat at the edge of society, observing the city of transients, the strange new species of animal that had evolved special organs of hunger and dying. They reassured each other that they were not mad, despite something delicate in their faces and some faint tremor in their hands, that they were healthy and ordinary and fine. Together, they yearned for the country, for fresh air, for quiet. They both sketched their impressions, though he sketched with words and she with charcoal and china white. When Augustus was in Paris visiting his wives, or when Ida sent Gwen letters, pleading for help with the babies, or Dorelia, walking in the Luxembourg Gardens with Augustus' two bastards in tow, made a rude gesture at Gwen, or when Rodin had neglected her for too long, Gwen ran to the Rue de l'Université and sat in the shade of the big horse chestnut tree outside one of Rodin's studios, H or J or M, talking with Rilke.

It had begun like this: the night Rilke first saved her from the asylum, when her mind was still windmilling, she had gone to Rilke's monastic room to thank him. Five flights up and at the end of a narrow black corridor. Her own terrible suspicion that she *was* crazy had left her unable to sleep, and now, pale and shaking, she knocked on his door and was invited in.

Sitting on the bench next to his table, her eyes were drawn again and again to the gas tube running across the ceiling and the damp blisters at the base of the wallpaper and the potbellied chest of drawers and the cot in the corner with its grey blanket. To the deep cleft in the centre of the mattress that held the impression of Rilke's body and the bodies of all of the other solitary men who had slept there over the previous century.

Rilke got up and pulled a curtain around the bed and returned to his seat. "Coffee?" he asked, though he had none. He put a hard-boiled egg on a plate and cut it in half and nudged one half towards her with the knife. The yolk fell out and he pushed yellow hemisphere back in again. When she prodded the egg with her fork, he offered her a flake of salt.

"Please, Monsieur Rilke," Gwen said, laying down the fork without eating the egg. The wax mock orange pinned to her bodice trembled in time with her heartbeats. "I am in need of help."

"You needn't eat the egg," he said, "just to be polite. I shall understand." He had seated her too close to the fire and now the little flowers were melting, dripping down the front of Gwen's rose silk dress. He tried to look away from the destruction, but couldn't avert his eyes until all that was left were the wire stamens and long streaks of white wax, as if a candle had burned over her heart.

Her mouth was open. She must have said something, but he had no idea what it might have been. "Stop drawing me," he said.

Now, tugging her left earring, rubbing her eyes as if to erase all she had seen, she asked him if he thought it was possible that people could live in more than one time, and, after thinking for a moment, as was his habit, he answered that everything is *possible.* We are grasped by what we cannot grasp, he said, serious as always, stooped over his inkwell, rolling his pen under his finger. He did not want to upset her. He had not known it was her when he opened the door and probably would not have opened the door, had he been aware it was her. He glared at the egg. In a nearby room, someone began to play on the piano. A girl, outside on the street, shrieked and laughed. *Ah! Tais-toi ne veux de votre saucisse!*

Rilke had been writing a letter to his wife when Gwen arrived and now he turned it around so that she could read it. "But it's in German," she said. He turned the letter back towards himself and scratched out a word with his pen. "Surely all art is the result of one's having been in danger," he read, translating carefully for her benefit, "of having gone through an experience all the way to the end, where no one can go any further." He looked up. "I was thinking of you when I wrote that, of your … recent time, for it seems to me that you, Gwen, live life to the point of tears, always, and as a result …"

"But you haven't been listening at all!" Gwen cried. "What about the child? Am I *quite* mad?"

"The child?" he asked faintly. Gwen would not be the first to have come to him with an emergency of this nature. Rodin was not a monogamous man. Neither were most of Rilke's friends. Rilke squirmed and cupped his hands in his lap. It seemed he felt himself wither, his own organ shrinking and diving within his body in terror of what a moment of careless passion might produce, this struggling, wriggling, unwanted tadpole. He leaned forward, turned in his chair and respread a white handkerchief over the back of his chair to protect the upholstery from his hair pomade. "Perhaps *a child* might not be something you should endure all the way to the end." Rilke swallowed noisily. A spire of bone bobbed in his thin neck. "I may not be the right person to talk to about this." The room, silent. The silence in the moment before a fall. Waiting. Tense. His heart beating.

Gwen opened her mouth, licked her lips, and then closed them carefully over her teeth. She was odd but so was Rilke. A tiny pulse in the corner of his eyelid wildly fluttering. What on earth was wrong with him? The second half of the yolk fell out of the egg. Gwen stared at it.

Rilke knelt and threw a few têtes-de-moineau into his little stove and finally, as Gwen's hands stopped shaking and the frost on her toes melted, she tried again to ask the question she had come about.

She lifted her portfolio and withdrew a handful of drawings, straightened them and put them on the table. "No one believes me about the children."

Rilke pushed back his chair and leaned forward to stand. The red of his cheek against the grey of his collar. "Wait," Gwen said, holding up her hand. "Please. Just listen. Maybe I was not quite right in the head today, but that doesn't mean that the children aren't real."

Her eyes looked into his for a moment. Was craziness some terrible prerequisite for artistry? Show me an artist and I'll write you a tragedy. A sigh and a nod. The creak of the chair as he sat.

"Tell me."

"I have been drawing them. And one child in particular. Renée. Who was the first one I met on the streets." She pushed the images across to him. "They are living in 1942." Artists claim to be sane like prisoners claim to be innocent.

"These drawings are ...?" Rilke looked at each one, simple sketches of children, in charcoal and red chalk, sometimes with a slight wash of colour, or brushstrokes of gouache, the children standing downcast, sad-eyed, taciturn. The drawings were similar in style to Rodin's drawings, done quickly and energetically, full of movement and tension, without backgrounds. Rilke was surprised how good they were, in many respects better than Rodin's own drawings. Gwen styled herself as a simple model, but she had brilliance. Greatness. He looked back at the drawings. He moved some to one side and spread some out on the table. He opened a drawer and took out a magnifying glass and leaned closer for a better look.

She'd brought the drawings of the children as evidence that her fantasy had substance, and that the children had tangible reality, if only through her charcoal. But it looked like he thought Gwen was patently mad. Insane, out of her mind, deranged, unhinged, a lunatic, non compos mentis, mad as a hatter, mental, nutty, off her rocker, around the bend, raving mad, batty, bonkers, cuckoo, loony, touched, at the very least, an odd duck. For her, a day without Rodin was a clock with no hands. "I often fear that I am crazy or that people will think me so," he said after a pause

Gwen felt strangely moved that Rilke was examining her work, asking questions about each child portrayed, as if he believed they were real. Gwen was an innocent, despite her long affair with Rodin. She hadn't *asked* for the children to appear to her, though she suspected that they did because she too understood what it meant to be invisible.

Now, in this overly warm little room, she felt like one of the children. So surprised to be *seen* by Rilke. His eyes huge behind the magnifying glass. She stripped off her gloves and loosened her top button. Rilke was, to her, what *she* was to Renée.

Rilke looked up. She pressed her fingers against her face and wiped something away. They both pretended she had poked herself in the eye. She didn't *feel* mad just then. She saw an image of herself in his eyes, small and surrounded by so much darkness, and understood that he wished to protect her. "I'll read more of your letters out loud to Rodin," he muttered to his collar, "and encourage him to respond to your letters more often." In an anguish of shyness, he nudged the egg towards her.

"You can have it," he said, meaning it this time. He was taller, thinner, more stooped than Rodin. His eyes were a more pure blue.

She pulled the drawings towards her and crossed her arms over them. The gas lantern hissed. The air dense with sepia smoke. "They disappear. When I was first here, there were thousands of children. Adults too. They lined the streets. Now there are only hundreds. One day, I am afraid, there will be none." She cleared her throat. "I can't bear it," she said. "Being the only one who notices when they are gone."

"Why do you think you are the only one who sees them?" he asked gently. He'd told her of his fear of tearing open an envelope and becoming a witness to something no one should see. He put a finger inside his collar and tugged.

But Gwen had been thinking about his question.

"I am an artist," she said. "No one else can make a record of who the children are."

"Paris is full of artists."

"No," she said. "Paris is full of people who draw and paint and carve. But there are very few artists. And of those who paint, I am the only woman."

"Is that all?" he asked.

Gwen paused. She was sure that if anyone would understand the reality of being invisible, it might be Rilke, who had his own secrets, his own tenuous grip on the world.

"It's something to do with my feeling for them. My understanding of what it is like. To be there but not there."

Rilke nodded. "The way Rodin makes you feel."

"The way *everyone* makes me feel."

"Including me?"

"Not you. Almost everyone. That is what it is like to be a Jew. Now and in that other time. As if you do not belong anywhere. As if you have no ownership of time and place. As if you are ..."

"Invisible," said Rilke.

"Yes," she said with a great exhalation.

She suspected that there must be some job she was meant to do. I'm weak and stupid! How can I help them if I can barely hold the idea of two times existing at the same moment in my brain?

"I am the wrong person," she cried. "Why me?"

"Because you care," said Rilke, and it was so true that she hoped perhaps there *was* something she could do to help. She hoped, perhaps, she might one day do something astounding, beyond even her art.

"People aren't born heroes," he said in response. "Those are shoulderblades on our backs, not wings."

On bad days, days when many children vanished, she visited Rilke in his room at 9, Rue Campagne Première, which was just past the cemetery, and he gave her books, or read his poetry out loud to her, to soothe. He helped her with her letters to Rodin, improving her spelling and grammar and suggesting better phrasing, more pleasing sentences, topics that he believed might be of interest to Rodin. On days when a child she had known vanished, she came to him downcast. And if she had not yet drawn the child, she was inconsolable.

"But where do they go?" Rilke asked. "Where do you *think* they go?"

He'd said that he thought the children were a projection of Gwen's own sense of self; that each time a child disappeared, Rodin or Augustus or Dorelia or Ida or some other member of her extensive circle had failed to see her as human, and on those nights, he gave her the whole egg.

"Yes?" he said. "Oh, Pauline is gone now? So sad! And what of her little brother, Jacques was it? Show me the drawing you have of her. So lovely." He'd push the egg towards her and suggest she eat it. Though every once in a while, Gwen would show him a drawing with such simple charm, such details of emotion, that he would say he was hard-pressed to believe she had merely imagined the child. And over time, it seemed that she must be telling the truth, and he came to believe that one day, Renée would walk in and sit down in Gwen's chair and he joked about how he would need to lie down on the bed.

"I lived near the ocean when I was small," she said when he asked her where she thought the children went. "I loved to walk over the mudflats, all the way to an island off the coast where there was a fort built over a great central cave that could only be seen when the tide was out. Cormorants had made their nests in the crags, wild masses of dried red seaweed and grass. On the rocks, a ten-foot-wide band of glossy brown barnacles. Desiccating on the sand, huge pale blue cauliflower jellyfish, white sack sponges, orange wrack, and everywhere, tiny holes in the sand from the cockles, though you couldn't see their shells. Green starfish and periwinkles and red noses and fat John Bulls and schools of the shy turquoise sand lances in the rockpools, their stones dense with dripping mustard yellow sea oak and anemones. And seagulls and waders and flycatchers and starts.

At low tide, it sometimes felt like a prehistoric forest was rising up through the sludge, as if worlds were hidden underneath or inside our world. Children pulled great branched antlers from the sand, and bones and fruits and flints from hundreds of years earlier. Petrified peat and tree stumps the size of houses. Glasswort and purslane and sea squirts and ancient moss and sandhoppers and lugworms and gorse. The eelgrass smelling of oranges and apricots. At dusk, the mauve horseshoe bats circling the sea, their squeaks like so many rusty doors opening and closing," Gwen said. "Thousands of years of tides, one day laid over another and another, somehow all stacked one on top of the other, and each time, everything I knew about that place, all the pathways and the best places to find cockles and the safest routes back to land, erased. I don't know what I'm trying to say here," she said. "I don't understand it, not really."

Rilke smiled at her. "You do," he said. "You do understand it. Or something about it anyway."

And a week later, he showed her a poem he had written as a comfort.

"That's beautiful," she said. "It feels right. Am I the small island?"

"Yes," he said. "No."

"You can be so mysterious."

"Well," said Rilke. "We are artists and outsiders. Surely we can tolerate a little mystery."

After a dreadful week where nothing had gone right, he loaned Gwen *Letters of a Portuguese Nun*, telling her that it was a volume of letters written by a nun several hundred years earlier who'd had an illicit affair with a soldier and was then abandoned. Initially, he said, the nun had been saddened, and then filled with yearning, but eventually, she felt stronger, and she'd become more proud, more full of self-worth, more capable of fine workmanship. "Perhaps," said Rilke tentatively, his knife hovering above an egg, "the book might be of assistance now?"

Gwen felt herself crumbling before him, ashamed that he saw so clearly her own terrible yearning for love, and also her anger over being abandoned for the horrible Duchesse Claire de Choiseul. She had a tiny flash of gratitude that she had never told Rilke about Augustus. She couldn't bear to be the object of his pity. Instead of crying out, as she wanted to, she gripped her elbows and tightened her lips and said, "I am not abandoned. I am not one of those whores on the Quai who wishes to throw herself into the water. Though, truly, this muddle of times is destroying me. But I am not ready to kill myself. Not yet."

"Of course not!" Rilke gripped his own elbows and hunched his shoulders and beetled his brows at her and wiggled his hips in the chair until she laughed at his mockery of her.

"Did you know that I bring Renée, into my room. To sketch her," Gwen said. Earlier that day, she had discovered that the entire Epelbaum family had been taken away on the trains. Jacqueline and Suzanne, the big girls, maybe nine and ten, and Jacques, and Andree and Henri and Arlette, the baby, from their waiting place near the Notre Dame.

Gwen had followed Rodin to church and sat in the back, admiring his beautiful white hair, and the great splashes of colour that fell from the stained glass rose high above them. After the service ended, Rodin walked slowly back up the central aisle, and her eyes had feasted on his face: on the pale pink blush of his cheeks, like a drop of rose-coloured watercolour paint on wet paper; on the way he had of stopping at every other step to run his hand over the smooth wooden ends of the pews, his great coarse thumb circling the knob. Rodin considered their relationship clandestine, and even though he had recently visited her in her room, even though he'd received a letter from her every day for three years, he passed by her without acknowledging her in any way and she stood there, her heart small, a tiny bird fallen from its nest and crushed.

And then, when she came outside, only half the number of children stood waiting in the line near the Seine, a line that had once held forty children and which now held five, and she ran over and discovered that the Epelbaums had all been taken an hour earlier while she'd been sitting inside the blasted church.

Gwen felt she had betrayed the children. If only she'd been *with* them, she might have saved them! She leaned over the parapet, staring into the swiftly flowing water, struggling with her face. They'd gone before she could draw them and now they were gone forever. The oldest child in that line was six, no age to be watching babies of two and three. No age to be carrying the infant. "No one comes back," the little children standing stoically in line told her. "No one."

In the water, the reflection of huge red flags hung from windows; a tiny flickering boat sailed through a barge and went about mid-stream; ripples from both; the slap of wavelets against limestone walls; a soldier threw a stick for his German shepherd; another soldier, his gun strapped across his back, rode a horse with tin buckets tied to the saddle; the flash of the horse's smiling silver shoes; the man's glittering black boots, the gold cord on his shoulders, a whiff of his cedar-scented aftershave; the roar of something mechanical overhead; the soldier pulled on the reins, the horse stopped, the buckets stilled, he aimed his gun at the little boat, the saddle creaked, the buckets clanked, a shot, a cry, a splash, a laugh. A group of well-dressed women did not even turn their heads. They pointed at Gwen. The policeman on the corner nodded as the women passed with their long baguettes and their long skirts and their long fingers, and then the policeman turned and walked right through the horse. Such hell.

Gwen closed her eyes and massaged her temples. Within, a painful dragging between her hips. There was nothing she could do. There was *nothing* she could do. How could she help when the objects of her assistance were as insubstantial as ash. She walked slowly along the street, shaking her head. It was always terribly hard to convince Renée to leave the line and come to her room, but once in a while she managed it. The girl liked to pet Edgar Quinet. She touched Gwen's charcoals and papers with reverence.

Renée! Gwen started and began to run. If the Epelbaums were gone, perhaps Renée was too? Gwen tripped on the hem of her skirt and twisted her ankle on the cobblestones. A man jumping down from a moving omnibus fell against her as she darted across the road and called, "I'm sorry, Mademoiselle!" She stepped in horse manure and slipped in fish guts that had been thrown onto the street and splashed through a stream of urine. She pushed through the crowds that thronged Boulevard du Montparnasse and turned the corner, and there was Renée, waiting as always.

"I gave Renée new clothes and some food today. Eggs, fruit, bread, milk for the baby. She is young, maybe thirteen. Fourteen. But still older than most of the others," Gwen said to Rilke that night. "Her brother, Naftali, is twelve, and Giselle is only seven. And the baby is a newborn." She was still struggling with her face and her sense of guilt. Was there really *nothing* she could do to help the children? "Her mother was sent away, first to Drancy and then to some other place, further away, in Germany or Poland. In a *cattle* train!"

"By who?" asked Rilke. "The French? Or was it the Germans?" he said and sighed. He rolled his pen again. A faint groove had been worn into the walnut table from the rolling of the steel pen. "I'm sorry that I keep on forgetting the details. It's just … it's a bit hard … you know." He hesitated, before adding, "I'm perfectly willing to believe that more than one time can exist in the same moment. I think it's an odd fact, a great and complex mystery that we cannot ever grasp. But do you not think it strange that only *you* can see the children? Surely others of great sensitivity …?"

"It *is* a lot," she said. "And yet you must believe me! Renée is no figment. She leaves an imprint on my bed when she sits there, and her dark hair is in my brush. I loaned her my toothbrush and now my toothbrush is wet."

Rilke closed his eyes. He felt the pulsing of his brain against his cranium. He rubbed his temples. "Take me to meet them," he said. "And if I cannot see them, at least show me where they stand."

The next morning, Gwen led Rodin's secretary to meet the children. They stood, she said, outside a school, on the curb, on the north side of the street, in bright sunlight. The cobblestones smooth and golden, but utterly without even the slimmest shadow. Gwen suspected she looked like a crazy cat lady, talking to herself in the street. The limestone wall with its crudely painted title and its mural of gleeful schoolchildren mocked her. "*These* are the children?" Rilke asked, pointing at the mural. She shook her head and droplets sprang from the corners of her eyes. "No. In front of that. Right here," she said, pointing. The great plane trees swayed in the slight breeze and their pods pattered down and rolled into the gutters. Small seeds floated in the golden air. Gwen cocked her head and listened for a long time to the one she called Renée, nodding. Rilke strained and strained to hear the girl's words. How he wanted to be a person who was witness to the invisible. How he wanted it to be *him* who saw the children. But instead, it was her. She would gladly have given him the talent, if only it would no longer be hers.

"What will you do?" he asked.

"Nothing," she said, and she began to cry. "It's unbearable. I can't do anything. Except draw them."

"I will give you what paper I can find," he said.

She looked at him then, and smiled. "You often tell me that you can't help me, but somehow, you always do." She wanted to say but did not say, *I love you.* She wanted to, but did not, kiss his cheek.

From that afternoon, Gwen spent frantic months sketching children all over the city, amassing hundreds, thousands of drawings of the children who waited in lines for the buses that would bear them away.

Another evening when she was again complaining to Rilke about the strangeness of two times existing together, he asked her to wait and then went to a shelf where he kept copies of his letters, and he searched through a file and drew one out. Gwen had returned the book about the nun, without any understanding of how her situation was similar to the nun's. She had begged him to assist her in writing a better letter to Rodin, one that would surely bring him running to her room.

"I miss my brother," Gwen said, angrily. She pulled her umbrella into her lap and beat her hand against it, once, twice. "*He* told me he understands. *He* does not think I am imagining things."

"I don't think you are imagining things," Rilke said to Gwen. "But you told me once that your drawings are the children you have with Rodin, and now you are obsessively drawing *actual* children. Well, actual children that no one else can see. It's hard not to see a parallel."

Gwen jumped up, almost overturning her chair. Her hands flew to her stomach. "It's not the same," she cried, gripping her flesh, tearing at herself. "How could I imagine things that haven't happened yet? What's the point of it all? First, a Great War, and then, a second war with flying machines that carry hundreds of men?" she said. "And the Hôtel Biron? A mansion that Rodin owns!" Gwen said. "If I am crazy, wouldn't I just see ghosts, or spectres?" She had a sudden very clear memory of the Joan of Arc on the Norman cupboard. *Joan* had seen the future. "If they aren't prophecies from God, then what is the purpose of such visions? Take them away from me! I don't want them! It's too hard!" She stamped her foot and from the floor below came an angry cry, telling her to stop, instantly, or there would be hell to pay. "Hell indeed!" she shouted back. "I am already in Hell every day, not being able to help these children!" And then, seeing Rilke's carefully neutral face, she pulled on her coat. She would not have him think she was insane. "One day you will believe me," she said. "Truly believe me."

Though she was angry with Rilke, she took his advice and began writing long stories about her life, instead of streams of endearments, to Rodin, addressing him as Julie. She told him about her walks in the Clamart forest, her little caves under the bushes, the way she lured Edgar Quinet back to her with scraps of meat. She told him about her new dresses and her odd landlady and the way her landlord screamed on the steps when he found out a friend of hers was a sculptor. "You've seen men naked!" the man shouted, his eyes bulging. She wrote about the small birds that nested under the tiles outside her window and the way rain glistened in every colour when the sun was behind it. She told Rodin about the bad men who followed her in the street, and about her friends in London and about Dorelia's new baby and about Miss Hart moving in next to her again. She wrote about her sorrow at the death of a lizard that had lived under a tile in her room and about her joy at finding a good bargain in the Bon Marché and about stories she was told when she was a small child. She wrote to him, too, of the Jewish children, of the little baby in his knitted blanket and of the way his hands tried to come together, to clasp in front of his eyes, and of the sweet scent of him, a combination of powder and soap and something indefinably young and lovely, and she wrote of the lessons she gave Renée and of the girl's progress and she even sent him an occasional sketch of one of the little boys in his bedraggled shorts, though she was careful, now, never to mention that they came from a different time. Every day, she sat and wrote and wrote and she began to think that she was as much a writer as an artist, for she surely spent more time writing than drawing now.

"Letter writing is a balm," Rilke said, the next time she knocked on his door with her portfolio tucked under her arm, complaining about the tangle of times. She was the one friend he saw almost every day. He relied on Gwen's company and on her gentle words of criticism about his poems. Both of them idolised Rodin, and it was pleasant, in the evening, to sit and talk about things they had seen and heard from the great man. "I wrote a series of letters to a young poet once. He had asked me a question about something that was unanswerable. I rather like what I wrote back to him." Rilke put on his glasses and pushed them up to the top of his nose. His dark eyes doubled in size and the flames from the fire were reflected in the glass. "One moment," he said. "I must think how to say this in French."

Gwen poured herself a glass of wine and sat down on the little cushion she had sewed him for his bench. "You could try English," she said. "You have been learning a lot of new words."

A fire burned in the grate, the kettle whistled, Rilke cleared his throat. Gwen liked the way Rilke spent so much time getting ready to speak. She liked his slowness, and she also liked the way, once he began to speak, he would forget himself, and become excited and speak loudly and with passion, and then, when he finished, he would go back to be ordinary Rilke again, Rodin's quiet secretary, in his muted brown suits and woollen vests and thin drooping moustache. He reminded her in some way of Ida, who was working on yet another baby, her fifth. Warm and generous with an undercurrent of disaster. The kind of person you couldn't help but love.

Rilke blew his nose and cleared his throat again. He folded his handkerchief and tucked the moist morsel inside the sleeve of his cardigan. "Have patience," he read, "with everything unresolved in your heart and try to love the questions themselves as if they were locked rooms or books written in a very foreign language. Don't search for the answers, which could not be given to you now, because you would not be able to live them. And the point is, to live everything. Live the questions now. Perhaps then, some day far in the future, you will gradually, without even noticing it, live your way into the answer." He cleared his throat yet again. "That's rather good. I wrote that two or three years ago. I sometimes forget what I write and am surprised when I pull it out again and it's decent."

Gwen's heart slowed. She could picture her own series of locked and empty rooms, extending in a row back all the way to Tenby. Why the death of her mother? Why all those nights with Augustus? Why the ongoing fight with Dorelia? Why the affair with Rodin? Why could *she* see Renée? Gwen wasn't at all sure that she wanted to live into the future that the children talked about. She was tired.

She reached over and pulled the kettle from the fire and the whistle stopped, sniffled and stilled. "I hate almost all my paintings when they are finished," she said. "Except for the children. With them, it's different. I don't know ..." she said. "I can't put what they mean to me into words."

"I don't think there is any way to understand these children of yours," said Rilke. He pulled at the ends of his thin moustache. The glass of wine that he'd been drinking when she arrived held a tiny inverted image of Gwen in its deep red surface. "Or even why you are the only one who sees them. No. They are a mystery, those little Jews of yours. We might say Jews are closer to God than Christians. Who knows or could begin to understand what might be possible, given such commune. Perhaps God Himself is looking for them to be saved from their fate in some way?" He pushed away the wine glass and drew a cup of tea towards himself.

Gwen sipped her own tea. "That would make me His little

saint and God knows, I am no saint."

They drank their tea in silence. The steam from his cup rose and fogged Rilke's glasses and he took them off and polished them on his shirt.

"My dear, you will just have to live with not knowing the answers to all of these questions."

"Live the questions now," said Gwen, agreeing. In the third and most beautiful locked room that Rodin rented for her, on Rue du Cherche-Midi, Gwen took out her finest sable brush and a tube of cadmium red and painted, in tiny letters near the skirting board beside her bed where no one else could see it, "Live the questions now."

LA CHAMBRE SUR LA COUR:

In March, despite misgivings, Gwen began walking around the corner to the rooms Augustus had rented for Ida and the babies the previous autumn. She'd successfully avoided the family for months, but now the birth was imminent. Ida was huge this time, much bigger than with the others, and her skin was orange peel, dimpled and discoloured. Her ankles looked like someone had rubbed them with a cheese grater. "I can't," she cried to Gwen. She lay splayed across the rumpled bed, panting from the heat, though it was only early spring. The windows were open, a cool breeze luffed over them, the clinking of milk bottles from the street, pigeons cooing from the rafters, the smallest boy rolling the seed of a plane tree back and forth on the floor, coffee roasting, sweat. "I just can't do this again."

Gwen resented the time she had to spend with Ida, because it cut, severely, into the time she could spend drawing the children. But Ida seemed so helpless, lying on her back, waving her hands in the air, for all the world like a beetle. Now, her head tilted back and she squeezed twenty drops of laudanum into her mouth as if it were pollen and her huge belly rolled from side to side, like a cotton-sheathed elytron. Twenty drops enough to kill a normal human being but Ida just smacked her lips. One child had fallen out of the window and was wailing in the dustbins. Another had almost been run over by the tram and a third had gone to investigate the Métro station being excavated across the road. He'd been missing for hours. It was dreadful the way some people had mothers and the mothers were appalling, careless, negligent, misery on wheels, while the little Jewish children had no mothers but craved them desperately. What a world!

"Come on," Gwen said, pulling the sheets tight under Ida and smoothing the pillows. "When you've popped this one out, we can make you a new dress, something pretty, for spring." Her mind boggled at the thought of passing even one baby through an entrance that seemed barely big enough for a banana.

"The baby will just vomit on it," replied Ida and she reached for the dark green bottle on her bedside table again and uncorked it. Her face was flushed a dark red. Her pupils had swallowed her eyes.

"Well, new curtains then," said Gwen, snatching the bottle away. A wild fierce stench. The whole flat reeked of the vile liquid. Nutmeg, sassafras, black poppy, myrrh.

"Have you seen my old dress?" Ida cried, beating at her belly. Gwen threw the bottle out of the window and ran to hold Ida's hands still. "The children cut it up for dolly clothes." Ida smelled almost like spice cake, but also of armpits and unbrushed teeth. Some other familiar smell lingered about her that made Gwen, after a moment, back away. Gwen began to scrub the floor, wondering at the source of the unusual odour.

It wasn't until the next morning when Gwen brought a baguette to the children that she recognised the smell that clung to Ida. It was the odd scent of frost and rotting leaves and burning hair and bones that the Jewish children carried on their flesh.

Augustus, fearful of the impending birth, had his own rooms on the other side of the Seine, and had vanished with his new conquest, Alick. There was comfort in that. Gwen didn't know what she would have done if her brother had suddenly shown up. The old difficulty.

Dorelia sometimes arrived to help, capably tucking babies into prams and wheeling them outdoors to howl in the fresh air, or whirling through the filthy piles of clothes and the stacked dishes in the sink, cleaning and tidying and sorting, but if Gwen was there, she frowned and excused herself. "Goodbye, dear," she said to Gwen at the door. Gwen the preferred mother. Or mother-substitute. "Give my love to Ida." They were very polite. Gwen thought of Dorelia at odd moments during her day, but they still hadn't properly made up after the Leonard episode. Gwen had not apologised for her outburst, and Dorelia had not apologised for her unfaithfulness. It was terrible to see Dorelia's beloved face but to feel almost nothing in response and even more terrible to realise that neither Dorelia nor Ida felt like proper family. The Jewish children had somehow become *her* children, *her* family. She had even read a book about Jewish holidays, so she could surprise the children with matzos.

Both Rilke and Rodin travelled away from Paris that March, and Gwen discovered that she felt the loss of Rilke more keenly than the loss of Rodin. "My dear friend," she wrote to Rilke, "I have given up my time at the desk to write to you, and I am looking forward to your reply." And he did write back, promptly. It was such a pleasure to receive thoughtful, detailed letters in the mail after years of only occasionally receiving a delivery of one of Rodin's terse messages, written in Rilke's wide flat hand. "I am not surprised that you write so often about family in your poetry. Conflict! Drama! Here I am, stuck in the thick of all the squabbles, and all I want is to sit in your little room by the fire with a cup of tea and talk about the children."

She ate an occasional evening meal with Miss Hart, who was still angling to get Gwen into her bed. "Will you ever give it a rest?" asked Gwen wearily one night after a dinner of kippers and mashed potatoes and innuendo. Miss Hart laughed and said, "I'm not dead yet," and Gwen was filled with a warm tide of gratefulness for having this rough woman, too, in her life.

Now, at the corner of her street, only Renée and Jacques and Giselle and the little baby were left. All the children near the Quai d'Orsay had been taken. Gwen was struck with the sense that these children were her true family, people from whom, like Rilke and Miss Hart, she derived her greatest and most uncomplicated joy. Perhaps, when one fell in love, one was ever and ceaselessly doomed to chaos. This was why it was called *falling*, an utter loss of control, a great tumble through emotion. Though she loved Rodin, their love was not peaceful and caused her as much anguish as pleasure. It was different, loving the children. There was peace in that.

Paris felt empty. Despite the howlings of the Ida John menagerie, there were silences everywhere else, and in the sparks struck from the carthorses' hooves and the scratch of the street cleaners' brooms on the cobbles and the whistle of the departing trains in the Gare Montparnasse, Gwen felt a sense of impending doom. "Come to my room," she begged Renée, and she sketched her repeatedly, over and over again, convinced that one day, she would vanish. "You can sleep here," Gwen offered. "You can bring your siblings. Please don't go back to the street."

Is there anything as painful as the sense that something you love will soon be lost? Her mother's cries from behind the bedroom door. Striking Augustus with the cooking spoon. Leonard putting out his hand to help Dorelia into the wagon. The Duchess' cruel laughter. Renée on the corner outside the school, cradling her baby sister.

Renée refused to stay in Gwen's rooms. "It's not good for you," she said. "We are better off by ourselves." Though Gwen did not understand why it wouldn't be good for her, and Renée would not explain. She wouldn't let the other children climb the stairs to Gwen's room and half the time, while she was doing her own work, she leaned out of the window, watching the road. "They will call me when the omnibus comes," she said. "Any day now. They are just putting together another transport." Stay, said Gwen. Stay with me. Stay or be lost. "We have to go with the trains. You know we do." Renée stitched golden stars to the clothing Gwen made for her. "But why such a heavy coat when it's such a warm spring? Why have you sewed coins in the seams?"

"I will explain the coins if you explain something to me," Gwen said. "Why don't you go to school?"

Renée stabbed the needle again and again into the fabric and only when Gwen insisted did she say, "I don't think people really care too much about us going to school."

"*I* care," said Gwen.

"You are just one person," said Renée. "And you aren't even French."

"What does *that* matter?" asked Gwen. "Sew a star on my coat too."

"They aren't for you," said Renée, but she smiled and took Gwen's coat and began to stitch.

"There are other good people," said Gwen, touching the coarse fabric of the star. "I'm sure if you went to the police ..."

Renée snorted.

"Rilke."

"I can't see him."

"He can't see you either. But if he could ..."

"*He's* not French either." Renée turned her back on Gwen, leaned on the window ledge and looked down the road. She pushed the needle through the cloth of Gwen's coat. "It wouldn't make a difference. You're just trying to be nice."

"I am *not* nice," said Gwen. "I am honest. It's not always the same thing. But I cannot understand why the French people would not stand up for their own citizenry. For *children*! It doesn't make sense, what you are saying."

Renée jabbed her finger and a spot of blood spread on the star on Gwen's coat. The girl sucked her finger and then spat on the floor.

"We Jews aren't liked because we are small and dark and different."

Gwen looked at Renée. Gwen was also a foreign-born citizen.

She was also small and dark and different. She thought about what it would be like if the police came to her door and took her away because she was an artist or a woman and she remembered that afternoon when the black motorbike had come with its coffin sidecar and her chest grew tight and her breathing ragged. She lifted her hands and patted the air, as if to part the curtains that separated her and this girl, but feeling nothing, she let her hands fall and now she thought only of graves in the air, gaping wounds wreathed in gauze, between which people passed, were passing like smoke, would forever pass. She felt dizzy and shut her eyes.

"Today, the trains took away Huguette and Fanny and Victor," Renée said. "They are going to go see their mother and their father now. They are happy," she whispered. *She* didn't sound happy. Every few days, Renée told Gwen the names of the children that she knew who had been taken away.

"Why do you have to cooperate?" Gwen asked.

Renée continued to stitch and now the only sound was the slight pop as the needle pierced the fabric and the rush of the thread as it was drawn through to the other side.

"Did they *want* to go?" Gwen asked.

The pop, the swish, the movement of Renée's arm.

"Do *you* really want to go?" Gwen asked, squeezing in next to her at the window. She was afraid that if the girl disappeared, *she* would also vanish. She would die if the girl said yes.

"Yes," said Renée, but she dropped her eyes. "We have been here in the city for a long time. It's hard taking care of my sister and brothers all by myself. Sometimes I can't find food for them, and they get so cold at night, and when they have bad dreams, well, I have bad dreams too. And there are bad men looking for children like us. I have to watch all the time. I'm tired. I miss my mother. I miss my father and my older sister, and my bed and my books and my little toy otter. I miss being taken care of. Of course I want to go." Still, her eyes looked away.

"You are not telling me the truth," said Gwen, very gently. She wanted to touch the girl's shoulder but didn't and instead her hands plucked at the tiny winged sporophytes that swayed above the moss on the soft old tiles, picking and picking at them, until the entire patch was fruitless. This moss, by her own hand, incapable now of reproduction.

Gwen brushed off her fingers, the pale green and red mossflowers scattering on the floor.

"Yesterday," Renée said, "a little boy came back. A five-year-old. He had been thrown through a break in the side of the train and he walked all the way back to Paris on the tracks."

Gwen waited. The girl said nothing further. Edgar Quinet jumped into Renée's lap and kneaded her leg before turning in a circle and lying down. Renée put her hand on the cat's neck. She stroked her fingers over his head. He began to purr. A tear fell onto him and then another and Quinet turned his head and licked the salt from his fur.

"The little boy said that the children don't go to their parents," Renée said. The cat, in Renée's lap, continued to purr.

"Renée," said Gwen and now she did touch Renée. Her hands did not sink through the child. Renée was not some cold phantom. The girl's arm was warm and solid.

"Renée." In all the world, besides Rodin and Rilke, this was the person Gwen loved best. She had hundreds of drawings of this one child. "Please."

"Don't touch me," said the girl, brushing away Gwen's hands. "We are fine. We do not need your help." She shimmered with emotion and for the first time since Gwen had spoken with her, the yellow star darkened and flickered and became merely a blur of colour over her heart, a smudged fingerprint, and Renée herself faded, became as translucent as a linen curtain in bright sunlight, and though Gwen wanted to reach out and grab her before she blinked out entirely, she was forced to look away.

LES SUPPLIANTES:

That night, March 8th, 1907, Ida went into labour. She'd felt the familiar pains dragging through her guts and a less familiar agony, a sharp and stinging sensation low down on her right hand side, and she drank a glass of water and called for Gwen and then, barefoot, walked to the Hôpital de la Maternité in Boulevard de Port Royal. Gwen did not know where Augustus was at that moment. She wasn't even sure where *she* was. She had a slight fever. The world was hazy, full of swirling colours. The Jewish children had, for the first time, seemed brilliantly shaded, even their fingers and necks sharp electric blues.

Ida's baby, a boy, was born in the early morning hours of March 9th. Ida looked at him folded into his blanket and cried. Another boy, thought Gwen bitterly, just when Ida could take no more, between Alick and the long string of hussies and Dorelia and the two household helpers, Clara and Felice, young, fractious, deliberately unattractive girls who had both gotten pregnant – at the same time! – and looked daggers at Augustus whenever he came near them.

Later that day, Ida's fever grew higher and her pain worse. "Gwen," she begged. "Please find Augustus!" Gwen ran to the Bobino theatre on Rue de la Gaîté and to all Augustus' favourite cafés, even the Café de la Regénce next to the Louvre, but Augustus was nowhere to be found. He had been temporarily arrested, it turned out, as a homosexual, and Gwen had to bail him out. He'd been walking with Euphemia, who was dressed as a man. Gwen remembered with a little thrill of horror, how close she'd come to the same disaster, back with Miss Hart, in The Monocle nightclub, but she had no pity for Augustus. "Your wife is *dying*, you bastard," she hissed. "Keep it in your pants or I'll cut it off myself."

Eventually, Ida's mother arrived and had Ida moved to a private hospital. She was operated on for an abscess, or perhaps it was peritonitis, but Ida failed to recover from that too. "You can't come in here," said Mrs Nettleship, pulling her skirts out of spitting distance of Gwen, barring her from the hospital room. "Smelling of cats as you do."

"Hardly," said Gwen. "And anyway, I rather like the smell of pussy."

When Augustus finally showed up, a little the worse for wear and reeking of Euphemia's cologne, he was horrified to see Ida so ill. Ida begged him to get her beef lozenges, a bottle of peppermint, eau de mélisse, violets, and he and Gwen ran all over Paris, frantic about her children, frantic about Ida, until they found all except the violets. Gwen watched from the door as he presented the presents to Ida like frankincense and myrrh, spreading them out on her bed and proclaiming their usefulness, though Ida's eyes were rolled back in her head from pain.

"I shall bring the children to her," Augustus declared, bouncing on the bed and patting Ida's thigh. "Her babies will buck her up!" Outside the door, he sobbed on Gwen's arm and made rash promises of good behaviour, if only Ida would be well. Gwen wanted to slap his face. "It's your fault," she said. "Don't you know how pregnancy happens *yet*?" At every moment, she had to force herself to stay by Ida's door, when all she wanted was to run back to her own children, to Renée and to Giselle and to Jacques and to Esther.

Neither the nurses nor Ida's mother thought it would be a good thing for the children to see Ida in her feverish state, and Gwen thought it wouldn't be good for Ida to see the sources of her distress. "I'll watch the children," she said and all of the adults rounded on her, aghast.

"You're not fit," said Ida's mother. "You have ..." she looked around at the door and then, when there were no strangers present, whispered, "… delusions."

"You might feed the children lead sandwiches. And put turpentine in their bottles." Even Augustus, of all people, was claiming to be a better parent than Gwen!

"Why don't you run back to your little studio," said the elderly Mrs Nettleship, "and do whatever it is that you do over there. Presumably with *cats*."

But though she was torn and wanted, most desperately to return and check on her own ghostly children, Gwen couldn't bring herself to leave. For here was her *real* sister-in-law, with a *real* baby that everyone could see. Maybe a baby that she, Gwen, would have to raise. If Ida died, maybe she would get to raise all of Ida's babies.

At night, she took out the photograph that had been taken right after the birth of David, the one where Augustus and Ida and she stood in a line with the infant, as if he had two mothers and one father. As if Gwen were a real mother. And in those moments, she remembered again, the soft curl of his body against hers, the warmth and weight of him in her arms, the fragrance that rose from the tender place under his chin.

Four days later, Ida's fever broke and she sat up in bed and said, "Take me to Dorelia. She'll cure me! She has always cured me of what hurt. We'll toast each other with a bottle of tonic wine mixed with Condy's and I'll give myself an enema. That'll do the trick." Though it had always been Gwen who had cured what ailed Ida.

Gwen and Mrs Nettleship had to hold her down with force and the doctor was called and he jabbed her with a dose of morphine that left her as limp as a week-old flounder. Sweat again streamed from her body. The sheets could be wrung out. Nuns came every few hours to change them. Ida's dark hair was matted from her tossing to and fro and wet strands wound around her neck, reminding Gwen of the black hair she still carried in her pocket and seemed unable to dispose of. "I'm drowning," Ida said, faintly.

Towards morning, Augustus came in from whatever new bender he had been on and laid a tiny posy of fresh violets on her bed. Ida motioned to Gwen, asking for a glass of Vichy water. "Here's to love," she whispered, raising the glass and smiling.

"Yes," Augustus said. He laid his hand on the back of hers. "Haven't we had a grand old time? To love!"

The corners of her lips turned up. She winked at him.

Love? thought Gwen. Was love, after all, a factor in their lives? Or had procreation been the focus? There were, after all, five baby boys and Ida only thirty.

Now it seemed Ida would recover after all and Gwen, thankful, slipped out of the hospital and ran all the way home to sit on her steps, waiting for dawn and the arrival of the Jewish children. She waited and waited, but they didn't come and in the meantime, the wind grew stronger and clouds scudded overhead like spume on a pot of boiling fat and rubbish raced down the street and leapt the fences and all the cats in the neighbourhood sheltered under the largest arch at the train station, yowling. The passage of the crowds on the close, dark streets like blood pooling in distended veins. Gwen was too tired to search for the children. She'd been up for several nights in a row, and needed to sleep. She climbed her stairs, took one last look out of the window, shook her head, closed the shutters and went to bed.

Paintings rise up out of her memories, out of the smell of the sea the morning you wake up and your mother is no longer alive, an empty beach outside Tenby on a grey afternoon with gulls tilting silently on the invisible currents of the chill air. Or the night you travel to London, to school, and across the sky there are so many stars that it looks as if there is a transparent ribbon of light through all that darkness. Out of memories of the love between two people; everything distant and curving, simplified and yet crystalline and bright, like a room in a painting by Vermeer, nothing extraneous, each detail wary and precise and vital; the alabaster hand of Ida in her bed after the birth of her fifth child, her lips the colour of veal.

Instead of recovering, Ida died a few minutes after Gwen left.

Augustus, looking at Ida after all the terror, said he felt only relief. He kissed her cheek, he said, and told her he still loved her, that he would *always* love her, and then he ran out into the street. After all the sadness, it suddenly felt like a holiday, the first day of spring, the most beautiful painting of the most beautiful day in the most beautiful city. With outstretched arms, he said he twirled around and around, shouting. He wanted to paint this gorgeous day! He wanted to toast being alive! He stepped into the nearest pub and got rip-roaringly drunk and did not come home for three days.

Gwen found out that Ida had died when the telegram boy knocked on her door the next morning bearing a yellow condolence slip from Rodin who had learned of her sister-in-law's death before her. She threw on her clothes, raced to the post office and wrote back savagely, telling him to save his energy for sex with her, with her, only with her. She didn't want to share him. Look how far non-monogamy had gotten Ida! Gwen wanted to piece together a family, with Rodin as the father and Rilke as the uncle and the Jewish children as the infants and herself as the wife. She would tell him so the moment she saw him.

It was only after she had already paid for the telegram and she was outside the telegraph office, in the weak spring sunshine, that she remembered the evening when she had stood and watched Rose Beuret move amongst the covered clay models. The moment had finally arrived when Dorelia should have had Augustus all to herself, but Dorelia would take no pleasure in

Ida's death or in the inheritance of her five children, just as Gwen would take no pleasure in the death of old Rose Beuret.

Her earlier understanding had been based on a false premise: that the mistress would replace the wife, should the wife die. But what if there was more than one mistress? The sky turned above her, there came a faint whiff of wood smoke and within, some new understanding clicked into place. Like Dorelia, though she was both mistress and muse, she was entirely forgettable, replaceable.

Gwen had seen Camille Claudel, Rodin's former lover once when she was walking along the Seine, seated on the little parapet that jutted low down next to the water on the Île Saint-Louis. Claudel looked ancient and fat and soiled. She had two cats inside the puffed sleeves of her nightgown and another inside her hat. Pieces of liver hung from a string around her waist. They had been bitten with cat-sized teeth and human-sized teeth. The woman's voice, when she called out to Gwen, who was descending from the Quai de Bourbon, had sounded as if it came down a long metal trumpet, echoing, harsh, inhuman.

Gwen slowly walked inside the telegraph office, a slick knot in the back of her throat. She knocked on the grated window, but just as she had suspected, there was no way of retrieving the telegram.

Old Mrs Nettleship snatched the oldest three children away to London. The two babies, Edwin and Henry, were left with Dorelia in Paris. "But what about me?" Gwen said when she came round to his apartment a few days later. "I could do it."

Augustus ran his eyes from the crown of her head to the tips of her toes. All of her clothing was black. His children, too, all wore black. Even Augustus had put aside his mustard-coloured boots and earrings. "I don't think so," he said. "You're an artist. Not a mother. Giving a child to you would be like asking the poor babe to snuggle up to the Eiffel Tower. One must have warmth when it comes to brats."

"I *am* warm," she said.

"You're like a ghost," he said. "Your kind of warmth gives me the shudders. No. It will never do. Stop your crying. That's the last thing we need right now, more tears. Dorelia is going to look after the bubs and I'll get her a nursemaid to help. Go back to whatever it is you do every day. You're not needed." Then, seeing that she was distraught, he pulled her against him and squeezed. "You have other skills, Gwenny. You'd be wasted on a kid."

"But what if I *want* to be a mother?" she mumbled into his shirtfront, a great cold place yawning within her abdomen.

"You were like a mum to me," he said. He rested his chin on Gwen's hair. Sometimes, even his most resolute efforts to hide his tenderness failed. "The best mother a lad could have. Wasn't I enough?"

Drawn from the crematorium on a stone slab, Ida's bones shimmered with heat. Though her body was gone, her hands were still bowed together, as if she carried an invisible child in the cradle of her arms. Swallows flew through the open windows, bringing flies to their nestlings, peeping and crying. She was alone, so alone, even at the end. To love, she had said. *To love.* On the street, Gwen's children lifted their noses in the air and sniffed. What was burning? Gwen, returning from the post office, turned the corner onto her street and looked automatically at the place where the children always stood, and there were three, instead of four. She sat down on the curb and covered her head with her arms and screamed. At Père Lachaise cemetery, the fossor hit the stone slab with his crowbar and Ida's bones crumbled to ash.

BOOK THREE: GWEN

PARIS 1908:

What she sold during her fourth year in France:

a packet of drawings of nuns, tied up with a twist of paper, for three francs;
a sketch of Miss Hart in a tuxedo;
a hat she no longer wanted, though first she clipped off the purple velvet violets she'd bought to please Rodin, and these she hid at the back of her closet, inside a shoe;
dozens of floral arrangements taken from the cemetery on Boulevard Edgar Quinet and sold to mourners for a franc each, when she was desperate for something to eat, though several others she took and left on Ida's grave and the rest she laid on the street where Renée had stood, a fresh bouquet every day;
a portrait of a general, on a postcard, to his child. The little girl had seen Gwen drawing in the Luxembourg Gardens and had offered her a franc to draw her father, who was sleeping in a chair with the neck of his uniform unbuttoned, slowly accruing a nasty sunburn;
her paint box that she'd brought on the steam packet from London, and which Dorelia had carried, most unwillingly, all the way to Toulouse and that had now, finally, been replaced with something larger;
several kittens;
her body, in untold erotic poses, to myriad men and women artists who hired her;
letters that she wrote for the injured soldiers at Les Invalides, at four centimes each;
a postcard of Rodin in his studio, next to King Edward VII;

an oil painting of Chloë Boughton-Leigh, for fifty pounds;
a self-portrait holding a letter from Rodin, written by his secretary;
an ancient gold coin that Rodin gave her by mistake;
herself

SELF-PORTRAIT IN A RED BLOUSE:

Renée was taken in the same hour that Ida was cremated.

"They came for her," Giselle said when Gwen asked her what had happened. "And she kissed us all on the head and then she walked away. That's all."

Gwen pushed away every thought of the girl. She packed away the drawings she had made of Renée in the very back of her armoire and covered them with clothing that was no longer wearable. But even that was not enough. One night, she took all of the drawings out of the wardrobe and laid them in the fireplace and struck a match and dropped it on the papers. The match went out and she had to try several times before one edge caught and then, sheet by sheet, each drawing curled and lifted and bent and rose, as embers, up the chimney and vanished, much like Renée herself.

Gwen kept one painting she'd made of Renée, the first one she'd made of her, when she was still wearing her own clothing instead of Gwen's, the purple jacket and the yellow leather belt. Gwen scratched off the star with a pallet knife and let the shavings fall onto the floor. She wrapped the canvas in brown paper she bought home from the butcher, and she tied it with the yellow belt that Renée had left in her room, and then Gwen put it on top of the armoire. When she lay down on her bed, she couldn't see the package. She could only see a tiny flicker of yellow, like a flame, and only when the light was good.

In June, Gwen celebrated her birthday with the remaining three children. Rodin was in Paris but, for the first time, he forgot the day and for the first time, she didn't care. Augustus and Dorelia and the children were all in Paris too, but she avoided them. She hadn't seen any of them since Ida had died.

Now, she tied fireworks in her hair and ran down the street, weaving in and out of the carts piled high with peas and radishes and new potatoes, shouting, "Happy New Year!" and Rilke again had to come and rescue her from people from Salpêtrière on black motorbikes. "It's my birthday," she said when he took her by the elbow, frowning. "They were all laughing. Didn't you see? It's the first time the children have laughed since Renée was taken away."

"Stop it!" he shouted at her as he dragged her up the stairs by her elbow. "Just stop it! There are no children! It's not your birthday! You could have lost your eyes!"

In July, she painted outside, stabbing the brush at the canvas, slashing the paint with her knife. "I used to be pretty," she said to one of the children. "But now look." She smacked a thick red line through the centre of the portrait. "Ugly. Ugly. Ugly." She had stopped eating when Renée disappeared and her skin had turned a pale yellow. A small crowd gathered to watch her hurl the painting into the Seine. "Good riddance!" she shouted. A yacht slid over the canvas and the small grey rectangle slipped sideways, the green water of the Seine covered Gwen's head and her face turned green and the frame sank. Now she painted other people frantically, but she never painted herself. Not anymore.

Salpêtrière: low buildings, courtyards with people in long white gowns and caps who look like convicts, leafless trees, leafless in spring and in summer and in autumn. Only in winter do they seem to bear leaves. A long dark room like a passageway, four windows of green bubbled glass, walls painted black. Startled benches crouch against the wall. Dim light, smoky, foul. All classes of people. An unwound clock. People with their heads in their hands, asleep. Bandages, gangrene, rictus, fear. Doctors in light gloves, coats to the ground, top hats.

In early August, for the second time, Edgar Quinet went missing, and in late August, Gwen could no longer find any children with the yellow star left in Paris, besides her three, though she walked up and down every street until her shoes fell apart and the hem of her dress was full of briars and sawdust and shit and she was sure her heart would burst.

Dorelia brought Gwen Edgar Quinet's kitten, Tigre, to replace the lost favourite. Tigre lay on top of the package that flickered at the top of Gwen's wardrobe, purring and toying with the end of the yellow belt.

In September, Gwen wrote to Rodin that she would like to die, that she would make sure of it, and he sent her a telegram. "Stop," he said. "I will come to you. Wait."

He came to her door, older, bent, shaking, his clothing loose on his frame, his beard sparser than she remembered. The veins on the backs of his hands stood out now, knife-like folds in ashen paper. Out of pity, he renewed his relationship with her and became more consistent about seeing her at least once a week, though he often only wanted to sit and talk for a few minutes and make sure she drank some tea. Gwen knew he did not want her suicide on his hands and it gnawed at her, that she had told him she wanted to kill herself, knowing he would return to her rooms. It was, she thought, beneath her. Beneath any artist, to substitute a symbol for real meaning.

She would never be Rodin's wife, nor even the mistress he presented to the public. Time passed and on tiptoe, she peeked through the windows of his studio as he took several new models to the Norman cupboard. Still, he continued to come to her rooms. She wrote to him every day, sometimes twice a day, with no expectation of receiving a letter in reply, just for the relief of being able to put down her thoughts. She yearned for him and chastised herself for this yearning, as if it were the worst form of weakness. It was not peace, but it was as close to peace as she could muster. She no longer believed Rodin read all of her letters, but she still thought he read some of them.

Mostly she searched, without rest, for a way to save the last children, Renée's brother and sisters.

BOY WITH A BLANK EXPRESSION:

In late November, Gwen found the solution.

She had been standing in her usual place, in the door to the café opposite Rodin's studio, wearing a pearl-coloured dress, waiting to hand him a letter, when she heard the young man seated at a table behind her say, "I don't mind them so much. I have known Jews who were very fine people."

Gwen turned. He was not from the city, but had evidently come to the city on business, as he was wearing a stiffly starched shirt and a tonsured suit. Perhaps he was eighteen or twenty years old, his face sweet, his hands nervous. His hat lay mangled on the table between him and another man with whom he was arguing.

"Do you like Jews?" she blurted and at the attention of this elegant redhead, he blushed, and blushed again, in waves.

He dragged at his cheeks with his hands. His chin was a pale blue. "Don't you?" His French, though perfect, had an unfamiliar accent.

"Don't I what?" she asked, twisting back towards the door, distracted. Rodin would leave the studio soon, and he would be expecting her.

"Like Jews?" he asked.

"I don't know," Gwen said, "if I like them or not. At least, many of my friends are Jews, but they are children for the most part. And I had one *very* good friend who was Jewish, and she was almost full-grown, and she, I loved."

Later, she was still sitting in the café. Rodin's letter was in her hand and now she had a cup of tea and a biscuit and the other man had left.

“Napoleon was an advocate for the liberty and respect of all people,” the man said. “Jews. Gypsies. Mohammedans.”

“Women,” said Gwen. She looked around for a clock but there was none.

“I’m not sure,” said the young man. “Probably women too.”

“Where are you from?” she asked. “You have an accent.”

He stared at her. “I just told you,” he said. “A minute ago. You keep on asking me and I keep on telling you. I am from Provence, from a small village. From Goult.”

“Tell me about Goult,” she said. “Forests,” she said. “How lovely. And streams, and mushrooms and berries and greens everywhere. You must never be hungry.”

“No,” said the man. “Never.”

“And it’s so far away from everything,” she said, a tickle of a plan emerging in her mind. “Are there even any police there?” She pressed her finger into the soft skin on the back of the man’s hand, just under the dorsal venous arch, the most beautiful of human chapels. He glanced up at her and blushed again, to the roots of his hair.

“Excuse me for asking,” he said. “But are you a coquette? My father warned me about the coquettes in Paris. He told me not to waste my money on them.”

“I’m a model,” Gwen said. “I am Auguste Rodin’s model.”

“You *are* a coquette!” he said delightedly. He put his finger in his mouth and bit down hard on the nail and then took up his hat and tried to straighten it and as a last effort, tried to put the crushed mass on his head.

Gwen smiled and patted his hand. “No. Just an ordinary lady. But I know some women like that, if you would like to meet one.”

The poor boy stammered and his hat fell off and knocked his teacup to the floor, and then he stood up, knocking the table so that Gwen’s teacup fell into her lap.

“Sit down,” said Gwen. “Please! I have a favour to ask of you, Mister ...?”

"Henri Girard. I am enchanted to make your acquaintance." He went to take off his hat and realised it was in the tea.

"My name is Gwendolen Mary John," said Gwen. "You may call me whatever you like. And it is likewise, a pleasure to meet you." And it was.

They sat and spoke for a while and Gwen reshaped Henri's hat for him, though he looked at it as if it were a tarantula, or an octopus. "It's not my hat," he admitted. "It's my father's. I'm not quite used to it."

It was almost dark outside, and yet still they sat, talking.

"I want to be famous," he admitted. "I want to make the world a better place."

"I have been lonely," she replied. "But I have also wanted to be brave, like Joan of Arc."

The café owner began to put chairs on top of the tables and a boy came out and began washing the floor in the back, whistling.

"Henri?" asked Gwen. "Perhaps I might help you. I think I know something you could do. To make the world a better place, I mean."

She took out a pencil and wrote down some names on a piece of paper and pushed it across to him. "One day," she said. "These children will come to you and they will need a place to stay and you will know that I sent them to you. What do you think of that? Will you remember?"

"Yes," said the boy in his innocence.

"Even if it's in ten year's time?" she asked.

"Yes," he said.

"Even if it's in twenty year's time?"

"Yes," he said.

"And thirty?" she said.

"I will *always* remember *you*," he said. "I have a good memory." He pulled the paper towards him. "Giselle," he read. "Jacques. Esther." He folded the note and put it in his wallet. "Are you sure this will this make the world a better place?"

Gwen nodded, thinking that it *was* possible to forget a mere meeting. He might not forget his first coquette, but even a year from now, the boy might have lost the paper.

"Putains wear red stockings," Gwen said, and they both stood and walked out of the café. "But see. I have blue." She lifted the edge of her skirt to show him.

"May I kiss you, Miss Lady-who-is-not-a-whore?" he asked, though even under protection of the night, his arms were awkward and his teeth chattered.

After a pause, in which many thoughts went through her mind, she said yes.

"A proper kiss?" It came out much louder than intended.

"Yes," she said, thinking of the tube of paint she had once refused to buy by trading a kiss.

"My first woman," he whispered after he'd touched his lips to hers and marvelled. "And an *English* woman. My brothers will not believe me."

"Like this," she said, guiding him. "Try again. Make your lips as soft as butter on a warm day." Of the Provençal brothers, this was the one who liked to travel, who had come to Paris, in search of adventure. Perhaps he wouldn't be home even if she managed to send the children to him. How could she make his resolution stick, and even extend it to his brothers?

"What if they were *Jewish* children?" she asked, when he pressed himself against her, took her hand. There were no more cicadas. The boy had come to Paris in the wrong season. "Promise me you will take them in."

"What will you give me if I promise?" he asked. Not *such* an innocent.

Gwen smiled. "Walk me home?" she asked. She put out her arm and the boy took her elbow and looped his own shaking arm through it. It was obviously his first time walking with a woman on his arm, and he kept stopping to readjust his hat and his bald suit, to take staggering breaths.

"Are you seducing me? I don't have very much money and my mother told me I must buy her silk threads for embroidery tomorrow at a special shop. But I would very much like to be seduced, if that's what you are doing."

Why did she want to do this now? It had something to do with learning to respect herself, to make her own choices. It probably had nothing to do with being a hero. But perhaps that is all a hero is, someone who learns to take the most difficult choice because it is the right one.

At her building, she asked Henri to come upstairs. "I would like to show you something," she said.

It wasn't quite a lie. Afterwards, she lit the lantern and pulled down the brown paper parcel and unbuckled the yellow belt.

"This was my friend," said Gwen. "My Jewish friend. Renée."

The boy did not know what to do. "Don't cry," he said, and then trying to distract her, "It's a very good painting. Who did it?"

"I did," said Gwen. Her spine, bent, the sharp bones breaking the surface of her flesh.

"I don't think you really *are* a coquette," he said then, looking around her room, at the paintings on the wall, at the fine photograph of Rodin, at the easel with its tubes and brushes. "You're an artist."

"Yes," said Gwen, turning the photograph to the wall. "I always wanted to be and now I am. But I was a model first."

"And who are Giselle, and Jacques and Esther?" he asked.

"Renée's family," Gwen said, "her sisters. And her brother."

MADONNA AND CHILD:

Early in the morning, after Henri left, Gwen put on her clothes and watered her ferns. She slid the package back onto the top of the armoire, and she printed Henri's address on a piece of paper and then she took out all of the money she had and counted it. None of it was from Henri. Instead of paying, she had made him promise to take care of the children. She looked at herself in the mirror. She did not look any different. A hero needed to be brave in some way, but bravery wasn't something visible. It was possible the change had taken place years earlier, when she first came to Paris.

She crushed her shame and went to Augustus and asked him for money for the children. He stared at her. "What mess have you gotten yourself into?" he said. "Is it an abortion you need?"

And when he understood that it was for the Jewish children, his lip curled. "Oh my God, Gwen. Really? Are you so far gone as to think that I would give Jews *any* money?"

"They're children."

"They're figments of a deluded mind. Perhaps it's syphilis you have."

She took hold of his jacket front and clung to it. "Please?" she said. "I would not ask for it if I did not need it. When have I ever asked you for *anything*?"

But in one smooth movement, he shook her free and slammed the door in her face. "You're crazy!" he screamed. "Thank God I didn't leave the baby with you!"

So she went from door to door, asking all of the artists in her building if they could contribute to help some children, though she didn't say which children they would be helping. She went to Rilke and to his friends. The only person she did not ask was Rodin, because she had been unfaithful to him, and could not look in his eyes. Even then, she did not have enough money, and so she stood, for several mornings, outside the train station, with a hat upturned under her easel, painting sketch portraits for tourists. Some of the men asked her if she would show them her other work, and she took them upstairs to her room and they paid her well for those types of viewings. It no longer mattered that she was invisible. It no longer mattered who she was or what she was. All that mattered to her was the chance to help the children.

When the pile of notes grew large enough, she sealed the money in an envelope and walked along the street to where Giselle and Jacques stood, with Esther in a basket at their feet, waiting.

"Here," she said, handing them the heavy envelope. "There must be someone in Paris in your time who you can pay to help you get to this address, and when you do get there, ask for the man Henri Gerard, or one of his brothers, and tell him that Gwen John, the putain from Paris, sent you. He will remember who I am."

She made Jacques repeat the instructions and then she kissed them all and walked back to her room and lay on her bed knowing that even after everything she had done, the children would not be saved. But she had nothing left to give. The wind blew over her, carrying the scent of autumn leaves and coming rain.

PROFILE OF A BOURGEOIS COUPLE:

Two years later, in October 1909, Rilke's wife, Clara, rented space in the empty Hôtel Biron on Rue de Varenne and within a month, Rodin had moved his studio there. He filled the walls with hundreds of tiny framed portraits. None of them were of Gwen. Eventually, the government of France gave the Hôtel Biron to Rodin, and it became the Musée Rodin, just as Renée had said they would.

"You forgot," Gwen said to Rilke. They were sitting in his room, at their usual place, a chessboard between them. The lamp was lit, there was a little bread on a plate, and a sliced pear, some hazelnuts and a chunk of green cheese. They were burning olive-wood prunings and the smoke reminded Gwen of her walk across France, when she was young and in love with Dorelia. She'd found a grey hair in her brush that morning, and was feeling her bones.

"No, I didn't," he said.

"You are getting senile and you forgot. Admit it, old man," she said, smiling.

"I rented that room in the Hôtel Biron just to fulfil your little prophecy," Rilke said. He loved Gwen very dearly. She was like a sister to him. "To please you. To make you think that your children existed and you aren't just a crazy old hag."

"No, you didn't," she said. "I can tell by your eyes that you completely forgot all about what Renée said. You're a horrible liar."

Rilke laughed. "You're right," he said. He *had* forgotten all about it, until he heard that the government gave the Hôtel Biron to Rodin, That day, though, their conversation came back to him and the hair had stood up on his arms.

"I told you I'd prove to you one day that the children existed," she said. "Checkmate."

And she took his king.

PAINTING 9:

Window wood – *jaune de Naples*
wall – *Ochre brun* darkened with sepia Hair
Window panes – sepia Hair
coat – *jaune de Naples ombre nature*
darks of coat – *ombre nature* – *noir*
Seat – *styl de Grain* – light of seal – *stil de graine* sepia Hair

Primrose = chromes, *verts*, bistre, gaboge, blues lacs, mole, caput mortum
Drawing of primrose – brown black (rusty blacks), sepia coloured
Greens of primroses = *terre verte* with its lining

Winter leaves. Ochres
Drawing of winter leaves – caput mortum, mole

Dead leaves. Terres. Sepia coloured
Drawing of dead leaves = Green, black

I dreamt of primroses last night. I am thirsty for the country and for Spring.

FADED DAHLIAS IN A GREY JUG:

Rodin died in November, 1917, fourteen years after Gwen first met him. Despite the Great War, despite bombs falling in the streets, and the allure of the Duchesse, and the advice of strangers and the nagging and imprecations and threats of Gwen herself, he continued visiting her in her rooms until the year before his death, and then his absence was only because he was too weak to walk. Amongst his papers were hundreds of drawings that were Gwen's and which were incorrectly identified as his, and over three thousand letters, still preserved in the boxes Rodin had made to show his appreciation, his love, for her grand effort.

In December of 1926, Gwen read in the newspaper that Rilke had died in Switzerland after pricking his finger on a rose. "Flair for the dramatic, my dear?" she muttered to herself. His king still stood on her window ledge, a reminder of the real game she had played with him and won. In the weeks and months to come, Gwen would fall into a deep melancholy at this loss, the latest of her friends to die before her. She wrote Rilke letters, and prayed to him, asking him to help her, to help the children, to help Rodin. "Wherever you are," she said. "You will know what is best." His name and hers, the same to Rodin, Marie.

In 1935, Ida's fifth son Henry, whose birth had brought about her death, fell or jumped off the cliffs in Cornwall. He was found wearing only shorts. Gwen wondered if she had been appointed his mother, if he would have died so young, twenty-seven. She didn't find out about his death until 1936, when Dorelia sent her a newspaper clipping. "Oh, Henry," she sighed. She didn't cry. She hadn't known him at all. He was not, after all, *hers.*

When, in 1939, Gwen read that France had been invaded, the horrors Renée had told her thirty years earlier flared in her mind and burned brightly there. She sat in her room shivering, remembering the children, Renée and Jacques and Giselle and Esther. She couldn't bear to see Paris filled with yellow stars that slowly disappeared. She couldn't bear to see her own little children again, lined up patiently waiting for the trains that would carry them away. And what would *they* think, seeing her old and frail at the same time as simultaneously seeing her, somehow, when she was still thirty and fresh and in love? Would *she* be able to see that young woman she had been, devoted, delinquent, obsessed? It was too confusing. It would be too painful for them, *and* for her.

She took down her painting of Renée, unwrapped it for one last look, kissed the girl's forehead and then re-cinched the yellow belt and put it back on top of the armoire. "Goodbye," she said to Renée and to her cats and to the little house she had bought in Meudon and to her wild, wild garden. "Goodbye," bending to touch the toe of Rodin's great *Thinker* with her lips. Then she knelt and rested her head on the grass where he was buried, beneath his most famous sculpture. She walked down to the station and took a train to Dieppe, hoping to find a fisherman who could sail her across the English Channel and away from all she knew was coming. But in the street, something sprung loose in her, some essential something that had kept her going through all the years, and she fell and was unable to rise. Above her head, swallows plummeted through the sky and all around rose a great chorus of cicadas.

"Are you alright?" asked a soldier, leaning down to help the terribly thin old woman.

"My Master?" whispered Gwen. The blue of the sky seemed to be a blue she had never painted it, and the swallows bigger, louder, more dazzling. The bells of Notre Dame rang wildly. There was no time to lose. The screams of the cicadas drowned out even the bells, and now all she heard was ticking, ticking, the beat of her own heart, slowing and slowing.

Rodin held out his hand. "Call me Auguste," he said, the sun pouring through his great halo of white hair and setting it on fire. "You have gone beyond anything I ever taught you. Now it is time for me to learn from you, little sister."

As Gwen took his hand, his greatest secret lay clear before her. Rodin was dyslexic and though he wanted to, he had never read *any* of her thousands of letters. And in the deep roar of the silence that filled her head, in the expanding past the glove of her skin and the washing free from the hard edges of her bones, she didn't care.

STILL LIFE:

The whereabouts of Renée's grave is unknown.

The whereabouts of Gwen's grave is also unknown.

Rodin is buried in Meudon, under *The Thinker*. He had asked to be buried under his Muse, but no one could remember why he adored that sculpture.

Rilke is buried high in a tiny churchyard in Raron, Switzerland overlooking a deep valley. He would have liked it there.

When Augustus went to Gwen's house after she died, he found hundreds of half-finished canvases mouldering from the rain in a room with broken windows, a few dozen cats, an apple, an unplanted rose bush that was blooming with a single white rose, and, on top of her wardrobe, a carefully wrapped painting that became known as *Girl with a Blue Scarf.* It was unsigned and undated and Augustus had no idea why it had been preserved when all of the other canvases were ruined. Experts guessed that it had been painted in 1920 but they were wrong about that and about much of Gwen's work. No one will ever find out who the girl in the painting was, though in 2009, a sixty-seven-year-old woman will pass an art gallery on East 60th Street in New York and see *Girl with a Blue Scarf* through the glass. She will be unable to go inside, unable even to do anything more than put her head against the window and sob at seeing this image of her dead sister.

EPILOGUE

OPHELIA, PORTRAIT IMAGINÉ:

In 1987, a woman sits in a café in Ménerbes, drinking tea with a business associate on a terrace overlooking the Luberon.

"I grew up here," she says.

"But you're an American," he says, squinting into the sun. "How is it possible you grew up here? I grew up in Goult and I know everyone there, even though I live in Aix now."

"I was one of those children," she says slowly. "The Jewish kids who were sent away by their parents during the war, and hidden in the country. This is where I grew up. Or someplace near here. I remember this place."

"You must have been very young. I've heard of people here who were hiding Jews during the war." He is uncomfortable with her now, and uncomfortable with the way she stares down the long valley as if she doesn't see it at all.

"I was a baby. By the time we left, I was three, maybe four. But I still remember the forest where we hid." A man who came every day bringing them food. Who left them small wooden toys to play with. Books. Once, an orange."

"With your parents?"

"No," she says, and a look comes over her face that leaves him completely unable to ask the next, most obvious, question.

"That smell of lavender, and the cicadas, that ticking like a clock gone mad, that's what I remember." The man is still squinting and she offers to change places with him, but he refuses. "Even within the forest, the smell of the lavender a presence like a hand on the nape of your neck." She is a writer, and can be excused for talking like that.

"So, who was it?" he asks, uncurious. "Maybe I know the family."

"I don't remember," she says, although she remembers the man's kind face, the way, when he blushed, his eyes seemed startlingly green.

"You must remember *something,*" says the printer. She can see he doesn't really believe her, that he is on the verge of getting up and excusing himself, and the deal will be lost. The flight down from Paris a complete waste of time.

"I think he was a miller or a baker," she says. "When he came to bring us food, he stood in the light coming through the trees and it was if he had an aura, a great penumbra of flour dust floated from his clothes and his hair and his hands. It always surrounded him. And he told us once that his mill had a sail. Like a boat. That's what my sister, Giselle, says anyway. I don't remember him telling us that."

Now the printer stares down the valley, unseeing.

"My uncle," he says, "has been the miller in Goult for sixty years. He just retired."

"Yes?" she says. She does not grasp the importance of his words and is still lost in the woods, lying on the cool, spongy moss, playing with a wooden aeroplane. She is still two or three.

"Esther," says the man, "Goult is the only town near here that has a windmill."

They get in his car and drive the short distance to the town of Goult, and he drives her up to see the mill.

"Is this it?" he asks. "Do you remember it?"

But she shakes her head.

On the way out of town, as he is driving on one of the new roads through an area where there are many large chestnut trees and a small stone hut shaped like a bee skep, she cries out. "Stop! Stop!" she says. "I remember this! I remember this place! Oh my God. This is it. This is where we were hidden."

"But this is my uncle's field," he says. "It's not a forest. I thought you said you were hidden in a forest?"

He takes the woman back into the town and up to his uncle's house and the low door is opened and they bow to go through into the cool darkness. She is not even sure if she will recognise him, if it *is* the man.

"Henri?" calls the wife. "Are you able to see some visitors?"

The miller is sick and in bed. His lungs are failing.

The wife leads the visitors into his room and the old miller makes an effort to sit up in bed and to straighten his pyjamas. He kisses his nephew and looks curiously at the unfamiliar woman.

"A girlfriend?" he asks. He winks at his nephew appreciatively. His hands look like the land in winter, all edges and walls.

Above, the windmill creaks and turns in the wind and the stones of the ancient house shake. Wisps of flour sift down through cracks in the ceiling. The miller coughs and a haze of dust rises from the covers.

"She says she was hidden in your forest when she was a baby," the man says, laughing. "I brought her here to prove her wrong. Uncle, you don't even have a forest!"

But the miller sits up straighter yet, and he puts out his hand to the girl.

"What is your name?" he asks and he takes her hand and draws her to his side. Even in the dark room, she can see his brilliant green eyes.

"Esther," she says.

"Esther," he says, and water runs from his eyes and he makes no attempt to wipe it away. "Esther. Yes. Of course you are Esther."

She tells him what she remembers and he tells her the story he has not told anyone, not even his wife. He is old now, and has been married to his wife for sixty years. She will forgive him almost anything, if only he will continue to live.

He asks for his wallet and when his wife brings it, he opens it and takes out a soft brown piece of folded paper. "Look," he says, giving it to Esther. And there, on the paper, are the names of her sister and her brother and her.

"A woman in Paris gave your names to me," Henri says, "and told me that one day you would come, asking for me, and that I should hide you. Somehow, she knew that I would."

What he does not say is that when the children were lifted, bedraggled and sleepy and ill, from the truck that had brought them all the way from war-torn Paris, that it was thirty-five years since he had received their names from a woman called Gwendolen Mary John, the first woman he loved. He does not say that Esther was a newborn, with her umbilical stump still attached. He does not say that he wondered for years afterwards how it was that Gwen was able to write down the names of three children who hadn't yet been born on that cold November morning in 1907 hoping hoping hoping that in 1942 he would take them in. He doesn't care anymore about the mystery of this. He only cares that the little baby he cradled in his arms and sang to in the forest, the child whose first word was his name, is here again now.

"Esther," he says. "My Esther."

ACKNOWLEDGMENTS

There were many eyes on this novel at various stages and I thank everyone who offered words of wisdom. However, there are some people without whom the book would not exist. The most important of these is my daughter Shterna who watched all of my other children in a rural cottage in Provence while I lived down the road in the extraordinary Dora Maar House and wrote twenty hours a day for a month.

For assistance with my research, I am grateful to Riva Lehrer who introduced me to Gwen on a summer afternoon filled with green skies and mammatus clouds; to the Musée Rodin in Paris, and its able archivist Sandra Boujot who gave me far more than she promised; to Cecily Langdale for providing me with catalogues of Gwen's work and clarifying points of her artistic technique; to my French publisher, Dominique Bourgois, and her brilliant daughter Victoire, who made every road in Paris smooth and whose enthusiasm for my project continues to make me want to make them proud; to my fantastic intern, Gina O'Neill of DePaul University, who translated thousands of Gwen's letters; to Gwen Strauss, who taught me about the deportation of Jewish children from Paris and who selected me for the fellowship that allowed me to write this book; to Dora Maar, who was surely breathing down my neck as I wrote, raising my hair in the middle of the night and giving me electric shocks; to my kind and responsive agent, Emily Forland, who is always patient with me; and to Dinah Voisin, in Peralta, who pointed out that I had been surrounded with busts of the John family all along.

My trio of editors, Fred Shafer, Shterna Friedman and Georgia Richter, deserve so much love and gratitude. Without you, I wouldn't be a writer and *Gwen* wouldn't be a book.

I am also deeply indebted to Sir Michael Holroyd, the premier biographer of Augustus John, for shoring me up just as I began to think I had taken a wrong turn, and for giving me a glimpse of what it was like to talk with the living – rather than imagined – Dorelia. Mesmerising, he said.

The National Endowment for the Arts and Dora Maar House provided the time and the space to write the first draft of this novel. They are remarkable institutions, generously supporting writers and artists during a period when such support is becoming more and more limited around the globe.

My beloved children have changed over the years I have been researching and writing this book. Without their ongoing support and their pride in me, I would be ashamed to spend as much time away from their lives as I do, shut up in my study, banging on the computer keys with two fingers. In the beginning they were curious about Gwen and wanted me to tell them all that I learned, but as time passed, they began to say, "Still Gwen?" and yes, it was still Gwen. My youngest son asked me a few months ago, "But are you *really* finished with Gwen?"

I don't want to be. It's hard for a reader to put down a book and say goodbye to a character, but it's even harder for the writer. I am grateful to the real Gwen John for insisting that women can be artists and can be taken seriously for their work. I wish I had known her.

FURTHER READING

A large catalogue of work was consulted in researching this novel. Many facts, images, journeys and interactions can be confirmed in the works that are available for reading and download on the author's own website.

www.goldiegoldbloom.com

www.ingramcontent.com/pod-product-compliance
Lightning Source LLC
LaVergne TN
LVHW041102080826
845145LV00007B/1655

* 9 7 8 1 9 2 5 1 6 4 2 5 1 *